Motherland

About the author

This is Maria Beaumont's third novel. After the mums from her kids' school have finished with her, it may be her last.

To find more about Maria and her books, go to www.letstalkaboutme.com.

MARIA BEAUMONT

Motherland

HODDER &
STOUGHTON

Copyright © 2007 by Maria Beaumont

First published in Great Britain in 2007 by Hodder & Stoughton
A division of Hodder Headline

The right of Maria Beaumont to be identified as the Author of the Work has been asserted by her in accordance with the Copyright, Designs and Patents Act 1988.

A Hodder & Stoughton book

1

All characters in this publication are fictitious and any resemblance to real persons, living or dead, is purely coincidental.

A CIP catalogue record for this title is available from the British Library.

ISBN 978 0340 92044 2
ISBN 0340 920 44 0

Typeset in Plantin Light by Palimpsest Book Production Ltd., Grangemouth, Stirlingshire

Printed and bound by
Clays Ltd, St Ives plc

Hodder Headline's policy is to use papers that are natural, renewable and recyclable products and made from wood grown in sustainable forests. The logging and manufacturing processes are expected to conform to the environmental regulations of the country of origin.

Hodder & Stoughton Ltd
A division of Hodder Headline
338 Euston Road
London NW1 3BH

This book is dedicated to all mothers. But especially my own.

Acknowledgements

Motherland was such an easy book to write. This is largely due to the fact that I am surrounded by some of the world's most, er, interesting mothers. Inspiration came from them all and my thanks go to each and every one of them. Especially to Vicky Emin, who is the funniest person I know Apart from David Emin, obviously.

Thanks also to Gráinne Fox, who is not as funny it has to be said, but is brilliant, clever, sharp and, more importantly, tall. Sara Kinsella, thank you for everything, but especially for that massage. And really, you shouldn't worry so much about having another woman's hands on you, but I guess here isn't the place to go into that. Thanks, actually, to everyone at Hodder, which is such a nice place to be.

And finally, my thanks to Matt, who made me countless cups of tea while I was working long into the night. Matt, I just wanted to take this opportunity to tell you that I bloody hate tea.

21

When we were young – very, very young, two or three years old young – what we looked like was of no consequence. But vanity kicked in and grew with each passing year until by the time we were teenagers, What We Look Like had become The Only Thing That Matters. This state of mind, by the way, was triggered by the very same hormones that were simultaneously pebble-dashing our faces with acne, which felt then like the end of the world, but now just seems pointlessly cruel.

Then the concern with appearance faded – along with the zits – as other things started to matter as well, until eventually What We Look Like is number nineteen or twenty on a list, above Phone Dentist but way below Buy Ariel.

And how brilliantly clever it is that reaching the inevitable point of No Longer Noticing coincides perfectly with Looking Like A Sack Of Shit.

I'm so lost in thought that when I first catch sight of the woman's face, I feel, for a moment, a stab of pity. When I realise I'm staring at *myself*, the pity is replaced by a feeling of pure, undiluted horror.

Don't get me wrong. I don't come from some Amish-type community that bans mirrors and all reflective surfaces. I *know* what I look like; it's just that I can't *believe* what I look like. My reflection has ambushed me and I'm stunned. The downturned mouth, the blue-grey sacks of skin under the eyes, the sag beneath the chin, the hair . . . the *hair*! I yank my cap down in an attempt to hide the shards of brittle hair that are poking out angrily from beneath. I'm just about to fix my collar, which I hadn't realised is half up, half down, when a voice makes me jump.

'I said, excuse me,' a man – more of a boy, really – says, apparently not for the first time. I realise now that I'm standing in a shop doorway. 'Are you OK?' he asks. He's wearing a nametag. I suspect he works here. 'It's just that you've been standing there staring at our sign for a while now.'

'Yes, yes, sorry,' I mumble, not sure why I'm apologising, but also not sure what he's talking about.

Then I see it. As I look past my reflection, I see a closing-down sign. It's a sports shoeshop. But not one that sells proper sports shoes. Technicolour parodies of sports shoes with inadequate ankle support and seventies-style platform soles. *Hilarious*. Why would I be sad about the closing of a shop selling comedy trainers with bling-bling buckles and rainbow-coloured laces? That's right; that's my viewpoint exactly.

Only last week I went through my shoe cupboard like a woman possessed and threw out every comedy trainer I owned. Five pairs, ten shoes. I felt so much better afterwards. And I did it because I wanted to. Not at all because a kid at school had been wearing the exact same pair as one of mine and another mother had remarked how ridiculous 'footwear for the young' had become.

'By the way, your cap.' The shop assistant is still looking at me. 'Limited edition, isn't it? My sister would kill our gran for one of those. Where'd you get it?'

'Selfridges,' I tell him, pulling down the peak of my Missy Elliott rhinestone cap in a vaguely conscious attempt to cover the lie.

'You're joking, aren't you? They sold out the minute they came in. Have you got, like, a contact or something?'

Meet Fran Clark, the personal muse of Missy Elliott. It's a little-known fact that Missy (as she's known only to her closest friends) designed the exclusive rhinestone-encrusted baseball cap around a mould of Fran's head.

I don't think so.

The truth is that my husband nabbed it for me (along with all the junked 'trainers'). He works for a marketing company that numbers adidas – and by association, Missy Elliott – among its clients. Ironic that limited-edition fashion designed for – and *only* for – street-smart teens ends up on the head of a middle-aged mum. My unwarranted perk fills me with embarrassment. This boy's sister would happily murder a close relative for what I didn't even ask for and – as Trinny and Susannah would gleefully point out – definitely shouldn't be wearing.

For a moment, I contemplate confirming that I'm down (in the *connected* sense, as opposed to being plain old depressed) with the right people, but, again, I don't think so. I end up mumbling, 'No, just got lucky, I guess.'

He grins at me, showing me his brace. How old is this boy? 'You sure you're OK, then?' he says. 'It's just you look a bit, you know, lost.'

I look at him and he seems so sweet and vulnerable that I feel suddenly overwhelmed by the injustice of the world. He has a brace, for heaven's sake, and shortly – presumably once the last shoe has been sold for a knock-down price – he will no longer have a job.

'Here, have it.' I take off the cap, ignoring the state of my hair now. 'Give it to your sister.'

'You're kidding, right?'

'No, really, I'm probably too old for this sort of thing, anyway.'

I give him a Lady Di eyes-down-head-slightly-tilted smile and wait for him to say the chivalrous thing.

'Hey, older women can wear this gear. That's what Missy'd say, anyway.'

He laughs and I rerun his remark in my head. Yes, he did just call me an *older woman*. Whoever said youth is wasted on the young was most definitely an old person. By the time this particular youth even learns to spell 'chivalry', he will have long forgotten the throwaway comment that so stung *this* older woman. I feel especially foolish now and want to get away. I shove the cap into his hand.

'Please, let me give you something for it,' he says, nervously stroking the black felt as if he's stroking the Queen of Hip Hop herself.

'Just think of it as a gift from a stranger,' I say in my best Marlene Dietrich voice. Don't ask me why. It just feels appropriate. Then I turn and walk out of his life.

I'm on a clock and mooning over myself in shop windows is not part of the schedule. Ha-ha, the *schedule*. I've already torn it up. I'm supposed to be somewhere else entirely, and, well, evidently I'm not. But there's no point dwelling on that, is there? Spilt milk and all that. No, best to move straight on. Which is precisely what I'm doing right now. Moving *away* from the sports-shoe emporium and *towards* shops where I might actually buy something. Having deviated from the schedule so disastrously, going home with carriers full of useful purchases is my only hope of salvaging anything from today. My shopping list:

present for Richard's sister
winter coat for Molly
outfit for me.

In that order, obviously.

I was close to getting a gift for the sister-in-law-from-hell

4

over half an hour ago, my plan being to spend ten minutes in Liberty, where I'd buy Richard's sister any old thing that looked reassuringly expensive. But as I stood outside, I felt Carnaby Street suck at my sleeve like the tube on a vacuum cleaner.

The person I *used* to be loved Carnaby Street – Memory Lane, then. Just over a decade ago, Richard worked in a glass-walled office round the corner in Great Pultney Street. My work often brought me into Soho, and when it did we'd meet, do lunch, mooch around . . . The person I used to be. A woman who wore funky baseball caps unselfconsciously, no matter who was looking.

But that woman is a million miles away from the one who sneers at platforms on trainers and wonders what has happened to the world. As I walk purposefully back towards Liberty, though, I realise that the world hasn't changed; it's me. Ten years ago, I spent real money on ridiculous clothes designed to make me look as un-whatever-it-was-I-was-supposed-to-be as possible. Because back then What I Look Like was still number two or three in the chart. Buy Ariel, incidentally, wasn't even bubbling under.

When I finally get round to it, finding a present for Fiona is easy: walk into Liberty, pick out ridiculously priced leather-bound photo album (ridiculous prices *matter* to Fiona), have it gift-wrapped, mission accomplished. Molly's coat is easier still. I stride into H&M determined to grab the first pink or fluffy thing that catches my eye. I walk out five minutes later congratulating myself on the double whammy of a coat that is both fluffy *and* pink. That still leaves a little time to buy something for me before I have to head back to pick the kids up from school. So I find myself outside Karen Millen – not a shop that sells the kind of ridiculous fashion-victim stuff I used to wear, but since I've so clearly moved on, surely a sensible place to start?

But obviously, it's not going to work out. I stare at the unarguably pretty, undeniably elegant outfits and panic. They look fine on the mannequins, but on me they will just look . . .

Maybe I should forget the new frock and wear any old rubbish; take the line that it's my party and I'll look crap if I want to. But that isn't the point of having a party, is it? The point is to utter a sartorial shout: *Hey, look at me, I'm a whole year older, but don't I look soooo much better than I did twenty years ago?* But tell me, who looks better than they did twenty years ago?

I veer away from Karen Millen's window, march into Starbucks next door and order a bucket of froth with a sprinkle of chocolate shavings. Then I take it outside, sit down at a little plastic table and enjoy my moment of defiance.

Richard despises Starbucks. He says that along with McDonald's and Gap, they are the advance guard of Armageddon. Or possibly something slightly less hysterical about globalisation depersonalising the high street. I know, I know, this is rich coming from a man whose wages are paid by adidas and several other global corporations. It's all right for him; he can condemn Starbucks from his room at the top, can't he? He has coffee on tap. But how can he be sure his secretary isn't pouring it from one of these very paper cups into the company cafetière? Ha! Justice, decaffeinated.

Richard should get off his high horse and remember one very important thing: before Starbucks, it was virtually impossible to get a decent cup of coffee *anywhere* in the entire United Kingdom. And as for his hatred of McDonald's, I've got this to say: if it weren't for the Happy Meal, several thousand women would have murdered their children – and possibly their husbands; HAPPY MEALS SAVE LIVES.

Sitting here thinking angry thoughts about Richard is useful. It stops me focusing on the real issues, which are: a) not only was I patently *not* where I was supposed to be several hours ago, but b) I am not going to get a party dress either. Now I have just enough time in which to drink coffee and have a cigarette. I'm supposed to be giving up, but I bought a pack at the Tube station. The thought of a cigarette always makes things better, even if the actual cigarette doesn't. I light one and take a long, slow drag. Ah, the luxury of thirty spare minutes . . .

Never a good idea to give me time, because I am the world's greatest waster of it, as my earlier failure to *show up* so eloquently demonstrated – wasting not just my own time, but several other people's while I was at it. Still, mustn't fret over that – spilt milk, etc. I form my mouth into an O and pop out a near perfect smoke ring. *Older woman* did the boy say? Never.

I'm early. In fact, I'm so early that I'm the first mum here and the caretaker has yet to unlock the gate. I think about having another cigarette while I wait, but that would be beyond redemption. Round these parts, women do their smoking in secret. Lighting up at the school gate would be only slightly less heinous than doing so in a cancer ward.

Sureya rolls up with an empty double buggy and though she isn't grinding a butt into the pavement, I'm reminded that the first time I ever saw her, she was in the middle of an argument ignited by a lighted cigarette. It was in the car park outside the gym. I'd joined in an effort to widen my social circle. After a year, I'd managed to make great friends with my yoga mat. After one particular session of trying to get in touch with my spiritual side (i.e. daydreaming pointlessly for half an hour), I stepped out into the fresh air and found Sureya, her confident voice yelling, 'I didn't light up in the gym. I waited till I got outside. What the hell's your problem?'

A woman in an expensive Ellesse tracksuit was yelling back, 'You were *in*side the door and your smoke hit me right in the face. The rules of the gym clearly—'

'Look, just . . . just fuck off.'

'Pardon?'

'You heard. I haven't got time for this. I've got a heroin deal to close.'

They both looked up then because I was laughing – they could hear me from all of fifty yards away. Ellesse Tracksuit stalked back into the gym, presumably to work the rage and secondary smoke out of her system. I walked to my car, which was conveniently parked next to Sureya's.

'Sorry, it's none of my business,' I said, 'but well done. If you ask me, there are too few people telling each other to eff off round here.'

'Honestly, I don't know where that came from,' she said, looking shocked – as if *she'd* been the one on the receiving end of the insult. 'I *never* use language like that.'

'Some people give us no option,' I told her.

'I suppose . . . I guess that when you know you've lost the argument and you haven't a leg to stand on, well, the F word is all you're left with, isn't it?'

We both unlocked our cars.

'You're off to close that deal now?' I asked.

'I could probably squeeze in a coffee first. D'you fancy one?'

She may have given up smoking and drinking coffee since then, but her smile is as warm as it ever was.

'Hi, Fran,' she says now. 'You're early. Have you been here since drop-off this morning?'

'I might as well have been for all the use today's been.'

'Some days are just like that, aren't they?' she says, though

I can't imagine that any of her days are like mine. One fundamental difference between us is that Sureya actually works. She teaches drama part-time. 'So, what's gone wrong?'

I think about telling her about the not-being-where-I-should-have-been thing, but since I never told her I was supposed to be there in the first place, why tell her I wasn't? She doesn't need to know. She doesn't need to know about my party-dress hell either. Much as she claims to be looking forward to my thirty-seventh, I don't think the event is pre-occupying her as much as it is me. I know I'm kidding myself that an expensive new outfit will miraculously transform me. There's no hiding the unwanted greys, the creases that I can't really call laughter lines – when do I ever laugh? – and the stomach that won't be sucked in no matter how hard I breathe. My thirties are slipping through my fingers like the sand in Thomas's Arsenal egg timer and there's nothing I can do to stop it. *Thirty-seven*. Only three years away from that mythical place where, it is told, Life Begins. Now *that* would be something.

'Have you signed my petition yet?' Sureya asks after I've answered her question with a shrug.

Sureya is a proper activist when it comes to local community issues. She writes letters to MPs, organises petitions and goes on marches. Sometimes she manages to drag me along too. The last thing was the demo against the erection of a phone mast in the park. I felt like a hypocrite as we chanted insults at Vodafone or Orange or whoever. I was pleased about the mast, you see. The reception round here is terrible. And if mobile phones are slowly frying our brains, frankly, so what? If they don't get us, the terrorists will. Or the car fumes. Or the deodorant. Surely before we spend our time campaigning against all the things that are killing us, we should be going out and getting a life that's worth fighting for? But I didn't say anything. I wouldn't, not to

Sureya. She's my friend, and true friendship demands patience and tolerance.

Her new thing is McDonald's, who want to open on the Broadway. She rummages in her bag and pulls out a sheaf of paper held together by a bulldog clip. She seems to have several thousand signatures already, which doesn't surprise me. Round here al-Qaeda would have a slightly better chance of opening a recruitment office than McDonald's do of getting their restaurant. I don't really want to sign it – you already know my views on McGlobalisation – but I do. Patience and tolerance, remember?

'Thanks, honey,' she says, as the caretaker unlocks the gate. 'Better be off to get the babes. See you later.'

I watch her wheel her buggy towards the Arlington nursery, which stands to one side of the main school buildings. I join the mothers who have gathered since I arrived and we amble into Arlington Road Primary. I feel a hand on my shoulder and turn to see Cassie. Cassie comes from Planet PC (not to be confused with PC World, which – despite the know-nothing staff – is a place that at least has some point).

'Francesca, excellent, I was hoping I'd bump into you today. I wanted to ask you a favour.' She doesn't wait for a reply. 'You may have heard I'm in charge of wardrobe this year,' she announces importantly.

'Right, good,' I say. 'So, er, am I dressed OK?'

'Pardon?'

'Well, you said you're in charge of wardrobe . . .'

She stares at me blankly.

'Oh, sorry, did you not mean wardrobe as in generally speaking?'

It's a joke, although I'm not sure where it came from. The woman I *used* to be cracked jokes all the time. Clearly, I'm out of practice because Cassie isn't laughing. I force myself to smile. 'Only joking, Cassie. What's up?'

'Right, well, I'm doing costumes for *The Wizard of Oz*. The Christmas production. Three of us from ARPS have volunteered, but we need a fourth.'

ARPS: Arlington Road Parents' Society, the crack team that is admirably (if bullying SS types are your thing) led by Cassie; its mission to raise money for the school in the name of charity. *Pur*-lease, Arlington is no charity case. Granted, it's a state school, but it is attended by kids whose parents are on at least a hundred grand a year, drive the obligatory 4x4 and holiday in Tuscan farmhouses. Isn't *charity* supposed to conjure up visions of skeletal African children with flies on their faces? Not chubby cherubs running around in Boden's finest.

But raising money for our wonderful school is not a matter about which one can be facetious. So when one is asked if one can make up the numbers for wardrobe detail, one must suppress the urge to tell Cassie to beam herself back to Planet PC, and, instead, smile. And nod. And offer one's services wholeheartedly.

'Of course I'll help,' I tell her.

'That would be wonderful,' she says, having expected no less. 'I thought the job would suit you, what with your talents.'

'Talents?' Now she's lost me.

'Didn't you used to work in television . . . or something?'

Ah, she's been picking up fag ends.

'Well, not exactly. Radio mostly. Although I did a bit of work on *Spitting Image*.'

'The *puppet* show?' She manages to make it sound like the crack-addicts-money-launderers-and-paedophiles show.

'Yes, that's right.' I smile.

'What sort of costumes did you do for that?'

Oh, I see. She thinks I made outfits for latex puppets.

'I can't sew to save my life,' I say. 'I did voices.'

I let it hang there for a moment, but I quickly realise she

isn't about to say, 'Wow, how interesting!' or, 'My God, what a gift!' or, actually, anything at all. She has this dead look on her face, as if she's been pumped with a gallon of Botox and has absolutely no control over her facial muscles.

'*Voices,*' she echoes eventually, for the sake of something to say.

I laugh awkwardly. 'I know. Silly thing to be good at, isn't it?'

Now, in the normal world, say meeting friends of friends in a pub, this snippet of info would be the perfect ice-breaker. Tedious small talk would be discarded as they threw names at me, trying to think of someone I *wouldn't* be able to mimic. Madonna, Marilyn Monroe, Mickey Mouse, Marge Simpson, Marlene Dietrich even. And that's just the Ms. Like I said, silly talent, but what can I say? It's my gift.

Cassie, though, isn't going to ask me to do my Jade from *Big Brother* or even my Judi Dench, not in a million years. No, that would be to admit she gave a damn. Which she doesn't.

'Hats,' she tosses at me as she walks off. 'I'll give you a list of how many and what types.'

Whatever . . . you stuck-up witch, I want to say but, obviously, don't.

I go to Molly's classroom and discover that despite being the first mum at the school gate, I'm now somehow late. Mrs Poulson glares at me as she hands over my daughter. Shot through with guilt, I grab Molly's hand and tug her off to the playground, where I know we'll find Thomas. He's there every day, kicking a ball around in the desperately few last minutes before home and homework beckon. He feigns not to notice our arrival and I decide to give him another five minutes of freedom. I watch him coax the ball with his feet, his thighs, his chest and his head, cajoling tricks out of it that still inspire awe in me. What can I say? It's *his* gift.

Molly pulls at my sleeve. 'Mummy, will you do Mrs Gottfried?'

'No, sweetheart, not here.'

'Aw, please. I *hate* Mrs Gottfried. *Pleeese.*'

I'm a soft touch. I drop to my knees and whisper, 'You vill sit in *total* silence until the bell,' in the faint German accent that everyone from reception upwards knows and fears. I wait for Molly's giggle, but it doesn't come.

'Mrs Clark, ve must talk ven you can spare a minute.'

Ohmygod. That wasn't me. Was it? No. So if it wasn't me, it could only be . . .

'Mrs *Gottfried*,' I gasp, looking up at her and having to shield my eyes from the September sun. 'Yes, of course, we must talk . . . Er, what about exactly?'

Did she hear me? Am I in trouble? Impersonating the deputy head is probably a hanging offence. I'm doomed, surely. My knees buckle as I try to stand up. I feel Molly quiver beside me and I put my arm round her protectively.

'Is it Thomas?' I ask unnecessarily. It wouldn't be the first time I've been hauled up to discuss my 'challenging' elder child.

'This isn't really the place,' she rasps, 'but ve must talk. If you give me a call, ve vill get something in the diary.'

She has death in her eyes, although whether it's me or poor Thomas she wants to kill is anybody's guess. 'I'll call you,' I say, as I hurry across the playground to gather my ten-year-old and get him to safety.

20

I peel back the duvet and Molly climbs gratefully into bed. She loves bedtime. I tuck the quilt up to her chin as she arranges two teddies on either side of her, tonight's chosen ones. Then I take one last look at her. Her hair, dark like her father's, is fanned over her pillow. Her face is an oasis of unspoilt beauty. You look at a sight like that and suddenly everything becomes all right.

'Goodnight, angel,' I say, stooping to kiss her.

'Mummy, will you just do Bart one more—'

'No more voices today. It's late, sweetie, go to sleep.'

I stand up and back out of her room, careful to leave the door wide open the way she likes it. I head for Thomas's room. Being five years older, he is allowed to read himself to sleep. Something educational usually, like the booklet dispensing wisdom on his newest PS2 game.

'Mrs Gottfried wants a word with me, Tom,' I say. 'What's that all about, then?'

I have to crane my neck to see him, and not just because he has taken cover beneath his camouflage duvet. The bed stands six feet off the floor. It's no ordinary bed. More an Ikea-designed space capsule on legs. Beneath the platform that supports the mattress are the integrated workstation and the cargo hold with its pods and cubbies. A cut-price Swedish miracle of engineering. NASA, look and learn.

'Thomas?' I ask again.

He emerges from the quilt in an explosion of petulance, infrared reading goggles strapped to his head, *Duke Nukem: Time to Kill* booklet in his hand. It's almost scary and I take an involuntary step back.

In my mind, he's chanting, '*Redrum, redrum, redrum.*'

In reality, all he says is, 'What?'

'Mrs Gottfried wants to talk to me. Something happen at school today?'

'*No*, nothing.' He turns his face to the wall and glares at the Arsenal badge on his Cesc Fabregas poster. Conversation over.

'OK. Is there anything you want to talk about?' I prod.

'No. Look, go away. I'm busy.'

And he's gone. Back beneath the covers with tonight's reading matter. Oh well, no bad thing, I suppose. He's jumped up two reading groups since we got him the PS2. It has to be helping.

'Night, sweetie,' I call out, shutting the door behind me, leaving him in pitch darkness the way he likes it.

I wonder how I could have produced two such different children. I'll have to have a serious talk with Richard at some point. He has some explaining to do because I'm coming to seriously doubt whether I'm really their mother.

I head downstairs and into the sitting room. Richard isn't home yet, but there's nothing unusual about that. With any luck, he'll have an *extra*-late one and I'll be safely tucked up when he rolls in, knackered from a hard day's marketing. You see, I wasn't where I was supposed to be today – I think I may have mentioned it. Richard won't be happy about that. Better he's unhappy while I'm asleep.

I settle on the sofa and pick up the remote, flicking channels with one hand, taking a cigarette from the pack with the other. As I put it to my mouth, the front door clicks open. A moment later, Richard is framed by the doorway, staring at me. His tie is pulled loose, his shirt is unbuttoned at the neck, and his face sags with disappointment.

'What the hell happened?' he asks, getting straight to the point.

'I'm really sorry,' I say in a voice that's quieter than a whisper.

'Do you know how many people you let down today? And it cost *money*, Fran. The studio had to be booked for an extra two hours while they waited for someone else to come and do it.' His teeth are tightly clenched, like little ivory dams holding back his anger. I wish he'd just let fly at me; get it over with.

He's talking about a voiceover job. His company has shot a test commercial at their own expense for some sexy new beer. They needed a voice to record the seven-word tag at the end. Enter me.

'Did they find someone, then?' I'm still whispering.

'Lisa I'Anson.'

'She's good.'

'She was completely wrong for the job. But she's professional. She *turns up*.'

But what does he expect? I haven't worked for years. I hardly even qualify as an amateur any more. But I don't say that. I should have known I wasn't up to it. I should never have said yes.

I nearly pulled it off. I got all the way to the recording studio – Saunders & Gordon, a place I've been to a hundred times before, though not once in the past decade – but I froze on the steps. It's only seven little words, I told myself. That got me to the door, my hand poised over the handle.

But. I. Just. Couldn't. Go. Through. With. It.

I'm Fran the mum now. Fran the housewife. Occasionally – not that often, given his work schedule – I'm Fran the wife. I realised too late that I am no longer Fran the voiceover artist.

So I ran. All the way to the shops.

Even though I knew I'd pay for it later.

Later as in now.

'You know, you only let yourself down today . . . Actually, that's crap,' he says, finally exploding. 'You let *me* down. I went out on a limb for you on this. I really didn't mind all the nepotism gags. So what, if it gets the job done? If the relative in question *turns up* and does the business. *So tell me, Fran, what the hell happened?*'

I'm flinching because he is furious.

'I just . . . Look, I was going to do it, I swear . . . but I just couldn't.'

'You *just couldn't.*'

'You have no idea how . . . how *terrified* I was.'

'I'm sorry, but what's so terrifying about *speaking*? Seven little words. It wasn't even on film. It's not even as if anyone has to *see* you say seven bloody words. You'd have walked it, Fran. You're brilliant at this. It's your thing, it's what you do.'

No, Richard, what I *do* is cook, clean, prepare lunchboxes. That's my *thing* now. I know that he and I have talked endlessly about me getting back into the Real World. But how could he have known that the Real World would instil such terror when even I didn't realise how scary it would be?

'Fran, talk to me,' he insists. 'What the hell happened to you today?'

'I don't know, Richard. I guess I just froze.'

'But *why*? It's your bloody job,' he says, complete exasperation taking over now.

'It *was* my job.'

'Well, perhaps you should have mentioned your *retirement* when I asked you to do it. What did your friends say? I mean, Sureya for one must think you're an idiot.'

'She didn't say anything . . . I didn't tell her about it.'

'Of *course* you didn't. Why on earth would you, when you

knew you'd end up bottling it?' He stops and runs his hand through his hair. Tries to calm himself. Then he looks at me and sees I'm about to launch into my explanation. 'Look, don't give me the I'm-only-a-housewife crap,' he says. 'We've got to move on from that.'

It's not crap; it's who I am! I want to scream at him, but don't. 'Look, I'm really sorry,' I babble instead, trying to appease him with yet more apologies. 'It won't happen again, I promise.'

He's not listening, just staring into the distance. 'Do you know what? I'm done with this. I'm sick and tired of pleading with you, jollying you along. Nothing's going to change, is it? So let's just accept it. You're in a rut and you're going to stay there.'

'I won't. Things *will* change. It's hard, but they will—'

'*Stop it.* Stop right there. I've heard this speech too many times. Please don't insult my intelligence with it again.'

Don't insult my intelligence. Exactly what Michael Corleone said to his brother-in-law . . . shortly before killing him.

Richard kicks off his shoes and I wait for him to continue, but it looks as if the conversation is over. He really has given up on me at last and instead he's putting a DVD into the machine, flopping on to the sofa. *The Sopranos.* He's a Mafia junkie and in his opinion *The Sopranos* is The Best Television in the World, Ever. A drama that chronicles the lives of woman-ising criminals who live like leeches on the backs of the honest and hardworking. What does that say about him? I wonder.

But I'm in no position to criticise – not tonight. I sit and stare uncomplainingly at the screen. I desperately want to apologise again. And again. But watching a DVD means there won't even be an ad break in which to beg forgive-ness. And by the time the programme ends, I'll have lost the will to bring up the matter again. I wouldn't say resolve is one of my strengths.

Just do it . . . but don't worry too much if you can't.

As we watch the opening credits, I pick up the cigarette I was about to have when Richard arrived home. When I light it, he fans the smoke away from his face, another thing to be annoyed about.

'Coffee?' I ask quietly.

He grunts his *no* grunt. I get up and head to the kitchen to make myself a cup and take my smoke with me.

I only opt for wine at the last minute because the bottle is already open.

19

Wednesday. Ordinarily, I'm not a lady who lunches. Today, happily, I'm breaking with tradition.

'So how's it going?' I ask, my mouth full of leaves that have been drizzled with balsamic vinegar. Not *splattered* or *haphazardly flicked at*, but *drizzled*. Obviously.

'The casting girl's doing the producer, lighting's shagging make-up, and I've had a grope with Phoebe the very cute hairdresser,' my friend tells me. 'The usual. I wouldn't mind, but all that attention I've lavished on her and my hair still looks crap.'

This doesn't wash with me. Unlike my mousey-brown curtains, Summer's luscious red curls always look movie-star fabulous; though I get to see them increasingly rarely. This is almost certainly because Arlington Road Primary is not the centre of her universe. She has a life.

Her life right now is a movie – a *proper* movie. She's starring in it alongside Clive Owen and Minnie Driver. Well, when they pass her in the market scene, she will actually be *alongside* them for about thirty seconds. 'It's no big deal, honestly,' she's been telling me. She's been playing it down, which is typical. It's all about not wanting to make me feel inadequate. I wouldn't be *that* surprised if when the posters for this movie go up, her name is above Minnie's.

'I could really do with your help,' she says. 'The dialogue coach doesn't know Eastern Europe from the East End. He's got me sounding like a Polish Peggy Mitchell. What's the secret?'

'There is no secret, *moja zabcia*.' I give this to her in my best Gdańsk. 'The trick is to speak from the back of the throat. Like you're about to gag.'

I haven't done Polish for ages and I'm pleased that I can still pull it off.

'How do you *do* that?' Summer shrieks. 'You are *brilliant*! What a waste.'

She doesn't know the half of it. Should I tell her about my failure to show last Monday? That's the question on my mind as she asks, 'What's "moja sab-whatsit", anyway?'

'My little frog.'

'How do you know all this stuff? How do you remember it?'

'Dunno. Must have a photographic memory or something.'

She stops, takes a sip of her water and gives me the kind of pitying look you'd give to a dying dog. 'I could so easily have got you this gig. We've got three different dialect coaches on the set – one for each accent – and you can do them all. You'd have saved the producers a fortune.'

'No, Summer, I'd have *incurred* them a fortune,' I tell her. She deserves to know the truth about her best friend even if it is only to get her off my back. I tell her about the test commercial, the seven little words and my spectacular no-show.

'Fran, how many times are we going to have this conversation?' she says when I've finished. She sounds like Richard. 'This is mad. Why are you running around having panic attacks? You've got nothing to be afraid of. You're the best.'

I'm not sure Tina Turner would agree with her . . .

'He's such a bastard,' she spits angrily after a moment's silence.

'Who?'

'Dick-head, who else?' she tells me. She has a habit of doing this: blaming Richard for everything, even my failings.

But what's her rationale this time? 'So how is it his fault?'

'Well, he could start by being a little bit more supportive, then you might not have felt so afraid to get back into the real world.'

'But he is supportive!'

'There you go again! Will you please stop bloody defending him all the time?' She's almost shouting. In fact, she couldn't sound angrier if I'd just told her that I'd lied to her twelve years ago; that, actually, *The Bill* was the bottom of the barrel, her Battered Wife had all the conviction of a soggy fish finger, and her Peckham accent was at least ten miles out.

I look around me to check no one in the restaurant is looking our way. 'Please don't shout, Summer,' I say, trying to calm her down.

'All right then, I'll say it quietly. He's a selfish pig. Why can't he be around more to help out with the kids? OK, let's face it, that's never gonna happen,' she concedes, before taking a moment to think properly about what she's saying. 'You know what you need to do? Forget Richard. You can't rely on him; we know this. I've got one word for you: *au pair*.'

'That's two words, actually.'

'Stop being flippant. North London's crawling with girls – mostly Poles as it goes – who'd love to pick your kids up from school.'

She's got a point, but I don't have an answer for her. Or at least, not one that I can give her in the little that's left of our lunch. She doesn't have kids, so she wouldn't understand what it's like to leave them to go out to work. That's what I tell myself. But really, when did I ever leave them and go out to work?

'Oh, never mind,' she says, tiring of waiting for me to respond. 'Maybe home is the best place for you. I'll be needing you around now, anyway.'

'What do you mean?'

'Oh, nothing. Just that the film's about to wrap and I'll be at a loose end, you know,' she says, waving a hand in the air, not wanting to talk about it any more. And actually, I don't blame her. She must be as sick as I am of talking in pointless circles about what I should do with my life.

I've been waiting to have an epiphany, a moment when the path the rest of my life should take will be laid out clearly before me. When it comes, Summer will surely be the first to hear about it.

Funny to think how much our lives have diverged since we first met. Back then she and I were in more or less the same place. That is, so desperate to make it we'd have done anything – even appear in *that* soap-powder commercial. Yes, it became the ad of the year, but unfortunately for us, only in the so-bad-it's-good category. She played the lazy-arsed delinquent who sat around in filthy clothes all day, and I was the soapsud. My face was hidden by costume, but poor Summer will never be able to deny her role. A dreadful ad that refused to die – it ran for years. But at least we kept getting the repeat fees. And better still, we had our friendship.

I'm staggered to think that was nearly twenty years ago.

Tension still lingers between us. But now Summer breaks into a warm smile. 'Let's change the subject before we argue really badly and then fall out, never to speak to each other again and one of your kids has to come after me with a machete to avenge your honour because I've been slagging you off for being rubbish at sorting your life out,' she says. 'So how are the kids, then?'

This is a rarely touched topic between us. Not being remotely maternal, Summer doesn't usually ask. It's not something I mind either. She isn't being selfish, quite the contrary actually. Summer's relationship with me is based on *us*. Having known the pre-marriage, pre-kids me, that's who she's interested in. She's the one person in my life who still views me as I used to be, so I guess I kind of like it.

'I've got to see the deputy head about Thomas,' I say, in answer to her question.

'What's he done?'

'I don't know yet. She's probably *concerned* that Thomas only thinks about football. But so what? He's brilliant. It's his gift.'

'Absolutely. And gifts ought to be nurtured, right?' she says, giving me a knowing wink.

'Absolutely.' I wink back. 'Don't worry, I'll sort it out.'

'I know you will.' She smiles. See? She still believes in the person I used to be, even if I don't. 'Listen,' she continues, 'why don't you come to the wrap party on Friday? You can meet my dear friends Clive and Minn and then we—'

'I can't. Richard's away Friday night.'

'So get a friggin' babysitter. They're ten a penny round here, surely.'

'More like ten pounds an hour,' I say, but she ignores the joke and makes a loud noise of furious exasperation.

The rise in volume means a bunch of women at a window table turn and stare at us. Rather, they stare at Summer. Maybe they recognise her from her six months on *Holby City* or the critically acclaimed costume drama she did with Bill Nighy or her short but disgustingly lucrative gig as the face of Asda. This happens a lot when I'm out with her. I take a sip of wine and bask in the reflected glory.

'Really, it doesn't matter,' I say. 'We'll go out another night. It'll give me something to look forward to.'

It sounds lame, but she goes along with it. 'OK, I'm going to hold you to that. Where's he going, anyway, this husband of yours?'

'Research group in Bristol . . . Don't look at me like that. He'll be back on Saturday morning and he's on full child duty for the rest of the weekend. I've blanked out the afternoon to go shopping. I'll be *gorgeous* for my party, you watch.'

'Anything would be an improvement on the way you look right now.' She wrinkles her nose. 'That sweatshirt is years old. No time to spruce up for lunch with your old pal, eh?'

'Sorry, but that's just life, I'm afraid.'

'No it isn't. It's you not bothering.'

'OK, OK, but like I said, I'm sorting myself out. By Saturday week I'll be totally transformed . . . You are coming, aren't you?'

'Wild horses, my little frog,' she says. She puts her hand over mine and I know that despite the jibes and the *not getting* certain things, she still gets me, the way only a real friend can.

I race home and start to cook. Well, I defrost the mince and chuck in the Dolmio. The mushrooms and parsley I add are my attempt to make something out of a jar look positively homemade. A touch of genius, or totally pathetic? I know what Summer would say. She has plenty of theories about me.

She was the only child of the warmest couple you could ever hope to meet. Summer, though, paints a picture of her father as a manic-depressive sociopath (gentle and slightly quiet to you and me) and her mother as a wilful exhibitionist (she sang while doing the housework). Summer also reckons her mum was a closet naturist. She used to cross the landing from bathroom to bedroom without a towel around her. So, obvious, really.

In truth, there was nothing wrong with her upbringing. She just needs to justify spending so much on therapy, which, as a Creative Person, is on a par with oxygen – *all I need is the air that I breathe and some therapy*. Her parents didn't get her, she – and her therapist – protest. Their failure to make a scene when she came out as a lesbian was clearly denial. And they didn't understand her need to change her name. (They'd christened her April, which, of course, was two long months away from who she really was. I asked her why she didn't just change her name to June, then. She told me not to be ridiculous – who'd want to be called a month when you could be named after an entire season? Whatever she's paying her therapist, it's clearly too much.) Her parents' worst crime was to die within three months of each other, as loved-up old couples often do. This wasn't nature taking its course, but an act of surrender – a refusal to understand her, right to the bitter end. Well, that's how Summer puts it, but hey, she's an actress: everything's a drama.

'Sensational' *The Times*
'Breathtaking drama' *Time Out* 'The London stage has never seen such a heart-rending performance. Summer Stevens in *Boiling an Egg*.'

Now that she hasn't got her parents to psychoanalyse, she makes do with me. Take my gift for voices. I've tried to tell her that it's just something I can do – like other people can draw or bend their thumbs back to their wrists – but she won't have it. 'I renamed myself Summer because I wanted to *embrace* who I am,' she said once. 'Your honing-the-voice thing is a subconscious act of denial. You're submerging your true self – hiding behind the identity of others.'

I didn't bother to argue. There's no point. That's the thing with people in therapy. They're all mad. For example, Summer would say that I'm stirring mushrooms and parsley into the Dolmio because I have no self-esteem, which comes from being abused by my parents, who had the audacity to split up when I was young, *deliberately* making me the victim of single-parent-family syndrome. And I thought I was doing it so my kids would get a bit of extra nutrition in their out-of-a-jar tea . . . But hey, what the hell do I know?

18

Fourteen years ago, when Richard and I met, my career was in full flow. I didn't have Summer's face, but never mind. My voice was in great demand and Adland loved me. You had a bank to flog? I could sound *so* trustworthy. A perfume? Just how breathily sensuous would you like me? Chirpy cockneys, acerbic northerners, southern belles . . . I could do the lot. I also did BBC nature docs, Radio Four sketch shows . . . I even did an early episode of *The Simpsons*. In those days, they weren't yet beating off the A-listers with a stick and they wanted my Maggie Thatcher. (Nowadays, of course, they get the real Tony Blair and they're doing *him* the favour.)

And the money! Not from *The Simpsons* or *Spitting Image*, but from Sony and Procter & Gamble. If a commercial ran and ran and the repeats rolled in, a half-hour stint in a sound booth could earn me a fortune.

Fourteen years ago, Richard had just about shaken off his graduate tag, but his salary barely covered his rent. So after we'd been seeing each other for six months, he moved in with me. For practical reasons, we said, but we both knew it was more than that. We were mad about each other. I remember the days when – *ha*, call us crazy-in-love – we even used to have baths together. We'd squash together like soapy sardines and the water would slosh over the side, soaking the clothes strewn on the floor. But did we care? *Ha*, we were crazy-in-love, remember.

These days, we have two bathrooms *and* a shower room, so we can take our pick. No one has to share any more. But that wasn't the point, was it? *Having to* didn't come into it. We *wanted* to do everything together.

What happens to chucking our clothes all over the bathroom floor and not caring that they'll end up sodden and trampled on? What happens to spontaneity?

'*Come here 'cause I want to fuck you right here, right now on the kitchen table and I don't care who sees us, but first I'll just put this knife away, and, ooh, better move this vase to be on the safe side. Oh, and I'll just get the chicken out of the freezer. And while I'm at it, I'll load the dishwasher, but* then *I'm definitely going to fuck you right here right now, etc.*'

Not exactly *The Postman Always Rings Twice*, is it?

But we've only ourselves to blame. By going with the passion, we nurture familiarity, which then spreads like cancer. Passion breeds familiarity breeds contempt. How sad.

For a couple of years, Richard was more or less a kept man. Then his career took off and so did his salary. Before we knew it, there was the big wedding and the flash cars and exotic holidays and then the children, and now fourteen years later, here we are. Saturday morning: Richard is at his research group in Bristol, and I'm on my own with the kids. Again. But I can't blame him. I suspect he's avoiding me because of the not-being-where-I-should-have-been incident last Monday.

I just texted Summer to tell her I hoped she enjoyed her wrap party last night. I sent it out of guilt – I felt bad that I hadn't made the effort to go. But even if I could have rustled up a babysitter, what on earth would I have worn?

An *outfit*! My party is a week away and the thought that I have *nothing to wear* puts me in a state of panic. I thought I had a solution. Sunday – being Richard's one day off, therefore *my* one day off – would be the ideal time to go frock-hunting while Daddy entertains the kids. But then, with a sinking heart, I remembered that Sunday is also his sister's birthday. I'll be trapped all day at a family gathering.

What the hell am I going to do? It's been nagging away at me all day and I've got to get my mind on to something else.

Thomas is moping, looking as if he's lost the will to live. He had football practice this morning, but two hours on, withdrawal is taking hold of his little body. It's a beautiful late-September day. I'll take him, his ball and Molly to the park.

I try Richard's mobile before we leave. I'd hoped he'd be back by now. Maybe he's stuck in traffic. Who knows? I get his voicemail. I don't bother to leave a message.

As we walk into the park, I look at the café ahead. It seems busy today. As we draw nearer, I spot Annabel, a mum from school. More precisely, the mum with the wart on the end of her nose. It's winking at me now in the low September sun. Obviously, she's with Cassie, who, despite not having a wart of her own, is Arlington's Head Witch. As we get nearer, I realise that I recognise every face at every table. It's like an Arlington mothers' convention. What are they all doing here?

'See you later,' Thomas yells as he hares off towards the football pitch without a backward glance. A game is already in progress, but I know it will stop the second he arrives. Then an argument will ensue over which side gets him. I have to agree with Richard that as ambitions go, football is hardly *feasible*. The chances of him making it are slim at best. But even so, I'm grateful for football on a daily basis. Thomas is complicated and sensitive – deep to the point of being unfathomable. He might be a mystery to me, his teacher and possibly to himself, but in football he has found an answer. It's a simple game, he's brilliant at it, end of story.

As he melts into the throng on the pitch, I steer Molly towards the café. 'Come on,' I say, 'let's get an ice cream.'

Before I know it, Annabel is beside me. 'Fran, can I have a word?' Now we're face to face. Or rather, face to wart. *Look into the eyes, into the eyes, not around the eyes and definitely not at the wart.*

'Of course,' I say. 'But what's going on in there?' I ask. I nod towards the café. Its French windows have been thrown open and inside I can see what looks like every single one of Molly's classmates cavorting around a man with a painted face as he twists balloons into animal shapes.

'It's Fabian's birthday party,' Annabel tells me authoritatively.

The shrieking from the café continues. I look down at Molly's sweet face as she stares at her friends and my heart sinks.

'Ooh, look, Fabian's got Mr *Punch*!' she squeals. 'And Maisy's in there! Can I go in, Mummy?'

Annabel's daughter, Maisy, and Molly are inseparable at school.

But what can I say?

No, you haven't been invited?

No, you aren't wanted?

I feel a stab of guilt. Poor Molly doesn't get invited to many parties. It's not her fault – she's pretty and so sweet-natured. I'm to blame. The few friends I've made at Arlington are women I actually like – quite a sensible approach to friend-making, you might suppose. But experience has taught me that befriending people whose company you enjoy is all wrong. If you want your kids to get on – that is, to get invited to the right parties – then you have to cosy up to their friends' mums because it is *they* who draw up the invitation lists. Witness Molly standing out *here*, party going on in *there*.

'*Please*, Mum,' she begs.

'Sorry, Molly,' I apologise. I try to fob her off. 'But we'll get an ice cream in a mo. I'm just going to have a quick word with Annabel.'

I turn to face her wart and quickly readjust my line of vision. She looks at me awkwardly, then gives me her most condescending smile. 'Look, this is a bit delicate, so I'll just get on with it,' she says. 'Maisy has been going on at me about the contents of Molly's lunchbox. Wine gums yesterday, Jammy Dodgers the day before . . . Freddie the Frog, I believe, the day before that.'

'Well, that's not all I put in there, but yes, go on.'

'I'm only trying to save your embarrassment, but were you aware that there's a movement to ban sweets and chocolates from the school? Including lunchboxes.'

No, I wasn't aware, but it doesn't surprise me. It would be madness to think that the mother-run police state of Arlington could ever condone sweets and chocolates as being part and parcel of the whole *being a child* thing. I picture Maisy's lunchbox filled with brown rice and tofu and her sad little face as she pines for a lump of chocolate moulded in the shape of a slimy amphibian.

'Mummy, the *party*.' Molly is tugging on my hand.

'Just a suggestion,' Annabel continues, 'but I've found yoghurts and little bits of fruit are ideal substitutes . . . and so much *better* for them.'

And you know what? I've had enough of being condescended and dictated to. I've had it up to here with her winking wart too. I'm going to say something.

'Molly's glucose intolerant,' I announce. Not exactly openly rebellious, but I'm standing my ground. Sort of.

'What am I, Mummy?' Molly asks, still staring at the party.

'Don't you mean lactose intolerant?' Annabel frowns.

Obviously, I'm not actually sure what I mean. 'Yes, that too, so it's really hard to find suitable things, to be honest with you, Annabel.' I feel my face burn red and turn away, pretending to be fascinated by the cavorting clown.

'Don't worry. There are plenty of alternatives these days. I'll give you a list and you can hit the health-food shops next week,' Annabel tells me.

I want to be anywhere but here, for Molly's sake and for mine. I can ignore Annabel's condescension but not Molly's desperation at missing the party. I'd love to tell her that Fabian's a stupid name, anyway. Stupid boy, stupid party, stupid—

'Oh, hi, Fran.'

I turn to see Natasha standing beside me. Fabian's mum.

'In you go, Molly.' She smiles. 'You're a bit late, but never mind. Here's your badge.' She peels off a white sticker bearing her name in fat orange felt-tip.

Oh God, I'm such a horrible person. There I was, thinking vicious thoughts about Fabian's mum for blacklisting Molly, and here she is, *expecting* her. Molly had been invited all along – the pre-prepared sticker proves it. Seeing the un-restrained joy on her face as she skips off makes everything better for a moment.

But only for a moment because I realise that – *shit!* – we have no present. And it's a well-known fact that the child who turns up to a party without a present faces eternal social oblivion.

'Would you like a drink?' Natasha asks as my head searches for a solution. 'I've brought wine for the mums. The café's prepared to turn a blind eye as long as we drink out of plastic cups. If anyone from the council turns up, it's apple juice, OK?'

She has a twinkle in her eye. God, I really *am* a horrible person, tarring everyone with the same brush, always thinking the worst of them. I barely know Natasha, but anyone who's prepared to defy the licensing laws by turning the park café into an illicit drinking den is all right by me.

'I'd love a glass,' I say, 'but I've stupidly left Fabian's present at home.'

Annabel narrows her eyes. She probably realises I've made a huge gaff here. 'We bought him the Twenty Questions game,' she says. 'They love educational stuff at this age, don't they?'

I want to tell her – preferably while punching her – that, *no*, at this age they'd much rather stuff marbles up their noses, but I don't.

'Thanks, Annabel, but you shouldn't have gone to any trouble,' Natasha says. 'He still prefers playing with the empty boxes. I thought that stopped at eighteen months.' She laughs and bends down to scoop up her toddler. 'Fabian's still got more in common with little Trist than he has with Quinn, hasn't he, Trist?'

I'd forgotten she has three boys. And look at her: slim, made-up, together.

I shuffle my feet and look at my dirty trainers and ripped jeans. I try to console myself with the fact that, OK, so she looks great, but her children still have stupid names. Strangely, the thought doesn't make me feel any better. Worse, in fact. Why am I always thinking such spiteful things about people?

'Don't worry about the present. Just sit down and relax,' Natasha tells me. 'I'll go and get you a drink.'

As she walks off, Annabel too rejoins her cronies, taking her wart with her. Head Witch Cassie half smiles at me, then looks quickly away. What's she looking so shifty about? Who cares? Molly's happy. And Natasha has just brought me a glass of wine. What more could I ask?

I settle myself on a bench away from the café and watch Thomas do his thing. I take a sip of wine and feel alcohol-tinged relief seep through me. I might still be wound up after Annabel's ridiculous lunchbox conversation, but a few more sips and relaxation will arrive.

I glance at the café and see Cassie, Annabel and the other witches, huddled together, heads down. Who knows what they are talking about? Maybe they're exchanging recipes.

'*Eye of newt, ear of bat, tail of frog, claw of cat. But let's not forget a spoonful of couscous and a handful of bean sprouts. After all, ladies, a healthy balance is so important.*'

But Natasha was a pleasant surprise with her warmth and her wine. Maybe I've been too blinkered. I'm resolving to search harder for like-minded mums when my mobile rings.

'What do you want?' Richard asks. 'The good news or the bad?'

'The good, I guess.'

'I've got you a pair of limited edition GHDs. The new pink ones.'

He pauses, waiting for me to squeal my undying grati-tude. Given that I let him down so badly last Monday, I know I should. But I don't.

Instead, I say, 'Lovely. Thanks. And the bad?' Like Richard's hero, Don Corleone, I'm a person who prefers to hear bad news immediately.

'It's been a total disaster. We've got to stay on and do extra groups today and then go back to the office tomorrow morning for a strategy meeting.'

'On a *Sunday*?'

But why am I surprised? It's not as if this is a first.

'I know, I'm so pissed off. And I'm knackered. Couldn't sleep at all last night.'

'Poor you,' I say, trying really hard not to sound sarcastic. I'm wound up now, because if he's working tomorrow, that means I have to go to *his* family gathering without him. In an effort to suppress my growing angst, I tune out of Richard's moan about work and watch Thomas score a goal – an athletic scissor kick that has his teammates burying him beneath a writhing pile of bodies. That's my boy.

'What's happening?' Richard asks, sensing he has lost me.

'Thomas just scored. We're in the park. And Molly's at Fabian's party.'

'Oh, yes, I saw the invitation in her lunchbox last week,' he says absent-mindedly.

'Well, why didn't you show it to me, then?' I snap involuntarily.

'I did!' he protests. 'I put it on top of your pile of papers on the counter.'

'That pile of papers, you idiot, was for the recycling bin.' My voice is raised now.

'What's the big deal?' he shouts back. 'She's at the party, isn't she?'

'Yes, but she very nearly wasn't. It was very nearly a complete disaster.'

'I was only trying to help.'

'Well, in future, you stick to your job and let me do the kids.'

'Fine, I'll remember that next time you're moaning about being bored because all you've got is the kids.'

'*Fine.*'

'Good.'

'*Good.*'

'*Jesus* . . . I'm going,' he says.

And he goes.

'Fuck you,' I say to nobody, draining the plastic cup in celebration of having the final word, even if he didn't hear it . . . and even though he's probably mouthing, 'Fuck you too,' to the air up in Bristol. No, not *fuck you*. He doesn't approve of swearing – apparently, it demonstrates a sad lack of vocabulary. Though he doesn't seem to mind that every other word Tony Soprano says starts with F.

Richard the gangster freak. He has a party trick: name any scene in *Goodfellas* and he'll quote you a line, possibly the entire scene. Although his accent is crap (but I would say that), he's word perfect. Having listened to him over the years, I've become something of an expert by default.

There's a scene in *Goodfellas*: Henry is walking with Jimmy when Jimmy asks, 'Do you think Maurie tells his wife everything?' And in the space of that throwaway remark, Henry *knows* that Maurie is going to get whacked. That's how easily, how quickly, life-changing (life-*ending*) decisions are taken.

It's as quick as that for me too.

No, no, no, I'm not going to whack Richard . . . Not yet, anyway. (*Joking!*)

But I am going to do something. I *know* that I have to sort things out. Now! Not next week, next month, next year, the way I usually tell myself. It's no longer just my sanity that's at stake, but my marriage too.

Look at us: we live in the same house, but we exist on different planets. And when we do come together, it's only to bicker. If I try really hard, I *can* remember when it wasn't like this . . .

Our first date: three hours in some crummy spaghetti

house *laughing*. To be honest, I used to find making people laugh a doddle – all I had to do was read out a menu in a Joan Rivers voice and they were *mine*. But Richard listened beyond the comedy voices. And he looked beyond my plain-Jane ordinariness – five foot nothing, thin lips, flat chest – and fell in love with *me*. And I fell in love with him right back. With his dry wit and perfect timing, he made me laugh until my eyes streamed. And I can remember it like yesterday. All that happiness and laughter . . .

But you know, right now, sitting on this park bench, I can't remember a single funny thing he's ever said.

I used to think he was a bit rock 'n' roll. He did coke, he smoked and drank; a real *fuck-you* spirit, which I loved. Then he caught someone's eye at work and got his promotion. Out went the cool T-shirts that showed off his tattoo and in came the suits and ties that showed off his profession-alism. I told him I liked the new him, which I suppose I did. All that winning new business meant he had to put in the hours but that was OK. Back then, he still had excess energy and he'd bring it home and inject it into *us*. And the pay rises and share options got us the big house and the wonderful life.

Ten years ago, when I was pregnant with Thomas, Richard – like Sureya, like *everyone* seemed to be doing – quit smoking. I told him I'd give up too and I did – for eighteen months in total. I endured two smoke-free preg-nancies. Yet, while my friend and my husband have remained resolute, here I sit, on a park bench with a cup of wine in one hand, a cigarette in the other. But at least, I tell myself, I did the right thing by my babies. Two gorgeous, chubby eight-pounders, they thrived and grew just as they were supposed to.

Unlike Richard's and my relationship.

What happens to couples when they have kids? How is it that children come between their happy, loving parents, forcing them apart like tiny human wedges? Honestly, Molly and Thomas are everything to me. I wouldn't want to be in a world without them. But where does that leave Richard? Stuck in Bristol, that's where. But what can I say? He may not be where he's supposed to be on this sunny Saturday afternoon, but neither was I last Monday morning.

Pots, kettles, black.

I force myself to smile as his gorgeous daughter bounds towards me. She's waving her party bag in triumph, as if she's just cracked the Da Vinci Code. 'Look, Mummy, look!' she yells, waving a giant yellow cellophane-wrapped monstrosity.

Whooping with joy seems the required response, so that's what I do.

Maisy joins her and they flop on to the grass and dip their fingers into the little sachets of white sherbet they find inside. I look on and wonder what the Sweet Nazis will make of that.

'I've given a box of that stuff to Annabel. Gift-wrapped, of course.'

It's Natasha, and I add mind-reading to her growing list of qualities.

I'm slightly embarrassed that she overheard our conversation earlier, but I bat it away. Instead, I laugh and say, 'They've had a great time. Thank you.'

'They enjoyed themselves all right. Here, have this.' She hands me another filled-to-the-brim plastic cup and adds, 'I need this one myself.'

She drinks hers back thirstily.

'Well, it's over now. Until next year,' I say brightly.

'These bloody children's entertainers are the vilest people

on earth. They hate us mums and they hate our kids even more. They're patronising, dictatorial . . . Mr Punch? Mister Bloody Wanker more like.'

This woman is OK. She's relaxed, she possesses an actual sense of humour, and, ooh, say it really quietly, she swears too!

'I can't believe I waited until the end to have a drink,' she says. 'I'm going back for another. I'll get you another too. Won't be long.'

I'm not going to get the next cup, as it goes. As she walks off, Thomas's game finishes and he trots towards me. 'Come on, let's go,' he urges sullenly – you'd never guess he's just scored six or seven goals. He isn't one to hang around, Thomas.

And I've learnt that there isn't much point in arguing with him, so off we go. I wave goodbye to Natasha, but she doesn't wave back. She looks as if she's about to head-butt Mr Punch, who seems to be taking her to task over the correct way to play musical statues. Best leave her to it.

I avoid eye contact with the witches, still at their table, their heads together. Good luck to them. They can't get to me now. The afternoon hasn't been such a wash-out after all. I've been wanting to make new friends and look what happened. I clicked effortlessly with Natasha, who until a couple of hours ago I'd glibly written off as One of Them. Sometimes it's a wonderful thing to be proved wrong.

For once, I feel as happy as all the other mums look. I decide that when we get home, the kids and I will bake cakes or do some painting. Or maybe we'll just play *Duke Nukem*. Who cares? We're going to have fun, even if it isn't of the PC variety.

Even the argument with Richard doesn't bother me now.

No, that was a positive thing. It sparked my resolve to change. And I'm going to stick with it: bake cakes, paint pictures, sort out my life. In that order, obviously.

17

There was a message from Cassie when we got home. Something about a woman from the National making the hats for the school play now, so thanks, but my services were no longer required. Is that why she was looking so shifty in the park? Well, that's OK. I never wanted to do her silly hats, anyway.

Ten o'clock. The kids are finally asleep and I'm contemplating calling Summer to see how her party went. Maybe she got off with Minnie Driver. No worries about it being too late to phone. Summer says sleep is for wimps. Or heterosexuals. Or are they the same thing?

As I put out my cigarette and pick up the phone, I hear the front door click open. It's Richard.

'You're home,' I say stupidly.

'Looks like it,' he says wearily. 'The whole thing was such a disaster we called it a day. We'll have to have a complete rethink next week instead.'

'Well, it's good to have you back.'

And it is. Because this is Day Zero, start-again time. I've played dressing up with Molly and three levels of *Duke Nukem* with Thomas. Now it's time to put Fight Night behind us and do some serious bonding. Starting from now.

He looks at the wide acres of empty sofa beside me, then flops down on the armchair opposite. I make a mental note to change my deodorant.

'I'm knackered,' he says, rubbing his grey face. He does look dreadful. 'Bloody traffic. The M4 was a nightmare.'

'Never mind,' says the new, invigorated me. 'Drink?'

'If there's any left.' He eyes the open bottle on the coffee table.

I laugh awkwardly and say, 'Well, of course there is.'

God, this is going well, I think, as silence obligingly fills the yawning chasm between us.

'Have you been smoking?' He's sniffing the air theatrically. Ex-smokers. The worst kind.

'I actually think I've done really well considering the day I've had . . .'

And I'm ready to tell him all about it. Not in a whingy, guilt-inducing way, but entertainingly; an amusing account of Lunchbox-gate and the mums and the party and whatever else I can send up, complete with witty asides and comedy voices. Honestly, I am so psyched up for this, but halfway through 'the day I've had' he turns away from me and picks up the TV remote. I feel my body deflate.

As I watch him channel-hop, I decide to ask him about his day instead. Show some interest for a change and be ready with genuine sympathy when he gets to the really dreadful bits.

But nothing happens.

And now I can't even remember how to run a sentence together. My mind is a total blank. I search my brain for something – anything – to break the silence, but there's nothing. This must be what it feels like to be Jade Goody.

Jesus, why the hell is *talking* with my husband of twelve years so difficult? Isn't conversation just supposed to, you know, *happen*?

Bad day at the office, dear? followed by a grateful unburdening of troubles, followed by mad, passionate, I've-missed-you sex.

'God, I hate that smell,' he says, tossing the remote aside. 'I'll take my bags up. I'm going for a bath.'

I stare at the ashtray on the coffee table. *Smelling* at me.

The phone is still on my lap. I could call Summer and get it all out. Or maybe Sureya is still up. I could have a heart-to-heart with her. But I know what they'd both say. Summer would tell me – *again* – what a pig Richard is. She's nothing but negative about him at the best of times. And Sureya would tell me – *again* – how lucky I am. She's nothing but positive about him all of the time.

But seriously, what's the point in talking to anyone about anything? What would it change? I'm going to bed. It was madness to think I could start rebuilding my marriage at this hour. I'll do it in the morning. Building work needs daylight.

16

Richard's father, George, is a retired petrochemical engineer. Nothing wrong with that, except that I have a horror of being trapped in conversation with him. I know from bitter experience that he can talk for two hours plus on the subject of Saudi Arabian oil refineries without hesitation, repetition or deviation. His mother, Elaine, is pleasant, easygoing, quiet . . . OK, her forehead bears the word WELCOME and the muddy imprint of George's gardening boots. And then there is his sister, Fiona, who is . . . well, you tell me.

She greets me in the hall.

'Fran, *hi*, don't you look well?'

'Do I?'

'Yes, the extra pounds suit you. Go on through. Everyone's been here ages. Oh, is that for me? Liberty again? *Lovely*. Where's that brother of mine?'

So, in just a couple of dozen words, we've established that a) I'm fat, b) we're terribly late, which is probably all my fault, c) I'm rubbish at buying presents, and d) who cares about a), b) and c) because, hey, where's her Richard?

It's Fiona's thirtieth. The baby of the family. She's already had the big party for her real friends. This is the secondary event for family. Bubbly, nibbles and chit-chat for aunts, uncles, cousins and a few old family friends who never quite went away.

George and Elaine arrive in the hall to greet us. Molly stands in the midst of us beaming at everyone, but Thomas hides behind me as I exchange stiff hugs with his grand-parents. We've perfected a technique over the years. From a few feet away, it looks like a hug, but actually, virtually no unsavoury bodily contact is taking place. It's the huggers' equivalent of air-kissing.

Richard comes in now, a case of Moët in his grasp – another client freebie. He gives me a grin. No big deal – it's just an automatic thing. The marriage rebuilding hasn't really started yet. Well, I took Thomas to football this morning, so we've barely seen each other. And a family do is no place to begin. I'll make a proper start tomorrow, Monday, when he's back at the office. Sounds like an excellent plan.

I grin back, but he doesn't see it because his sister has jumped on him. Now *that* is a hug. A hug the like of which my husband hasn't given me for . . .

Jesus, is that jealousy? Of my *sister-in-law*?

They peel themselves apart and follow their parents into the huge sitting room at the back of the house. Richard grabs Molly's hand and tugs her along with him. Cast adrift in the empty, echoey hall, Thomas and I stand alone. The look on his face. Is that jealousy? Of his sister?

Richard is crazy about Molly. But it's so easy to be crazy about her, isn't it? She's sunny, straightforward, pretty, clever . . . Molly is most definitely his daughter, whereas Thomas is . . . Well, to Richard, Thomas is a riddle wrapped in an enigma wrapped in a hard outer shell of surliness. A puzzle that he cares not enough about to crack. No, that's not fair. It isn't that he doesn't care about Thomas or loves him less, it's just that . . . Actually, he probably loves him less.

Oh God, I don't know. Our son is a mystery to us both. I don't know why he's so sensitive and moody and dark. But I'm trying to understand him; make a connection. I'm even making some progress. Last night, we watched an old episode of *Friends* together. I'm not sure exactly how many gags he got, but he laughed out loud three times. *Three* times! Unprecedented – a year's worth of laughter in one half-hour period. In fact, the image of his teeth is still with me. Mismatched, oversized slabs that have somehow squeezed themselves into his tiny jaw. Where had they come from? The last time I saw him smile he still had cute, white mini-squares arranged in two neat rows. As unfamiliar and misshapen as these new teeth were, they were beautiful. *He* was beautiful.

Thomas and I sit in a corner. I'm cradling a glass of wine. Thomas is a Diet Coke junkie, but this house is a fizz-free zone so his hands are drinkless.

We watch Richard and Molly work the room – she's her father's daughter all right. His looks, his charisma, his ability to make people warm to her by simply *being*. I put my arm round Thomas's shoulder. It's a reflex, a response to Richard taking Molly's hand as he encourages her to tell Elaine about her performance as a tree in her assembly last week. What can I say? She was a great tree and so she should be telling her grandma all about it. Especially in that great tree voice she came up with all by herself. A sort of raspy, woody whisper. Exactly as a tree would sound if it could talk. People gather around her, impressed, amazed and patting Richard on the back for the marvellous job he's done by simply *being her father*.

But where's Thomas's praise? What about the hat-trick he scored in his match this morning? I want to stand up and shout. Listen, everyone, Thomas scored *three* goals in *one* match AND ALL WITH HIS LEFT FOOT! But I could yell it at the top of my voice and no one would be impressed. This is rugby country. Balls are banned unless they're oval.

Richard knows less about the offside rule than I do and cares even less that Thomas might just be the next Wayne Rooney.

'Shall we go out to the garden for a kick-about?' I whisper.

His face lights up and then quickly drops. 'But there's no ball here.'

'That's what you think. There's one in the boot. I'll smuggle it in. Wait for me outside. Rendezvous by the apple tree in two minutes.'

We sneak out of the room in full view of everyone, but seen by no one.

15

Bob Geldof might not have liked Mondays, but I do. Especially Mondays that come after Sundays as crappy as yesterday. I'm doing the laundry. At the washing machine, I go through pockets meticulously. God, I'm good at this. You won't catch *me* leaving a scarlet paper napkin in a pair of jeans and turning an entire wash pink . . . er, like I did two weeks ago.

I pick up the trousers Richard arrived home in on Saturday and pull out a crumpled fiver, a business card from some guy at ITV, a sheet of computer printout that, once I've unfolded it, turns out to be a bill from the Langham Hilton, itemising, among other things, snacks, sweets and drinks from the minibar. It throws me so I check the date at the top. Friday, 23 September. My stomach flips.

Research groups in Bristol, he said.

Nightmare traffic on the M4, he cursed.

A tacky room in a Travelodge, he moaned.

Definitely not a deluxe double in a five-star hotel in the heart of London.

Jesus. What kind of custard-brained *idiot* am I? Any woman with an ounce of intelligence would have twigged he was lying, wouldn't she? Wouldn't she?

But hold on, STAY CALM. It really is possible that I might just be jumping to the wrong conclusion. That's what I'm thinking as I check the bill against the calendar on the kitchen wall. But, no. The dates definitely tally. I slump forward on to the kitchen counter, my head swimming with the real-isation that I haven't got the first thing to feel calm about.

If I'd imagined this might happen, I might have been better prepared for it and wouldn't now feel like such a fool. And somehow, that's the worst feeling of all.

Unbelievable but true: I've never imagined Richard cheating on me. Honestly, it hasn't once crossed my mind – not even as I gazed into the shop window last week and saw the world's most undesirable woman staring back at me. Because if Richard was screwing around, well, that would just make him like every other man and haven't I always thought he was different?

Jesus, just how many kinds of idiot can I be in the space of five minutes? What woman *doesn't* think her husband is different? But they're men. And screwing around is what men do best, isn't it?

So here I am, jumping from feeling sick to wondering if it could all be a ridiculous mistake to hating All Men to thinking that what would *really* make things better – at not quite ten in the morning – is a nice glass of wine.

I almost called Summer for advice, but decided against it. I knew what she would say. She'd have told me to arm myself, shoot first, ask questions later. Because if he's having an affair, he would have to die.

I didn't know what to think. My head was pinging point-lessly back and forth between conflicting positions until for some inexplicable reason, I decided that confronting Richard immediately was the way to go. Which now actually seems like a really stupid idea, I think, as I stand outside his office block.

I'm not normally this impulsive. I don't normally arrive at my husband's place of work unannounced. But this isn't *normally*. Sitting on the Tube, I listened to the voices in my head. Little comments Richard has made lately, helpfully replayed for my edification. That I care too much about what others think of me. That I am (*'And you wonder where Thomas gets it from'*) too sensitive. And most often of all, that if I'm so bored, why don't I get off my backside and *do* something? Meanwhile, another voice totted up the months in which we haven't had sex. Because Richard is always out and when he isn't, I told the voice, he's too tired. *Hmmph*, the voice replied.

As the train rattled on, I told myself to stop listening to the stupid voices. I told myself that there can't be another woman. Maybe he just needed to get out of the house because I've been such a misery lately. And I've been feeling dreadful since Fight Night; why shouldn't he have been feeling just as bad? I clung to the thought. As specks of light at ends of very black tunnels go, this one shone pretty brightly.

I thought about how miserable I've been. Richard has always tried to encourage me back to work in the hope that it would lift me from my pit. I've resisted in part by telling myself that the fulfilment that supposedly comes from working is way overrated. Arlington is full of mums who have hopped off the career ladder to do the school run and bake cakes – and don't they seem happy enough?

Then I thought of Sureya and how she's managing to combine having a life with raising kids. Why have I always been so defensive? *You can't work* and *be a good mum. One or the other would suffer.* But Sureya's twins seem to be doing just fine.

A whole train journey spent batting thoughts back and forth, no conclusion reached. And now, here I am.

As I look up at the building – the eighth floor, Richard's office – I've decided to use another West End shopping trip as a pretext for *just happening to be in the area.* Then I can ask – in a way that suggests I've only just thought of it – if he's free for lunch. And as we relax over a light, healthy snack, I can nonchalantly mention the Langham Hilton. And maybe then he'll hit me with his totally innocent explanation, and we'll laugh and slap our foreheads and then laugh some more. It'll be fine.

So why then do I feel sick?

I've got to pull myself together. There must be an innocent explanation – he wanted some Fran-free time in a hotel room; that *must* be it. OK, so we aren't as close as we used to be, but we still have two gorgeous kids and a beautiful home and all that history. Richard hasn't made it to the eighth floor because he's an idiot. And only an idiot would jeopardise all that history for a quick shag with some office girl.

Office girls . . . they're all around me, clicking along the streets of London in their heels. Slim, tailored, confident office girls . . . I look at myself. God, I didn't even get changed before I came out. I'm wearing— No, it doesn't bear description. Let's just say *tailored* doesn't come close.

There's a Next across the street. Not exactly D&G, but beggars can't be choosers and all that. Have I got time to nip in for a five-minute makeover?

Forget it – I'll need a hell of a lot longer than five minutes. Let's just get this over with.

Richard is on the phone. He waves me into his office with one hand while scribbling on a pad with the other – proving that here, if not at home, he *can* do two things at once.

His office is big and the floor-to-ceiling glass on all sides means I can see Richard's people outside. Busy, important people with real jobs to do, reasons to be here. What am I doing here again? Oh, that's right, I'm playing amateur detective.

I feel ridiculous. He puts the phone down and looks at me and I want to run.

'Hi, how's it going?' I say, as breezily as I can.

'What are you doing here, Fran?'

I try to read his face. Is he pleased to see me? He's inscrutable, so I plough on. 'I just happened to be in the area . . . shopping . . . you know, for an outfit . . . for the party. I just wondered if you fancied lunch.'

I feel like a spotty, gawky twerp who's been dared to ask the school hero out on a date. *Relax!* I tell myself, this is no stranger. And even though he was undoubtedly once the school hero, he is now your husband.

'You know how busy I am, Fran.' He speaks slowly, the way the school hero would speak to the school twerp. 'I'll be lucky if I have time for a sandwich, never mind lunch.'

'Oh . . . OK, just a thought . . .'

I peter out as Richard looks past me. I turn to see a woman framed by the doorway. She's beautiful and shockingly slim. The light streaming through the big windows illuminates her perfectly, as if this is all rehearsed, as if a top cinematographer has spent the entire morning setting up the shot. Then, in a move straight out of a shampoo ad, she tosses her hair over her shoulder and delivers her line: 'Ready for you, tiger. Got your charts?'

The camera pans to me now. I'm cast in the role of Block of Lard, and though I don't have a line, my face says, *Did that woman just call my husband tiger?*

Is it her? Did she spend Friday night at the Langham Hilton getting it on with Richard? I look at the bustling office behind her. There are women everywhere. It could be any one of them. But only this one just called my husband tiger.

I realise now that, Richard apart, I recognise no one here. But why should I? I don't visit him at work any more. In the old days, I'd meet up with him and his crowd for lunch or a drink. But that was another age – BC, as in Before Children. The people he used to work with have long gone – probably to do the school run and bake cakes – and they've been replaced by the next generation.

'Karen, great,' Richard says. 'Yes, I'm ready . . . This is Fran, by the way. Have you met?'

Of course we haven't. When would we have met?

The woman – more of a girl, really – smiles. 'Hi, nice to meet you,' she says. Her smile is dazzling – straight out of a toothpaste ad. I give her one back, but it probably resembles something out of an Anadin commercial – tense, nervous and all that. She looks over my shoulder at Richard. 'We're in room one,' she says. 'Adam's joining us when he's out of his meeting.'

I find myself listening to her accent. Not American. More Canadian. The way she made 'out' sound like 'oat' . . . definitely Canadian. But so what?

'Be there in two minutes,' Richard calls out as she turns to go.

It can't be her. He wouldn't introduce his wife to someone he was screwing, would he? He'd have gone all shifty and awkward and the truth would have been irrefutable. But actually, he didn't introduce me as his wife, did he? And she didn't hang around to make conversation either.

God, my head is a mess. Spinning around faster than Kylie's bum in the video.

'Sorry, Fran, but you should have called first,' Richard says. He's not looking at me, but searching through piles of paper on his desk.

'Never mind. Just felt like being spontaneous, that's all,' I say, as merrily as I can manage. 'Canadian, is she? That girl?'

'What?' he says, distracted now. Still searching. Tiger has lost his charts. I can't believe the state his desk is in. Every inch is covered in papers, layouts and documents. Something in me wants to lunge forward and tidy it up.

'Sorry, but I've got to get on. The pitch is at five,' he says. 'You know how it is.'

Er, no, actually. How is it, Richard? What pitch? The days when he would come home and tell me about his job, *really* tell me stuff, have long gone. Nowadays he gives me it in soundbites; brand synergy and blue-sky thinking and optimal targeting of upmarket ABs, the ones with all that disposable income. Well, good for them. But what does it all mean?

Actually, it's not all his fault. Do I ever ask what he's up to? No, is the answer. And my waning interest coincided perfectly with him not having the time or the inclination to tell me.

He's MD to this lot. Managing Director. But to us at home, all it stands for is Missing Dad. And not necessarily in the longing-for sense, either.

'Fran?'

I snap back to the present. He's standing in front of me clutching his charts. 'Sorry, miles away,' I say. 'Right, yes, I'll get out of your way, then.'

'Sorry,' he echoes. He leans forward and kisses me on the cheek, and then I watch him leave the room.

My stint as an amateur detective is over.

14

Sureya and I sit in my kitchen. I have a glass of white wine in front of me. Sureya prefers, as is her way, herbal tea. And, as is also her way, she's smiling. You'd never guess we're talking about infidelity.

'I really don't believe it,' she says, oozing hope. 'He's the last guy I'd have down as having an affair.'

'Really? Why?' I ask, desperate for some of her optimism to rub off.

'Would he really risk everything you've built together?'

'Men take those sorts of risks all the time, Sureya,' I tell her flatly. 'I thought Richard was different, but . . .'

'*But* he *adores* you,' she says with absolute certainty.

Is that the best she can come up with? I've been on the receiving end of precious little adoration of late.

'He's never *here* to adore me,' I say, taking a sip of wine and enjoying the chill as it slides down my throat.

'Yes, work, the big promotion, all that,' she replies, with a bat of her hand. 'Men define themselves by their jobs. They can't help it. It's in their chromosomes. But just because he's always at the office doesn't mean he's stopped caring.'

I raise an eyebrow. 'That's easy for you to say. You see your husband from time to time.' I hear the bitterness in my voice and immediately want to take it back.

'Rubbish. Mina called the TV repair man Daddy the other day,' she jokes. 'Look, do you know how many times Richard has called me – from the *office* – to make sure

Michael and I will be at your party? As if we'd miss it. I'm not the only one either. He's been through the invitation list several times. He's agonising about every detail, you know. He's *desperate* to make it the best night of your life, believe me.'

The thought of my husband wasting precious work time agonising about my party gives me a glow, I must admit, but not nearly enough to overwhelm the hard evidence of the hotel bill.

'I've got a bit of paper that says he's having an affair, Sureya,' I remind her.

'It says nothing of the sort. There could be any number of explanations, most of them innocent. You have to talk to him about it, give him a chance to explain. Don't prejudge anything, Fran.'

She's right. I have to talk to him. 'I will,' I say.

'*When?*' She sounds exasperated. 'When did you find the damn thing?'

'Monday.'

'And today it's?'

'Yeah, yeah, Thursday. Look, I've barely seen him. He won his pitch and you know what it's like.' I use Richard's line on her. Well, it worked on me. Shut me up a treat. I take another long, slow sip of my wine. I will the alcohol to seep into my head and help me achieve total amnesia. I'd dearly like to forget the fact that I haven't talked to my husband for three days. I'd also like to forget the fact that my thirty-seventh birthday party is two days away and I still have nothing to wear. But the wine, as usual, is going in the wrong direction, heading straight for my waist, maybe even going as far as the tops of my legs. My thighs are drunk, while my head is as clear as a summer day.

'Fran, what are you waiting for?' Sureya implores. 'This is too important.'

'Why? I thought you said he wasn't having an affair.' I think I'm being obtuse now.

'No, I don't think he is, but clearly you do and clearly it's doing your head in. So *talk to him.*'

'It's complicated, Sureya.'

'No, it's simple. You've got something on your mind. Talk to him about it. Look, I know confrontation can be . . . *difficult*. But the longer you put it off, the harder it'll be. I know you, Fran. This isn't something you can hide from.' She laughs. 'And aren't you always saying you don't want to turn into your mother?'

My mother. Someone else who never talks about anything. Well, she talks a lot, but never about anything that matters. The Brushing Things Under the Carpet Gene, one I have surely inherited.

Sureya sips at her tea and runs a weary hand through her thick, glossy hair. Which of us is more exasperated at this point is anybody's guess. 'What did Summer say?' she asks.

'I haven't told her.'

'I don't blame you. She's never liked him much, has she?'

Sureya loves Summer. Of course she does. Spunky actress and feisty drama teacher is a match made in heaven. The few times that we've all gone out together, you'd have thought it was those two who'd known each other for nearly two decades.

'Look, you've talked to me. That's a good start,' she says. 'But you know it's Richard that counts.'

She would say that. She comes from a family who shouted and screamed at each other about everything. All grievances were aired on a daily basis. It was a healthy, *open* atmosphere, she tells me. But that's the way feisty, hot-blooded ethnic people behave, I tell her. It's not the British way, is it? But Sureya doesn't buy it.

And the thing is that Summer – who is as British as a red telephone box – doesn't buy my strong, silent (as I like to think of it) approach either. Summer and Sureya, both, are inhabitants of therapy country. Having It Out – whether with husbands, lovers, parents or £50-per-hour psychotherapists – is the answer to everything.

It seems that I'm the only cynic around here, British or otherwise.

But it really is complicated. Since his pitch on Monday, work has been crazy for Richard, not exactly the best scenario for *talking*. Last night, he was still at the office at midnight. He called me to say he might as well stay in town, given that he had a seven o'clock breakfast meeting this morning. There's nothing unusual about this. It happens all the time. So why should this week feel different? Because of one silly hotel bill?

I think about all the nights I've sat alone with the TV remote since Richard was made MD. How well do I really know him? He could be the world's best cheat for all I know. Fitting in countless fleeting affairs between trips to France to see his other wife and three children. But if he is, if we are talking worst-case scenario, do I really want to know?

I take a gulp – no longer a sip – of wine and Sureya gives me a look. 'What is that? Your third glass?'

'Sureya! Are you counting?'

'Sorry, no. Just you seem a bit . . . thirstier than usual,' she says with a laugh.

That's one way of putting it, I suppose. But, hey, lots of women need a drink or two in the evening, don't they? Just to aid the unwinding process?

A sudden flash. I remember the one piece of good news I've had this week. I let out a little yelp. 'Ooh! I didn't tell you about Ron.'

'*Ron?*'

Ron isn't the sort of name you get round these parts.

'He left me a message today. He's a scout for Crystal Palace.'

She gives me a blank look.

'They're a football club. He came to watch Thomas a couple of weekends ago and was so impressed he wants me to take Thomas for a trial. Can you believe it?'

'You need to be focusing on your marriage right now, never mind FA Ron.'

'I don't think David Beckham's mum would've said a thing like that.'

'OK, but you've got to have it out with Richard,' Sureya says, ignoring me. 'The sooner you have confirmation that he loves you, adores you, can't live without you and that everything is lovely in the Clark household, the better.'

She's putting her drama training to good use. And her uplifting performance is wonderful, but rather than filling me with an optimistic glow, it makes me feel worse.

'I didn't tell you, but I let him down last week,' I say. 'Really badly.'

She looks at me, concerned. 'What did you do?'

'It was just a work thing,' I tell her flatly.

'Work?' she gasps excitedly. 'How long have I been going on at you to revive things on that front?'

You, Summer and Richard all, I think. 'Oh, it was just a tiny little job,' I say. 'But I let Richard down. And now he's . . . *disappointed*. I think he just doesn't want to be around me.'

'Even if he has to book into a luxury hotel to escape?'

'Well, room service won't let him down, will they?'

'This is the last time I'm going to say it, Fran. *Talk* to him. *Tonight*.'

'I will,' I submit.

'Good.' She drains her cup. 'Are you all set for your party?'

Am I all set for my party? Well, I've done bugger all about an outfit and bugger all about anything else. 'Yes, I suppose so,' I say half-heartedly.

'Fran, come on, you were really looking forward to this. Look, why don't I have Molly and Thomas on Saturday morning and you can go and get your hair done? How about it? Get yourself in the mood?'

Friends really couldn't come any better. 'Thanks, Sureya, but Richard will be home. He can entertain them for a couple of hours. But you're right. I'll make an appointment.' So I've got no dress. At least I'll look OK from the neck up.

'You do that. Now I've got to go. Helen has to leave by ten.'

She's got Helen babysitting? I'm confused. 'I thought Michael was home.'

'He is. But he's a layabout who can't be trusted to look after two small children. Besides, I'm going out three times next week. I'm using a babysitter so he can't throw tonight in my face too.'

I can't help laughing. She's only been round for an hour. 'You're unbelievable. You've organised cover for *one hour*?'

She doesn't laugh back. 'Yes, Fran. It's about knowing how much you can ask for without being greedy. Your trouble is, you never ask for *anything*. And if you don't ask for anything, you know what you'll end up with, don't you?'

And that's about the size of it.

13

Friday: I bump into Natasha on the way to school. Or rather, she bumps into me. She has her head down, her slender frame leaning into a double buggy. It's gigantic. Like a sitting room on wheels. Two-year-old Trist sits in one side. Fabian, just five but looking older, is in the other.

'Oh, I'm so *sorry!*' she cries out as a wheel scrapes my ankle.

'Don't worry, I'm fine.' I smother the pain with a forced laugh. If anyone else had crashed into me I'd limp pointedly all the way to school.

'In a hurry, are we?' I ask.

'Gottfried's threatened us with a red card if we're late just once this term,' she explains. 'Why do you think Fabian's in the buggy? He's way too big for this thing, but when you're in a rush, it's a lifesaver.'

Molly looks up at me. 'Baby,' she whispers. The trouble is she whispers as loudly as most people talk. And through a loudhailer at that.

To her credit, Natasha laughs. 'Isn't he just? But this is a new term and I'm not going to start it by giving Cassie another thing to gossip about.'

'What do you mean?' I ask. I'm a little confused. I thought she was tight with the Head Witch. And if she is, why would Cassie gossip about her?

'If she finds out we've been officially reprimanded, well, life just wouldn't be worth living. Don't get me wrong. I'll take on any number of vile children's entertainers, but Cassie . . . ?'

Once again, I find myself marvelling at Natasha. Not just at her ability to laugh at everything, but at *her*. It's almost nine o'clock and she's wearing full make-up. And a slinky, bum-hugging skirt. And are those Jimmy Choos? I try not to look down at my battered jeans, and pull the peak of my cap over my naked face. Why do I look as if I fell out of bed and rolled straight out of the front door? Molly woke me at six thirty. I can hardly blame the lack of time.

We're at the school gate. Thomas, who has been walking ten yards ahead of me, breaks into a sprint towards the junior playground, determined to squeeze in two minutes of football before the bell rings. He gives me a tiny wave. No kiss, no backward glance. At least I got a wave today.

'Actually, if Cassie worried less about what others are up to and paid more attention to her appearance, she might be a happier person,' Natasha says. 'You've got to make the effort, haven't you?' she adds matter-of-factly.

And, of course, I so know what she means. I make the effort to put my shoes on every day.

'The secret is to prioritise,' she says, turning and calling out to her eldest. 'Quinn, come on, give it here.'

He's been lagging behind and it's only as he trots to catch up that I realise why. He's clutching a cereal bowl and licking the last few Cheerios from a spoon. He hands both to his mum, who chucks them into her buggy's basket, where they nestle alongside another two bowls and spoons.

'Breakfast en route,' she explains, seeing my stare. 'They'd love to eat at the table like normal kids, but this is the only way I get half an hour to myself in the bathroom. Like I say, you've got to prioritise.' And she laughs all the way across the playground.

★   ★   ★

Mrs Gottfried catches me on the way out of school.

'Mrs Clark, ve must have that chat.'

'Yes, we *must*,' I enthuse, thinking that having a sit-down to discuss Thomas's inattentiveness/surliness/any-other-ness is the last thing I need right now.

'Are you free now?'

'No, sorry. Busy. On my way to the dentist,' I say. I have the school gate in sight now and I up my pace.

'You *vill* call me?'

'Yes, *definitely*,' I yell as I break into a brisk trot.

That's why I wear trainers and not Jimmy Choos on the school run. How would I flee in heels?

What an inspiration Natasha is. She manages to combine total self-interest with getting a balanced breakfast into her kids. She looks like a model, yet her children remain happy and nourished. And I have never met anyone who laughed so much first thing in the morning. That's it. If she can do it, so can I.

I've decided to drive up to the Broadway. I'm on a mission. A mission to – *finally* – find something to wear to my party, which is – don't panic, deep breaths – TOMORROW!!!

Actually, there's nothing to panic about. All the organising is being done for me. The venue and caterers are booked, a DJ has been briefed on my favourite tunes, and a stylist is preparing to transform our local tennis club into the Rio Carnival or something.

All I have to worry about is myself: get outfit; do hair.

The party was Richard's big idea. He works in marketing. Big ideas are his business. I wouldn't be surprised if he brainstormed this one with his hottest teams. Objective: GET WIFE OUT OF RUT. I must admit, I thought a party was a great idea. I told myself that it might not change my life, but at least it would fill an evening with several consecutive hours of *pleasure*! I imagined the new outfit and hairdo that would transform me from walking dead to swaggering bombshell. And all our friends would be dazzled by my appearance, telling me how stunning I look without even tacking on *for your age* at the end.

I'd said I needed to get out more and what better place to start than at my very own party? It was going to be great.

And it is going to be great. OK, so I'm nervous about being the centre of attention – haven't been that for a while – but it is going to be great. It is going to be great. It is going to be . . .

Isn't repetition the basic principle of brainwashing? Hey, whatever works, right?

So I'm finally doing something about finding a new outfit. The shop I'm in is a factory outlet that sells cut-price designer items. When I say designer, I mean that someone *designed* them, yes, but that someone being a man in a sweatshop, somewhere in China.

'Ah, that looks lovely,' the shop assistant tells me as I emerge from the changing room wearing the trousers she gave me. *Forced* on me. She's got greasy hair and spots, and her tracksuit makes mine at home look haute couture. A fine person to take fashion advice from.

I don't think so. I look ridiculous. Does my bum look big in this? Jesus, even my ears look big in this.

'Have you got them in black, maybe?' I ask hopefully.

'But yellow's so, like, *in*,' she tells me as if I'm stupid. 'And it really brings out your eyes.'

If I wear these, the only eyes that will be brought out will be those looking at me. On six-foot stalks.

'Hey! You could wear this with them,' the girl tells me excitedly. 'Beyoncé wore something like this to the MTV Awards.'

She's holding up a shimmering sequinned top. Also yellow.

I'm going to resemble a glittery egg yolk. Not exactly a look Beyoncé has come to be known for.

'Maybe something less . . . spangly,' I suggest.

The girl turns up her nose. 'Well, what sort of look were you going for?'

'Anything that doesn't make me look like a glittery egg yolk?' I offer.

'Eh?' She frowns.

'Sorry, but look at me. I'm not exactly Beyoncé, am I? I'm not even the other one.'

'You mean Kelly?'

'No, the *other* one, the one whose name nobody can remember.'

'Michelle?'

'Er, yeah, her,' I mumble.

Suddenly, a body explodes from the cubicle behind me. 'OhmyGodIhavegottohavethese!'

I turn to see another spotty sixteen-year-old wearing exactly the same trousers that I'm modelling. And the funny thing is, she does actually look amazing in them. Exactly like Beyoncé, but in a designed-in-China-on-the-cheap sort of way.

That does it. I'll take them. And they're only £18.99. A bargain! (I bet Beyoncé paid a hell of a lot more for hers. Mug.) I've got this little black top at home that will go great. Chuck a belt round it and I'm sure it will be perfect. Job done.

That's what I thought in the shop.

But driving home now, I think I might have just indulged in what is generally known as a panic purchase.

Yellow trousers. You'd never catch Natasha in a pair of those.

What was I thinking?

*   *   *

I'm in bed. The digits on the alarm twinkle at me – 2.09 a.m. I hear the front door being closed ever so quietly. Richard's home. Good. I get out of bed and put on my dressing gown. His arrival gives me the opportunity to do what I've been wanting to do all night: *talk to him*. Sureya's right. I've got to give him a chance to explain.

But I stop at the bedroom door. This is stupid. He's been working so hard all day – all *week*. We can't have this conversation at gone two in the morning.

I've talked myself out of it.

Because if I get back into bed and feign sleep, I'll be safe. Eventually, real, dreamless sleep will arrive, where nobody is up to anything and mysterious hotel bills don't exist. Well, they do, but they're unexplained. Like UFOs. Plenty of sightings, photos even, but who knows what they're all about? No one. Exactly.

Feigning sleep won't be necessary, as it goes. I hear Richard creep up the stairs . . . and go into the spare room. I tell myself he does this because he doesn't want to wake me. What other reason?

I wait a full half-hour to make certain he's asleep himself before going downstairs for a glass of water. Or whatever.

12

Goodbye thirty-six, hello thirty-seven.

As soon as I wake up I'm feeling anxious. Birthdays do that to me. This one only seems worse because I'm having a big party, I guess. Long time since I had one of those.

I try to put my nerves aside and shake the fuzziness from my head. I get dressed and head downstairs, trying to put myself into a better frame of mind. It'll be fine. OK, so I didn't find an outfit – *yellow* trousers?! – but so what? Maybe we'll just keep the lights dimmed so no one will actually be able to see me. Oh God, just thinking about it and I feel sick all over again.

'*Mummy!* Daddy's making pancakes!'

Molly is sitting at the island in the kitchen. Richard stands at the Aga. He's wearing a pinny and a blob of batter decorates the tip of his nose. 'Morning . . . And happy birthday,' he says.

'Happy birthday, Mummy,' Molly says, flinging her arms towards me. I lean down and let her hug me. 'I made you a card.'

She hands me a folded piece of paper. A felt-tip drawing of a stick woman decorates the front. She's wearing a pretty dress, but her hair is a manic mousey-brown scribble – could only be me, then.

'Thank you. It's beautiful, sweetheart,' I gush, trying to put thoughts of my outfit to one side.

'Oh, some girl called Vicki rang earlier,' Richard says. 'Said she can't do you, but Ginny can. Make sense?'

It does. After I'd spoken to Sureya the other day, I rang about a thousand different salons, desperate to find someone who could fit me in at such short notice *and* on a Saturday. I got one eventually. I've never been there before and I wonder how good they can be if they've got spare appointments on a Saturday? Anyway, I explain all this to Richard. Well, apart from the bit about not bothering to book a hairdresser because I thought I'd do it myself and then changing my mind and having a nightmare trying to find one with a spare slot, I explain it all to Richard. Actually, what I say is, 'Hair appointment.' The rest is just detail. Men don't really do detail, do they?

'Oh,' he says flatly, staring down at the frying pan.

I'm sensing there's a problem here. 'What's wrong?'

'Well, it's just that I wouldn't mind putting in a couple of hours at the office. It's a golden opportunity to get stuff ready. You know, for Monday.'

'Oh,' I say, my turn now. 'Well, if you'd told me, I could have got Sureya to have them after all. She offered, but I thought you'd be home.'

'If Sureya doesn't mind, well, do you think you could ask her?'

Really, I should have known.

But my party-dress panic must be taking up all my brain space because I've only just registered something. 'What's happening on Monday?' I ask.

'You know, the Milan thing,' he says nonchalantly.

News to me. 'What *Milan* thing?'

'Jesus, Fran, I told you. Me and a couple of the guys are going on a recce with the new client. They need us to see their flagship store in Milan because they're opening up a similar one in London. I did tell you about it.'

When does he imagine that he told me? During one of the many evenings we've spent having heart-to-hearts this week? During one of our hour-long telephone chats? Or was it during one of our regular telepathy sessions?

It might possibly have been during one of the evenings when I'd had a couple of glasses of wine and so had promptly forgotten about it, but this thought barely registers, obviously.

As I watch Molly tuck into her honey-coated breakfast, another surge of panic hits me. I've just realised I'd forgotten about football practice.

If Richard wants to dump our children on Sureya, he'll have to call her himself. I'll execute the other, much harder task: informing my son that he'll have to live without football this morning.

'Tell Sureya I'll be back by two, latest,' I tell Richard as he picks up the phone. 'Where's Thomas?'

'In his room . . .' Molly informs me.

Drawing me a card, perhaps?

'. . . playing *FIFA Streets*.'

I kiss her and head apprehensively back upstairs. Thomas isn't good with bad news. Telling him he has to miss football is as grim as it gets. A death in the family would be guaranteed a sunnier response.

I've been getting my hair dyed for a few years now. Early grey. Sounds like a nice cup of tea, doesn't it? I spotted the first white strand in my mid-twenties. A single hair amongst tens of thousands screaming, '*Brace yourself, babe, it's all downhill from here!*' I told it to shut up and plucked it out, but reinforcements weren't far behind, an army of reminders that I wasn't nineteen any more. They say, you can run, but you can't hide . . . but actually, that's rubbish. You *can* hide beneath a tub of 'honey golden blonde' and that's a fact.

So although I haven't been for ages that's why I've always loved going to the hairdresser. I get to sit under layers of chemical paste and scraps of tinfoil and kid myself that, temporarily at least, I *can* turn back the hands of time. (Sorry, is that a line from an ad? If it isn't, it should be. It's naff enough.)

I'm not much enjoying this particular trip, though. It's giving me too much time to think. And I *think* that I definitely should have talked to Richard last night. It didn't matter that it was late. Eleventh hour, gone midnight, whatever. If we still love each other, time of day is immaterial, isn't it? *We should have talked.* We'd have cleared the air . . . and then had mad, passionate making-up sex. And I wouldn't now be thinking regretfully that *we should have talked.*

My phone rings – a good excuse to stop *thinking* – so I answer it.

'Happy birthday, angel,' Summer announces.

'Thanks. Where have you been all week? I've been calling you.'

'Long story. I've been in Tenerife with Phoebe.'

'Phoebe?' I repeat hesitantly. Sorry, but who is she talking about? Her love life is harder to keep up with than Jude Law's.

'Phoebe the hairdresser. I told you about her at lunch.'

'Oh, OK.' I'm not sure I remember, but I don't fancy being told off again today for not paying attention. 'And how did it go?'

'God, it's a bit of a story, Fran. We'll talk tonight. So, are you all set?'

'Yes, going from mousey brown to golden-honey fabulous as we speak,' I confirm.

'Good. And have you sorted out the rest of your life yet?'

'I haven't really had an opportunity to fill my diary with

bookings, Summer, but give me time.' I think I'm slightly overdoing the sarcasm.

'You've had all week. What have you been doing?'

'Children. I've been doing children and home things and, well, all sorts.'

'Stop bullshitting me. I'm really cross with you.'

'Don't be.'

Silence.

'At least you're getting your Kate Bush head sorted out,' she says at last. 'But we have got to sort *you* out. Once and for all. New year, new start. Yes?'

God, will she ever give it a rest? What gives her the right? Sitting on some hairdresser's face in Tenerife all week and then coming back all recharged and taking it out on me? Summer, the eternal party animal. No ties, no responsibilities, no worries. Forever on at me to sort my life out. You know, sometimes I just wish she'd get off my case.

'I do love you, you know, Fran. I'm only joshing. I'm not really having a go at you . . . Fran?' she asks when I don't reply.

But sod it. Sod *her*, with her proclamations of love. I didn't come to the hairdresser to get choked up.

I feel an inexplicable sob threaten and quickly gulp it back. 'Sorry, what did you say?' I frown theatrically at my phone, dipping my head as if straining to hear.

'I said, I *love* you. I was only joking about—'

'Sorry, Summer, losing you . . .' I give my *What can you do? Bloody useless mobiles* shrug – not that anyone is paying a blind bit of notice – and flip my phone shut.

That'll teach her to try and help me with my life.

When I walk out of the salon at half past one, Summer's call is still bouncing about my head. Why do I find it so hard to talk to my friends? Why do I find it so hard to *talk*? Jesus, I'm not turning into my mother . . . I *am* my mother.

I'm now also filled with renewed party nerves. I'm feeling something that vaguely resembles a panic attack, when something occurs to me. The house will be empty, which means I have just enough time to get back and have a quick drink before I pick the kids up from Sureya.

A quick drink never hurt anybody, did it?

'Why did you leave us round there for so long?' Thomas is furious. 'Where've you been?'

'God, Thomas, I was only getting my hair done. D'you like it?'

'You've been *hours*,' he shouts, ignoring the gorgeous new me.

The hairdo isn't bad, actually. Not sure about the colour – a bit *too* honey – but generally, I can't complain. It worked out pretty well for a panic purchase.

Molly plays happily with two bits of string and a twig. In her mind, they're priceless items of jewellery and she's the Queen of Sheba or something. Her imagination is boundless.

As is Thomas's fury. 'Don't *ever* leave me round there again!' He was already mad with me over the missed football. Leaving him hanging at Sureya's has just rubbed gritty, abrasive rock salt into the wound.

I'm determined not to shout at him. My head is woozy enough as it is. I had half a pack of Polos before collecting them. I don't think Sureya smelt the evidence. Well, she didn't say anything. She didn't mention that it was nearly four o'clock either. 'What was so bad about it, Thomas?' I ask with deliberate calmness. 'You love going round to Sureya's, don't you?'

'Where the hell did you get that idea? I hate it round there,' he shouts.

'Thomas, please don't speak like that.' He'll think I'm referring to his language, but it's actually the shouting I object to. Fragile head and all that.

'Yes, I *will* marry you, Prince of Thieves,' Molly says to the imaginary man kneeling before her. She thrusts out my feather duster as if it's a sword or a sceptre. 'I name you my husband, Prince of my Land.'

It won't last, sweetheart. He'll get promoted, fly off to Milan and leave you at home with the kids and the wine box.

'Will you stop playing that stupid game?' Thomas yells, before running from the room. 'This house is full of *crazy* people,' is the last thing I hear before his bedroom door slams shut.

I could go and talk to him, but I don't. Guilt gnaws away at my stomach. Is he this way because of his father and me? If I can't sort out my own problems, how am I going to help Thomas? That reminds me. I must phone FA Ron and sort out that trial business. That will be a good start. I'll do it Monday. Definitely.

The panic attack refuses to budge. I feel sick at the thought of being the centre of attention. I have *got* to find something to wear. *Now!* I arm myself with a fresh glass of wine and cigarettes and go up to my bedroom. The alarm clock tells me I have two hours and seventeen minutes. *Right, let's get to work.*

I fling open the wardrobe doors. There must be something in here. Some sexy little number I've forgotten about, perhaps. Or some tired old faithful I can jazz up with a belt or a scarf. But as garments pile up around my ankles, I realise it's hopeless.

I stop and stare at myself pointlessly in the mirror on the wardrobe door. Nice hair, shame about the face. Big brown dewy eyes that used to be called saucers now just look plain old sad. Lips, cracked and dry, to match my skin.

God, my head is foggy. *Need to think*. Need to lie down. That'll help. I stub out my cigarette, collapse on to the bed and surrender to the dizziness . . .

'Jesus Christ, what the hell are you doing?'

What?

I sit up too quickly and the sudden rush of blood from my head achieves the same effect as the couple of glasses of wine I had earlier. I look up and my eyes swim into focus. Richard is standing over me.

'What?' I ask.

'Molly has virtually annihilated the kitchen. She's got the bloody *knives* out and you're up here sleeping! Jesus, Fran, do you know what time it is?'

Outside, the light is fading. Not a good sign. I look at the alarm: six thirty. We're supposed to be at the tennis club at seven checking the vol-au-vents or whatever.

'Oh God, I'm so sorry. Must have nodded off,' I say feebly, trying to shake the fuzziness from my head.

'God, that *stench*,' Richard says, screwing up his nose. 'Have you been drinking?'

What to say? Hard to deny really, given that *stench*. And that's not all. I catch sight of myself in the mirror. Amazing what a little lie down can do to a £130 hairdo. It's sticking up on one side like an asymmetric Mohican. I look down at the crumpled bed, the clothes strewn across the floor. What a complete and utter mess. And I don't mean the room . . .

I hate myself. When did I turn into such a lush? I'm thirty-seven, for God's sake, and, children apart, I have nothing to show for myself but a failed career and a husband full of contempt.

Of which I'm feeling enough for the both of us.

'Helen's already here,' he says. 'She's doing tea for Thomas and Molly. You'd better get ready.' He marches to the window and throws it open.

I stand up and walk purposefully over to the wardrobe. Trying my damnedest to make it look as if I know what I'm doing. But I don't. I don't know anything. About what to wear, what to do, how to act . . . *everything*.

I can't do it any more.

I crumple to the floor on top of my discarded clothes and sob. The frustration of the week floods out of me and there is nothing I can do to stop it.

I feel his arm go round me. He strokes my devastated hair and then hugs me tightly. 'What's the matter?' he asks eventually.

'*Everything*.' The sobs intensify, as if he's squeezing them out of me.

He lets me cry for a bit. 'Come on, get up,' he says, lifting me to my feet now and leading me to the bed. He sits me down and asks, 'What is it?'

It feels strange. *He* is strange. Awkward, yet full of love. How he can be both at the same time I don't know, but there it is.

I can't stop the tears. I know my eyes will be puffy and crimson and in an hour's time we'll be at the party of the year (well, of my year, anyway), but I don't care. All I care about is that right here, right now, in my bombsite of a bedroom, Richard is holding me for the first time in months.

'Come on, what is it?' he prods gently.

'I haven't got anything to wear,' I say. And because that sounds utterly pathetic, I add, 'And you don't love me any more.'

Which also sounds pathetic now it's out, but thankfully he doesn't let his arm drop from round my shoulder. 'You're being silly,' he says quietly.

'What, about not having anything to wear, or about you not loving me?'

'Both.' He reaches down and picks up something from the floor. 'Look, I got you this . . . Happy birthday.'

The bag has 'Gucci' on the front. I take it from him and untie the ribbon that holds the handles together. I pull out a pile of loosely crumpled black tissue and reach inside. Carefully, I lift out the most exquisite top I've ever seen. *Top* doesn't do it justice; it's a beautiful work of white silken art.

'That bad, is it?' he jokes because fresh tears are flowing now.

'No, it's lovely . . . gorgeous. It's just that . . .' But I can't finish the sentence. I've just seen the label and read the number ten. I can't tell him I've jumped up two sizes while he wasn't looking. So I just squeeze out, 'Thank you,' between the sobs.

He looks anxiously at the clock again, then he takes hold of my shoulders. 'Listen, here's what you're going to do. You're going to go into the bathroom and wash your face. Then you're going to get dressed. If you don't want to wear this –' he tosses the Gucci top aside '– fine. It doesn't matter. You just have to get yourself together and when you're ready, we'll go to this party and have the time of our lives. Got that?'

He speaks gently but confidently. Just as he might to a terrified junior minutes before her big presentation to the company's wealthiest client. It's no wonder he's done so well at work. So *professional*.

'I don't want to go to this stupid party. I just want . . .' What do I want? '*You.*'

'Fran, this is ridiculous. This party, it's all for you. What does that tell you?'

His breathing quickens, he's agitated now. 'This is the

recording session all over again, isn't it? You're bottling out of your own party . . . *Jesus.*' He runs a hand through his hair and takes a deep breath. 'Look, tell me, what is it?'

I can see pain in his face. The thought that he still cares for me gives me hope.

'I don't know,' I say eventually, though I know exactly what's got into me. The hotel bill is just two feet away in my knicker drawer. I have to tell him. OK, my timing isn't ideal, but Sureya's right. I have to get it out in the open.
Now.

What comes out instead is, 'Do you still love me?'

'You're pissed. I think you should go and wash your face.'

'A simple yes or no will do.'

'Fran, do you really think we've got time to sit here and dissect—'

'You don't, do you?'

'Jesus, I haven't even said anything and you're reading—'

'*Jesus*, Richard, if you don't love me, why don't you just admit it?'

A horror-movie-type cry fills the room and we both look up. Molly's pink ankle socks flash from the doorway towards the top of the stairs. How long was she standing there? How much did she hear?

'Sort yourself out, Fran,' Richard snaps. 'I'll see to Molly.'

11

I had to leave the top button undone, but the skirt looks OK. Top-to-toe black. It's slimming, apparently. Oh, how times have changed. Or rather, the size of my midriff has. Richard's beautiful white Gucci top lies sadly on the bedroom floor where he discarded it.

'You look lovely, Francesca,' Sureya says, giving me a hug.

And I have to agree with her. Kind of. It's a miracle that I'm here at all. A double miracle that I look, well, *half* decent.

Michael gives me a big hug too, and Sureya thrusts a beautifully wrapped present at me, a shiny silver bow tied round it. 'Now, don't take this as an insult. I do hope you like it. And *use* it.'

'Thanks, Sureya,' I say, putting the present on the side table with the others. 'For having the kids today, and for the present. I'm sure I'm going to love it.'

Actually, I'm sure it's yet another self-help book about finding your inner bollocks as well as your grey roots or whatever. Sureya does so love all that rubbish.

'All that matters is that you enjoy tonight. *Your* night.' She smiles.

'To be honest, I think I just got myself into a bit of a state about it all,' I tell her, taking a sip of my champagne. 'A silly panic attack, that's all.'

She frowns at me. '*Panic*. Yes, I could smell the *panic* when you came to pick the kids up.' Oh. So much for the

Polos. 'I'm going to get myself a mineral water. See you in a bit,' she says, dragging Michael off towards the bar.

They were one of the first couples to arrive, Richard and I getting here seconds before them. It took a while to calm Molly down. He and I had to hug each other profusely to convince her that we were very much in love, just as mummies and daddies should be. Molly's perfect but fragile world cannot be rocked with the news that Daddy thinks Mummy is a useless, flaky piss-head and Mummy thinks Daddy is a lying, cheating scumbag and that neither has the courage to tell the other, truthfully, what they really feel.

Molly soothed, I slapped on some make-up, said a hasty goodbye to Thomas (who still wasn't talking to me) and left the house. *With* Richard. Luckily, the tennis club is only two hundred yards up the road, because I could barely walk in the shoes I'm wearing – another Richard freebie. Although not a word was spoken, we made it to the club, my heels and our marriage just about intact.

Sureya and Michael join Richard on the other side of the room. Momentarily alone, I take another sip of my drink and enjoy the sensation of happiness and relief that fills me. Before we got here, Richard put his arms round me and told me that I had to forget my bad feelings and *enjoy myself*. That I'd forgotten how to, that was all, and just needed to be reminded. Then he held me tight and this time it wasn't because I was hysterical and I felt a warm feeling I haven't felt for a while.

Maybe he's right, I think now.

Everything's going to be OK.

Another sip and I feel even better. Like an elastic band that has been stretched to snapping point, I'm slowly relaxing, unwinding nicely. Music plays, people mill and noisy banter fills the elegant, panelled room. Everything is perfect. Well, *almost*. My glass is empty. Just find a passing waiter and . . . there you have it. *Perfection*.

'What the hell's going on?' Summer hisses when she's sure nobody is listening.

'Nothing.' I smile, the champagne doing its stuff.

'You can't kid me. You've got foundation caked on your face like cement and you're knocking it back like you're fresh from the desert. What's happened?'

'Nothing. In fact, everything is lovely.'

'Really?'

I nod a very affirmative nod. 'Richard loves me and everything's wonderful.'

'*Really?*' she drawls sarcastically.

'Yes. Anyway, can you please get off my back? I'm just starting to enjoy myself.'

'How did I ever let you marry him?' She shakes her head. 'God, look at him, working that crowd.'

On the far side of the room, Richard works his magic and several beautifully groomed women I barely recognise throw their heads back and press their manicured hands on to their ribs to stop their sides from physically splitting. I feel a tiny stab of pain because, well, he used to make me laugh like that, didn't he? But the night is long. He'll be making me laugh soon enough, I know it. I take another sip.

'You've got him all wrong, you know. Earlier, we had this . . . *moment*.'

'Oh, *pur*-lease. You're going to make me throw up. I've had enough of feeling sick to last me a lifetime,' she says, gulping at what looks like an orange juice – perhaps to make the nausea go away.

I'm about to ask her what she's talking about when we're interrupted. An auburn-haired, pretty slip of a girl appears

at Summer's side. And I do mean *slip*. She's very young.
Barely legal, surely?

'Phoebe!' Summer's eyes nearly pop out of her head.
'What the hell are you doing here?'

'My mates blew me out. I hope you don't mind, but I
thought I'd surprise you!' her girlfriend says, bobbing up
and down like a puppy on springs.

'Well, yes indeed. Surprised I am,' Summer says, looking,
it has to be said, extremely surprised. 'Fran, meet Phoebe.
Phoebe, Fran.'

'I've heard so much about you. Thank you for not minding
me just turning up,' she fizzes, shaking my hand vigorously.

I don't mind at all. Any friend of Summer's is a friend
of mine. Besides, they've been seeing each other for, what
is it? A whole fortnight? Summer measures her life in dog
years. To her, two weeks constitutes about five years, so this
girl must be a serious thing. Why then does Summer look
so awkward?

'Hello, who's this?' Richard appears at our side.

I introduce him to Phoebe and it's all very amiable and
you'd never guess that Summer feels only loathing for my
husband.

'Enjoying yourself?' he asks me.

'Yes,' I reply. '*Yes*, I am. It's actually quite lovely.'

And Summer may well roll her eyes behind his back, but
I mean it. He's holding my hand and looking at me as if he
really cares. That look, plus the nth glass of champagne are
giving my world an ethereal glow. Everyone around me shim-
mers and sparkles magically. Even Sureya, who has now joined
us, must be able to feel the energy between Richard and me.

'Everything all right?' She beams.

'Absolutely,' I tell her. Then I whisper in her ear, 'You
were so right. About talking. I promise never to scoff again,'
I laugh.

She gives me a big hug, before being dragged off in search of drinks by Summer, who looks as if she doesn't want to be left alone for too long with Phoebe.

'Thank you for doing this,' I tell Richard when we're alone. 'And I'm . . . sorry about earlier.'

He shifts uncomfortably. His eyes flicker off me momentarily, but then they're back. 'Hey, have you seen Isabel and Harvey?' he asks excitedly. 'I've just been chatting to them. They're directing again and you'll never guess what they've got coming up.'

'Tell me,' I say, feeling as if I've been covered in fairy dust, not really listening, but loving his enthusiasm anyway.

'They're making a feature. An animation – CGI. But not a kids' film. They've bought the rights to some cult sci-fi novel. Harvey told me it'll be *Toy Story* meets *Blade Runner*.'

'Sounds brilliant.' What do I know about science fiction, and what on earth is CGI? But it does sound brilliant – right now everything does.

'Doesn't it? Anyway, they're desperate to talk to you about one of the parts,' Richard explains. 'They've got some big names pencilled in already, but Isabel says there's a small but crucial role for you. Written with you in mind, she reckons.'

Look at that. Him in his gorgeous Ozwald Boateng suit, more attractive and important than any man I've ever known, and all he cares about right now is sorting me out. Of course he loves me. Summer is so wrong about him – much as I love her, she's just behaving like a stereotypical, man-hating dyke. All he's interested in is bringing me back to life.

'I thought you'd given up on me,' I say. 'After my, er, no-show.'

'That? Ancient history. Forgotten.' He smiles.

I throw my arms round his neck and enjoy just hanging there for a moment. Then I pull myself up to his face and kiss him gently on the lips. As I pull back from him, I'm not sure what I was expecting to see, but I didn't reckon on the same look of pain I glimpsed earlier.

'Do you think we can get it back?' I ask, still holding on, not wanting to let go.

'What's that?'

'The passion. Remember that? You know, kissing, cuddling, S, E, X.'

'I think you're pissed,' he says. He still has a smile on his face, but there's nothing behind it. He lifts my hands from his shoulders and holds them in front of him, effectively a barrier between us now. His eyes dart nervously around the room. 'Just keep it together, Fran. Harvey's looking over.'

'OK, I'm to*gether*,' I reply a little too petulantly. Actually, I'd better slow down with the champagne. If I'm not careful, I'll be on the floor in no time.

Richard lets go of my hands, which isn't the way I wanted this moment to end. He doesn't notice my disappointment because he's being pounced on by Fiona. Where the hell did she spring from? And who invited her, anyway?

'Hey, sis!' He hugs her as if last Sunday was a lifetime ago. As if she's just been flown in *all the way from Australia* by Cilla.

She virtually throws a present at me, blows me a pouty kiss and drags her brother off to talk to someone else I don't remember inviting. Like half the people here. Who the hell are they? Sod them. I drain my glass and swap it for a full one.

'So, the big four O. How does it feel?'

'Excuse me?'

Who is this man and what is he talking about?

'The big four O . . . *forty* . . . Bit of a landmark, yeah?'

'I'm not forty,' I spit. 'It's my thirty-seventh.'

'God . . . I'm *really* sorry. I just thought . . . you know, big bash like this and everything, it had to be a special one,' he squirms.

No, you creep, you just thought I look forty. Who the hell is he? I glare at him, too drunk to care that I'm making him uncomfortable. 'Who are you?' I ask a little too aggressively.

'Pardon?'

'What's your name? I don't remember you.'

'I'm Chris . . .'

I stare at him blankly.

'Chris Sergeant . . . TV department . . . Saatchi.'

Chris Sergeant, head of TV, Saatchi & Saatchi . . . Shit. How the hell could I have forgotten Chris? My favourite person in Adland, ever. Chris used to book me for virtually every job that required an accent . . . A hundred jobs, a thousand laughs . . . Sergeant Chris! Lovely, gorgeous, *fantastic* man. Of course, he was a bit thinner back then, but weren't we all? And *I* made Richard put his name on the list. Oh God, now it's my turn to squirm with embarrassment.

'Chris!' I shout, the pitch of my voice rising to squeaky. 'I'm *so* sorry.'

''S OK. Listen, I'll just go get a refill, Fran,' he says, backing off. 'Back in a mo.'

I watch him work his way through the throng until I lose him. I feel terrible. I really want to catch up with him, reminisce . . . I'm sure we'd be at it all night, if he'd only give me another chance.

I'm about to go find him when I feel a hand on my arm. '*Fran.*' I look round and see Summer. She's looking over her own shoulder nervously.

'Summer,' I gasp. 'I have *so* put my foot in it.'

'Whatever, listen, I know this isn't a great time, what with it being your big night and everything. I was going to leave it, but I need to talk to you. Tonight.'

'Talk away, girl, talk away.' I'm slurring, but only ever so slightly.

'Are you completely smashed, or what?'

I'm about to tell her how stupid she's being and explain how champagne does that to you on an empty stomach, but I realise this would be tantamount to owning up to being completely smashed so I don't bother. I just laugh some more. Quite a lot, actually.

'Boo!'

It's Phoebe, arriving between us like Tigger on amphetamines.

'Fran, I've heard so much about your voices,' she bubbles. 'Do Cher! I *love* her and Summer says you do the meanest Cher.'

Summer groans audibly. Whether it's because she's embarrassed by the request or she's bored to death by my voices is anyone's guess. Phoebe is so frothy I want to oblige, but when I open my mouth, all that comes out is the loudest hiccup, which makes me want to collapse with laughter, which makes Summer visibly wince.

But she forgets what she wanted to talk to me about moments earlier because she's spotted Sureya again. Did I mention how much she loves Sureya? 'Let's go. I want to talk to Sureya about this dream I've been having lately.'

'You haven't said anything about a dream. What's it about?' Phoebe asks, head bobbing about in time to the music.

'One where I'm dead. Or I think I am because no one seems to notice me. Come on, let's go.' Summer gives me a look before dragging Phoebe off.

I'm standing alone. Again. And I'm starting to know what Summer means about being dead because nobody seems to have noticed me for ages. Or maybe everyone else is dead and I'm the only living person here. Like *The Shining*. I'm Jack Nicholson, talking to a bunch of people who no longer exist at a party that isn't really happening. Have you heard my Jack Nicholson . . . ?

I don't know how long I've been standing here, but I am seriously wondering if I'm invisible. I can't be, though, because the waiters can see me. They seem to be queuing up to offer me drinks. How many have I had now? I watch people swim around me, laughing, drinking, celebrating.

The music cranks up in volume. 'Play That Funky Music, White Boy' pumps out from the speakers and it's a cue for all the funky white boys to hit the floor. Only they're not remotely funky. They're dancing like those nearly-dead people in *ER* whose bodies spasm uncontrollably as they're blasted with megawatts of electricity. I want to run on to the dance floor and shout, '*Clear!*'

I can't watch without giggling. I decide, instead, to go off in search of food, but when I get to the buffet, I find I'm too late. Empty plates are being stacked and removed, so the only available stomach filler is liquid. So on I drink.

I scan the room for Richard. Haven't seen him for a while. He's not on the floor with the others – thank God. Now they're twitching spastically to 'Living In a Box'. I like this song. Takes me back. I close my eyes and . . .

'Fran, at last!' A shrill voice cuts through the bass line. It's Isabel of Isabel and Harvey fame. They're a directing duo who made their names shooting TV ads and pop promos. They were This Year's Thing for, oh, years; so cutting-edge you could shave your legs with them. Then, when they were at the top of the tree, they decided they wanted out so they gave it all up to go live on a ranch in Idaho. Or Bogota. Or somewhere like that. I can't quite remember.

My eyes focus on Isabel. What *is* she wearing? Some kind

of African robe thing by the looks of it. Was it Angola they escaped to, maybe?

'*Isabel*, fantastic to see you.' I smile. 'How long have you been back?'

She beams high-priestess-ly at me. 'Oh, maybe six months . . .'

Where the hell did they go? Was it Egypt, maybe?

'. . . although it feels like six minutes. It's been mad. You just don't know where the time goes, do you?'

'No, you certainly don't,' I laugh, thinking how right she is. All that food gone without me even noticing the evening slipping away.

Harvey arrives at her side. He's wearing a loose muslin two-piece, beaded at the ankles and neck. Where would he have bought an outfit like that? 'Francesca!' he booms. He hugs me and I smell something vaguely oriental . . . Got it! *Turkey*. They've been farming goats in Bodrum.

He looks me up and down. '*Gorgeous* sight. Makes me glad we came back.'

'Really?' I ask.

'Absolutely. Cornwall's great, but you can't surf for ever, can you?'

Oh . . .

'So, how's my favourite French whore?' he asks.

Ah, how could I ever forget her? A commercial for Renault. It never ran, but it was the job that launched them both into the stratosphere. The film they shot – complete with me in fishnets and an asphyxiating bustier – wasn't quite what Renault had in mind for their family runabout. It was slightly *off*-script. Actually, Isabel and Harvey tossed the original script on day one and as soon as Renault realised what they were up to, they fired them. Normally, nothing kills a director's career quicker than a firing, but a tape of their ad did the rounds of the agencies and they were made.

I'm not surprised. It was a very funny commercial. And – with the help of some extremely artful lighting – I didn't look too bad in that bustier.

After that, they saw me as their lucky charm and they cast me whenever they could get away with it. But the last call I got, Thomas was only about two months old and . . . excuses, excuses.

'We've been dying to talk to you.' Isabel beams. 'Did Richard mention anything about *Black Planet*? Our feature.'

'Oh, yes the . . . GIC . . . thing,' I say vaguely.

'*CGI.*'

'Sony Pictures are committed now.'

'It's gonna be *amazing*. A total genre-buster.'

'*Shrek* meets *The Matrix.*'

'*Snow White* meets *Predator.*'

Poor bloody Snow White, I think. Not what she had in mind when she went for a walk in the woods. My eyes flicker from Isabel to Harvey and back again as they hit me with their pitch. Why me? Shouldn't they be saving their energy for the guys at Sony?

'We've got some serious names pencilled. Alan Rickman—'

'Totally loves the concept. *Desperate* to be involved.'

'Colin Farrell, Gary Oldman, Sarah Michelle Gellar—'

'And Francesca Clark.'

'We need you, Fran. No one does South African like you.'

Well, apart from the South Africans, I think.

I'm confused. 'But . . . Richard said . . . Isn't it sci-fi?' I say.

'Absolutely. It's apartheid in *space.*'

'*ET* meets *Mississippi Burning.*'

'We've got this character. Really dark. Pure evil. But sexy with it.'

'A sadistic racist alien that talks like . . .'

Isabel trails off, presumably unable to think of any South Africans who aren't Nelson Mandela.

'Zola Budd?' I supply.

'Exactly!' Harvey exclaims. 'Total mind-fuck.'

'She's *you*, Fran.'

Really? I've thought myself a lot of things lately, but funnily enough sadistic racist alien (with a Jo'burg twang) hasn't been one of them.

'How about it?' Harvey asks.

What can I say? I can't go back to work. The kids need me. Besides, I probably wouldn't even know which end of the mic to speak into. Jesus, I'm the woman who has panic attacks about lunchboxes! Honestly, what do I say to them?

It really doesn't matter that I can't speak because they're off again. On another torrent of *Star Wars* meets *SpongeBob SquarePants* or whatever. I smile and nod and laugh in what I hope are the right places as, dizzily, my attention flits from my rumbling foodless stomach to the whirling disco lights to the flailing body parts of uncoordinated people in party mode. Not one of them belonging to my husband.

'Sorry, guys,' I interrupt as politely as I can, 'but have you seen Richard?'

'I think I saw him outside on his mobile,' Isabel says as Summer joins us.

'Fran, can I talk to you?' she says.

'Sorry, Fran. We've been monopolising you,' Isabel apologises.

'We'll talk, yeah?' Harvey says. 'You've *got* to read the script.' And with that, they're gone.

'What did *they* want?' Summer asks.

She knows who they are. She's in the business, she knows who everyone is. And she must be livid that they don't know who *she* is.

She doesn't wait for me to answer. 'Never mind, I'm sorry, but I'm in such a state, I need to talk to you, Fran.'

And I'll be happy to listen, but right now, my head is swirling. Can't think straight.

'I can't talk,' I say. 'Not now. I have to find Richard.'

'Bu—'

'Sorry, Summer. Got to go,' I say as I head for the exit.

Richard is on the patio, bathed in the glow of the flood-lights that illuminate the tennis courts. It's drizzling and he has his jacket collar pulled up. One hand is deep in his trouser pocket, the other holds his mobile to his ear. When he hears my heels click, he turns round to see who it is, sees me and turns away again.

I stand twenty feet away from him feeling uncomfort-able. Wondering if I should go back inside and leave him to it. But who's he talking to? What call is so important that he has to leave his wife's party at almost midnight to make it?

He flicks the phone shut and turns towards me.

'Was that Karen?' I ask. God, where the hell did *that* come from?

'Who's Karen?' He looks confused – very *convincingly* confused at that.

'You know, *Karen*.' I give it to him in my best Canadian – north Ontario, to be precise. 'Drop-dead sexy, calls you tiger.'

'What the hell are you getting at?'

'I don't know, you tell me.' I'm starting to shiver. I'm not sure if it's the cold or the conversation. One that *I* started and now desperately wish I hadn't.

'How much have you had to drink?' he asks, looking me up and down.

But I'm not drunk. I'm sobering up unpleasantly fast.

The drizzle has turned into proper rain and it's acting as a very effective cold shower.

'Stop changing the subject,' I say. 'Are you fucking her?'

Oh God. What did I say that for? Richard looks as if he might explode.

'You're mad, do you know that? It's no wonder things have . . . No wonder I . . . Karen is an employee. A *colleague.* Jesus, you think I'm *screwing* her?'

He looks at me, his head shaking from side to side.

'Your phone.' OhGodohGodohGod, who is this talking? Because it certainly isn't *me.*

'You what?' he asks, looking confused.

'Your phone. Let me see it.'

Last caller, I'm thinking. If KAREN flashes up on the display, I'll finally know I'm married to a cheat.

'This is insane,' he spits. But I see it in his eyes. Not sure what, but there's no denying it's something. 'Absolutely insane.'

Insane, yes. But I've pushed this conversation over the crest of the hill and now that it's gathering speed I realise there are no brakes. Nothing else for it now but to let it run to the bottom and crash.

'Let me see it . . . please.'

He pulls his phone from his pocket and thrusts it in my face, deftly flicking at a couple of buttons with his thumb.

'See? Do you see it, Fran? Happy now?'

Raindrops dapple the display and I have to squint to read the word. But it's not KAREN. It says GUCCI.

'Gucci, Fran. My *client.* I've been at their beck and call since the pitch. They call, I jump. Whether it's chucking down with rain or sleet out here, I *have* to take the call because that's my job. *That's what I do.* Do you get it now?'

My mouth hangs open as I picture the beautiful top lying crumpled on the bedroom floor. The pitch he worked so hard to win – the one he was in the middle of preparing for when I waltzed into his office with demented notions of infidelity.

After what seems like far too long, I rediscover the power of speech. 'I didn't realise,' I say pathetically.

'That's your trouble, Fran. You go jumping to conclusions, but in reality you don't know anything. Do you know me at all any more?'

I've been such a total idiot. Shooting my mouth off and all based on nothing. OK, there's the slip of paper that started all this, but it must have a completely innocent explanation attached to it. Oh God, I've just realised. It's probably not even his. He's the MD. *He signs off expenses.* Someone gave it to him as part of a claim. *Duh!* Why couldn't I stop and think before I dived in? Did I say *dive*? More like the world's most spectacular bellyflop.

'Sorry,' I mouth.

'Jesus,' he spits. 'If you got yourself a life, maybe turned up to the odd recording session . . .'

Oh, I thought that was ancient history.

'. . . Why am I even bothering? This is crazy. We've got ninety-five people in there. Our *friends*. I think at least one of us should be looking after them.'

He pushes past me angrily and I watch him shove open the double doors and return to the party. I should follow him. Act like a grown-up. Put this stupid row behind me and tend to my guests. But I can't move. I look down at myself, watch the rain lash at my top and gradually turn the fabric transparent.

The doors crash open and I look up, hoping it's Richard having a change of heart, coming to save me from humiliation and pneumonia.

But it's Summer.

'Hey, look, it's the one-girl wet T-shirt contest. Sexy bra, babe.'

'Thanks. Just needed some fresh air,' I say, feeling a need to explain myself.

'Good idea,' she says. 'Dead smoky in there.' She pulls a cigarette from a pack and lights it in her cupped hand. She inhales deeply, looking as lost as I feel. What's eating her?

'Good move, inviting Harvey and Isabel,' she says after some silence. 'Dick-head tells me they love you.'

I nod and smile. Or try to, given that I'm soaked through and still reeling with humiliation.

'Fran, brace yourself, my love, because I've got some-thing to tell you.' She's grinding her barely smoked cigar-ette out into the paving slab, not looking at me. 'I can't believe it myself,' she says. 'I never thought it would happen. I've been so careful. And now I've got Phoebe yapping around me like a puppy and I can't get rid of her. I thought she was a good idea. A way of reaffirming who I am. I couldn't have been more wrong.'

'You don't like Phoebe, then?' I ask, trying to adjust to her wavelength, and not think about the fool I made of myself with Richard just now.

'I *like* her, but I don't feel anything for her. If you know what I mean.'

'So why go away with her?'

'It was one of those good-idea-at-the-time things. I sort of panicked.'

'Well, just tell her. Say sorry nicely and move on.'

How hard can it be? It's not as if she hasn't had the prac-tice. Summer has ended more relationships than a divorce lawyer.

'It's not that simple. She's only twenty. Just a kid. I'm worried she might kill herself. Or at least scratch at her skin with her nails a bit. She's slightly flaky.'

So that's her problem. She's hooked up with a nutter. I wonder if my behaviour – standing in the rain and falsely accusing my husband of adultery – counts as bunny boiling?

'Actually, I don't really care how she takes the news. It's you I've been bothered about telling.'

'That you want to dump Phoebe? Why should I care? I hardly know her.'

'No, you idiot, about me being pregnant.'

Silence . . . for, oh, at least a week.

'Well?' she finally asks.

'You're *pregnant*?'

How I manage to get the word out I don't know. *Pregnant*. It just does not belong in any sentence that refers to Summer. It makes no sense. Yes, yes, I know lesbians have babies, they make great mums, blah, blah, blah . . . but Summer? Never. She has the maternal instincts of a shop mannequin. I'm not being horrible. SHE'S JUST NOT INTERESTED. This is too shocking. Too far out. It's like . . . I can't think of an analogy. There isn't one that comes close.

'*Pregnant*,' I repeat, though this time it comes out as a whisper.

'I can't believe it myself, but three different tests can't be wrong. And I've been sick as a dog.'

'How many weeks?'

'Eight.'

'You knew when we met for lunch?'

'I wanted to tell you. That's why I met you. I got such a bollocking for leaving the set that day too. But you had your no-show-at-work drama and you were upset and . . . Well, you know how it went, you were there.'

Yes, I was there. And I didn't notice a thing. But what was there to notice?

'Look, I'd better get back. It's taken me all night to lose

Phoebe, but if I leave her alone for too long, anything could happen . . . You coming?'

As I trail damply behind her, the true shock of what she's just told me is only just hitting me. *Summer pregnant.*

Yet another thing I never dreamt would happen.

My God, whatever next?

10

It's two o'clock. I lie in bed and feel a hangover kick in.

I didn't have another drink after I followed Summer back inside. People were starting to leave, thanking me for the great party, must get together again sometime soon, blah, blah. I left on my own as Richard was staying behind to settle up, organise a cab for his sister and her two friends, look for other excuses not to be with me.

I know he's home because I heard the front door open and close half an hour ago. What's he doing down there?

The self-inflicted humiliation of earlier still hasn't left me. What a fool I've been. But I have a plan, one that will surely make things right. I'm going to start with sorry. I'll say it repeatedly if necessary. Then, I'll move on to the promises. No more insecure paranoia. A Brand New Me. Life begins at forty? *Pah!* By totally reinventing myself at a sprightly thirty-seven, I'll be *years* ahead of schedule. And on Monday I'll call Isabel and Harvey about that job. I am so ready for this. A shame it's taken the stupidity of tonight to show me, but you have to hit the bottom in order to bounce back up, don't you?

I'll tell him all this just as soon as he comes upstairs.

Of course, I'll show him the hotel bill, but only as a means of demonstrating where all this unhappiness began. And it doesn't matter any more because I've moved on. (Obviously, I'll pause briefly at the end of this bit, giving him a cue to offer up his perfectly innocent explanation.) Of course he's not screwing Karen and it's perfectly natural that workmates call each other tiger. Or foxy. Or poodle. And there will be no need to suggest that they stick to their given names in future to save us wives any unnecessary jealousy because, well, the Brand New Me is so not the jealous type.

No, it's going to be a beautiful conversation and we'll make up by having a love-in. We'll stay in bed all day, curled up like John and Yoko without the politics. Molly will love it. She's a sucker for romance. And who can blame her?

Romance is a wonderful thing. Look at Summer. What the hell is all that about? But you know what? It doesn't matter. She's having a baby! And if in the process she's fallen in love with a bloke (Summer and a *bloke*?), that is marvellous. I'm going to finish the conversation we started in the rain by telling her all that matters is her happiness, be it with a man, woman or beast. OK, maybe not a beast. That would be taking the whole romance-is-wonderful thing a step too far, but you get where I'm coming from.

I'm ready to sort my life out. Or, to coin Richard's favourite line, like the new Don Corleone, today is the day I take care of all family business.

Don't get me wrong, I'm not planning to litter North London with corpses as per the film. Richard garrotted with his favourite Paul Smith tie; Summer lying limp, her brains splattered over her copy of *Stage*; Sureya slain in her herb garden. No, I'm simply going to make amends with everyone I've either ignored or neglected, starting with myself.

It really is an excellent plan and I'm ready to kick it into action the instant Richard comes upstairs.

It's two forty-five. Richard obviously isn't coming up. To talk to me, sleep with me or anything else. I've been lying awake thinking. I'm thinking that Summer's a fraud and a liar. What's her game? *She has had sex with a man.* She *hates* men – or so she's been telling me for the last twenty years. Has she been lying to me all this time? And has she been stringing Phoebe along with her lies too? Poor kid's only twenty. Well, I'm thirty-bloody-seven and I'm not going to let her get away with it.

She's not the only one who's in for it. Bloody Richard. He's a complete fucking liar. I'm looking at the hotel bill. Not a figment of anyone's imagination – it was there where I left it in my knicker drawer. *Part of some minion's expenses claim.* What was I thinking? It has Richard's name at the top. He is a lying scumbag because it is irrefutable proof that he *has* been screwing Karen. I'm certain of that now and I'm not going to let him deny it again.

I stand up and pull my dressing gown around me. I tiptoe past the children's rooms and make my way down the stairs.

He's in the sitting room, asleep on the sofa. Even with the expensive suit all crumpled and creased and his face squashed uncomfortably against the cushions, he still looks beautiful. Molly's face but with a touch of grey. But how come his greying temples only add to his appeal? How fair is that? Why doesn't his grey make him look haggard and undesirable the way mine does to me? And why is his torso so lean? Muscular through no particular gym regime and despite several lunches a week. I never lunch and look at my torso. And his hands – tanned, smooth and un-callused. Where have those hands been? *Bastard.*

'Richard, wake up.'

He stirs, shifting his body uncomfortably. He half opens his eyes and his hand goes up to his neck, rubbing the spot where it was bent at a painful angle.

'What time is it?' he asks blearily.

'Time we talked.'

I sit down on the coffee table in front of him, my bottom half resting on a pile of magazines. We stare at each other, waiting for someone to make the first move. Evidently, he isn't going to say anything. It's up to me to get the ball rolling.

'OK, so maybe you weren't talking to Karen earlier, but I know you've lied to me. Something is definitely going on with her . . .'

No response, just a dead-eyed stare.

'I found this.'

My stomach flips as he takes the now-crumpled bill from me and looks at it.

'Oh,' he says at last. He forces his body upright on the sofa and winces as he straightens his legs. 'Right . . .' He's drawing this out, buying himself time.

It's like one of those dawn raids where the police drag suspects from their beds and interrogate them before they've had a chance to wake up and get their lies in order. 'So what's going on?' I prod. I'm damned if I'm going to give him the luxury of time to dream up an alibi.

He pinches the bridge of his nose and sighs deeply. 'You're right,' he says. 'It is time we talked.'

And as those words come out of his mouth, I realise I've reached the point of no return. I'm not going to get the innocent explanation that I've been so desperate for. There *is* something to talk about.

'Nothing's going on with Karen,' he says. 'But there is something . . . someone.'

Oh God . . .

'Who?'

'She's called Bel. Short for Belinda. She works for Gucci. She's the client. Well, she wasn't when I first met her, but that was, well, it was a while ago. She got promoted. Now she's their head of brand development.'

Jesus. What's he doing? Giving me her CV? Stupid, stupid bastard . . .

'How long?' I demand.

'I've known her for about a year. But nothing happened for ages.'

'How *long*?'

'Really, it's only been a couple of months. Maybe three. At the most.'

Only three months. Is that supposed to make it all better?

'What the hell does it fucking matter?' I shout.

'Fran, the kids.'

'*Tell me.* What does it matter how long you've been shagging her? Three months. Three years. So what? YOU'RE SHAGGING HER!'

'I'm sorry . . . I'm really sorry. Honestly, I didn't want this to happen . . .'

So why did it?

'. . . I tried to stop it . . . We both did. But we were spending a lot of time together. With work. And you know, these things happen . . . She does know about you. I made it clear from the start what I had at risk.'

'At *risk*? What are we? Part of your share portfolio?'

'No, it's not like—'

'Because if that's how you feel, this is your Black fucking Monday, Richard, because you can just fuck off out of here right now!'

Yes, still shouting.

'I thought you might say that.' He rises slowly to his feet, looking everywhere but at me.

'Is that it? You're just going to walk out?'

'Well, that's what you want, isn't it? Isn't that what you just said?'

I want to scream, but I don't have any words. I have no idea what I want. But I do know one thing. Just like Al Pacino says in his stupid *Godfather Part III*. No, Richard, THIS IS NOT WHAT I WANTED!

'We need some space,' he says quietly. 'Let's face it, things haven't been . . . *right,* not for a while. Long before Bel, if we're honest . . . You're right, Fran. I should go.'

I can't believe this. He's turning it on me. Like it's my decision that he leaves. Isn't he going to beg me to let him stay? Plead for forgiveness now he's had the courage to confess? Isn't he going to try to fight for what he's losing?

That's the thing that shocks me the most. That obviously, he doesn't think he's losing anything at all.

'I'll go and get some stuff together,' he says as he walks from the room.

And ten minutes later, he's gone.

9

I don't know where Sunday has gone. Like a cheap magic trick, it just seems to have disappeared. But unlike pulling strings of coloured hankies from a hat, I'll never be able to bring it back.

As if I'd ever want to.

I stayed in the sitting room after Richard left. I had no sense of passing time until I heard birdsong. At just after six o'clock, I tiptoed upstairs and climbed into bed. When Molly came in at six fifteen, I put on a superb act of waking up after a hard night's partying.

'Did you have a lovely, lovely time?' she asked.

'Yes, lovely, thank you,' I replied. *I made a drunken idiot of myself, your father left me . . . the perfect way to welcome middle age.*

'Helen let me stay up and watch *Millionaire*. Where's Daddy?'

'He had to . . . go away. For his job.'

'Can I have Frosties?'

I couldn't face the kids. So at nine o'clock, I phoned my mum. She was delighted to have them for the day, of course. She regularly begs me to visit more so she can see her grandchildren. She lives in Radlett, forty minutes up the road in Hertfordshire. She sells the benefits of country living as if she's an estate agent and I'm buying. And she's right. Her house *is* pretty and backs on to open fields and woodland, and there *is* horse riding within genuinely easy walking distance. Thomas and Molly love going there and I should take them more often. But you know how it is. Time disappears, leaving you feeling too guilty to pick up the phone and you swear that you will *soon*, but soon never seems to come and on it goes. Besides, Richard never wanted to visit. His fault, then.

But Richard wasn't home, so maybe all that could change. No time like the present, I thought as I picked up the phone.

I kept it together until Mum arrived for the pick-up. A mud mask cleverly hid the telltale signs of impending hysteria – the attack I was going to have just as soon as I shut the door behind them. I told her I was having a 'me' day. She told me what a great idea that was and Al rolled his eyes.

'Bloody ridiculous,' he said. 'What the hell's a "me" day?'

I might have felt intimidated if Mum hadn't slapped him playfully on his arm. She knows how to make him smile. All she has to do is hit him. Maybe I should have tried that with Richard.

We were standing in the hall waiting for the children to get their shoes on. Al's large frame filled the doorway where he stood jangling his keys impatiently. What is he? Sixty? Sixty-two? He's a big guy. Aren't people supposed to shrivel with age?

'Thanks for having them, Mum,' I said. 'Just the birthday treat I need.' The mask was doing exactly what it was supposed to do. Masking my face. I was helping by holding my hands up just above the surface of my skin as I spoke, as if I was frightened the mask might crack. Which, actually, it was in danger of doing.

'Don't speak with that thing on, love. Besides, having the kids is a treat for *me*. We'll catch up later. Al wants to get off.'

Al can't abide waiting. He had already moved to the car, rubbing at a spot on the bodywork with his cuff.

They've been together for three years now. Al – Alan – is a man's man. He hunts, shoots and fishes, and when he isn't out killing things, he's locked away in his garage tinkering with a relic that is, Mum assures me, a collectible. He's not the type of guy who understands why a woman would need 'me' time, despite the fact that pretty much his entire life is devoted to 'me' as in him. He's taking a rare break from himself now by acting as a cabby for my kids.

But I don't want to sound as if I don't like him. Whatever he's like, the fact is that Al has transformed my mother's life. From shabby Bethnal Green to the real green of Radlett. From a tiny terrace to a sprawling cottage filled with stuff she had previously only ever seen in magazines. She's like a before-and-after transformation in a TV ad.

'You'll never believe you used to chop, slice and dice when you try the new Kenwood Chefette with its revolutionary three-in-one action! It chops, blends and liquidises with just one – yes, one! – touch of a button.'

Al likes his gadgets. Mum does too, though I think she's still enjoying the novelty after a lifetime without. In short, she's made a remarkable – even revolutionary – transformation. And all it took was twenty-one years of being on her own. Well, I've got it all to look forward to, haven't I?

Al used to be a builder's merchant. His shop was on the Mile End Road, not so far from where Mum lived. He sold up not long after they met and that's when they moved to Radlett.

Despite the overbearing alpha-male thing Al has going on, I'm just happy that after all these years, Mum has found a companion. One who's given her a beautiful home and lovely holidays. And the revolutionary Kenwood Chefette.

As she left, she told me she'd have the kids home by eight and said she hoped Richard was enjoying his business trip.

Why didn't I tell her? Because to tell her the truth would

have made it real, and why would I want to do that when I can pretend otherwise? Besides, like I've said, Mum and I talk a lot, but we never really *talk*. It's just our way.

I waved madly as they drove away. Molly blew kisses and Thomas scowled, although I'm not sure why. Al is originally from Yorkshire and he's a mad Leeds United fan. It may not be Arsenal, but it's football. He and Thomas have something they can *do* together, which is more than can be said for the time Thomas spends with his father.

Or should that be *used to* spend?

Jesus, what the hell was going to happen to us now?

That thought must have spent the morning circling above my head in a holding pattern. As soon as they drove away it descended on me like a crash-landing 747.

Richard the weekend dad.

Fran the single mum.

Suddenly the future was clear: gushing taps in the middle of the night; heavy deliveries sitting on the drive, waiting for someone strong enough to bring them into the house; a punctured tyre on the motorway, a woman who doesn't know a jack from her elbow, a huge articulated lorry thundering towards her and her children, going out of control, they're sitting ducks on the hard shoulder as the truck smashes into them causing immediate, body-mangling death . . .

They'd been gone five minutes and I was hysterical. Not wailing and screaming, but internally I was in a panic. If I'd been calmer, I'd have thought it through.

- Richard was never able to fix a tap. He always did what I'll now have to do – call a twenty-four-hour plumber.
- He was never around when heavy deliveries arrived, yet somehow they'd always be in the house by the time he got home.

- He did know how to change a tyre, but the operation used
  to take him so long that the hypothetical runaway truck would
  have mown us down anyway.

But calm, clear thinking obviously wasn't going to be the
order of the day.

I went to the kitchen sink and frantically scrubbed off
the ridiculous mask. Then I took some deep breaths, sat at
the island and smoked. Smoking was good. It calmed me
down. I tried to think *calmly* about Richard and me. Where
had it all gone wrong? Could it ever be put right? But why
would Richard want to put it right, when he was now having
his brow stroked by a beautiful woman? Was she beautiful?
Well, she worked for Gucci. Not Matalan or Dorothy Perkins.
Gucci. See? Thinking was not the answer. I needed to *do*
something.

So instead, I drummed my fingers on the worktop and
listened to the sound echo through the house. Did the place
always feel that empty with only me in it? No, because no
matter how late Richard's home-time was, there was always
an eventual home-time to look forward to.

As I smoked and drummed my fingers, I looked out of
the window and noticed the umbrella over the table on the
patio was rocking backwards and forwards ominously in the
wind. I really ought to have gone outside and put it away.
But I didn't because I noticed Myra the Cabbage Patch Doll
– *Myra*, Richard's idea of a joke – leaning on the toaster.
Her arm was falling off and Molly had been begging me
for weeks to sew it back on. Here was a chance, finally, to
get a needle and thread and fix it. But I didn't because the
cigarettes caught my eye. Oh, good, cigarettes! So I lit another
one and glanced at the clock on the microwave. My children had only been gone a few minutes, yet somehow that
was nearly two hours ago.

It was one minute past twelve. My heart was aching. Literally. Another panic attack? Or does devastation really do that to you? Make your heart physically hurt.

Don't know if any doctor would have prescribed a glass of wine for my symptoms, but there you go. That's what I did. I poured myself a glass of the rosé that was open in the fridge. For some reason, rosé always makes me think of the summertime. I remembered a period of optimism earlier this year when I had planned the summer holidays. I was sure that the fortnight in Nice I was organising would give the four of us the chance to see that, *yes*, we were a very special family indeed. As I recall, my burst of energy was sparked by sex. It was the first time Richard had been near me in months and I was sure it marked a new beginning. I wasn't to know then that what it marked exactly was the last time we'd have sex.

And of course Nice didn't happen because Richard's job did instead. The idyllic two weeks I'd hoped for turned into five days in a mildewy cottage in Devon. Richard couldn't come. The kids and I spent the rest of the holidays hanging around North London's array of parks. Thomas and Molly counted the days until they went back to school and their friends. I counted the days until they went back to school and I could stop pretending that hanging out in parks was the best thing in the world.

So the rosé just opened a can of worms, but I finished it anyway. Then I wrenched the cork out of a bottle of red to wash away the foul taste of summer. It was a Beaujolais. These days, Beaujolais reminds me of a château tour we went on four years ago. It was just the two of us. We had a wonderful time. We ate and drank like Frenchmen and I believe we screwed like them too. So there it was: another bottle of gut-churning memories to drink my way through. Once it was empty, I opened a bottle of white. Like a self-assured artist, I'm not afraid to mix my colours.

But I'm not going to be able to make a proper start on the white because it's ten to eight. Where has the day gone? I need to have a drink of water, brush my teeth, wash my face . . . Basically, I need to clear my head before the kids get home.

I'm gargling mouthwash when I hear a fist hammering insistently at the front door. I go downstairs and see Thomas through the stained glass. I open the door and he rushes past me and up to his room. Molly follows, but not before she's bear-hugged her granny.

'Thanks for having them, Mum,' I say as Molly disappears into the sitting room to turn on the TV in search of cartoons.

'No, thank *you*. We have had the *loveliest* day.' She beams. 'Those kids are a credit to you and Richard, you know.'

Funnily enough, I haven't cried all day, but that last remark has triggered an urge to collapse to the floor and sob my heart out. I fight it. I really, really fight it. Luckily, Mum isn't looking at me. She's fumbling with a carrier bag.

'Here, take this,' she says, handing it to me. 'It's just a few bits and bobs I bought for Molly and a video of some football match for Thomas. It's Al's and he says not to tape over it. It's a classic, apparently.'

'Thanks, but you really shouldn't have.'

'Oh yes I should. And more often too.'

That's as close as my mother ever gets to a dig. If she thinks it's odd that I'm not asking her in for a cup of tea, she isn't about to say so. I'm managing to hold my emotions in check and I'm bracing myself against the doorframe to stop from swaying, but I have got to get this goodbye over with.

Al comes to my rescue. He's in the car and he gives an impatient little blast on the horn. He isn't one to endure long goodbyes. Or short ones. Things to do, people to see, animals to shoot.

'Best be off,' Mum says brightly. 'You need to get those two to bed. They've run themselves ragged today.'

'Thanks again, Mum. And thank Al too, won't you?'

She looks at me strangely, then says, 'Are you all right, Fran?' She's peering at me now. Fortunately, the light in the hall is gloomy. 'You look worse than you did this morning.'

'I just had a bit of a reaction to the avocado. You know, the face-pack thing,' I say, patting my cheek. 'Anyway, like I said, say thanks, won't you?'

Al toots his horn again. Mum, looking concerned but never one to pry, backs away – both physically and metaphorically. 'So, you're OK?'

'Of course I am!' I say really, *really* brightly. 'I've been doing nothing else all day. I've just had a *me* day!'

Talking loudly really works, doesn't it? You can spout total nonsense, but do it loudly and with enough gusto and you can get absolutely anyone to believe it. Why do you think politicians get so vocal? *'I have said it before and I will say it again, this week's weather is unacceptable. Under this Labour government, rainfall has increased to record levels, despite their pledge to tackle the issue. The people of Britain can rest assured that the next Conservative government will guarantee Better Weather. Our two-year plan will ensure not only that it never rains on weekends, but also any surplus precipitation is re-directed to where it is needed most – i.e. to Europe, which for too long has seen this country as a dumping ground for its own unwanted weather.'*

If my little 'me day' speech doesn't completely convince Mum, at least it gets her off the premises. I wave her off, close the door and lean against it. Now all I have to do is put the kids to bed.

And then I can cry as much as I like.

8

The sunglasses I'm wearing have nothing to do with the sun, which is nowhere in sight, anyway. They have everything to do with the fact that yesterday I consumed more alcohol than I should have.

I've never viewed enjoying a glass of wine as a problem. When a man comes home after a hard day's wheeling and dealing in the City and says, 'I need a drink, honey,' is it so different to the mum – namely me – who has one in the evening just because her feet are killing her? I never thought so.

But this morning, I'm thinking that this weekend's drinking is bothering me.

But then again, yesterday was something else. Does that excuse me? My husband *had* just left me. What woman wouldn't go on a bit of a bender?

At seven o'clock this morning, I gave Molly her breakfast. My body was in the kitchen, but my head was somewhere else entirely. I was thinking about Richard.

Richard has spent years thinking about me. Not just thinking, but actually *doing* as well. He has made real, time-consuming efforts to lift me out of my hole. Look at the party. Look at the recording session I never turned up to. And they are just the latest in a long line. Even in the depths of my despondency, I was always *aware* that he was trying . . .

Why didn't I *respond* – just *once* – when he was calling

in favours to get me back to work or arranging surprise child-free weekend breaks or ringing old forgotten friends and telling them we were dying to see them again because I was too shy to pick up the phone?

God, I have so had this coming. I've driven him away as surely as if I'd climbed into the car and started the ignition myself.

I feel pathetic. Because when I was faced with a husband who'd become so exasperated that he walked into the arms of another woman, I finally responded. Oh, yes, I responded big time. I turned into someone worse. I don't know who that was drinking in my kitchen last night, but she wasn't me.

But if she wasn't me, why the hell am I the one with the hangover?

Molly's bubbly chatter on the walk to school pounds at my skull like a pneumatic drill. And now something jagged is scraping at my ankle.

'Oh my God, I've done it again!'

I look round to see Natasha's double buggy-cum-breakfast bar and in the nick of time stop myself from crying out in pain. Again.

'I'm so sorry. Are you OK?' she asks, stopping abruptly.

'No worries, I'm fine.' I force a smile. 'How are you?'

'Oh, you know, mad, mad, mad!' she says, mascara-ed eyes sparkling, laughing merrily, looking anything but mad.

Looking quite stunning, actually. Today she's gone for barely-there lip gloss instead of last week's chocolate brown. And in place of the Jimmy Choos are yellow – *yellow!* – espadrilles. The colour complements the lime green in her Diesel skirt, which I remember she was wearing at her kid's birthday party . . .

Amazing. I can't remember the last time my husband made me laugh, but I have perfect recall of every detail of this woman's daily wardrobe. *Shit!* There's something else I almost forgot. *Ron*, football coach, answer to Thomas's prayers. I make a mental note to call him today.

'*Love* the rock-star shades,' Natasha says, jolting me back to the present. 'Still getting over Saturday night? I hear your party was a smash,' she says.

'Oh, how do you know about that?' I ask, taken aback.

'Ha, nothing gets past me,' she laughs. 'No, I'm joking. I know Amanda and Adam.'

I look at her blankly.

'Adam the designer? Works with your Richard. We had them over for lunch yesterday and they told us all about it.'

Who the hell are Amanda and Adam? Well, they were at my party evidently. But what did they see there? Did they sense the tension between Richard and me? Did they notice just how drunk and disconnected the birthday girl was? And, God, my *rudeness*. I was rude to Chris. Who else? This guy Adam? And did he and Amanda give Natasha a full tabloid kiss 'n' tell over Sunday lunch? I feel blood rush to my head, making my cheeks glow red and my headache pound all the more viciously.

'Well?' Natasha prods. 'Was it as fantastic as they said? I'll take the shades as a yes, shall I?'

'Oh, you know how it is. Can't drink like I used to,' which, when you think about it, is actually the complete and utter truth.

I tell myself to calm down. I tell myself that Natasha would hardly have hurried to catch up with me if this Adam and Amanda had outed me as a deranged bunny-boiler. It works because I feel my heart rate gradually return to normal.

'Listen, what are you doing after school?' she asks. 'I'm free if you'd like to bring the kids over. It's supposed to be sunny later.'

We're at the school gate now and I'm wondering how to

say thanks but no thanks. Thomas has run off for a kick-about. He has only seconds before the bell that marks the end of his freedom.

They think it's all over . . .

He could score three goals in that time.

'How about it?' Natasha presses. 'The kids can play in the garden and we can have a gossip.'

'Say yes, Mummy, let's go!' Molly squeals at my side. 'Fabian's got a tree house. *Please* let's go!'

'Excellent,' Natasha says before I can decline. 'Come round at four. I'll have a bottle open.' She winks at Molly. 'A bottle of Fruit Shoot, that is. Strawberry OK?'

'*Hooray*, Fruit Shoot!' she screams, running off towards her classroom, blowing me kisses as she goes.

I'm feeling even more shell-shocked as I walk out of the school gates. Sureya has to physically grab my arm to get my attention. 'Fran, I've been calling you,' she says, panting slightly after her run to catch up with me.

'Sorry, I didn't hear you.' I try to smile. 'How are you?'

She gives me a worried little frown. 'Fran, you and Richard seemed so sorted on Saturday night. What's with the shades? What's wrong?'

Friends, eh? I usually feel lucky to have one like Sureya. But not today. Today, I'm happy to morph back into my mother; I want to push her sweet, beautiful, concerned face as far away as possible. 'No, I'm fine.' I beam. A great actress. 'Just need to get home and get some much-needed sleep.'

'Fran . . . I think we should talk.'

'Definitely. Later this week. Maybe tomorrow?'

'I can't. We're going to visit Michael's parents in Bath.' She stops. I don't answer. 'OK, we'll talk when I get back, then. I can wait.'

Oh. *She* wants to talk to *me* about something. I thought

she was going to get on my case, like Summer does on a regular basis. Now I feel bad. Sunny, selfless, sweet Sureya. And me, the liability.

She peers closely at me. 'Are you sure you're OK?'

'Of course.'

I'm not sure she buys it, but the important thing is, she drops it. Some small talk is made. While she's away can I use my spare key and water her tannis root or whatever witch herb it is that she grows. Honestly, I have my suspicions. She's watched *Rosemary's Baby* too many times and it really does stink in that greenhouse of hers. Maybe I should look for some secret panelling in a secret wall in a secret cupboard when I go round . . .

'I'll only be gone a few days. I'll call you as soon as I get back,' she tells me. 'And you're sure, *sure* you're OK?'

'Yes,' I lie again.

And yet again, she drops it.

Weird. That is *so* not Sureya.

When I get home the phone is ringing.

'Hi, it's me,' Richard says.

The sound of his voice so stuns me that I can't reply.

'My plane's boarding, but I couldn't go without talking to you.'

My heart is pounding again. I want to say something nice. Not desperate or needy. Just nice.

'Is she there? Standing next to you? Listening?'

I didn't want to say *that*.

'Don't be silly. I'm on my own. I just wanted to—'

'But she's at the airport, isn't she? Waiting for you to finish so you can go get your seats together?'

'Please don't be like this—'

'She is, though, isn't she?'

'*Yes*. Yes, she's here. But so are Grant and Susan from

the office. This is a business trip, Fran. It's not a romantic mini-break . . .'

OK, so she's there. I knew she would be, though. And I still want to say something nice.

'I'm worried about you,' he says.

'What on earth for?' I spit. 'I'm not your problem any more, am I?'

A sigh . . . a long, deep sigh. 'Are the kids OK?'

'The kids are fine. They think you're doing business. They don't have to know that what you're *doing* is your client.' *And I love you, Richard. Have I mentioned that lately?*

Silence. And more sighing. But this time from me.

I have pushed the thought of the Other Woman into an unlit corner of my brain. I've wanted to keep her well away from my mind's eye, which has the ability to distort things horribly. But now she's all I can see and I desperately want her to go away because Richard is calling me and all I want is to say something nice.

'Sorry,' I say at last. It's all I can think of. *Nice* isn't coming easy.

'Don't say that. You've got nothing to apologise for . . . It's me . . . not you. That's why I'm phoning. We really need to talk about . . .'

Silence. Again.

'About what, Richard?' I prompt. He sounds troubled and vulnerable and this gives me a tiny glint of hope.

'About *this*. We need to reach some kind of . . . I don't know, some kind of a place where we can sort this out.'

'What do you mean, *place*? To sort it out? *How*, exactly?'

I'm not being obtuse. I don't know what he means. He sounds as if he's reading lines from a textbook. A self-help manual he picked up at the airport bookshop, perhaps. *It's Not You, It's Me: 10 Easy Ways for the Busy Executive to Dump His Wife.*

'I don't know,' he says, frustration creeping into his voice. 'But we need to sort it out so I can see the kids, for a start.'

Well, what was I thinking? That he was phoning to attempt a reconciliation? To tell me he's made a terrible mistake? This isn't a make-up phone call. He's at the airport with his mistress, for God's sake.

'What have you told them?' he asks.

'I haven't poisoned their minds against you, if that's what you're thinking.'

'That's not what I meant. Look, it's probably best not to tell them anything. Not until . . .'

'Until what?'

'Until, you know, we've talked . . .'

A thought strikes me now. Maybe I never have to tell Thomas and Molly that their father has left. They haven't questioned his absence. Why should they? He's always away. *On business.*

'I know you must hate me now, Fran . . .'

Yes, I do. But I only hate you because I love you.

'. . . And I don't blame you at all. But I'm not the bastard you think I am. OK, this thing has happened, but you and I have been suffering for a long time now. Way before Bel and me . . .'

It's like a punch to the stomach. What was once *Fran and me* has become *Bel and me.* After all these years, is it as easy as that? Delete one name, insert another?

'We need to talk about how we move forward from here.'

That's right. *Move forward* to a *place.*

'Haven't you got a plane to catch?' I say.

I don't want to talk about *moving forward.* I want to stay right where I am. OK, so this is limbo land, but if I stay here, it means he's still with me. Well, it means he isn't *not* with me – not officially. And as long as it's not official – as long as I haven't told the kids, my mum, my friends – it means there's still a chance he might come back. This is all true. I'm certain of it.

'Get off the phone. Catch your plane,' I say, not viciously, but decisively. 'We'll talk when you get back.'

'OK,' he says slowly. 'I really am sorry, Fran. I didn't want to hurt you.'

I hang up before he finds out exactly how much he has.

The phone has rung several times today, but I've been too busy to talk to anyone. I've been busy doing four things: lying on my bed, smoking, drinking and looking out of the window. Like most women, I'm good at multi-tasking. I have, however, been careful *not* to think. Thinking is just too painful. I get off the bed and head downstairs. I stop by the answering machine in the hall and press play . . .

Summer wants to talk to me about her pregnancy and a man called Laurence – the guy who got her pregnant? And something about George Clooney – surely it wasn't him? The message is garbled and crackly, but I do catch the bit about her finishing with Phoebe. She's warning me against opening the door to anyone young, crazed and armed with super-heated curling tongs . . .

There are several other crackly messages. One from the bank trying to sell me something I don't need. One from Ruby or Wendy telling us what a great party it was, one from someone called Don or Ron – wasn't I supposed to be calling someone called Don or Ron? One from Mum telling me how much she enjoyed having the kids, and one from someone called Isabel.

Isabel! *Star Trek* meets *Coronation Street* or whatever. The job Richard was trying to sell me on.

I've just had a thought. Richard was trying to get me back to work to give himself one less thing to feel guilty about. It doesn't take me long to convince myself. I no longer hate him because I love him. I hate him because he's despicable.

And I hate his stupid, glamorous bloody girlfriend. Her image, which I've done so well to suppress, now punches its way to the front of my mind. She's supermodel slim, and when they make love, which is most of the time, it's wildly erotic and uninhibited and the lights are on. Why would a woman who oozes Gucci from every pore ever turn the lights off? And when they finally finish – because even lovers as hot as those two have to stop sometime – she lights up a cigarette, and it looks so amazingly sensuous in her naturally plump lips that Richard doesn't fan the smoke away. Rather he lies next to her, drinking in the smell of her, smoke and all . . .

Thinking is a really bad idea. I need to get on. Pick up the kids. Get to Natasha's. Just time to change my top, which is crumpled beyond repair after spending the best part of the day in bed.

I rush back upstairs and throw on a fresh T-shirt. Not so fresh, though. I don't notice the stains on it until she opens her front door . . .

'Hel*loooo*!' Natasha whoops. 'Go through into the garden, kids. Quinn's in the tree house, Thomas. Go on up and join him.'

Molly sprints through the house, while Thomas slopes, his shoulders hunched. Being in the year below and therefore subhuman, Quinn holds exactly the same amount of appeal as a tree house; that is, none whatsoever.

'Let's sit outside,' Natasha suggests as she leads me into her big kitchen and towards the French windows.

I walk into the garden and see Thomas visibly drooling. The lawn is the size of a football pitch and at the far end stands a goal the size of most lawns. He'll be fine, then.

'We've got sun on the bench over there and shade on the patio here,' Natasha says. 'Take your pick.'

I pick the patio and sit myself at a big teak table beneath a huge umbrella. I watch Natasha disappear back into the kitchen for refreshments. I notice she's swapped this morning's espadrilles for a pair of sensible Birkenstocks – pale blue to match the little denim skirt she's now wearing. I find myself marvelling at her yet again. *This woman makes time in the day to do actual costume changes.*

I'm glad now that I came. The less time I have to torture myself with my own company, the better. For as long as I've lived here, I've been surrounded by women who are everything I'm not – Cassie and Annabel to name but two. But Natasha's different. She too is everything I'm not, but for once that's an invigorating thing.

She reappears with a jug of Pimm's. That's all right. Pimm's doesn't count as proper drinking. It's just fizzy pop for grown-ups. She pours two glasses and hands me one. 'Here's to the last bit of sunshine we'll see this year. Cheers!'

We chink glasses and I take a small sip of the fizzy stuff.

'I'll just get us some nibbles,' she says. 'Then you can tell me all about the party.'

I tense at the P word. I may be a former actress, but lying my way through an account of the worst night of my life is surely a challenge too far. But I force myself to relax. I take my mind off the horror of Saturday night by taking in my surroundings. Natasha's house is a grand double-fronted affair. It's the sort of property you walk into and have to suppress the gasp of wonder for fear of appearing unworldly.

I look out over the garden. Molly is following Fabian up the ladder that leads to the tree house, which is big enough to sport its own estate agent's board and sell for a six-figure sum. Quinn and Tristram hang out of the windows, looking down on Thomas. They're counting out loud: 'Twenty-six . . . twenty-seven . . . twenty-eight . . . ' They'll count themselves hoarse – Thomas is brilliant at keepy-uppies. It could be several hours before the ball hits the ground again.

Right now – with his best friend at his feet and an awe-struck audience in the grandstand above – he's at his best, and that fills me with hope. For him, and for me.

'Here, have some of these. They are divine,' Natasha says, reappearing with a dish of marinated olives. 'Yes, just put it down there, Anna, thank you.'

A girl, as tall and thin as a lamp post, with short hair and a pierced eyebrow, puts a tray of several bowls of crisps and nuts on the table before disappearing back inside.

'Anna's fantastic,' Natasha whispers. '*Czech*. I don't know what we'd do without her. Actually, I do. My children would die of starvation. She's a lifesaver. And she's introduced me to a friend of hers who has the greenest fingers.' She holds up her beautifully manicured hands. 'I think mine must sweat weedkiller because they murder everything they touch.'

So Natasha has staff. Two of them. Maybe there are others. A butler? A social secretary? A cushion-plumper? She has *staff*, she does *costume changes*; she's like a suburban Britney Spears.

Stop that, Fran. I could have had a cleaner or an au pair. Or even a cushion-plumper. But for whatever reason, I've never bothered. It occurs to me that if I'd had some help around the house, I might have been able to spend time on sorting my shit out. Look at Natasha. It works for her.

It's never too late, I tell myself. I think back to Richard's phone call. Maybe the *place* he wants us to *move forward* to could be *staffed*. Aided by a stylist and a chef, I could lure him home with costume changes and gourmet nibbles. I am being deadly serious here. IT WORKS FOR NATASHA. I cannot stress that strongly enough.

'Eighty-nine . . . ninety . . .' Quinn, Molly, Fabian and Tristram chant from the tree house. Thomas looks exhausted, but isn't giving up. And neither will I.

There's still everything to play for.

It's a beautiful afternoon, Natasha seems to really like me, and the kids are having a normal, happy time. And I'm certain that Richard and I will find a way through this mess.

I'm certain of it.

'Your home is wonderful, Natasha. And you look so great. You make it all seem effortless.' I say this without a trace of bitterness because I don't feel any at all.

'Don't be ridiculous. You're the one who's got the effortless look going on.'

I'm about to tell her that, actually, it is very literally effortless, but she doesn't give me a chance.

'Me?' she continues. 'I look as if I've been worked on by a blind makeover artist. I'm a total mess.'

Her necklace matches her bracelet, and her hairband coordinates with her top. Which bit of her is the total mess? Her ears? Well, I do see a mole on her lobe. Maybe that's her problem.

'Do you ever miss working?' I ask.

She laughs. '*Retail?* Why would I miss that? Besides, I've got my hands full with this lot.' She makes a sweeping gesture across house, garden and assortment of sons. 'But if I were you, I'd miss it,' she says. 'You were a voice artist, weren't you?'

'Something like that,' I reply, wondering how these things get around. 'Actually, I have been thinking about going back to work.'

'Fantastic. So what's stopping you?'

Good question. I didn't have much luck explaining it to

Richard the other day. What chance do I have now?

'Oh, you know, it's hard with the kids. Know what I mean?' I say, hiding behind the two handiest excuses a woman ever had.

'Nonsense!' she cries. 'Get yourself an au pair and off you go,' she laughs.

Those were Summer's words too, as I recall.

She refills my glass, which is somehow empty. That's the thing with Pimm's: it just gets glugged back – though Natasha's glass is still pretty much full, I notice.

'You really should get back to work, if that's what you want. Adam tells me that Richard really supports and encourages you about these things.'

'Oh, yes, definitely,' I say, wishing I could remember Adam from the party.

'And so he should. It's all right for them, swanning off to work, pretending that being waited on by PAs is stressful. If you ask me, this is the hard bit. This staying at home and raising their children and dealing with all the day-in-day-out crap.'

'Do you really think so?' I ask, hope surging through my body again. Because it does give me hope that I'm not alone in finding this motherhood lark so difficult.

'Bloody hell, yes.' Natasha nods. 'They're never here, and when they are, they expect you to submit gratefully whenever they're in the mood, no matter what your day's been like. So selfish.' She closes her eyes and gives a little shudder. 'Men, eh?'

I'm almost speechless. How can someone who looks so up all the time feel so downtrodden? There is a part of me that thinks she's slightly spoilt. If it weren't for her husband's high-flying job, she wouldn't have the tree house in the field and the army of cushion-plumpers or whatever. But there's another bigger part of me that tells me we're not so very different, Natasha and I.

Before I can offer my total agreement, she turns to me angrily. 'Jesus, never mind the men, what about some of the women around here? Can you believe Cassie dumping *hats* on me?'

My heart gives a little skip. 'What do you mean?' As I ask the question, I'm thinking I already know the answer.

'For the Christmas play. Honestly, it's so annoying. Doesn't she realise I've got enough to deal with without the bloody *Wizard of Oz* to worry about?'

Cassie must have had second thoughts as soon as she'd asked me. She didn't waste much time calling to fire me, did she? Look at that. I can't even keep a crappy little volunteer job. What the hell am I doing entertaining notions about going back to proper paid work? I didn't want to do her silly hats, anyway. So why then am I feeling so hurt?

'Bloody Cassie. I must have "mug" tattooed on my forehead. I don't know how I'm going to fit it in with all the other crap I have to deal with,' Natasha says, and as she speaks, as always, she's laughing.

I think about the working mothers who have all that crap *and* a job to deal with. Not the mums round here who work for *self-fulfilment*, with hours designed to accommodate the school run. No, the ones who work fifty-, sixty-hour weeks to keep their kids in shoes. I had a mum like that once.

Natasha is presenting the sort of target that back in my twenties and not long out of Bethnal Green, I would have enjoyed ripping to shreds. I'd have done it with comedy voices and everyone would have laughed, even the victim. But not today. I'm a grown-up now. I'm drinking Pimm's with a friend rich enough to own a tree house that twenty-five years ago my mum and I could have moved into thinking it a step *up* the property ladder. But Natasha is going out of her way to be my friend and the feeling is quite comforting.

And Richard always said that I'd make friends easily if I'd only get out there.

Richard.

There's still everything to play for . . .

'God, *Cassie*. That reminds me,' she says, taking a tiny sip of her drink. 'The ARPS meeting is tomorrow morning. She wants to allocate jobs for the Autumn Fair. I've been roped in. Again.' She lets out a ladylike groan. 'Hey, why don't you come with me?'

'*Me?*'

'Please say you will. It'll be much more fun if you come too. I need someone I can make snidey jokes with.'

Me get involved with ARPS business? I may be trying to put my head in a more positive place, but I don't think I'm ready for *that* just yet.

'I haven't been invited,' I say.

'So? They'll be delighted with the extra help.'

I'm really not sure. Somehow it feels like too big a step.

'And we all get together for a drink afterwards,' she prods.

Well, put like that. 'OK, I'll come.'

She whoops with delight and I find myself whooping too and for the first time in ages it's entirely involuntary.

'One hundred and ninety-nine . . . two hundred!' Quinn and co. chant.

Thomas finishes by dropping the ball from head to foot and smashing a fierce volley into the top right-hand corner of the full-size goal.

As I lie in bed, that feeling of hope is still with me.

We didn't get home from Natasha's until gone seven. The children didn't want to leave. Doesn't surprise me about Molly. She'd be happy anywhere. Stick her on a waste tip and she'd turn it into Neverland. But Thomas? *Thomas did not want to leave.* As we walked home, he talked about Quinn, who may be a *whole* year younger, but he reckons he has hidden talent – and who better to coax it out than my Thomas, the football coach? OK, he was really intense and his little body was all bunched up while he talked, but, hey, he was talking! And the conversation went on for, ooh, minutes.

He was coming out of himself before my very eyes. I could do that too. Three hours with Natasha had flushed away the heartbreaking thoughts that had filled my head all day. It had nothing to do with the two jugs of Pimm's we got through – fizzy pop for grown-ups, remember?

As we left, I decided I wasn't going to let the heartbreak back in. OK, I'm not so much of an idiot that I think it will be easy. I have serious problems, starting with a husband who isn't here any more, and continuing with me, the only reason he isn't here any more.

But there's still everything to play for.

Natasha hardly knows me, but she really opened up to me this afternoon. It felt so good to be *trusted*. And good to get out of my own head and into someone else's. Because while I've moped, she's coped – which sounds like one of Sureya's catchphrases, but so what? Natasha has got on with life. With a smile. I asked her what her secret is. Her answer knocked me sideways.

'Prozac.'

That's right. Her smile is medicated!

She looked at my shocked face and laughed. 'It's no big deal,' she said. 'Actually, it is. Prozac is a fucking miracle. It makes you feel happy, but it doesn't stop you feeling yourself . . . if that makes sense.'

It did. I felt enlightened. And honoured. She was trusting me with stuff that only she and her doctor knew about.

And here I am lying in bed feeling honoured and enlightened. And *inspired*. It really is time I took control of my life.

Tomorrow, I'm going to phone Isabel and talk to her about that job. Wherever it was I misplaced my bottle all those years ago, I'm going to find it and I'm going to get back to doing what I do best: voices. That's Step 1.

Step 2: I'm going to cut down the drinking, which I've noticed has crept up lately. I've already made a good start. I've not had anything to drink today. And before you say anything, *the Pimm's doesn't count.*

Step 3: I'm going to get staffed up. Well, I'm going to get an au pair. This will help with the childcare when all the jobs start rolling in, and she can also do some of the housework, which will give me time to make myself look gorgeous. OK, I know that if I wanted to waste time making myself look half decent, I could easily get on with it without having an incommunicative Czech girl lazing about the place, making me feel guilty because she misses her family and only earns ten pence a week . . . Actually, I've no idea what I'm talking about. God knows what having an au pair will be like, but the point is that Accepting Help is a Psychological Step Forward. I know what I'm talking about this time because I read it in the blurb of the stupid self-help book Sureya gave me for my birthday.

And Step 4, the big one: the moment he gets back from Milan, Richard and I are going to sort this mess out. He's going to realise that Gucci Girl is just a stupid fling and we are going to Make This Marriage Work. He won't take too much persuasion because before his visit, I will have spent two hours fixing my face and hair, as well as finding an outfit that doesn't make me look size sixteen. (Obviously, Step 3b should be Go on Diet, but he's only away for three days and I don't think there's much chance of losing two stone in that time. So being realistic, deceptive clothing will have to do.)

Finally, Step 5: reintegrating myself with the world – or at least the world of Arlington Road Primary, and let's face it, what other world is there? Tomorrow's ARPS meeting is going to signal the start of my new proactive approach to life.

I know it's been a long time coming, but I'm ready now to change everything. I'm sick of the pain that comes from thinking about how I got into the hole I'm in. Now I'm going to give myself over completely to the task of climbing back out of it.

Natasha, you have no idea what you've started!

7

If Cassie thinks it's odd that I'm here, she doesn't say so. But perhaps she hasn't spotted me. There are twenty or so mothers gathered in the school dining hall. Muted chatter bounces off the art-filled walls. Natasha sits next to me looking like she's just flown in from Paris Fashion Week. She's in white today – a flowing gypsy skirt that folds itself over her long legs and a matching top with daisies appliquéd to the cap sleeves. With her hair in a ponytail, she looks about fifteen – a very well made-up fifteen, true, but the make-up suits her. It's not a bit overdone.

I've taken a leaf out of her book and put on some lipstick. I feel totally transformed. OK, more like slightly improved. Actually, the only difference is my lips are a tiny shade darker and no one has noticed anyway, but so what? Small steps and all that. The fact that I'm here at all – let alone in lipstick – is proof of my new state of mind, and silly as it may sound, I'm feeling sort of proud of myself.

Cassie claps her hands together. 'I can see lots of new faces today, which is *wonderful*. ARPS would be nothing without your efforts and this excellent turnout is proof of your dedication to raising the funds our school so *desperately* needs.'

She says this like she's Bob Geldof, we're Band Aid and our children are starving, fly-specked Africans.

Don't just sit there. Give us your feckin' money!

She stops and turns to Annabel. It's wart nose's cue to

stand up and take the floor. 'Thank you, Cassie. Now, we have a lot to get through if this year's Autumn Fair is going to be as stormingly successful as the last one, so if I race ahead and mention the Christmas play, feel free to stop me!'

Was that a joke? I laugh because everyone else does.

Blend in, Fran.

Natasha leans in to me and whispers, 'If she mentions bloody hats, I'll have to kill her.'

I smile and feel a tiny glow. For the first time as an Arlington mum, I am on the *inside*. Even better, I'm here with a friend. It is the best of all possible worlds.

The most amazing thing, of course, is that I'm feeling this good at a point in my life that can only be described as rock bottom. But maybe I'm not there any more. Maybe I'm already swimming back up. Just keep swimming. Break the surface and take in huge gulps of beautiful fresh—

Hands have shot into the air, Natasha's among them. *Damn.* What have I missed? I wasn't paying attention – too busy analysing.

'Excellent, that's food, cakes and hot beverages taken care of,' Cassie says as Annabel takes down names. 'The food stalls are our top earners. You're such *marvellous* cooks, it's a wonder you aren't all as overweight as I am.' She draws her hand across her frame – all seven and a half stone of it.

'Don't be so silly. You're an absolute sylph,' Annabel cries – just as she's expected to – and Cassie smiles modestly.

'Next item,' Annabel announces, all businesslike again, and – *shit!* – is she looking at me? *She is.* 'We had a wonderful stall last year. It really lent an air of *style* to the event. Designer gear. It would be wonderful if we could have more of the same, please?'

'Of course, Annabel,' Natasha says. 'I thought you might ask, so I've already started sourcing things. How organised am I?'

She laughs and so do I, the danger of another panic attack subsiding.

'And, Francesca—' Annabel says – now she *is* talking to me. 'The Hook a Duck stall. It doesn't take any particular expertise and it's pretty self-explanatory. The children just hook a duck and win a prize. Would you man that for us?'

Ooh, that was a bit below the belt, wasn't it? *No particular expertise.* Unlike being a witch, obviously. OK, so telling her to stick her stupid ducks up her skinny backside isn't an option, but I could have a cheeky laugh here by answering in a voice. But which one? Holly Hunter? Cilla? Ruby Wax? Decisions, decisions . . .

'Any problem?' she nudges, her witch smile firmly in place.

'Not at all,' I finally say in a voice that's all my own. It's all about playing the game. *Blending in.* And it isn't so hard to do. Natasha gives me a little smile and unlike Annabel's, hers is genuine.

Annabel isn't finished, not by a long way. 'Other stalls that need manning are as follows . . . '

And on she goes.

And then some.

Maybe this being on the inside is overrated. When I was outside looking in, I had no idea it would be this . . . *dull.*

Could it get any worse? Annabel has got to the matter of the Ice-cream Cart. 'We'll be having a *cart* this year. Last year's van was so tacky. Now, Rowena's father has kindly built the most beautiful piece – he's customised a genuine antique costermonger's cart, and Harold's mum has run up an exquisite striped silk canopy for it. But it needs to be painted . . . preferably by someone with an eye for Victorian colour schemes. Any offers?' (I think she goes on to say that the wheels – which are Stone Age – have been donated by the British Museum, but I can't be certain.)

I want desperately to laugh, but there is not a trace of humour in this dining hall. Just Mums on a Mission. Is this what happens to women who used to have careers? Who used to Be Something? They no longer have an office to thrust in so instead they do their thrusting at school?

But I'm on the inside now. I should be empathising with them, not slagging them off. I should be blaming the government. Of course, it's their fault for not providing enough opportunities for intelligent, professional women like these to get back to work.

That's better. A bit of positive thinking lifts me. Nice thoughts are *energising*. I should have tried it years ago.

But that doesn't mean this isn't deadly boring. When is it going to be over?

Cassie stands up and clears her throat. 'And finally . . .'

Yes! The magic words!

'. . . the MC. Who's going to man the mic? A very demanding job. We need a clear speaker, someone who can think on his – or *her* – feet. Any suggestions?'

'What about Martin? He did a terrific job last year—' someone offers.

'We'd love to have him, Susanne, but he's away with the BBC that weekend – I've already checked,' Annabel interrupts, as if she's the DG and the Martin in question is her best friend Martin Bashir.

Suddenly my most positive thought of the morning pops into my head: *MC? I could do that.*

'Anyone else who's good with a microphone?'

Me, me, me! I'm good with a mic.

'What about Linda?' someone suggests. 'She's done motivational speaking. She'd love it.'

'I'm afraid I've given her the entire arts and crafts area to run. I couldn't take her off that. She's the absolute lynchpin,' Cassie says.

I really could do it, you know.

'Oh, I know,' Annabel pipes up, 'what about that lady . . . you know, the one who drives the sporty BMW?'

'Who's that, then?' Cassie asks.

'*You know*, the lady with the BMW – it's blue. She has a son in year two.'

Cassie, none the wiser, looks at her sidekick blankly. Annabel's wart seems to throb with frustration. 'You *do* know her,' she goes on. 'She's really pretty, wears really nice clothes. She did something on the TV a while back . . . remember? One of those property programmes on Channel Four.'

Cassie's brow furrows, a sure sign of brains being wracked.

'Oh God, what *is* her name?' Annabel says pleadingly.

'Do you mean Marianne? The blonde lady?' someone suggests.

'No, not Marianne.' Annabel's face is screwed up in frustration now. 'You *do* know her. She's stunning. Lovely clothes, *BMW* . . . And she's got one of those bags with all the buckles on. And she's got that lovely laugh . . .' Annabel surveys a sea of blank faces. 'And she just had her hair cut really short.'

Oh! I know who she's talking about. I almost jump from my seat I'm so eager to tell them. 'You mean that black girl, don't you?'

And suddenly *everyone* knows who Annabel is talking about. And we'd have got there ages ago if she'd dared to mention a small but telling detail, one teeny-weeny word. Political correctness gone mad? It's in a straitjacket, bouncing off the walls of the padded cell.

I want to laugh. Because it's funny. It is ridiculously funny, yes, but also I want to laugh because suddenly I'm feeling very nervous. The room is silent, everyone looking at me. Except for Natasha, who only has eyes for her shoes. Little white mules, which I notice are spotless. Spotless white shoes? Just as unheard of in my world as mentioning a person's skin colour is in this one.

'It's Marcia, isn't it?' Cassie says. 'Marcia Robinson.'

'You're right, well done, Cassie,' Annabel tells her, pushing me out of the frame. 'I'll call her today. I'm sure she'd love to do it.'

I could have done it, I think, but obviously don't say.

After my tumbleweed moment, I have no desire to hang around the school. But as I walk along the corridor in the junior block, I can't resist stopping at Thomas's classroom and peeking through the glass in the door. He's at his desk by the window, but for once he isn't staring longingly out at the playground – or more particularly, at the goalposts in the playground. He has his head down over his work. His teacher wanders up and stoops over his desk. She nods approvingly and gives his shoulder a little pat and I feel good feelings well up . . .

And I feel a hand on my own shoulder.

I turn to see Mrs Gottfried. 'Are ve *ever* going to have that chat, Mrs Clark?' she asks, a deliberately weary look on her long, thin face.

'Yes, of course . . . I'll give you a—'

'Tomorrow, three o'clock. I'm free then.'

She turns and walks away, not giving me a chance to say, 'Look at him now, Mrs Gottfried, just look at him. He's working so *hard*. And his teacher just gave him a little pat. I *swear*, I saw it with my own eyes.'

As I watch her disappear round the corner, I hear the rapid click-click-click of heels behind me and before I know it Natasha is at my shoulder.

'God, wasn't that just ridiculous in there?' she pants.

'What's that?'

'You know, Annabel, her mental block on the B word. *Ridiculous.*'

'Embarrassing more like. Why was I the only one who'd say it?'

'Because you were the only normal person in the room, that's why. I was so thrilled you were sitting next to me, though! We've never had such excitement at an ARPS meeting before. I love it.'

She didn't look as if she was loving it when she was staring at her shoes, but what do I know? She's laughing now so I relax a little and smile back. It's amazing that just being with this woman lifts me.

'Will you let me return your hospitality?' I ask her. 'Bring the kids to tea tomorrow? Say you will.'

She throws back her head and laughs some more. 'We'd love it.'

'Excellent. It's a date.'

And just like that, I have something to look forward to. That wasn't so difficult, was it?

6

Summer in shades. It's usually such a celebrity affectation – such a hey-look-at-me thing – but I know that today it's nothing of the kind. She took them off when she arrived at the restaurant, took one look at the shock on my face and put them straight back on again. Summer Stevens is showing the classic signs of early pregnancy: whopping great bags under the eyes.

'Is everything OK with the baby?' I ask.

'Jesus, Fran, keep it down, will you?' she hisses.

I hadn't exactly been pumping up the volume, but that's another classic symptom: paranoia – everybody can tell, everybody's looking at *me*. Her outburst causes the two girls on the next table to look round. Do they recognise her from TV? Whatever, staring is definitely what they're doing, so I lower my voice to a whisper.

'Sorry, Summer, but you look rough. Why didn't you call me sooner?'

'I did, idiot. Several times. Have you given up listening to your messages?'

'Sorry. I've just had a lot on, what with Richard being in Milan and everything.'

'Well, that's good. Busy is good.'

That's two people I've lied to now. Mum and Summer. Although technically, I haven't lied. I just haven't told them what's happened. Why should I? I tell myself I don't want to worry them, but I know there's a ridiculous, childish thing going on here; that if I don't talk about it, it isn't really happening. Like when Molly broke Grandma Elaine's heirloom vase. What's good enough for Molly . . .

Summer takes a long sip of water. Funny. She can – and does – usually drink any man under the table. But not today. Today, she is *with child* (her description. Well, she's an actress, so how else would she put it? *Pregnant?* Ha! That would be for mere mortals) and she isn't happy about it either.

'God, I'm knackered,' she groans. 'Here I am creating a life and it's killing me. How twisted is that?'

'You're only doing what millions of women have done before you.' I wince as soon as the words are out. What was meant to be funny just sounded patronising. I wonder, when did *funny* become so difficult? Obviously, I shan't be attempting that again this lunchtime.

'Everything's gone wrong,' she says bleakly. 'I can't even enjoy a fag any more.'

'What does the father say? Or was it like, you know, assisted conception . . . of some kind.' I'm fumbling here. 'A test-tube baby or something . . . Is it?' Well, I have no idea, do I? We haven't talked about it. And I presume she arranged this lunch – our second in two weeks – so that we could.

'What are you like?'

She thinks I'm joking. I laugh, pretending that I am. Maybe that's the secret to being funny. Being serious.

Suddenly she looks at me, her face taut with anxiety. 'Listen, he doesn't know,' she hisses. 'And you mustn't tell him either.'

'Calm down. How could I tell him? I don't even know who he is.'

'I told you. It's Laurence.'

'Right, Laurence. Who's Laurence?'

'God, do you ever listen to anything? Laurence is directing *Angel Face.*'

'*Angel Face?*'

'Urrgghh! The Clive fucking Owen film.' She's sort of shouting and sort of whispering at the same time, not such an easy trick to pull off.

I don't think I'm being much help here.

'OK, let's just stop and go back to the beginning. You slept with the director?'

She gives me a tight little nod, as if anything more expressive might let loose too many unwanted emotions.

'Why?' I ask.

She takes her glasses off and I see her face properly. Summer is six months older than I am, though usually she looks years younger . . . *usually*. Not today.

'Because I'm a fucking idiot, that's why. That's what you're thinking, isn't it? You should see your face.'

I must look as shocked as I feel. I try to change my expression. I'm desperate not to get this conversation wrong any more. 'No, sorry. I'm just surprised . . . You must admit, you and men, you haven't exactly got a long history of . . . er, getting on.'

She sighs heavily and waits for the waitress to put down our pasta. 'Laurence is the *director*,' she says at last. 'Shallow, I know, but there you go. He came on to me on the first day of shooting, and at first it was like, "Oh, right, Minnie's turned you down, yeah?" but actually, it was a complete aphrodisiac . . . God, attracted to *power*. It's pathetic.'

'Stop it right there. None of us can be responsible for our feelings,' I say. I can remember – and wish I couldn't – the surge of aphrodisia I felt when Richard suddenly started to get ahead at work.

'I felt despicable . . . cheap, if you must know,' she continues.

'I didn't know why I was doing it, but I knew I couldn't help myself. I wasn't expecting much from the sex, but . . . God, this is a total mind-fuck.'

Try as I might – and I can't believe I'm trying – I just cannot conjure up a vision of Summer having sex with a man. If it's doing my head in, I can't imagine what it's doing to hers.

'He's an amazing guy, Fran. I never thought I'd say that about a man, but he really is. He's got this air of authority about him, but I've never once heard him raise his voice. He's talented, funny, madly creative, and he really seems to . . . *get* me.'

'Does he know you like girls?'

'Uh-huh. He came on to me as a dare. The first AD put him up to it – I worked with him on that stupid zombie movie. Anyway, it was supposed to be a one-off. But get this, the other night he told me he loves me.'

'*Wow*,' I say quietly, aware of burning ears on the table beside ours.

'I know. Can you believe it? I fucking hate men and there was one telling me he loves me!'

It really doesn't surprise me. As far as I'm concerned, diva tendencies aside, Summer is so damn loveable.

'Jesus, it's all so fucking complicated. I only slept with Phoebe because I was trying to sort things out in my head. Poor girl. There was him running after me, her running after me, me running around in circles trying to keep one from bumping into the other. Not easy when you're all on the same set.'

'So, did Phoebe help you sort things out?'

'Oh, yes. Phoebe helped me realise I didn't want to be with Phoebe. Big mistake.'

'Right. So does this mean you're not a lesbian any more?'

She's cross again. 'What do you think? Laurence came

along and *cured* me? God, that's the sort of idiotic thing my mother would have said.'

I wince, feeling like someone who's just noticed the BEWARE: THIN ICE sign just as the frozen lake starts to crack beneath her feet.

'Jesus, Fran,' she spits, 'you're rubbish, do you know that?'

'I do,' I confirm. 'I do know that.'

And I do. I am *rubbish*. I've had plenty of crises in the time I've known Summer and she's always been there for me. She's always seen through the confusion and known exactly what I should do. Now here she is having a crisis of her very own and where am I? Cowering on the other side of the table, terrified of opening my mouth for fear of making things worse.

OK, in my defence, she is very hormonal and we all know how deadly hormones are. Tiny chemical weapons of mass destruction. If Bush and Blair had declared war on hormones, they would have been on much safer ground.

But even so, I should be coping better than this.

'Look, I'm sorry,' Summer says, seeming to sense my despair. 'This is so confusing even I don't get it. I don't love Laurence, but I don't want to be *without* him either. I've never felt this way about *anyone*. And this pregnancy thing . . . I have never understood all that biological-clock bollocks . . . *Babies*.'

'That's cool. You are what you are and all that.'

'That's what I always thought. So why the fuck am I feeling like this?'

'Like what?'

'Like putting my hand across my stomach every time I cross the road, like wanting to buy baby clothes, like lying in bed thinking about what to call it . . .'

Now I'm completely thrown. Before this conversation started, I hadn't allowed for even the vaguest possibility that she might have any maternal instincts. The realisation that very clearly she has makes me feel terrible. Honestly, until now, I'd assumed that this pregnancy was heading only one way, and that *wasn't* the redecoration of her spare room into a nursery.

'So, what are you going to call it?'

'Britney, of course . . . I don't bloody know. I still can't take it all in.'

'It's so lovely,' I say, giving her hand a squeeze. 'Well, *I* think it's lovely.'

'It *is*. I can't believe I'm saying it, but it is *lovely*. But there's this thing . . . There's already a huge complication.'

'OhmyGod, is something wrong with the baby?' I'm having visions of Summer pushing a buggy with a two-headed, three-legged twin gone wrong.

'No, not the baby. It's Laurence. He's directing the next George Clooney. A cop-buddy thing with Samuel L. Jackson. It's amazing. His big Hollywood break. He's out there now prepping it. Anyway, he wants me to fly over next week.'

'That's fantastic, Summer.' I beam. I'm truly knocked out by this. 'It's all your dreams come true. But what's the complication?'

'He wants me to fly over for a test. He really wants to use me. George has seen some of the dailies from *Angel Face* and he's really up for it too.'

'But I thought you didn't have much of a part in it.'

'Don't be ridiculous. I just told you that so you wouldn't go getting all depressed because you aren't doing anything with your life.'

I'm saved from responding by the waitress, who has come to clear our plates. I've only had one glass of wine

so far, but this conversation is exhausting me, so I ask for
another.

'Blimey, Summer,' I say when the waitress has gone.
'George Clooney *loves* you.'

'Well, it's not cut and dried. Universal wants Sharon Stone.
I mean, they've never heard of me. That's why I've got to test.'

'Well, what George wants must count for something,' I
tell her hopefully. *George Clooney loves her!* And to think,
she was once in an Asda commercial.

The girls on the next table get up to leave, but pause at
our table. 'Excuse me, but are you off the telly?' one of them
asks.

Summer is in no mood to sign autographs and she looks
at me pleadingly. 'We do not know about what you are
talking,' I say in my best Spanish, taking up Summer's hand
again. 'My lover and I live mostly in Madrid and sometimes
in Barthelona. Do you know Barthelona?'

Since they've spent their lunch break straining to hear
our conversation, English accents and all, the girls scuttle
off giggling, surely having us down as a pair of lunatics.

'Look, Summer, the screen test is *fantastic*,' I say to her
when they've gone. 'What's the problem?'

'Well, the fact that the director who wants me for the
part doesn't know I'm pregnant is a bit of a glitch,' she says,
going for maximum sarcasm. 'Fran, the role I'm up for is
a member of a terrorist cell. I'd have to do four fight scenes
and a helicopter crash. I don't see that working with a bump
and swollen ankles, do you?'

Ah, I see now.

What a mess.

To give myself time to think, I take out a cigarette. When
I see the look on her face, I put it straight back.

'If I'm not allowed to smoke, neither are you,' she says.
'Anyway, I thought you were giving up.'

'I am,' I reply, fully intending to give up . . . one day. 'Look, Summer, do you want this baby?'

'Yes . . . *No* . . . I don't fucking know.'

'OK, right, here's what you do . . .'

She looks at me hopefully, tears banking up on the rims of her eyes.

What am I going to say? She's the one who's always got brilliant advice – what would she tell me if I were in her shoes? I only wish I could ask her . . .

'Here's what you do . . .' I repeat, stalling. 'Nothing.'

'Nothing?'

'That's right, absolutely nothing . . . for now. You don't tell Laurence a thing, you fly to LA, do the test, then decide. I mean, if Sharon Stone ends up with the part, all you've got to worry about is telling Laurence about the pregnancy . . . or not.'

'And if I get it?'

'Well, you worry about it then. It'll be really tough . . . But the thing is, you don't have to decide now. Just try to enjoy the moment. Hollywood, Rodeo Drive, lunch with George and Samuel L. . . .'

She's thoughtful for a moment. 'You're right. If the tables were turned, it's probably exactly what I'd be telling you . . .'

Really?

'I mean, what the hell else can I do?'

'Whatever happens, Summer, I'll be here for you. You know that, don't you?'

'You already are,' she says, tears trickling down her face.

Summer puts on her sunglasses as the waitress brings us our bill. When she's gone, Summer smiles at me through the tears. 'Sorry, Fran.'

'For what?'

'Having to put up with this. It's all been a bit me, me, me, I'm afraid. Tell me, how have you been?' she asks.

I consider for the briefest moment telling her the bad news – the Richard news – but decide that, no, the Molly-not-telling-then-it-hasn't-really-happened thing has worked for me so far . . . I'm going to focus on the good. Because there has been *some* good news today. And if I have a few more days like this, I'm positive I can make the bad news disappear completely.

'I made a couple of calls this morning. *Work* calls,' I tell her, beaming at the memory.

'Really?' she says, perking up. 'Who?'

'Remember Chris Sergeant?'

'Head of TV at Saatchi?'

'Uh-huh. I used to be his favourite VO in the world, ever. Anyway, he was at the party on Saturday and I was so rude to him I had to call to apologise. He wants to meet for a drink. He's going to call me in a couple of days when he's less busy.'

'I'm really pleased. How long have I been nagging you to get your arse out there and do a bit of schmoozing?'

'It's not schmoozing. He's just an old mate.'

'Yeah, an old mate who happens to run the TV department in one of London's biggest ad agencies. That's schmoozing, babe, and it's nothing to be ashamed of. Anyway, you said a couple of calls.'

'I rang Isabel . . . you know, Harvey and Isabel.'

I really can't believe I did it. Can't believe I made a call, the mere thought of which had me so terrified I wanted to throw up. I tell Summer about *War of the Worlds* meets Willy Wonka and the part as a Sarth Effrikkan in space and how Harvey and Isabel are convinced I'm their woman.

'That's amazing, Fran. So, what happens now?'

'They're sending me the script. I have to do a read-through for the execs on Monday and I am absolutely bloody terrified.'

'Of what? Your South African's amazing. You make

Winnie Mandela sound like a fraud. This is *it*. This is where you rejoin us working stiffs. I *know* it.'

'I'm not so sure. It's such a big leap. If it was just a little voiceover job, something to get me back into—'

'Stop it, Fran,' she says, reverting to the hard-as-nails Summer I know and love. 'I'm telling you, if you bottle out of *this* one, I am a hormonal time bomb at the moment and I *will* kill you. Promise me you won't let me down.'

'OK. I promise.' And I mean it. She's right. No more excuses.

I look at my watch. 'Shit, I'm late,' I exclaim.

'What for?'

'School. I'm supposed to be meeting the deputy head about Thomas.'

'Your poor children. You've got to blame the parents when they start acting up at school, you know,' she says. Two minutes pregnant and such an earth mother already. She'll be giving me handy little tips for what to do with aubergines next.

'Piss off, Summer,' I say, and still, she gives my hand the biggest, warmest squeeze. You insult people and look what you get. Maybe I should try it on Richard.

'Don't worry. I'm sure it's nothing,' she says. 'Thomas is a fantastic kid.'

I think so too.

'I'm so proud of you,' I say. 'About Hollywood and every-thing.'

'No, I'm proud of *you*.' She gives me a faint smile. 'Now, you go. I'll get the bill. And don't worry. Everything's going to be fine. For *both* of us.'

But why doesn't she look like she means it?

5

I needn't have worried about being late because it's the deputy head who's keeping me waiting. I sit outside her office and wonder how to play this. Thomas isn't a *bad* boy. He doesn't bully, spit in the corridors or start fights. But they worry about his *below average socialisation.* In old terminology, he's the quiet kid at the back of the class. And they fret over his inattentiveness. Despite the fact that – thanks to PS2 – his reading has come on in leaps and bounds lately, his schoolwork is in *the lower quartile.* In old terminology, he's the quiet, *thick* kid at the back of the class.

I have pointed out that his concentration levels might improve if his desk didn't give him an excellent view of the football pitch. I wasn't being entirely flippant. It was my way of steering the conversation on to something positive. That is my son's talent. He's being scouted by Crystal Palace, for God's sake! (Shit, *must* phone Ron.) Shouldn't the school rejoice that – in the humble opinion of his mother – it has in its midst a young Pelé? I shouldn't have wasted my breath. Football is lovely, wonderful, splendid . . . save for one fact. At the final whistle, there is inevitably a winner. Which means that there is also a loser. In the Arlington philosophy, competition is embraced . . . provided *everyone* can win.

'And the score in this season's FA Cup Final is Arsenal 2, Liverpool 0. So the trophy goes to Arsenal . . . and also to Liverpool,

who played an excellent game and – let's not forget – turned up on time, and in lovely clean strips too!'

But what do I know? I ask myself as Mrs Gottfried marches towards me in her defiantly sensible shoes.

'Mrs Clark, thank you for coming in,' she says – quite charmingly for her. 'I know how busy you must be.'

I'm not actually, but I don't say that. I follow her into her office and take the offered seat.

'I'm so sorry to be calling you in so early in the new school year,' she says as she sits behind the desk. She smiles and I find myself warming to her. I know she's a hate figure for most of the kids at the school, but playground opinion is no basis on which to judge her. And neither is her very slight German accent. I mustn't dismiss everything she says just because she speaks in a comedy voice. No, that would be silly and childish and not the sort of thing I'd do (today). Today, I'm going to give her a chance.

I'll begin with a little pre-emptive defence work on Thomas's behalf.

'No, I'm glad you called me in,' I say. 'I think it's *excellent* the way Arlington so readily involves parents in, er, school issues. But can I just say that Thomas has promised me he's going to turn over a new leaf this year. He still loves his football, of course, but he's going to knuckle down and—'

'Mrs Clark, please, I must stop you. Ve're getting off on the wrong foot. I don't vant to talk about Thomas . . .'

Jesus, it must be me, then. What is it? I look at my clothes. Denim jacket, cargo pants and scuffed Timberlands. Summer gave me the once-over at lunch and scoffed. Is Gottfried about to do the same?

'. . . No, it's Molly.'

Did she say *Molly*? Impossible. Unless she's overachieving and they want her to hang back while her classmates catch up – purely in the spirit of *everyone* being a winner of course.

'What's she done?' I ask, genuinely surprised.

'This is very delicate, Mrs Clark,' Mrs Gottfried says *delicately*, as if I'm an eggshell she's obliged to step over, 'but Molly is displaying alarming signs of racism.'

'*Racism?*' I gasp.

I'm astonished. Molly doesn't even know what race is outside of the egg-and-spoon sense. She certainly doesn't know that it's also an -ism.

'She is running around the playground and calling out "rice and peas".'

I smile. It sounds so wrong in a German accent. It's *rice an' peeeeas!* You have to really give it some welly, Jamaican stylee. I can hear Molly doing it with perfect inflection. Her father's looks but her mother's larynx, bless her.

'I'm sorry, but it isn't funny,' Mrs Gottfried says in response to my mild amusement. 'The other children are copying her . . .'

Not half as proficiently, I bet.

'. . . and von of the mealtime assistants asked vere she had learnt this saying. She said from her mother.'

'She did,' I confirm.

Mrs Gottfried lets out a little gasp.

'It's off the telly,' I explain. 'You know, *Bo Selecta.*'

I'm met with a blank look. A little more explanation is necessary, I feel, and *then* we can put this matter to bed.

'He takes off Trisha . . . talk-show Trisha. "Rice and peas" is a kind of catchphrase. I did it for Molly and she found it funny, and, well, I guess you know the rest.'

'At Arlington, ve vill not tolerate racism,' Mrs Gottfried says quietly.

'Neither will I, Mrs Gottfried. God, never in a million years. But this isn't racism . . . It's . . . I don't know . . . It's just silly. It's what a lot of white people think black people eat, as if it's *all* they eat. It's just a joke.'

'No, it is racial stereotyping,' she corrects, 'of Afro-Caribbeans.'

'But it's also sending up white people for *doing* the stereotyping,' I try to explain.

'That vould also be racist.'

My jaw hangs open. I really don't know what to say. Am I really on such a different planet here? I want to scream with outrage. My sweet, innocent five-year-old daughter has been branded a racist. Where the hell do I go from here?

'Mrs Clark, you must appreciate that ve cannot allow this behaviour to continue. Ve must nip it in the bud . . .'

Nip *what* in the bud? By next week she'll have moved on. She'll be taking off Scooby Doo. Will they haul her up then for being cartoonist?

'. . . Believe me, this is exactly vere the Holocaust started.'

Really? I was under the impression that the Holocaust began with a murderous lunatic persuading his followers that Jews were subhuman – not with a five-year-old cheerfully calling out, 'Gefilte fish,' in the playground. But, you know, she's the bloody teacher. What do I know about history?

I'm struck mute. Partly out of disbelief, but also out of fear that anything I say may be taken down and twisted beyond recognition before being used against me.

'Ve must ask that you speak with Molly,' Mrs Gottfried informs me.

'I don't know . . . This just seems a bit . . .' I want to say 'crazy', but I don't.

'Please, if you don't, I vill have no choice but to take the issue to the headteacher . . . and perhaps to Social Services.'

'*Social Services?*'

'This is a *very* serious matter. One that doesn't just concern Molly either.'

'Thomas? Why, what has he said?'

'Not Thomas, Mrs Clark . . . you. Apparently, at yesterday's ARPS meeting, you said something that vas . . . perhaps *ill-advised.*'

'What are you talking about?' I ask, even as the B word is flashing through my mind. 'Mrs Gottfried, referring to someone as black is not—'

'Please, Mrs Clark, *Afro-Caribbean.*'

Jesus, this is the biggest load of garbage I've ever heard. Why the hell am I taking it? This is the new me, after all. The new me who's going to do a read-through in front of high-powered movie executives (though it's probably best to gloss over the fact that it's for a part as a brutal bigot). And the new me is not someone who stands for the suggestion that she or her sweet, unsullied daughter is a racist.

'How many *Afro-Caribbean* friends have you ever had?' I demand.

'I don't think that's at all rel—'

'I'm sorry, Mrs Gottfried, but it's completely relevant,' I say, up and running now. 'When I was growing up, my best friend's family came from Jamaica and her mum virtually raised me. We all used to laugh at each other – the food we ate, the way we talked – and we were not racists. I *know* what racism is. The National Front was very busy in my neighbourhood, so I know what I'm talking about. I will not have anyone accuse my children or me of being racist.'

It's a big speech, but it's something I *do* know a little about. I lived in multicultural Britain before the term was ever coined. There were fifteen different languages spoken in my street alone. I'm sure that if I'd been raised in a vanilla neighbourhood such as this, my career would never have happened. Sure, I was born with a gift for voices, but the fact that I was surrounded by fifteen different languages and a thousand different accents brought it out of me. My best friends Chanda and Amita loved it. 'Go on, do Rasheed when he's angry,' they'd demand, or, 'Hey, do Mr Patel when we nick his Black Jacks . . . Go on!'

Our other best friend, Sharon, lived with her mum and older brother, David. We'd invade his room and wind him up and he'd yell at us to piss off and then his mum would start yelling at *him*: 'Hey, David, learn some respec' now, man, and leave them kids alone or I gonna come wup your black arse, you hear?'

God, taking off Jamaican like that around here would have us marched to the gallows.

Sharon used to love it when I took off her family. First, her brother ('Just fuck off, you stupid lickle pickney') and then her mother (see above). Then her mum discovered my talent and got me to take off her sister, who'd always be coming round with saucepans of food. And while she laughed herself senseless, Amita, Chanda and Sharon would get bored and wander off to play in the street without me.

But I guess it was a different time. A different place.

There's no room for multicultural gags in this office. All I can do is reiterate what I know in my heart. 'We are *not* racists, Mrs Gottfried. It's as simple as that.'

She sighs deeply. 'I am not suggesting that you are, Mrs Clark.'

'What the hell are you suggesting, then?'

'Molly's playground behaviour is *inappropriate*. You must talk vith her.'

She hasn't listened to a word I've said. 'Molly is *not* a racist,' I say, wearily rising to my feet. I don't hear her reply because I'm closing the door – quite hard – on my way out.

4

Natasha loves my kitchen. 'It's *amazing*. Just look at it,' she purrs, seeming to forget that hers makes mine look like a studio-flat kitchenette. 'You've done so well with the space you've got. Did you design it all yourselves?'

'Yes, all our own work. We did it about five years ago,' I tell her proudly.

We were a good team, Richard and I. And we will be again.

Natasha and I are sitting at the island. Its painted legs have been distressed to create the illusion that it saw sterling service during the century before last. Overhead hangs the complete set of copper pans that looked so great in *House & Garden*. They give the room the aura of the Serious Cook, as does the Aga, which sits majestically off to the side. This kitchen is handcrafted, bespoke, state of the art, and it contains everything you'd need to create any dish in the world.

Mostly, I create junk food. But unlike me, Richard is a fantastic cook. Five years ago when we were renovating the house, we comforted ourselves through Builder Hell with a dream. In this dream, Richard was effortlessly throwing together a mouth-watering seafood dinner, infused with Mediterranean herbs (*infused*, mind you, not just chucked in) and, yes, *drizzled* with balsamic vinegar. As he *created*, I'd be sitting in floaty chiffon, rocking our baby girl to sleep in her Moses basket with one hand, a glass of white in the other . . .

So you see, we just *had* to have the stupid dangly thing with all the copper pots hanging from it. The dream wouldn't have come true without it.

What happened to the dream? Well, the baby girl never slept. I never used the Moses basket because a curious and playful (let's not say jealous and vengeful) five-year-old kept tipping her out of it. I never got any floaty chiffon because when you have three perfectly good pairs of leggings, you just don't, do you? And of course, Richard has never cooked any gorgeous meals, infused, drizzled or otherwise. The only part of the fantasy that materialised was the glass of white.

I have one now. I try to top up Natasha's, but she puts her hand over it.

'Thanks for inviting me to the ARPS meeting,' I tell her. 'It was fun.'

'You were bored out of your mind, you liar,' Natasha laughs. 'As was I, it has to be said. But you have to show your face at these things, don't you?'

Do you?

Well, I might have thought so at one time.

I'm glad I invited Natasha back here. The children are playing in the garden. It's turned chilly today and unlike kids, who are a bit freaky and don't feel the cold, we've opted to stay inside.

'I love what you've done to this place,' Natasha says, looking about the kitchen, her face beaming, and I think she really means it.

'Oh, it's nothing compared with yours,' I say with just as much sincerity.

She wrinkles her nose. 'Well, it's only bricks at the end of the day, isn't it? I'd much rather have what you've got. A husband who supports you unconditionally. That's what really counts.'

I feel twin stabs. The first is a stab of pure pain. My husband isn't here and I *so* wish he was. The second is a stab of guilt. I've told Natasha nothing about what's happened. Though we've barely begun to get to know each other, I feel as if I'm betraying her by not confiding.

'You're lucky, Fran,' she continues. 'You've got such a close-knit family.'

I watch Tristram, Quinn and Fabian playing with Molly on the decking outside. Her sons might have stupid names (much as I like her, I can't excuse the names), but at least they're playing together. I think about Thomas in his room, alone with his PS2, and wonder what exactly Natasha sees that makes her think we're so close-knit.

'You know, I have so enjoyed these past few days,' Natasha says.

'Me too,' I agree. 'Why on earth didn't we get close before?'

'Who knows? But this is our moment, so let's make the most of it.'

We chink glasses and I take a long sip from mine. I notice that her barely-there lips scarcely brush the rim of hers.

'You're friends with that pretty, dusky girl, aren't you?' she says. 'Oh dear, I can say that around here, can't I? No cameras or anything, are there?'

'No cameras. Just the written report I'll be handing over to ARPS later on . . . Sureya, yes, we're good friends. She's half Malaysian. She's away at the moment, so you've got me all to yourself.'

'Poor Fran. Everyone's left you,' she jokes. 'Richard's away as well, isn't he?'

'Yes, but he'll be back tomorrow. Maybe Thursday. He's not sure at the moment how long it's all going to take, but it won't be long now . . .' I'm waffling. The thought of Richard, who seems to be elbowing his way into this conversation, is throwing me off balance.

'You really miss him, don't you? How sweet.' She laughs

and I notice the crinkly lines round her eyes are like mine. But not really. Hers are laughter lines, not crow's feet. 'So, what's he up to, then, this Richard of yours?' she asks.

'Oh, groundwork for a new client. It's a great opportunity. It's all go, go, go.' I laugh extra merrily, hoping it will smother the sounds of my insides churning.

'Aren't you good? There you are supporting him as much as he does you. No wonder you're so close. I am so envious. If I weren't such a nice person, Fran, I'd seriously consider killing you and stealing your identity.'

I laugh extra, *extra* merrily and desperately scour my brain for a subject that has nothing at all to do with Richard or marriage or supportive bloody couples.

'I've been thinking . . .' I say, though I have no idea what I've been thinking. This is like an improv exercise at drama college. Think quick, be sharp . . .

'Go on.' She leans forward, intrigued.

'I've been thinking . . . how does a girl get her hands on some Prozac?' I ask, then immediately feel very uncomfortable.

I feel uncomfortable because all of a sudden I'm having to fight the urge to open up to Natasha. *Absurd!* I haven't told my two closest friends what I've been going through, but for some reason – maybe it's because Natasha has trusted *me*, maybe it's because the mention of Richard has knocked me sideways – the urge to talk, to *really* talk about him, is overwhelming.

'Why are you asking me about Prozac?' she says. 'What is it? What's wrong?'

I laugh nervously. When I look at Natasha, I see a woman who is everything I want to be. She's permanently jolly and well put together, and she's popular. Maybe Prozac isn't such a bad idea.

'Oh, nothing really. It's just that not everything's what it seems, is it? We all put on a bit of a face for the world, don't we? And, well . . . I've been thinking about it . . . and Prozac . . . Why not?'

'Because it's not a *why not?* thing,' she says seriously. 'My doctor asked me a thousand questions before she wrote the prescription. What's wrong, Fran?'

I am standing on the very edge, teetering at the point of no return. Natasha has trusted me with stuff, maybe I *should* trust her right back. She really likes me – I can feel it. So why the hell not?

Because you never tell anyone outside the family what you're thinking, that's why.

No, that's silly. That's Richard (and the much lesser-known Marlon Brando) talking, not me. I *should* talk more to people – and talk more openly.

I take a sip – OK, a gulp – of wine and begin . . . slowly. 'I don't really know what I'm talking about, but . . . well, isn't Prozac just like a sort of pick-me-up?'

'My GP might balk at that description, but I suppose, sort of . . . Look, I don't mean to pry, but is there something you're not telling me?' Her eyes seem to moisten with concern.

'I, well, I guess I have been having . . . a rough time lately,' I stammer, wanting to open up but still uncomfortable with the thought. Natasha's eyes are on me. I take another gulp of wine to steady my nerves. Sorry, Richard, but you asked for it. Never mind devoted husband. I'm telling her what a slimy, cheating bastard you really are.

I notice my glass is shaking in my hand. Nerves? Sadness? I don't know.

Natasha takes a stab. 'Fran, are you drinking too much? Is that it?'

'Well, I have been drinking more than usual lately,' I tell her truthfully.

'I did notice the Pimm's go down quite quickly the other day.' She smiles. 'But that's OK. We all need a bit of a lift, us desperate bloody housewives. I pop my pills, you've got your wine. It's no big deal.'

'My father was an alcoholic,' I say . . . And God knows where that came from. The words just tumbled out before I could stop them. I know I wanted to open up, but I meant about Richard. Not about my sad and pathetic family history.

'You're worried that you might be, too?' she probes gently.

'No, no, it's nothing like that,' I splutter.

She tilts her head and looks at me with concern.

'Well, I suppose I do need a drink most days . . .' I say hesitantly. 'But like you said, who doesn't need a glass of wine in the evening, right?'

'Where do you draw the line, though?' she asks.

What line? I think. What is she getting at here?

'Have you thought of talking to someone?' she continues.

'What, you mean like AA?' I say indignantly. 'Honestly, it's not that—'

'No, no, that's not what I meant,' she says awkwardly. 'But some sort of professional . . . if you're worried . . . Because, well . . . alcoholism can run in families . . . can't it?'

God, why on earth did I tell her about Dad? I never want to think about him, let alone talk about him. Was it my subconscious pushing out the first thing it came up with in order to stop me confessing about my cheating husband? But Richard is the issue here. *Not* drinking – not mine and definitely not my long-gone, long-forgotten father's. How the hell do I move this conversation on?

'Look, honestly, I don't think it's that bad,' I protest, trying to claw back some ability to express myself properly. 'It's just that I ought to keep an eye on my intake. For the sake of my waistline.'

She slides her hand across the island and rests it on mine.

'You don't have to feel bad, you know. I don't know anyone around here who doesn't have some kind of prop.'

'Even Cassie?' I attempt a smile, hoping she hasn't read too much into what little I've told her.

'Even her . . .'

Glad that we seem to have moved the conversation away from me, I wait for her to tell me what Queen Cassie's crutch is, but she doesn't.

'You know Maureen?' she says. 'Lucy's mum?'

I shake my head.

'Well, anyway, she binge-eats. She's been doing it for years now. Her husband's never there, and once she's put the kids to bed, she more or less empties the fridge – she'll get through a whole Sara Lee cheesecake on her own. Then she'll head for the bathroom and chuck the lot down the toilet.'

'That's terrible. Poor woman.' I feel bad now. I've been so self-absorbed – as if I'm the only person around here with troubles. 'Did she tell you about it?'

'No, Mia did. They're good friends. Mia only told me because she knows I'm absolutely discreet and wouldn't tell a soul. I hardly know you, Fran, but for some reason I trust you completely,' she says, giving my hand a squeeze. 'You can trust me too . . . You know that, don't you?'

'I know I can,' I say, and I'm really fighting the tears now.

'Alcoholism is nothing to be ashamed of,' she whispers. 'OK?'

Whoa, wait up a minute. I'm *not* an alcoholic, I want to say. She has *so* got the wrong end of the stick. I want to explain about the panic attacks and the lack of confidence and the husband who has left me for a flashy upgrade and all the rest of it. I'm going to tell her everything right now, so that she'll better understand. But a stampede shatters the moment. Four pairs of feet thunder in from the garden.

'We're starving!'

'We want tea!'

Any chance of finishing this conversation ends as the feeding of four hungry children begins. Five if you count Thomas, who'll have his on a tray in his room. What better way to eat than alone?

It's not until Natasha has left and I'm clearing away the tea things that I notice, amongst the clutter on the island, two empty wine bottles next to Natasha's glass.

Which is as full as it was when I first poured it.

3

Friday. Cold autumn drizzle spatters my face as I head for home after the school drop-off. I'm walking quickly, but not because of the weather. I am a woman on a mission.

The kids and I passed Gottfried in the playground, but she didn't see us. I could so have taken a blowtorch to her iceberg face. I thought of talking to Natasha about her, but she was busy talking to a group of mums I don't know. She didn't acknowledge my wave – I must be invisible this morning. Maybe I'll talk to her later.

The reason I'm on a mission is because of my conversation with Thomas. Although conversation is the wrong word . . .

I looked at him after we'd passed Gottfried. His face was ashen. I assumed it was terror at what she wanted to see me about. I put my arm round him and I told him not to worry – she didn't have any complaints about him.

'I don't care about her,' he said, shrugging his shoulders and dumping my arm. 'Have you phoned Ron yet?'

I only just managed to stop myself saying, '*Ron who?*' Jesus, how could I have forgotten? I've been so busy trying to sort out my own life I'd forgotten Thomas has hopes and dreams too. Well, one hope, one dream.

'You haven't done it, have you?' he spat before I could reply. 'God, you're so crap sometimes.'

Only sometimes? I thought, as he ran off without saying goodbye. He was right. I have been crap.

So that's my mission: call FA Ron.

I let myself into the house and march straight up to the phone. As I reach out my hand, the phone starts to ring. I pick it up.

'Hello, Fran.'

It's Richard.

I wasn't prepared for that. I half-expected it to be Summer with a pregnancy update. Or possibly a George Clooney update.

I've got to pull myself together here. Be strong.

'Hello?' Richard says. 'You still there?'

'Yes, sorry, miles away,' I say breezily.

'Yeah, I know how you feel.'

Except you have literally been miles away, haven't you, Richard? But I don't say that. I'm being strong.

'Good trip?' I ask. Strongly.

'Yes, very useful,' he tells me, going on with the charade that we're friends and he's talking about a business trip that was expected to be dreary but turned out to be quite fruitful, strictly from a business perspective, of course. 'I got you some of that seaweed face cream everyone's going on about,' he continues. 'You know, the brand Jennifer Aniston endorses. I'll give it to you when I see you.'

When he sees me.

'Great,' I say. Still strong.

But no one's in the mood for charades and we lapse into silence.

'I thought you were going to be back days ago,' I say after a while, trying not to sound accusatory.

'Yes, but . . . well, that's not the way it worked out.'

And just how did it work out, then? Did you knock work on the head and hire an open-top Ferrari in which you and the beautiful Bel drove – her long hair blowing in the breeze, your hand stroking her knee – through olive groves and vineyards to an out-of-the-way trattoria where you . . . ?

Silence is not a good thing. The sound of his voice has crushed me, yet I need to hear him speak. I need to hear him say something pleasant. I force myself to think of Natasha and the positive effect she has had on me. I force my head back to where it was only a couple of days ago.

At last, we both speak, but at the same time.

'Listen, I just want to say—'

'I'm calling because—'

'Sorry,' I say, 'go on.'

'I want to come round tomorrow . . . if that's OK with you. I want to talk to you. And I want to see the kids. I've missed them.'

'I bet you have,' I say and immediately regret it because it sounded so bitter. Another obliging silence fills the chasm between us as I try to think of something nice to say. But it isn't happening.

I listen to the sound of breathing. His? Mine? I can't tell. He sighs. 'So, can I come over? Maybe on Saturday?'

'We'll be home early evening, after football.'

'OK. Maybe we'll get the kids a takeaway or something? Eat together?'

Well, that's good. Isn't it? Eating together. That is definitely a good thing.

But something occurs to me now and without thinking I ask, 'What are you going to tell them?'

'What about?'

'About you not being here.'

It's all I really want to know. Has he left me for good, or . . . what?

'I don't know . . .' A sigh as deep as an ocean. 'I thought we could discuss what we tell the kids now.'

Oh, fuck. I shouldn't have asked. Talking to the kids means we've reached a decision. About the future. I'm not ready for decisions.

My legs give way. What happened to being strong? I have to sit. I stumble back to the staircase and flop down.

'So . . . shall we talk about—'

I cut him off. 'Any other reason you want to come round? Apart from seeing the kids.'

'Well, I need to pick up a few shirts, if that's all right.'

Shirts. He's been missing his shirts.

'What about me?'

The words just spill out. I'm desperate to hear him say he's missed me, but terrified he's going to say he hasn't. I'm *desperate* for some hope, but the silence tells me there is none.

'Oh, there's someone at the door,' I say. 'We'll see you tomorrow. About five.'

I hang up, none the wiser.

I'm ironing shirts. *Angrily.* I'm livid with myself. Why didn't I seize that conversation by the balls and show him what a changed woman I am? Why didn't I tell him about ARPS and the calls to Isabel and Chris Sergeant? But I console myself with the fact that he's coming tomorrow and I can tell him then. And he'll also be able to pick up a stack of crisply laundered shirts. I even went to the shop and bought a can of spray-on starch – something I've never done before.

Does Gucci Girl starch his shirts? Does she even iron them? Of course not. Who ever heard of a mistress who wastes time doing her lover's laundry? OK, the fact that she doesn't waste her time on domesticity is part of the reason he left me, but that's not the point. He can shag her all he likes, but what's he going to wear at the end of it?

Exactly.

Ha! I'm one up already.

Excellent. Now I'm feeling better. And now that I've ironed

the last shirt, it's time to get the day back on track and phone Ron. Time to turn Thomas into a football star.

But once again, as I reach for the phone, it rings.

'Hello, sweetie, I'm back,' Sureya gushes. 'Have you missed me?'

'Of course I've missed you,' I tell her as warmly as I can manage, because it's true. Obviously, I still need to phone Ron, but he can wait a few minutes while we catch up. Well, he's waited this long . . .

'What's been happening, then?' she asks.

Jesus, where do I start? With the fact that my husband has left me? With Gottfried's accusation of racism? Or with the fact that I can't even sort my kids out, never mind myself? 'Nothing much, really,' I say, reverting to type. 'Boring, boring. What's new with you?'

'Oh, nothing much,' she says, but this time she sounds strange. 'Except, well . . . there is this one thing. You know I wanted to talk to you before I went? It's the reason we had to go and see Michael's parents . . . I'm pregnant, Fran.'

I scream out. Can't stop myself. 'That's incredible! Wonderful! Fantastic! I can't believe my two best friends are pregnant at the same time!' And as soon as the words are out, I clap my hand over my mouth.

I promised Summer, hand on heart, on pain of death, that I wouldn't tell *anyone*. And Sureya didn't even have to twist my arm. I just came out with it. Jesus, something else I can feel terrible about.

'Are you talking about Summer?' Sureya sounds confused, which isn't surprising.

'Yes,' I say, 'Summer . . . Look, I swore I wouldn't tell anyone. Please, if you see her, you've got to pretend you don't know. I feel dreadful now.'

'Summer! The man-hater. *Ha.* Jesus, what the hell is going on?'

'It's complicated,' I say, squirming, thankful that she can't see my shame.

'Don't worry, you don't have to say anything . . . But, oh my God, did she actually sleep with a man, or was it . . . ? OK, you don't have to say.'

'Look, I'm really sorry, but I can't.'

'Please don't apologise. It's fine . . .' And then, 'Was it a . . . you know . . . a do-it-yourself thing?'

'Sureya!'

'OK, OK, I'll stop. She'll tell me herself in her own good time, I guess.'

We're both quiet for a moment, Sureya stunned, me regretful for opening my big mouth.

'So. You. Pregnant, huh?' I say to break the silence.

'God knows how I'm going to cope with work when this baby arrives,' she says, sounding tired already.

Sureya runs drama groups in and around Hackney. They're for kids who have nothing . . . like the kid I used to be. Funny, but she works a stone's throw from where I grew up, but I could never do the job she does. I know more about one-parent families, welfare and poverty than Sureya ever could, but she's the one who hauls herself to endless seminars and workshops at inner-city schools and youth clubs while I sit on my fat behind feeling sorry for myself.

'I've barely got the twins settled in nursery and now this,' she sighs. But Sureya isn't one to dwell on the negative for long. 'But I'll work something out. I've talked to Helen and I might take her on full-time when the baby arrives.'

'So *Helen* knows?'

'I told her last week,' she says quietly, knowing the implication of the question. 'Look, I was going to tell you – the night of your hotel-bill drama, actually. But I couldn't say anything then, could I? Is that all sorted, by the way? You two seemed very loved-up at your party.'

'God, yes, just a stupid misunderstanding. It was nothing.' Well, I can hardly tell her now, can I? I move the conversation back on to safer ground. 'Anyway, never mind all that. How many weeks are you?'

'Twenty-one'

'*Twenty-one?*' I almost shout. 'Why didn't you tell me before?'

'Fran, I already explained. I was going to—'

'Not last week. I mean *before* before. Like maybe when you were only *four* months gone.'

I can't believe I'm attacking a pregnant woman, but I'm stung. She told Helen, the childminder, not me, her friend. What the hell does that say about me?

'I'm really sorry, but I just wanted to be sure before I said anything. So much has been happening, and, well, you've had enough on your plate.'

'What's that supposed to mean?'

'Well, you have to admit, you've been a bit . . .' she searches for a word '. . . disengaged. Be honest, it didn't start with the hotel bill, did it?'

Silence from me. I'm too choked to speak.

'Fran? I understand, really I do – Richard's promotion has been tough on you. In lots of ways.'

'What's that got to do with anything?' I ask.

'Look, I know you're a real cynic when it comes to therapy, but I think you're depressed. I think you should talk to someone.'

'That's what I've got you for, isn't it?' I say. This is my standard line whenever Sureya brings up therapists, but it doesn't come out in its usual joking way. It just sounds spiteful and I immediately regret my tone.

She lets it pass, though, and says, 'You know, I'm wondering if you ever really properly recovered from the post-natal depression after Molly was born. I've heard that it can last for—'

'I don't know what you're talking about,' I interrupt

166

petulantly. Sod being strong, the new bloody me. I don't want to talk about my supposed post-natal depression or therapy or anything for that matter. 'Listen, I've got to go. I left the iron on upstairs.'

'Oh,' she says, and the sadness in her voice fills me with guilt, but still I can't take it back.

'Sorry,' I offer stupidly.

So stupid it's met with silence.

'Congratulations, anyway. Let's talk later,' I add. And then I hang up.

Immediately, I walk to the fridge and take out the Chardonnay. If only problems could be solved with cigarettes and alcohol. If they could, I'd be laughing. But, no, I hate myself. How could I have been so horrible to the sweetest friend I've ever had? Sureya has always been there for me. I remember when we first truly bonded. It was right after the birth of Thomas – my beautiful, Bambi-eyed and incandescently angry newborn who never slept and, consequently, whose mother didn't either. I'd see mums in the park or at the supermarket looking so *sorted*. They'd make standing at the checkout, trolleys loaded with groceries and kids, look like a trip to Legoland. And then there was me. Miserable as sin, the presence of my gorgeous, longed-for baby failing utterly to lift my spirits. Days merged seamlessly into nights. An endless merry-go-round of feeding, changing, rocking, feeding . . .

That was the first time in my life I felt useless. I couldn't cope with one tiny baby. I wasn't a single mum. We weren't broke. What the hell was wrong with me? It was Sureya, naturally, who suggested post-natal depression; a hormone-induced thing; nothing to feel guilty about. But I was sceptical. I had a baby who was a very small but profoundly unhappy person . . . who would not sleep. I was exhausted. I didn't need *hormones* to make me depressed!

Richard didn't understand. Mostly, probably, because I couldn't articulate my feelings properly. Sureya, on the other hand, was wonderful. She took time out to sit with Thomas so I could get my head down. She took me shopping. Phoned me lots. And as that dark cloud above my head slowly lifted, I knew I had the truest of friends. When the same depression happened all over again with Molly, history repeated itself in more ways than one. Sureya? There she was for me again.

Will she now be worrying about the possibility of post-natal depression? God, she's probably worrying about a thousand things: giving up work, coping with the twins *and* a newborn – and, *Jesus*, look how I treated her.

But her news was a slap in the face. A stinging reminder that the rest of the world is moving forward – adding new family members – while I'm stuck in reverse – family members decreasing. Then another slap as it dawned that she'd withheld her news for months – too much for a flake like me to take. She must have felt vindicated when she finally did tell me because . . . well, I was disgusting.

Who needs enemies when you can have a friend like me?

I want desperately to call her back and grovel and apologise, then grovel some more. But I feel so heavy-hearted, what would be the point? I don't want to speak to her until my head is in a better state. I have to get a grip. I have to do something – just *one thing* – that's positive today.

I pick up the phone again and dial Ron's number. A tired-sounding secretary answers. She tells me Ron isn't there.

'When will he be back?' I ask.

'He's a scout,' she says. 'He's hardly ever here. He's out scouting.'

'Have you got a mobile number for him?'

'If you want to tell me what it's about, I'll pass on a message,' she says, sounding as if it's the last thing she wants to do.

'Oh, OK . . . Will you tell him that Francesca Clark called? I'm Thomas Clark's mum. He wanted me to arrange for him to come in for the trials.'

'They were last week.'

For the nth time today, I feel the life go out of my legs.

'They can't have been,' I say weakly.

'I'm sorry,' she says, not sounding sorry at all, 'but you've missed them.'

I laugh. I don't know why, because this is not funny – this is, in fact, a complete disaster. 'There must be some mistake,' I say. 'Ron definitely wants to speak to me about Thomas. I must have got it wrong. Maybe it wasn't about the trials.'

'Well, I can't think what else it'd be about,' she says.

'Please just tell him I rang,' I plead. 'Ask him to call me back . . . *please*.'

'I'll give him the message.'

Then she hangs up.

Then the same old familiar feeling of panic sets in.

Oh God, what have I done?

I go to the kitchen and pour myself another glass. I stand at the island. Next to me on the countertop is a bound wad of A4 paper: *Dark Planet* by Isabel Parlour and Harvey Duncan. It arrived two days ago. I haven't so much as glanced at it yet. I pick it up and take it upstairs, along with the Chardonnay and my cigarettes. Might as well force myself to read it. Use the pathetic notion of reviving my career to suppress the realisation that I've almost certainly killed my son's.

The doorbell wakes me. Blindly, I rush downstairs, fleeing my nightmares. I open the door. Natasha stands on the other side, smiling. She has the double buggy with her, fully loaded. Why aren't her kids in school?

'Fran,' she says, managing to increase the wattage of her smile. 'I woke you, didn't I?'

'Yes . . . er, no . . . Jesus, what time is it?'

'Four o'clock.'

'Four? The kids!'

I turn round to grab my jacket and make the sprint to school, but she puts her hand on my arm.

'The kids are here,' she says with her trademark laugh.

I force my eyes to focus and see Molly and Thomas standing with Quinn at the garden gate. They're playing catch with a tennis ball.

'Don't worry,' Natasha says, sensing my confusion and panic. 'Mrs Poulson was in a right old flap, all set to call out the dogs when you didn't show up. Well, I wasn't having that and I told her you'd arranged for me to pick Molly up. Then we went and collected Thomas and here we are.'

'My God, thanks, I'm so sorry, I don't know what happened,' I gabble. 'I wasn't feeling well. Had a lie-down, must have—'

'For heaven's sake, *don't worry.* These things happen. And the kids are fine.'

'Thank you, thank you so much, Natasha.' I'm not gabbling now, just gushing.

'Don't be silly. You'd do the same for me. Look, you're not well. I could get Anna to pop over and cook the kids' tea. Give you a chance to get your head down.'

'Thanks, but really, I'm fine now. Just had a bit of a dodgy tummy earlier.'

I'm so grateful to her. I want to invite her in, thank her properly. But suddenly I'm aware of myself. My crumpled clothes and crusted eyes. And I'm aware of the taste in my mouth – the bitter coating of wine on my tongue. I take half a step back because I'm convinced I'm surrounded by a cloud of fumes so thick it's probably visible.

But if it is, Natasha isn't giving anything away. She's just smiling at me sweetly.

'Mummy, can Fabian stay round and play . . . ? Please, Mummy, *please!*'

'Not today, Molly,' Natasha says. 'Your mummy's a bit poorly. But why don't you come back to mine? You can play in the tree house if you like.'

'Can we, Mummy?' Molly's face has lit up like the Blackpool Illuminations.

'No, really, it's—'

'No arguments, Fran. You need to sleep off that bug. Come on, kids. Let's go.'

And so I let them go. Partly – no, *mostly* – because I'm not yet ready to face Thomas and tell him I've screwed everything up. As I watch them walk down the path and turn into the street, I'm overwhelmed with gratitude and shame.

I hated lying to Natasha. If only Richard leaving *was* a bug that I could sleep off. How long has he been gone now? Six days and counting.

2

Saturday. It's freezing. I'm huddled on a bench in the park watching Thomas do his thing. Molly is in the playground behind me, sliding, swinging and totally impervious to the cold. As is Thomas. But he's just scored his first goal. Goals imbue him with a kind of Ready Brek glow.

Normally, on a day as cold as this I'd go home. My dedication to my son's obsession isn't so great that I'm prepared to risk frostbite. But today is different. Last night, I told him about Crystal Palace. That he didn't scream, swear and throw things at me was because . . . well, basically I lied to him. I told him that Crystal Palace weren't taking on any new boys this year. Cutbacks, I explained – that old one. It worked in as much as it deflected the blame away from me. He retired to his room to brood, only emerging this morning in his football kit.

'I know Palace are rubbish,' he said quietly on the way here, 'but I don't care who I play for. Even someone more rubbish than them.'

My heart ached for him. He's so desperate to make it *he'll play for anyone*. I felt so shabby for having lied to him that I decided to watch every single kick of his session, even if it means they have to chip my frozen body from the bench with an ice pick.

He has the ball at his feet. He dribbles it past a couple of players, seeming to marvel at his own ability, as if he never knew he could do that. He looks up and directs a pass towards a teammate, but for once, the ball ends up with the other side. Immediately, his body language changes. He goes from loose and lithe to tight and angry. The easy joy that only seconds ago he derived from his own skill has evaporated. That is *so* Thomas . . . I look at him trudge across the pitch, his shoulders hunched, angry and intense. Although he has slightly more hair now, he has barely changed from the day he was born.

But the world can change in an instant, can't it? A terrorist bomb can go off, a lottery ticket can come good, or Thomas can suddenly find the ball at his feet and instinctively lob it over the head of the goalkeeper.

He accepts the back slaps of his teammates with an awkward smile and ignores his mother, who's clapping and cheering like a lunatic.

I'm tempted to bolt for the café now, warm myself up with a coffee. But although a lot of Arlington mums are in there this morning, there's no one I really know. It's a shame Natasha isn't up there. I could do with a fresh injection of her energy. Or Sureya. I have some *serious* apologising to do. I've made up my mind. After football practice, I'm going straight round there. I'm going to tell her how sorry I am for my behaviour and that I love her dearly. Maybe the fact that I've had such a shitty week mitigates my behaviour. I'll let her be the judge. Because I've finally decided to be honest and tell her the truth. But we'll get it over with fast and then focus on *her* news. Which is exactly what I should have done in the first place.

Today's icy wind is a good thing. Maybe it'll blow away the fuzz in my head – alcohol-induced, of course. I can fool the kids – *Mummy has a headache* – but I can't fool myself any longer. I never wanted to have that conversation with Natasha, but since I did, it's been on my mind.

Do I have a drink problem?

Before we had kids, Richard and I always went for a drink after work. Professional people are *allowed* to need a drink after a hard day at the office/recording studio/wherever. And it was practically mandatory that every Friday night we went out with our mates and drank ourselves stupid. It's just that weekend-blow-out thing. The mark of being sociable, of being young and carefree.

But at exactly what point does drinking stop being a way into society and become the way out of life?

Did my father ever ask himself that question? He was a man who could only get through breakfast without a drink if he was still drunk from the night before. He didn't have a job that defined him. He was, in a single word, an alcoholic.

Mum put up with him until the eve of my thirteenth birthday. She sent him out to buy me a birthday cake. She wouldn't normally have trusted him, but she had a double-shift that day – she worked in the kitchens at Homerton Hospital.

I never heard Mum raise her voice to him. Most days, she'd come home to find him still drunk and still jobless and she'd tell him to sort himself out. But when he came home pissed and *cakeless*, she packed him a small bag and quietly told him to leave. But she never yelled. Maybe if she had, he'd have come good on one of his thousand promises. Maybe he'd have sobered up and got a job . . .

But probably not.

On my final day of being twelve, he *swore* he'd stop drinking. It would be easy, he said. He just wouldn't do it any more. He'd stop 'just like that', he joked in a slurred Tommy Cooper. He was good at voices, my dad. Funny that . . . But Mum had heard it too many times and she wasn't listening any more.

I was. I knelt on the landing and strained to hear every

word. And I cried because I knew it was over. Stupidly, I was crazy about the man in a way that I wasn't about my mum. She was never there, was she? She was always working. But my dad was always home when I got in from school – well, the pubs hadn't opened yet. And he adored me. Mum was never affectionate – she was probably too knackered for kisses and cuddles. But the alcohol permanently swilling through Dad's veins made shows of affection come easily.

When Mum chucked him out, I was devastated.

'Please make him come back,' I begged. 'I don't want a cake, anyway. *Please* just stop him going.'

In a rare display of emotion, she put her arm round me. She didn't talk. She just let me cry. Looking back, I wonder what sadness and pain she was feeling. But at the time, I didn't care. I was just a kid and my only worries were for myself. Because, like so many of my friends, I too was now going to be fatherless.

I haven't seen him since. I have no idea where he is or even if he's alive. Mum and I never talk about him, but then, we never talk about anything that matters. And these days, I rarely think about him. Just occasionally. Like now.

And the tear in my eye may just be from the wind.

I twist round to check on Molly. She's at the top of the climbing frame with Maisy. That means Annabel and her wart must be close by – probably in the café. Reflexively, I turn my jacket collar up and my attention back to the pitch. The coach has stopped the game and is showing the boys how to head the ball. Or rather Thomas is. While the coach barks out tips, he tosses balls towards Thomas, who times each leap to perfection and firmly directs each ball back into the coach's hands.

'Skinny little kid, but he's a great player, isn't he?'

As a warming glow of pride oozes through me, I look round at the woman who's joined me on the bench. She's young, pretty and bla— *Afro-Caribbean*. Big brown eyes, big hoop earrings and an expensive sheepskin coat.

'Is this a proper football club?' she asks.

'Yes, it's a really good one,' I tell her. 'They practise every Saturday and play matches on Sundays.'

'Well, that might just swing my decision about which area to move to. My son's football mad.'

'You're looking round here, are you?'

'Yes, but it's so expensive. Harrison turns three next year and we'll have to move now if we're going to get him into the Arlington nursery. It's the best school for miles, isn't it?'

'Yes, I've heard that,' I say.

I marvel at her forward thinking. Richard and I only moved into the area because we loved the house. It was by pure, blind chance that we found ourselves in the Arlington catchment. These days, you have to start planning your address the day after you've had sex. The day before if you're really sharp.

'I honestly don't know if we can afford it,' she says as the coach starts up another game, this time giving Thomas to the other side in the interests of fairness. 'Mind you, anywhere would be better than where we're living now.'

'Where's that?' I ask.

'Bethnal Green. What a dump!'

'Oh, I grew up there,' I tell her instinctively.

'You know what I'm talking about, then. Mind you, it doesn't matter what your postcode is, some things are the same everywhere, aren't they?'

'What do you mean?' I ask, wondering what Bethnal Green could possibly have in common with here, apart from, perhaps, zebra crossings.

'I've just been warming up in the café— Don't they do great cappuccinos? But those women . . . I don't know.' She shakes her head and laughs. 'You should have heard them gossiping. They were ripping some poor woman to shreds. God, I am terrible, aren't I? I mean, eavesdropping makes me just as bad, doesn't it?'

'No it doesn't,' I say. 'You can't help overhearing stuff, can you?'

'I suppose . . . But, God, the *things* they were saying.'

'What?' I ask, interested now.

'See? Now we're doing it. *Gossiping.*' She laughs.

'Yeah, but it's not as if we know each other,' I say. 'And we don't know who they were talking about, so it's not *real* gossip. It's kind of hypothetical.'

She smiles at me indulgently. 'OK, you've convinced me. Some woman they know forgot to pick up her kids from school yesterday and they were saying, well . . .'

Oh, please no.

'. . . they were saying she'd passed out from drinking too much. Apparently, she's an alcoholic. And this witchy-looking woman – even had a wart on her nose – was slagging her off something wicked. Reckons she's a bit of a racist, too. Sad, isn't it? Racism isn't something you'd expect round here.'

I want to throw up. I don't want to hear this, not another word.

But she hasn't finished yet.

'They were saying she's been bad for a while, with the drinking and stuff, but things have got out of hand since her husband walked out. He's gone off with some six-foot model and it's just tipped her over the edge, poor cow. That happened to my sister last year. Bastard ran off with their babysitter. And the babysitter was fifteen years younger than him. *Fifteen* years! Can you believe it?'

I want to reply that yes, I can believe it, but speech is no longer possible.

Where did this girl come from? There are dozens of

benches in this park. Why did she have to pick mine to sit on? She could be having this conversation with any other perfect stranger. *I didn't need to know any of this.*

A blast of noise rips through my head. The final whistle. *Thank God.* I stand up, my legs unsteady. Thomas trudges towards me and I mentally urge him to hurry up so we can get the hell out of here.

'Good luck,' I manage to say to the woman – the one busy forward-planning the next stage of her life, having just annihilated mine.

'Oh, thanks,' she says, oblivious to the damage she's wreaked. 'Bye, then.'

I need to get home. I need to put the children in front of a video so I can lock myself in the bathroom and sob. Or smash things. Or sleep. I don't know what. I just need to get there.

My eyes scan the playground for Molly, but they find Fabian first. Where did he come from? Who cares? I just need to get the hell out of here.

'Molly!' I yell, spotting her. 'Come on!'

She trots towards me, and the three of us begin the long walk past the café.

If I just keep my head down, I'll be OK. Just keep walking. Don't look.

But the café is like a magnet and I can't resist its pull. I turn my head and there it is. A couple of women are outside, putting coats on to their children.

And there's my *friend* Natasha, holding her youngest, talking to Annabel and someone else I don't recognise. She sees me and waves. A big, happy Prozac grin on her two-faced face. I make out I haven't seen her and turn my head back to my trailing son.

'Thomas, come *on*! We're late.'

If I can just get home, I'll be OK.

1

I'm pissed of course. It was the only way to make it through the afternoon. Who gives a shit, anyway? Actually, Summer does.

'Jesus, look at you, Fran. You have got to pull yourself together, honey. He's going to be here in a couple of hours.'

'Fuck him,' I slur. 'Fuck the lot of them.'

'That's right, fuck 'em. Those women are a bunch of whores. But you can't be like this for Richard. You need to talk to him and you need a clear head.'

She holds the mug of black coffee up to my lips, tries to make me drink, but I twist my head away.

'Why the hell didn't you tell me about this sooner?' she demands. 'I can't believe your husband's left you and you didn't say anything.'

Well, why do you think I didn't tell you, Summer? Because we're always talking about *you*, that's why!

But that's just nasty. It's also rubbish. I didn't tell her because it was easier not to. It's *always* easier not to say anything. Everyone knows that!

'The miserable, cheating bastard,' Summer fumes. 'He should have his dick cut off and fed to the— God, now I need a fucking drink.'

She's livid. But who is she angrier with? Richard, or me? The mood she's in, she'd be cross with Mother Teresa for . . . I don't know, for dying or something. What else could you be cross with Mother Teresa for?

When I don't respond, she says, 'Look at the state you're in. You couldn't speak if . . . Actually, fuck it. Force yourself. Why didn't you tell me, Fran?'

Blah, blah, blah, talk at me all you like, I'm not answering. I'm just going to carry on sitting on this stool, making sure I don't fall off. Easy. Just hold on and focus on the horizon like when you're on a boat and feeling seasick. Forget the waves, just focus.

'This is *mad*,' she snaps.

She's right. This is mad. I called her because I wanted to talk. But in between me phoning and her arriving I compensated for having no one to talk to by having a drink. And now, guess what? I don't want to talk any more.

She thinks deeply for a moment. 'Right. This is what we're going to do. I'm taking the kids. Right now. And they can stay over with me tonight. Got that, Fran?'

'Don't be silly. You're going to *Hollywood* tomorrow, honey,' I say. 'George, Sam . . . *Sammy!*' How could she have forgotten a thing like that? She's crazy!

'My flight's not till the evening. Plenty of time. Listen, you've got the rest of the afternoon to sober up and then you've got all night to talk to Dick-head in peace. We'll meet, dissect and analyse when I drop the kids off in the morning.'

Dream on, baby. I don't *want* to spend all night talking to Richard. I just want to sleep.

'Are you listening to me?' she snaps again. 'I'm being serious, for fuck's sake.'

'You *swear* too much,' I say. 'Not sure I approve of you looking after my children . . . Anyway, what are you going to do with two kids? Have you ever spent five minutes with anyone under the age of sixteen?'

'Of course I have. I did that fruit-juice commercial with that bratty ten-year-old last year. Taught me everything

I need to know. Besides, it'll be good practice for when mini-me arrives. Come on, let's go and pack their things.'

'Don't be ridiculous,' I tell her firmly. Well, it sounds firm in my head. 'You don't have to do this.'

'Yes I do. *Look* at you . . . Did you say Thomas is an Arsenal fan?'

'Y-es,' I say slowly.

'OK, that's where we're going.'

'What, you've got tickets?'

Now, if she has a *proper* plan, I'll be delighted. Several of Thomas's classmates get to watch every one of Arsenal's home games, but Thomas has never been. If Summer has got her hands on a couple of tickets, Thomas will follow her through the fires of hell to get there.

'Of course I haven't got tickets. We'll go by Tube. It's on the Piccadilly Line, right? There's bound to be a hotdog stand outside the ground. We'll do working class. Hang around and soak up the atmosphere or some-thing . . . I don't know. It'll come to me when we get there. I'll improvise.'

Well, it's a plan. Half-baked, but *football*-related . . . *Aaaars-en-al!*

'But you have to promise me that you're going to sober up,' she commands. 'Promise me!'

'I *promise*,' I say, the way Dad used to.

Our cellar is well stocked. Racks of wine, cases of beer, bottles of obscure brandies and liqueurs that come out at the end of dinner parties. Keeping it stocked is— *was* Richard's thing. Seems it's my job to empty it out.

I'm down there now. Searching for a robust yet fruity red to complement an utterly fucked-up life . . . Château Déstruction . . . 1970 . . . an excellent year for sour grapes . . .

Where's Richard when I need him? He always knows the perfect wine for any occasion . . .

Sorry, Summer, but I'm drinking myself into oblivion.

I've looked, and, well, there really is nowhere else to go.

0

'Fran . . . *Francesca* . . .'

I can't move. My body is numb . . . paralysed. Can't even open my eyes.

'Jesus, Fran, wake up.'

The voice seems distant . . .

'*Fran!*'

. . . Miles away. I will move when it gets nearer.

1

Something cold and wet on my forehead. I force my eyes open. A soft-focus Richard is up there above me.

'Hi,' he says quietly.

I want to say hi back, but my mouth won't work.

He wipes the damp flannel across my forehead again and then over my cheeks. I close my eyes and lose myself in the tenderness of the moment.

'I thought you'd never wake up,' he says.

'What time is it?' I just about manage.

'Just gone eight. Where are the kids?'

I don't know. In their rooms? Hasn't he looked?

It comes to me. '*Summer.*'

'Summer?'

'She took them to the football . . . and a sleepover.'

'Jesus,' he says quietly. He's never felt entirely comfortable with Summer.

I open my eyes and adjust to the light. Then I focus on him, sitting on the edge of the sofa, looking down at me. He looks *rough*. I've got clean shirts for him upstairs. I'll tell him so he can go put one on. Straighten himself out a bit. Why does he look so awful? What's happened?

'What's wrong?' I ask.

'You passed out . . .'

Not with me. With you.

'Here, drink some of this.' He slips his hand beneath the back of my head and raises it slightly, lifting a glass of water to my lips. I take a sip.

'What's wrong?' I ask again.

A barely perceptible dry laugh. 'Nothing. Nothing's wrong.'

He stands up and walks out of the room. I try to sit up, but my head seems to have trebled in weight and I slump back down. The curtains are drawn. I didn't do that. Must have been him, then. I twist my head round and look at the glass coffee table.

Wine bottles. A few of those. One glass.

Oh God, I have to get up.

Quickly!

On shaky, barely functioning legs, I move as fast as I can out to the hall and into the downstairs loo. I only just make it.

Later – maybe ten minutes? – there's nothing left. I feel weak. Exhausted. But definitely better. Well, I do now that I've brushed my teeth. I splash some water on my face and dry myself with a towel, enjoying the feel of it on my skin. It's warm from the rail – a *heated* towel rail. How spoilt can a person be? I have a cellar, a downstairs loo with a heated towel rail and a garden adorned with elegant hardwood furniture. A garden that's *furnished*.

I don't deserve any of it, do I?

I am a waste of space, and if I didn't have two beautiful children to care for, there would be no point being here. Not just in this house, but on this planet.

And if that's true, what hope do I possibly have of holding on to the one man I have ever truly loved?

When I woke up this morning – which actually feels like several days ago now – I was looking forward to his visit. I was excited at the thought of talking to him about all the things that have been going through my mind this past week. I was looking forward to listening too. Hearing him tell me how *he* really feels. Long ago, wasn't our love built on honesty? We've been glossing over our feelings for too long now, just going through the motions . . .

Yes, when I woke up this morning, I was really looking forward to talking; *getting it all out.*

Ridiculous idea.

Twenty-four years ago, I let my dad walk out without trying to stop him. Maybe I should just do the same here today.

Bye, Richard, have a nice life.

I find him in the kitchen.

'Here, I've made you some toast.' He offers me a plate.

'No, thanks. Really, I couldn't.'

'Please, Fran, just eat it. What have you had today?'

'Nothing,' I say without looking at him. 'Richard . . . I'm sorry you had to see me like that. I guess it was the pressure taking its toll . . . Look, why don't you come back tomorrow? The kids will be home by lunchtime. You can see them then.'

He leans forward on the island. His chest heaves with the sheer magnitude of his sigh. 'Please don't say sorry again, OK? This is all . . . *me.*'

You're damn right it is, I think, but don't say.

He looks at me, clearly filled with self-rebuke. 'God, but what do I expect? I deserted you, Fran. It's no wonder you passed out from—'

'I was *asleep.*'

He looks up at me and raises an eyebrow. 'Whatever . . .' he says eventually. 'Look at what I've done to you. This is terrible.'

I look down at myself and I see a mess. Ill-fitting, scruffy jeans, crumpled T-shirt. He's right about that much. I do look terrible.

'You've got completely the wrong idea,' I tell him, shaking

my head. 'I'm just very tired and it was just a stupid one-off and—'

'We need to talk,' he says.

'*No.*'

It's way too late for that now.

'Yes we do, Fran. I've got to explain myself. I'm feeling dreadful here.' He stops and looks at me imploringly. 'Please sit down.'

He pulls a tall stool out from the island. Its metal legs scrape across the tiled floor and the noise vibrates through my skull. As I climb up on to the seat, he slides the plate of toast towards me and puts the kettle on.

'I've betrayed you,' he says. 'I know that. But . . . I have to put it into context.' He takes a slow, deep breath. 'Do you know what was so appealing about Bel?'

The mere mention of her name makes my heart catch. Giving me a list of her amazing qualities is just sadistic. Why is he doing this?

'She was an escape. She took me away from you, Fran—'

'Don't, *please.*'

'No, this is important. For the past . . . for ages now, every time I've come home, I've looked at you and felt like a failure—'

'*You've* felt like a failure?'

'Yes, me. I've looked at you and just watched you drift further away from me. You've been surrounded by all these worries and insecurities and I just couldn't reach you. I've desperately wanted you to be a happier person, Fran. Do you know that?'

He looks at me, waiting for a response that I don't give him.

'But it wasn't working, was it?' he says. 'I suppose being with Bel has been like stepping into another world. A place where . . . I just didn't have to worry about anything. I have wondered if I'm the reason you've become so unhappy . . .'

He puts a cup of coffee in front of me. He looks wrecked. His face is drawn and grey, he could probably do with a shave, his hair is lank and uncombed . . .

He looks beautiful.

'Do you know how badly I've wanted to get things back to how they were?'

Do you know how much I love you?

'I was aware,' I say quietly.

'I'm sorry, I really am. But I couldn't go on like this.'

His face is ashen, as if the speech he has just given me has drained him. It made me feel pretty lousy too. It was no revelation, though. He was only telling me in his own eloquent way what I already knew. He reached out to me plenty of times, but . . .

Well, I blew it.

He's pacing now, anxious, as tightly wound as a ball of elastic bands. He stops suddenly and looks at me.

'Have you been drinking like that a lot lately?'

'Don't be ridiculous. I told you, it was a one-off.'

'Some one-off,' he says, staring out of the window. 'Jesus, you were passed out. *Comatose.* What if Molly and Thomas had been here? What were you thinking?'

'*What?*' I can't believe what I'm hearing here. How dare he? 'What do you think, Richard? You left me for your client. I think I'm allowed a little reckless drinking under the circumstances.'

'Fran, *please.* I'm not excusing what I did, but you have to accept that things haven't been right . . . *you* haven't been right since . . . probably since Molly was born.'

'I don't accept any such thing,' I snap.

'No? OK, so why didn't you go back to work?'

'Because I wanted to be with my *baby.*'

'But you could have had it *all.*'

'You don't know how it feels, Richard. You never gave birth. You don't understand at all, do you?'

He slumps down on the counter and says, 'You're bloody right, I don't.'

And how could he? It's not as if I was ever able to articulate it . . .

Over the years, I may not have been working, but I've still been able to do any voice. Jesus, I can even take off people taking off other people. I can do Joan Rivers doing Zsa Zsa Gabor. Roni Ancona doing Victoria Beckham . . .

But if you ask me to explain how I'm feeling – to *do* myself – I've found it – still find it – impossible.

After Thomas was born, the post-natal depression—Yes, that's what it was. Whether it was caused by hormones, an impossible baby or a cocktail of both, it was undeniably depression and irrefutably post-natal. Anyway, the *post-natal* depression hit me so hard that it was four years before I was brave enough to try for another baby. I'd naïvely thought having Molly would lift me from my hole. And would you believe it? There it was *again*. Lightning does strike twice.

My confidence was shattered. Failure – because that's how I saw it – is a difficult thing to admit. Even to your husband of twelve years. Richard tried, he really did, but I wouldn't let him in. Then, a year ago, he was promoted. Promoted as in physically removed from the house and turned into a passing ship.

One that has now sailed off into uncharted waters.

'Do you love her?' I ask.

He turns his back and looks out into the blackness of the garden.

He's saying nothing.

'Do you?'

He keeps his back to me. 'It's complicated . . .'

I wait for him to elaborate, but he doesn't.

'Jesus, Richard, you could at least give me something here,' I scream. 'You're the one who wanted to *talk*!'

I don't know where the rage is coming from, but I want to lash out at him. I want to *really* hurt him because he's right. Everything that's happening here is entirely of his making.

'What do you want me to say, Fran?' His voice lacks the volume of mine, but it's every bit as intense. 'That I'm crazy about her? Do you want me to run through a side-by-side comparison?'

'Fuck you, Richard. I fucking hate you, do you know that?'

'Well, that's just great because I loved you, Fran. I only wish you'd saved me the bother and told me a long time ago.'

His voice is cold. There's fury in his words, but it's contained behind a wall of ice. And he still has his back to me, refusing to turn round and look me in the eye.

'Well, I'm telling you now,' I scream. 'I FUCKING HATE YOU!'

Still he won't turn.

I pick up my coffee cup . . . hold it for a moment . . . then fling it on to the tiles. It shatters. Shards of white china skid across the floor and coffee splashes on to Richard's trousers.

And still he doesn't turn.

The room is silent now.

After a long moment, instinct finally kicks in. I slide off the stool and set off to fetch the mop.

Still without looking at me – sensing what I'm up to – he says, 'Leave it . . . Just leave it.'

I sit back down and watch him whip the tea towel off the rail on the front of the Aga. He bends down and mops up the pool of coffee.

I light a cigarette as he stoops again with a dustpan and

brush and sweeps up the fragments. I blow smoke into the air above his bent body, daring him to complain about the smell.

He doesn't.

As he tips the dustpan into the bin, I ask, 'Where are you staying?' My voice is calm now, as if the fight never happened.

'The agency's just bought a flat,' he replies. 'Wigmore Street.'

How about that? Does the agency anticipate the disintegration of its employees' marriages to the extent that it's *provided* for?

'But I'm staying here tonight,' he continues. 'I'll sleep in the spare room. Call Summer. Tell her to bring the kids back early in the morning.'

'I will,' I say, when all I want to tell him is that I love him.

'You're not touching another drop while I'm here. OK?'

'OK. But like I said, don't go getting the wrong idea about the drinking. It was just a blip, that's all.'

I stub out my half-smoked cigarette in the ashtray – I don't have the appetite for it any more. As I grind the butt into submission, I'm startled to feel him behind me. I wasn't expecting to feel his arms around me, pulling me in close. I lean back into him, feeling overwhelmed by his smell, which seems weirdly alien and heartbreakingly familiar all at once. His stubble brushes my cheek, now wet with my tears. Or maybe they're his. I can't tell any more.

2

The kids are in the morning room . . .

I remember the first time we looked round this house. How impressed I was by the sheer number of rooms. The estate agent had names for them all. A *cellar*. A *second* reception. A *home office*. That was a government department, wasn't it? Well, this house had one of its very own. But what really got me was the *morning* room. The house had so many rooms it could afford to have one with restricted hours. Honestly, I wondered if shutters came down at noon.

But the place is actually nothing special, not by the standards of the area. Most houses have rooms to spare. No wonder park-bench girl wants in.

Richard and I experienced that rare thing, love at first viewing. Obviously, I was excited at the prospect of moving here. Until I was twenty, I lived in a regular two up, two down: bedroom, bedroom, front room, kitchen. Oh, and there was a bathroom squeezed in somewhere. But I use the tag 'bathroom' loosely. Don't go imagining anything fancy. There was a plastic avocado bath, an almost matching sink and a blue loo that Dad, in a rare burst of usefulness, had found in a skip.

But it's only because I've gone on to live somewhere fabulous that I have a point of comparison. Back then I lived in a street of identically tiny houses, packed with family members who jostled for the available space. And we had variety too. It was Multicultural Britain at its best. And in my present *mono*cultural neighbourhood, they have the audacity to lecture me on racism. What the hell do they know? What our children learn about other cultures, they get from books or the odd guest speaker who has travelled from a place far, far away where foreign people live. Like, say, Leicester.

Despite the best efforts of the white fascists in our area, race was never an issue for my friends and me. We lived by one very simple rule. We divided people into two camps that had *nothing* to do with colour: the ones we liked and the ones we didn't.

At the time, I didn't appreciate any of this. It was just *life*; not there to be analysed, but there to be lived. Looking back, I can see that I have a lot to be thankful for. I may not have had much in the way of toys or clothes or holidays, but my world had a richness that my cosseted children will never know.

Simple days.

No money, no toys, just friendship. People we liked and people we didn't.

But, oh, how I've come on. I now live in a house that has a cellar and a morning room.

Where the children are now.

Thomas is watching the tape Al lent him. Molly is comforting Myra the Cabbage Patch Kid, whose arm has finally fallen off. This actually gives Myra VIP status in the dolly pecking order – she's Molly's first amputee. Well, it does until Molly is reminded of Chloe, her Baby Born, who, unlike Cabbage Patch, is conventionally pretty and still has four fully functioning limbs. If I were clearer-headed, I might give her a little sermon on how all God's dollies are created equal, but I'm not, so I don't.

Summer didn't wait to be asked in when she delivered the kids. She saw Richard in the kitchen and scarpered, mouthing, 'I'll call you,' as she went.

'Wait,' I shouted as she ran down the garden path. 'I wanted to wish you luck.'

'No time. Plane to catch. I'll phone.'

'Give my love to George,' I called, but she was gone.

She can talk for England when the fancy takes her. The only place her fancy was taking her this morning was away from my house, which ordinarily she loves. But not with Richard in it.

He was making a full English. The kids – yes, even Thomas – shrieked when they saw him.

'*Daddy*, you're making breakfast!' from Molly, who does like her food.

'*Dad*, are you taking me to football?' from Thomas, who does like his football, although I'm not sure it needs restating.

Kids have a habit of getting their priorities right, don't they? Richard could have been away for three months and have come back with a different nose and no ears and they wouldn't have noticed.

We ate breakfast together and if you didn't know a thing about us, you'd have thought we were the perfect family. A Sunday-morning fry-up cooked by Dad, while Mum stayed in her dressing gown and the children ribbed each other playfully. My God, were those Thomas's teeth? I must have seen them three times as he laughed at something silly Richard was doing with his scrambled egg.

I can almost fool myself into thinking everything is perfect. In fact, you can rewrite anything if you really try.

JR (Richard):   I've sure missed you, honey. It's great to be home with the people I love.

Sue Ellen (Me):   I love you too, JR. Hey, John Ross, Daddy's home from his big oil convention in the city.

John Ross (Thomas, showing teeth):   Hey, Dad! Are you done doing kind and wonderful things for other people?

Can you come play soccer with me now?

Sue Ellen: Oh, honey, Daddy has to phone the children's hospice first. They want to thank him for his multi-million-dollar donation.

JR: Shucks, I get all the thanks I need when I look into the eyes of those poor little sick kids. Right now, all I want to do is hug you, Sue Ellen, and tell you that you're neither a drunk nor a tramp and you're actually a very fit mom indeed.

Perfect families. I can close my eyes and pretend that Richard isn't making coffee in preparation for a conversation about child access and financial arrangements.

I fooled myself as I lay in bed last night. He may have been in the spare room, but at least he was back home. But the pretence is over now. Richard puts the mugs on the island. He doesn't sit down next to me. Or even opposite. He paces.

He's a man who runs a company. He chairs meetings and makes assured decisions on the fate of millions of pounds of client money, yet I've never seen him look as edgy and nervous as he does now.

'I've got a big pitch to Shell on Monday week,' he says, surprising me with talk of work even though that's what I've been thinking about. 'We've actually got through to the final round – pitching to the chairman.'

'That's good.'

'Yeah . . . But it means I've got to go into the office in a while. Run through things with the team.'

'Right,' I say. As we're on the subject of work, I'd like to keep it here a bit longer. 'Do you know what I did last week? I called Isabel about that job.'

'That's good,' he says quietly, still pacing.

'She sent me a script. I'm going into town for a read-through tomorrow.'

'That's brilliant.'

'It's *terrifying.* They've got a bunch of Sony execs coming to hear me.'

'You've got nothing to be scared of. They're just a bunch of suits. You, on the other hand, have the most amazing voice I've ever heard.'

He's not patronising me. He *means* it. I manage to give him a smile.

'It's great news. I'm really pleased.' And now he stops pacing. 'But I'm a bit worried about leaving you.'

Crunch time, it seems.

'Please don't be. We're fine. It's not as if we're not used to it.'

'Fran, I know you said yesterday was a one-off and I know why you did it. And for that I'm sorry, I really am. But how do you know it won't happen again? I'm a bit worried about leaving you with the kids and—'

'Oh, *please*, leaving me with the kids is what you do. It's what you've been doing day in, day out for the last ten years . . .'

He looks stung.

'I'm sorry, but you are so overreacting.' I'm in my stride now. 'Yes, it was a one-off, but you're wrong about knowing why. You have no idea what set it off.'

'What are you talking about?'

Well, I wasn't going to say anything, but since he's asking . . . 'Yesterday, I sat on a park bench and listened to a complete stranger telling me that less than a hundred yards away all my so-called friends were ripping me to shreds. Ridiculing me behind my back about what a crap mother I am, how crap my life is . . .'

'What do you mean? You're not making sense.'

'This woman . . . she just struck up a conversation with me. She'd overheard them in the café. Obviously, she didn't know it was me they were talking about, but I did.' Just the memory of it makes tears sting my eyes.

'How do you know? They could have been talking about anyone.'

'It was me all right. There was too much . . . *detail*. Everything. They knew about it all.'

Molly runs into the kitchen. I don't want her to see me crying so I look away quickly. I needn't have worried. She doesn't have eyes for me. She wraps her skinny arms round the bit of Richard's waist that she can reach and buries her face in his stomach. 'Love you, Daddy,' she says earnestly and skips back to the morning room.

'But how would they know anything about our . . . our situation?' Richard asks when she has gone.

I shrug. What can I tell him? That I confided in a woman I barely knew? That I'd closed myself off from my closest friends but given the intimate details of my life to the first woman who'd flashed her designer labels at me?

'Jesus,' he says as something dawns on him. 'I know what this is about. It's Adam.'

'Adam?' I repeat. And actually, what is he talking about?

'One of our designers at work. He goes out with a really tall girl, Amanda. They were at our party. She works at HSBC with that woman Natasha's husband. He must have heard rumours and gone and shot his mouth off. The *bastard*.'

While Richard is seething, I'm working out exactly what he is talking about. It takes almost a full minute for the realisation to hit me.

He's talking about his affair and how it got out. I can't believe I didn't ask myself that same question. While I've been wallowing in shame because Natasha has told everyone that I'm a middle-aged lush who neglects her children, I didn't stop to think about how they knew Richard had left me.

Now I'm filled with renewed anger. 'Don't you dare blame Adam for picking up fag ends. That's what happens when you fuck about at work,' I spit angrily. 'People gossip. It's what they do.'

'Whatever, he's a slimy bastard. *Jesus*, he was all over me about the party when I got back from Milan.'

I can't listen to this. So Adam's two-faced. So bloody what? Is that any worse than being a lying, cheating, *also* two-faced scumbag? I don't think so.

Inwardly, I'm quivering with rage. And desperation . . .

Ever since the conversation with Natasha, I've been worried that maybe she's right. Maybe I *am* an alcoholic. Maybe the day when I can't function without a drink in my hand isn't far away. Or maybe it has already arrived. Because right now, at ten in the morning, all I want is a drink.

'I'm really sorry you had to go through what you did yesterday,' Richard says, sheepish now. 'Jesus, no wonder you . . . It would have been enough to send anyone over the edge.'

His concern is quite soothing. I let it wash over me, wanting more than just sympathy, but making do with it, anyway.

He looks at his watch. 'Fran, I've really got to be making a move. I'm sorry . . . We've got such a lot to talk about. Once this pitch is over, we can get together properly and try to make sense of things . . .'

I still can't look at him.

'Are you seeing her?' I ask.

'What do you mean?'

'Are you seeing her today? After your thing at the office.'

'No . . . No plans. If you must know, I haven't seen her since we got back from Italy . . . I've just been too busy.'

Yeah, right. Why am I even asking? As if he'd tell me the truth, anyway.

He goes to the morning room. I listen to him say goodbye to Thomas and Molly. He gives them some bullshit about another business trip. Their disappointment is muted. I wonder if they're picking up a vibe.

He returns to the kitchen and I follow him to the front door.

I wonder if he's really going to work, or is he heading straight round to Gucci Girl? And I notice the overnight bag on the floor in the hall, discreetly nudged into the corner next to the umbrella stand. When did he pack that? And did he put in the shirts I starched and ironed for him?

'I'll call you,' he says, picking up the bag.

'You do that,' I say. I watch him leave, not moving until I hear the car engine start.

3

Friends come no better than Sureya.

I called her first thing this morning. Only to ask her to take the kids to school. I couldn't face the knowing looks, the judgement of Cassie's gang.

When Sureya arrived, I was theatrically clutching a bunch of tissues, props to support the lie that I was too bunged up with cold to chance a school run. But she knows me too well and didn't buy it for a split second. A split second being all the time it took for me to dissolve into tears. 'I'm so sorry. About that awful phone call and . . . everything.'

'Never mind all that. Go round to my place *now*,' she insisted. 'Wait for me there . . . And stick the kettle on.' She wouldn't take no for an answer. She just threw her keys at me, gathered Molly and Thomas and shot off.

I watched them go, then put my jacket on and set off for her house.

When she arrived home, I told her about Richard. All of it. Now that I've finished, she looks as if she might spontaneously combust . . . or something. I have never seen her so shocked and angry. Shockingly angry.

'I could kick myself. All that stupid optimism I plied you with when you showed me that bill. You'll never listen to me again, will you? God, how come my radar didn't pick anything up at your party? I'm usually so good at spotting the signals.'

'Sureya, please forget it. I missed them too, even when

they were right under my nose, printed on Langham Hilton headed paper.'

'I don't understand it, Fran,' she says, hunched over the table, her head in her hands. Anyone would think *her* husband had just left her. 'He gave you such a wonderful night. It doesn't make sense. Does he love this other woman?'

I gloss over the fact that we haven't properly spoken about the other woman by changing the subject. I do this by telling her about what I found out from the girl in the park.

She is outraged, as I knew she would be. 'Those disgusting, evil cows need to die slow, painful deaths for what they've done to you.' I'm not sure that pregnant women should be giving out such bitch vibes, and, really, it's quite a revelation. Sureya *never* does bitch vibes. She is the original Little Miss Sunshine.

'I feel so guilty. I've been obsessed with this pregnancy and I've neglected you horribly.'

'Rubbish. Saving me from the ARPS witches and Richard's wandering dick isn't your job. None of this is your fault. How could it be?'

Sureya is emotional at the best of times. Now, her hormones get the better of her and she starts to cry, which sets me off. If aliens were observing us through the slats in her kitchen blinds, they would think us ridiculous. '*While ingesting many cupfuls of a hot, brown beverage, they engage in discussion for several earth hours, during which they contort their faces and liquid droplets fall from their eyes. They appear to have no control over this production of moisture.*'

'Please let's talk about you now,' I say after we wash our faces. 'I haven't even told you how happy I am for you. And I so am.'

'I know.' She smiles, letting me change the subject. 'You know, I can't believe I'm twenty-four weeks already.'

'You're kidding. It was only twenty-one last week, wasn't it?'

'Oh, you know what doctors are like,' she says breezily. 'You give them your dates, then they tell you you're wrong, like you don't know your own cycle. It's all mad,' she says, dismissing the issue with a flick of her hand. 'The point is, the baby will come when the baby comes. Give or take a few weeks. Who's counting?' She laughs merrily to illustrate her point. Which doesn't make any sense at all to be honest.

'You're sure you're OK?' I ask.

'Of course.' She laughs yet again.

I fear she doth protest too much, if you know what I mean, but I can't work it out. I'm so annoyed with myself. If I'd bothered to take a proper look at her earlier, I'd have noticed that her dusky complexion is more than usually bleached and her usually sparkling eyes have become circled by grey.

'So you don't want to talk about anything, then? Get some textbooks out, do some pregnancy research, anything like that?' Sureya is big on textbooks. She has an office full of shelves devoted to them.

'It's all going to be fine.' She bats the issue away again. 'Actually, I want to ask *you* something, Fran. About what those women said. Is it true?'

'What, that Richard has left me? Of course it is.'

'No, I mean the stuff about . . . you know, hitting the bottle.'

Obviously, I knew that was what she was talking about. And naturally, I edited my account of the weekend – I didn't tell her how Richard found me on Saturday.

'Of course it's not true,' I exclaim, as if she's Cassie and she's just asked me if it's true that I use Dolmio in my bolognese. 'Do I *look* like an alcoholic?'

'Sorry, sorry, of course you don't. No more than I do, anyway. Although, not any more.' She pats her tummy. Her bump is still tiny. She's not so pregnant-looking yet that you'd offer her your seat on the train.

'God, Sureya, it's been freaking me out,' I blurt suddenly, feeling myself head off in an entirely unplanned direction.

'What has?' she asks.

'The thought that I'm an alkie. Ever since this conversation I had with Natasha last week—'

'That bitch,' Sureya hisses.

'I told her some stuff and she made a diagnosis, and, well, she got me thinking – going out of my head, if you must know. I'm an alcoholic, aren't I? One step away from the Priory.'

And now that I've said it – made an admission of sorts – I feel nothing but relief. It's like squeezing a huge, over-ripe zit. A gross analogy, but the feeling is exactly the same.

'You told her about your father, didn't you?' Sureya says quietly, her arm going round my shoulders. In all the years I've known her, we've only ever talked once about my dad, but she's not one to forget.

And now that she has brought him up, I'm crying so hard I can't speak. I nod and put my hands over my face.

'And you're worried that now it's your turn, sort of thing?' She's got it in one.

'Talk to me about it, Fran. *Honestly.*'

I calm myself, and then I tell her. Honestly. About how in the weeks leading up to my party, the drinking has been creeping up – how the daily glass of wine has turned into the daily two, maybe three. About how I overslept and missed school pick-up. About how Richard found me after my trip to the park.

'It just doesn't bear thinking about, Sureya,' I tell her, still crying. 'So I haven't been thinking about it. I've been having a drink instead. I just don't know what's happening to me any more.'

She doesn't answer, but takes a deep breath and steps back from me. Christ, is she judging me, too?

'Look, Fran, I'm going to ask you some questions and I want you to be absolutely straight with me,' she says at last, her voice firm.

I give her a curt nod.

'How many drinks do you have a day?'

'I have no idea. It varies. I don't count.'

'You don't count or you *lose* count?'

'I don't lose count,' I protest. 'Well, apart from on Saturday. That was just . . .'

'Hell?' Sureya supplies when I trail off. 'I can imagine. But tell me, Fran, how many drinks today?' she asks, sternly returning to the point. Suddenly I'm a little bit scared. Of Sureya! Mad, but there it is.

'Well, none. So far,' I add ominously.

'How do you feel in the morning? What are you thinking when you wake up?'

'About the school run, what I'm going to put in their lunchboxes, the usual rubbish. Why?'

'No shaking or sweats, anything that makes you want to reach for a drink?'

'First thing in the morning? Are you mad? I can't even drink a whole mug of coffee first thing,' I tell her, wiping the tears from my face.

'OK, so when you do have your first drink, do you need to continue, you know, like you can't stop?'

'Well, Saturday . . .' I feel shame remembering it.

'Not a typical day, though, was it? Has that happened before?'

'No, never.'

She pauses and shakes her head. 'That bloody Natasha,' she says after a moment. 'How dare she?'

'What do you mean?'

'What gives her the right to make a pronouncement – never mind to broadcast it to the bloody world? She doesn't have a clue what she's talking about. Alcoholism – *any* addiction – is a very complex issue. She's not a doctor, a professional.'

'Neither are you, Sureya,' I say. She's a drama teacher, for heaven's sake, but the way she's talking you'd think she was a founder member of AA. I want to laugh, but I daren't.

'Excuse me, but I do know what I'm talking about,' she says indignantly.

'You did *theatre* studies,' I tell her tentatively.

'Yes, and at uni one of my placements was with a group that did workshops in rehab clinics.'

Now – as I picture her persuading the junkies to *really* BE *the needle* – I desperately want to laugh. It may be the nerves, or it may just be funny. I can't tell.

'You may well laugh . . .'

Yes, I'm afraid that I may.

'. . . but I saw a lot of stuff. And I learnt a lot. A damn sight more than bloody Natasha. Plenty of experts will tell you that any sort of regular alcohol intake constitutes a dependency. Frankly, that makes most of the adult population alkies. But full-blown alcoholism – the inability to function on any level without a drink – is something else. And believe me, you are *not* an alcoholic.'

'Aren't I?'

'*No*. And don't go thinking that just because your dad was, it automatically follows that you will be too. Alcohol is a prop, something we reach for in times of stress. And tell me, when have you been more stressed than you are right now?'

I give her a shrug.

'Exactly. I'd be amazed if you weren't drinking a bit more than usual. I bet you're smoking more too.'

She's right, I am. I feel some relief because this is Sureya talking. She never spouts off about anything unless she's sure of her ground. And she's the queen of therapy. If she had her way, she'd have us all in counselling just for wearing shoes. ('But *why* are you hiding your feet? Please don't tell me your feet are cold without socks. That's classic Jungian displacement.') Yet here she is denying me her I-really-think-you-need-therapy speech.

'Actually, I know when I've seen you as strung out as this,' she says. 'Remember after you'd had Thomas . . . ?'

How could I ever forget?

'The post-natal depression—'

'If that's what it was,' I say, the cynicism kicking in instinctively.

'The *post-natal* depression lasted for months. We were getting together a lot back then and a glass or two of wine was always part of the routine. If you were ever going to become an alcoholic, it would have been then. Your drinking would have escalated and we'd be booking you in for the liver transplant now.'

Accurately, she reads my silence as scepticism, and carries on, eager to convince me.

'You're *depressed*, Fran. You're stressed and suffering from a severe self-esteem deficit, but you're not an alcoholic. That's a huge leap to make. God, the more I think about it, the angrier I get. Natasha's known you ten minutes. She has no business making any sort of judgement. She needs to get a life of her own instead of pulling other people's to pieces. You'd have to feel sorry for her if she weren't so poisonous.'

Her words throw my stupidity into painfully sharp relief. What was I thinking pouring my heart out to a virtual stranger when I was keeping the very same stuff from a true friend like Sureya?

'I'm sorry, Sureya,' I say.

'What on earth for?'

'I should have talked to you before.'

'Yes, you should have. But we're talking now. Look, you have been honest with me, haven't you? About the drinking, I mean.'

'I swear.'

'Good. But I'll be keeping an eye on you. First sign of trouble and we're straight off to see Dallas, my counsellor buddy.'

I almost choke. 'I am *not* seeing a therapist called Dallas!'

'OK, then, I'll find you someone called John,' she laughs, then gives me the tightest hug. 'You know I'm here for you, Fran, don't you?'

Yes, I do.

'I'm going to focus all my energy on you. Much better than worrying about Michael, anyway.'

'What do you mean? I thought you two were all loved-up?'

'We are . . . But you never know what they're getting up to, do you . . . He's in New York. Had to fly out first thing this morning. How do I know he won't be getting it on with some Manhattan minx?'

'That would never happen. Not Michael.'

'How can you be so sure? I said exactly the same thing about Richard a few days ago. You can never say never.'

'Look, Michael just wouldn't. He's crazy about you,' I tell her certainly.

Come on, this is Sureya we're talking about. Who wouldn't be?

It's lunchtime and Sureya has made us sandwiches. I'm having a glass of wine with mine – a small one, mind. She's having herbal tea. Obviously.

I'm feeling very emotional as I eat. My two best friends are pregnant – and they have their own different reasons to be stressed about the fact – and yet they are the ones running around looking out for *me*. I make up my mind now to pull myself together. I'm going to be there for them both. I tell Sureya as much.

'I mean it,' I say. 'Whatever help you need, I'll be there. I promise.'

'I know you will be, Fran.' She smiles, and although she looks drawn, I can see the love in her eyes.

Which, of course, makes me cry again.

'Just let it all out,' she soothes. 'I told you, talking is good. You should do it more often.'

Depends on whom you talk to, though. Look where it got me with Natasha.

Unlike Natasha, though, Sureya is a friend worthy of the name. The type of friendship that evolves over years without you even noticing how close you're growing. Not the sort that's force-fed with stuffed olives and Pimm's over the span of a few days.

All that *opening up* has left me feeling floaty and light-headed and I kind of like it. It's better than feeling leaden, which is how I've felt too often lately. Maybe there is something in this talking malarkey after all.

I feel like hugging her. This beautiful, selfless woman with more than enough problems of her own to deal with has just given up an entire morning and half an afternoon to sit and listen to my crap.

Why do I always have to be the most miserable person in the room?

Why can't I take my head out of my hands for a second, look around me and see that I have the most amazing friends? And why can't I be happy for that one simple fact?

But I am!

At this moment, I really am happy to count my blessings. My life could be so much worse. I have a wonderful home, two gorgeous children and the two best friends who could ever have walked into my life. What more could I ask for without being impossibly greedy . . . ? Well, a faithful, loving husband, maybe . . .

But, no, I'm going to count my blessings, even if it kills me. Sureya's usual optimistic outlook is spot on, and I make a decision to start thinking about my life in terms of my glass being half full.

And as I look at it, that's exactly what it is. I've hardly touched a drop.

'Do you think that glass would be so full if you were an alcoholic?' Sureya asks, sensing what I'm thinking.

'Thanks, Doc, for being so thorough with your diagnosis,' I joke, glass half-full-ishly, 'but I think my time is now up.'

We both laugh as we get up. It's time to collect our children.

She flings her arms round me and squeezes me tightly.

My fabulous friend. And she's having a baby! I can't wait to tell Summer. She'll be delighted. They can be bump buddies.

Walking into Arlington is tough. I feel as if the eyes of four hundred mothers are upon me. How far has Natasha's venom spread? But talking to Sureya has helped. I feel as if she gave me back a little of my self-esteem. And she's by my side now, which gives me the strength to hold my head up. Well, actually, I'm wearing a baseball cap and my head is angled downwards, but you know what I mean.

Ten yards into the school grounds, Sureya peels away and heads off for the nursery. I'm on my own. I head for the infant block at a very brisk walk, careful to look neither left nor right . . .

I'm nearly there. The corridor outside Molly's classroom is empty. I'm the first to arrive. I'll be able to whisk her away before the mob turns up . . .

But the fact that I'm carefully looking neither left nor right means I don't see Gottfried approaching until she is right in front of me. She blocks my path.

'Mrs Clark,' she rasps. 'Have you had a chance to think about the matter ve discussed last veek?'

Right on cue, a bunch of mums crash through the double doors behind us. Now we have an audience and I have an excuse to be as hoity-toity as I like.

'This is hardly the time or the place, is it, Mrs Gottfried?'

I can't believe I'm being so patronising. She still scares the hell out of me, but it feels good to stand up to her. She looks at me, furious, as if she's just caught me with a can of spray paint spelling out FUCK SHIT CUNT WANKER in three-foot letters on the wall in front of me . . .

Now there's a thought.

I'm joking. I'd never do that. Spray paint is so expensive. I'd have to use chalk.

'Please give me a call,' she says. It's not a request but a command. 'This matter has not been resolved satisfactorily . . . the head shares my concern.'

'*Rice an' peeeas!*' I yell as she spins on her heel and walks away.

Of course I don't. In truth, my legs are trembling. Thank God my trousers are baggy. Jesus, how can five minutes in a primary school be so *stressful*?

Mrs Poulson flings open the classroom door. I jostle through the mums and grab my daughter's hand. We head off to the playground in search of Thomas. Freedom beckons . . .

Miraculously, my son appears by my side and we walk towards the school gate. Or should I say run? Out of the corner of my eye, I've seen the sitting-room-on-wheels. Sylph-like Natasha is pushing it manfully, struggling to catch up with me, one child in the buggy, two in her slipstream.

She's determined, I'll give her that. I won't be able to outrun her unless I break into a sprint, and how would that look?

'Fran, I haven't seen you for ages,' she calls out brightly, slightly breathless.

I look at her properly now. Manolo Blahniks today. And look at that: her hair scrunchy matches her chocolate-brown handbag. What a gift this girl has with accessories.

'How have you been?' she asks.

Where do I start, Natasha, you two-faced, deceitful, gossiping . . . ?

'Oh God, where do I start? So much has been happening!' I gush, as if I'm Businesswoman of the Year and my company's share price has tripled overnight and I've not only decoded the human genome in a spare minute, but I've also invented these spindly six-inch heels that are really easy to walk in.

My tone probably throws her. She's spent the weekend telling anyone who'd listen that I'm the human equivalent of a condemned building, and here I am doing wide-eyed exhilaration. I don't think she was expecting *breezy.*

I should have been an actress.

But so should she. 'Oh, that's great!' she trills, stumbling in her efforts to keep up with us. 'You must come round and tell me about it.'

'Mummy,' Molly pants. 'Why are you walking so fast?'

'Got to keep up with Thomas.'

He's way ahead of us. I thank heaven once again for PlayStation. Thomas never wastes a second in his rush to get home and switch it on.

'How about it?' Natasha asks. 'Tea at mine? It'll be fun. We can have Pimm's!'

She laughs her infectious laugh. Infectious like Ebola.

'Some other time.' I smile, pulling ahead slightly. 'We've got a lot on today.'

'And the Autumn Fair,' she calls out as I put clear pavement between us. 'We need to get together and have a chat about it.'

Oh, yes, we need to chat all right. We need to talk at some length about what a twisted bitch you are. We need to find out exactly what the words 'trust', 'discretion' and 'friendship' mean to you because I believe we're working from very different dictionaries.

But I make do with, 'Yeah, gotta rush, *bye*.'

I close the front door behind me and feel sweet relief ooze through my body. But the pleasure doesn't last for long. The answering machine is blinking at me. I press play.

'*Fran . . . Isabel here . . .*'

Oh, fuck!

'*. . . Where the hell are you? I have three execs from Sony waiting. I don't know how much longer we can keep them entertained. I hope to God the fact that you're not home means you're stuck in a taxi or something. Why isn't your mobile switched on? Just . . . get here soon.*'

Oh, fuck, fuck, fuck.

A second message:

'*Fran . . . No, I'll handle this, Izzy . . .*'

Harvey this time.

'*. . . Fran, thank you for making us look like a pair of fuckwits in front of our backers. You'll be pleased to know they've left now. I will not forgive you, you know. Trust me on that. Oh, and if you think you'll ever so much as voice a fucking ten-second tea-bag commercial again . . . It is over. You can trust me on that too.*'

'Who was that, Mummy?' Molly asks.

The Grim Reaper, I think. 'No one,' I say.

'Did he say the F word?'

I ignore her. I grip the banister at the bottom of the staircase until my knuckles turn white. I want to scream . . .

How could I have been so stupid? So stupid and self-absorbed. Self-*obsessed*. Talking about me, me, *me* all bloody day. It's good to talk, is it, Sureya? She must be insane because all talking does is make you forget – FORGET! – the appointment that was going to *save your life*.

What a stupid, pointless mess.

Harvey will never forgive me? I'll never forgive myself.

I just about made it through teatime without breaking down in front of Molly and Thomas. I didn't bother to make them do their homework. Instead, they sat in front of the TV while I chain-smoked in the kitchen.

What's the big deal about letting your children watch telly all night, anyway? That's what my friends and I used to do when we were kids and it didn't do me any harm. That's what I told myself as I lit another cigarette. But when I thought about it – when I considered what a mess I'd become – it crossed my mind that perhaps I wasted too much of my youth watching *Wacky Races* and *Scooby Doo*. That decided it. I whisked them upstairs for a bath and a story. Well, Molly listened to the story and Thomas shut himself in his room.

They've been in bed for half an hour now. I'm sitting downstairs stewing.

How the hell could I have been so stupid?

It wasn't a dentist's appointment. It was a major film corporation. An audition for a part in a proper film. OK, maybe also a completely stupid film, but that's not the point. And OK, I'd never have got the part because I would have been so rusty at the read-through, but that isn't the point either.

I should have at least turned up.

I think about Summer in LA and her screen test tomorrow. You can bet she won't forget to show up.

I pick up the packet and light another cigarette. I'm about to pour myself a much-needed glass of wine when the phone rings. I don't want to answer it. I'm sure it's going to be Harvey with a fresh list of curses. But it persists and I don't want it to wake up the kids, so I pick it up.

'Hello, am I speaking to Mrs Clark?'

Oh, get lost, you stupid telesales bloke. Can't you see I'm busy beating myself up here?

'Who's that?' I ask, ready to have a go.

'It's Ron. Ron Penfold. At Crystal Palace.'

'*Ron!*'

But it won't be good news, will it? He's only phoning me to tell me how useless I am for screwing up my son's chances.

'I was disappointed you didn't get back to me in time for the trial . . .'

See? What did I tell you?

'. . . only your lad's got something a bit special and I really wanted the guys down here to get a proper look at him.'

'I'm sorry,' I say weakly, 'but, stupidly, I got mixed up with the dates.'

'These things happen . . .'

Yeah, I'm sure mothers up and down the land are forever blowing their kids' dreams because they get their dates mixed up.

'. . . I thought perhaps you weren't interested. You know, some parents aren't keen on their sons getting too involved with football. They'd sooner they stuck to their schoolwork.'

'No, no, it's not that. Honestly, I just got the dates—'

'Don't worry,' he laughs, sensing my desperation. 'Janice told me you called, so I figured you and Thomas were still up for it.'

'Yes, *yes*,' I gasp, not caring how desperate I sound.

'OK, this isn't normally the way things are done, but I had a word with Terry Kember – he runs the academy down here. He's doing some training sessions with the lads on Saturday and he says if you want to bring Thomas along, he'll give him the once-over. That all right with you?'

Is that all right with me? Is he mad? No, of course he's not. He's an angel. OK, I'm being dramatic, but really, I could kiss his halo because I'm certain he has one.

'Yes, *yes*, of course,' I gabble excitedly. 'Saturday. We'll see you on Saturday.'

He laughs again. I love this man. 'OK, midday, twelve o'clock. Thomas can show Terry what he's made of and then we'll take it from there. How's that sound?'

'It sounds amazing, brilliant—' S l o w   d o w n, F r a n. 'That'll be fine,' I say – *almost* calmly.

'I can see where Thomas gets his energy from, Mrs Clark.'

'Fran, *please*.' I *so* love this man!

He laughs and I detect a slight accent – yes, even in a laugh. Midlands . . . Black Country . . . Oh, who cares?

'Right, I'll stick a map in the post, but it's easy to find – it's in Beckenham . . .'

Beckenham? Where the hell's that?

'. . . Any problems, give me a ring. I'll give you my mobile number . . .'

I grab a pen and as I write the number down I realise my hand is shaking. But it's good shaking. I want to explode with happiness. My heart is bursting and I can feel blood surging around my body in a rush to get to the next organ and the next and the next. Adrenaline. The greatest drug known to man. I *so* do not need – want – this drink. As I put the glass back in the cabinet, and the wine back in the fridge, I'm feeling quite triumphant. How about that, then, Natasha? Tell that to the cronies at school.

Once I've hung up, I creep upstairs and open Thomas's bedroom door. I peek into the darkness. I can't see a thing, but the sound of rhythmic breathing is drifting down from his ceiling-high bed. I can't wake him now.

The best news in the world and I can't even give it to him.

Never mind. It will wait until morning. Breakfast is going to be just magical.

I have a smile on my face as I sink into the sofa.

I press play on the DVD remote. *Goodfellas.* The third best movie ever, according to Richard, kept off the top spot by a pair of *Godfather*s. I'm going to pretend we're watching it together. I'm going to pretend it's my third favourite film too. Maybe it will be by the end.

It hasn't been a bad day, given the current circumstances.

OK, there's been a blip or two, but . . .

I'm a glass-half-full girl now.

And I'm not even drinking.

4

I open my eyes and see that the TV screen has turned to black. *Goodfellas* are long-gone fellas. I must have nodded off. The clock on the VCR tells me it's well past midnight.

So why is the telephone ringing?

And whoever heard of good news coming at this hour?

I run to the phone in the hall and grab the receiver. 'Hello?' I say, unable to hide my anxiety.

All I can hear are muffled sobs – a child crying in the background.

'Sureya? Is that you?'

The child's cries are louder now.

'Fran, something's happening,' Sureya whispers.

My heart lurches. 'What is it? What's wrong?'

Molly appears on the landing, her eyes half-closed. 'Who are you talking to, Mummy? Is it Daddy?'

Briefly, it occurs to me how strange it is that Molly doesn't question her father's absence. She doesn't wonder why he now lives at the other end of a phone line, but seems simply to accept it.

No time for that now. 'Sureya, tell me what's happened.'

'I didn't know who else to call,' Sureya whispers, trying to keep the panic away from her child. 'I'm bleeding . . . I need to get to the hospital.'

'Give me fifteen minutes,' I tell her immediately.

'What about Molly and Thomas?'

It doesn't take any thought at all. 'Fifteen minutes,' I repeat, before putting the phone down.

But what about Molly and Thomas? I haven't got a plan . . . I *have* to think . . .

Molly ambles sleepily down the stairs.

. . . *Think* . . .

They have a father, don't they?

'What's happening?' Molly asks.

'I'm calling Daddy.'

Her face breaks into a smile as I pick up the phone again and dial his mobile number. I only hope it's switched on . . .

'Who's that?' his sleep-fogged voice asks after half a dozen rings.

'How quickly can you get here?' I ask.

'Fran . . . ? What's happened?'

I don't have time for questions, whether they're his about why I'm calling so late or mine – *is he alone?*

'It's an emergency, Richard.'

'Jesus, the *kids*—'

'The kids are fine. I've got to get Sureya to hospital.'

'My God, what's happened?' He's wide awake now.

'No time. Can you come?'

'I'll be there in twenty minutes. Half an hour tops.'

I hang up and think.

Half an hour. Sureya didn't sound like she could wait that long.

'Why are you breathing funny?' Molly asks. 'Have you got a cold?'

I must be hyperventilating. I take a deep breath and try to calm myself.

'Darling, we're going to have to wake Thomas and get you both dressed,' I explain. 'Daddy's going to be here soon, but I just need to go out, so I'm going to leave you at Sureya's till he gets here. OK?'

OK? Of course it is. Getting dressed in the middle of the night, Daddy coming home – she couldn't be more excited if I'd just offered her a midnight trip to Disney World.

'Come on, let's wake Thomas,' I say.

I watch her scamper up the stairs. Oh, to be five again. A world where stuff just happens. It's just either good stuff or bad. No explanation necessary.

As they're dressing, I call Helen, our babysitter, who doesn't need to be asked twice.

We get to Sureya's just within the promised fifteen minutes. The house is quiet. She's managed to get the fretful twin back to bed.

'Helen's on her way,' I tell her. Then I turn to Thomas and Molly. 'Kids, I want you to sit down quietly on the sofa until Daddy gets here, OK? Then he'll take you home to bed.'

After I'd spoken to Helen, I called Richard again. He's a fast mover when he has to be – he was already in the car.

'What's going on?' Thomas asks. In the world of a ten-year-old, stuff – good, bad or indifferent – requires *detailed* explanation. He stares bug-eyed at Sureya, whose face is bloodlessly grey.

'God, this is terrible,' she groans. 'Here it comes again.' She grips hold of the stair rail and closes her eyes tightly.

'In the front room, kids,' I snap, physically shoving them through.

Oh, Sureya. This can't be happening.

'You're having contractions?' I ask stupidly.

She nods through the pain.

'Look, maybe it isn't. Maybe it's something else,' I say, clinging to the thought myself.

The wave passes and her body straightens out.

'I don't know what the hell's going on,' she pants. 'This

219

is all so wrong. I didn't say anything, but I haven't felt her move for ages.'

Oh my God. Bleeding and contractions at twenty-four weeks . . . It doesn't take a genius, does it? But I don't say that.

'Stop it, you're just panicking. This could be anything. The doctors will fix it, whatever it is.'

Maybe I shouldn't really be saying that – just in case – but what else is there? Surely false hope is better than no hope?

There's a light tap on the door. I see Helen's silhouette through the frosted glass and I let her in. She looks as worried as I feel. But we don't hang around to chat. As she goes to check on Molly and Thomas in the sitting room, I wrap a coat round Sureya's shoulders and get her into my car.

We barely speak on the journey to hospital. The roads are booby-trapped with traffic humps. Every time the car jolts over one, it sends a shock of pain straight to Sureya's abdomen. Fucking *humps*. Whose brilliant idea was it to turn suburban London into an assault course? When this is over, I'm going to seek him out and kill him.

Where did the daylight come from? I stand in the corridor outside Sureya's room, wondering where the night went. I left her a few minutes ago. I needed to make some calls. Helen first. She was fine. She'll stay with the twins for as long as necessary. And, yes, she'd already called Michael. Being on New York time, he hadn't yet gone to bed. He was at dinner with his clients. Of course, he cut it short to get back to his hotel and find a flight home. Easier said than done. He called back to tell her he can't get a seat before tonight – he won't be with Sureya again until tomorrow morning.

By the time I'd finished talking to Helen, I was in deep awe of her. She's one of those rare people whom nothing seems to faze. She didn't bat an eyelid at being dragged out of bed in the middle of the night. She didn't need to be told where anything was, to be briefed on routines or even to be reminded to call Michael. She just got on with it. But she's a pro. Stepping into other people's lives and minding their kids is what she does for a living.

Somehow, though, I don't think she'll be putting in a bill for this one. Sometimes it takes a catastrophe to find out who your friends are. Proper friends, that is. Not the type for whom you're just a name to be shuffled on a dinner-party seating plan, but friends who appear simply because you need them.

I called Richard then. I don't know what I was expecting . . . '*Look, Fran, I really can't be doing with this. I've got ten pitches, a dozen board meetings and fifteen lunches to get through today.*' . . . But he was great too. He'd taken Thomas and Molly to school. Even did their lunchboxes. *Unprecedented.* I can categorically state that Richard has not made one packed lunch in ten years. I wondered what he put in them – I almost asked him. But then I thought, sod it. He could have stuffed them with nothing but chocolate bars and I'd have been happy. Let Annabel take it up with *him*.

As if she'd dare. Genteel bullying is what she does to weak, insecure mums like me, not to thrusting, go-getting guys like Richard.

It was a little stilted, but it felt good to be talking to him about stuff that wasn't *us*. It's what we Brits are good at, isn't it? Putting our problems aside and pulling together in times of adversity. Like the Blitz all over again, only on a microscopic scale. I'm not sure I'd run that analogy past any war veterans, but you get the idea.

Practicalities out of the way, he asked me about Sureya.

He choked up when I told him. But there was nothing he could say. What can *anyone* say?

'Are you going to the office now?' I asked.

'Don't be silly. I've told them I'm off until further notice.'

'But . . . haven't you got a pitch or something?'

'Shell? God, don't worry about them. They're a huge multinational oil company. I'm sure they'll cope without me for a day or two.'

'What? You're going to miss your pitch?' I asked . . . *Unprecedented.*

'*Fran*, Sureya's just— What do you take me for?' A moment of silence. 'Look, there's a whole team of people working on it. It'll do me good to delegate for once. I have this tendency to . . . er . . . want to do everything myself. Why do you think I've hardly been home this last year?'

Well, I thought that had something to do with a girl in head-to-toe Gucci, but I didn't say so.

'What if they blow it for you?' I asked. 'You know, lose the pitch.'

'Simple. They'll all be fired.'

We both laughed. Then I asked, 'Is it OK if I hang on here?'

'*Fran, please!*' He sounded as if he wanted to shake me. 'Stay for as long as you need to. What time do I pick the kids up, again?'

'Be there for three fifteen. And Molly has Gym Slips today.'

'*Excellent,*' he said. 'What's that?'

'An hour of roly-poly, basically. Just drop her off in the infant hall.' Then I added, 'The smaller hall at the back of the school. The one that's marked *Infant Hall,*' just in case.

'Got it. Anything else?' he asked.

'Yes, there is. Some *good* news, actually,' I said, remembering that amidst the gloom there was the glint of some genuine, twenty-four-carat good news. 'It's about Thomas. You can tell him when he gets home.'

I explained about FA Ron's phone call and Saturday's trial.

'That's great. Brilliant,' he said without sounding entirely convinced. 'I'm sure he'll be thrilled.'

'He will be. I'm just sorry I won't be there to see his face.'

He sighed then. 'I'm really sorry, Fran,' he said, his voice cracking.

'About Sureya?'

A pause. 'Yes, about Sureya.'

'I know.'

That was five minutes ago. I'm still in the corridor, still blinking in the daylight. Still unable to comprehend what Sureya has been through. Hell, basically.

There wasn't anything the doctors could do. Her baby had died inside her, possibly days ago from what they could tell. A baby girl.

You know the cruellest thing? Not only did she have to deal with the realisation that her baby had died, but at twenty-four weeks, she also had to go through labour. Labour, for anyone who hasn't been there, is no barrel of laughs. Sureya had to endure all of that pain in order to give birth to death.

The doctors and nurses did what they could to make it as painless as possible. But they could only alleviate the physical. Pethidine helps, but the only thing that gets a woman through childbirth is the thought of the new life at the end of it. There was no such light at the end of the tunnel for Sureya.

And I was next to completely bloody useless throughout. I knew then how pointless Richard must have felt as I screamed from the effort of pushing out Thomas and Molly. Like he did with me, I held her hand and soothed her as best I could. But what use were words?

It was just a sick, tragic parody of childbirth. I watched the nurse clean the baby and wrap it in a blanket – just as she would have if the tiny, *tiny* thing had had a heartbeat. Then – just as she would have if, etc. – she asked Sureya if she wanted to hold her. It's the right thing to do, she explained gently; part of coming to terms with what's happened, apparently. Sureya – exhausted, her face streaming with sweat and tears – held out her arms and accepted her child.

I sat on the edge of the bed, my arm round her shoulder. And for the first time since I'd been there, I cried. But how could anyone gaze at that minute thing and not weep? She was *perfect*. She had everything – ten fingers, ten toes, a fragile button of a nose, lips that formed a perfect Cupid's bow . . . *everything* except a heartbeat.

As I cried with Sureya, I remembered my own tearful explosion of joy when I'd brought Thomas and Molly into the world. Part relief that the ordeal was over, but mostly just . . . *joy*. Joy at the life that was about to be lived; all that *potential*. But those ten tiny fingers were never going to wrap around Sureya's. Those gorgeous lips were never going to curl upwards into a smile.

Why had it happened? Perhaps the placenta had broken away from the uterus, it was often impossible to tell. Sureya wasn't to blame in any way whatsoever; it was all too common, the doctor said. One in six pregnancies ends in miscarriage, blah, blah. Who was listening? Not Sureya. I put my arms round her as her baby was taken away, and I thought her tears might never stop. But the doctor returned with a sedative and as she gratefully slipped into unconsciousness, I slipped away too.

I went to the loo and splashed my face with cold water. In the mirror, I saw dark, sunken eyes and hollow cheeks that had nothing to do with lack of sleep and everything to do with the horror I'd just been witness to.

I emerged into the day-lit corridor, desperate for a cigarette. Of course, in the rush to leave home, I hadn't picked them up and a hospital is no place to buy them. So without the benefit of nicotine relief, I made my phone calls.

It's time to return to Sureya now. I make my way to her room, hoping she's still asleep. For her sake of course, because heaven knows she needs the rest, but I have my own selfish reasons for wishing it. You see, I have no idea what I'm going to say to her. Where would I even begin?

I quietly open the door and peek round. She's sitting up on banked pillows. Awake. Staring straight ahead. She doesn't turn her head as I slip into the room.

'How are you feeling?' I ask.

She doesn't say anything. I sit in the chair beside the bed and listen to the sound of my own breathing. I search for some words of wisdom, maybe something comforting, but my head is empty. I feel so completely useless . . .

'Maybe you should get some sleep,' I say eventually.

Stupid, stupid me! I could kick myself. What use is sleep to her? I wait for her to yell at me for being such an idiot, but she doesn't.

'She's called Rosa,' she says softly. 'My favourite flower. Selfish, eh?'

'I don't think anyone would call you that.'

We lapse into silence.

'I've called everyone. The twins are fine. Michael's coming back tomorrow morning,' I tell her. 'First thing.'

No reply.

'And Helen's cool about staying on. For as long as you need her.'

She still doesn't say anything, but now it's because she can't. Her eyes are no longer staring blankly, but are screwed up tight, and her body is heaving with jerky, silent spasms. I jump out of my seat and go to her.

'She was perfect,' she sobs. 'So completely bloody perfect.'

I wrap my arms round her, hold her tight, turn my face to hide my own tears.

'What did I do wrong?'

'*Nothing*. There was nothing you could have done. You mustn't blame yourself.'

Stupid, useless, pointless words. There are no words to make sense of such senselessness. And all that Sureya is left with is this devastating tidal wave of grief.

The rest of the day? Not one I'll wish to remember; one I'll never be able to forget. Shortly after Sureya had refused her lunch, a counsellor came to see her. I sat with them and listened.

Pointless words.

The counsellor broached the subject of the funeral. For the first time, Sureya organised herself into something that almost resembled normality. She didn't want to hang around. Rosa will be buried tomorrow.

I slept on the chair in Sureya's room last night. Not what I'd really call sleep. I drifted in and out, shifting positions every few minutes, trying not to make a sound. Sureya was sedated again, but I didn't want to risk waking her.

The doctors checked her out this morning. She was pronounced fine. Just a shattered heart. I helped her dress and brought her back home. Helen opened the door, took one look at her and made a unilateral decision to take the twins for a long walk in the park. They didn't want to go and clung to their mother as Helen struggled to put their shoes and coats on. But the woman is a pro. She has a thousand ways to get small children to do what they don't want to do. They were out of the door within ten minutes of our arrival.

When they'd gone, Sureya went up to her bedroom as I

went to make her a cup of tea. Michael arrived home then. He stood in the hall looking drawn and ashen, but with none of the usual complaints about jet lag.

'I am so sorry, Michael,' I said. Then, 'She's upstairs.'

Without a word, he dropped his bags and raced up the stairs, two at a time.

I left them to it.

And now I'm putting the key in the lock. Thirty-six hours since Sureya called me, I'm home.

5

My kitchen island has been transformed. Richard's laptop takes centre stage. Next to it is his Blackberry, his Dictaphone, his iPod and something sleek and silver that looks as if it might be for getting stubborn stains out of space suits.

'This is alien body matter. It'll never come out, not even on a boil wash.'

'Have you tried the new Lasermatic Stain Phaser 3000?'

Scattered around the hardware are stacks of papers that have presumably arrived here by motorbike. So much for Richard delegating. In this digital age, he can set up mission control anywhere, even in a neo-Victorian country kitchen.

He slides off his stool as soon as I walk in. He comes to me and I fall into his arms. 'Poor Sureya,' he says, hugging me tight. 'How is she?'

'As crap as can be expected. Michael's home now.'

'Jesus, Fran. I can't believe it. I didn't even know she was pregnant.'

'Neither did I until last week.'

'I thought you two told each other everything.' It isn't an accusation. Rather a statement of fact.

'She didn't want to say anything until she was sure it was going to be OK. I must be the kiss of death. Don't you think it's ironic that it didn't go wrong until she'd told me?'

'Don't be ridiculous . . . You are joking, right?'

I laugh to show that I am, but actually, I'm thinking I have a point.

'By the way, Chris Sergeant called about an hour ago,' he says as he puts the kettle on. 'I didn't know you were seeing him.' He sounds impressed.

'I'm not. Well, we were supposed to be getting together for a drink, but somehow I don't think our relationship is meant to be resurrected. I expect he was just calling to blow me out.'

'Not how I heard it,' he says. 'He said he's sorry he's been too busy to call sooner, but he wants to talk to you about something. *Urgently.*'

My heart does a little flutter, but I stay quiet.

'What's that all about, then?' he asks.

I shrug as if I have no idea, but really, when you think about it, why would the head of the television department at a top London ad agency need to talk to me *urgently*? A job? Oh God, just the thought makes me feel sick. My recent track record on jobs is . . . er . . . poor. One booking that I was too terrified to turn up to. One audition that I was too ditzy to remember. Actually, *forgetting* a read-through with Sony. How rubbish was that? I panic, remembering that I told Richard about the read-through – what if he asks me how it went? Best to move off this subject asap. Best not to say *anything* about me and work until *me* actually *works*.

'Kids all right?' I ask. I've missed them.

'Yeah, fine . . . except that Thomas has been bouncing off the walls since I told him about Crystal Palace. I think his teacher must have thought I'd given him a couple of lines of charlie for breakfast.'

I laugh, and feel a simultaneous pang – I wish I'd seen Thomas's face when he heard the news.

'What's Molly's teacher called?' Richard asks.

'Mrs Poulson. Why?'

'*Cow.* She challenged me this morning. Made me feel like

the local bloody paedophile. Said she hasn't seen me before, which is ridiculous.'

'Is it?' I ask.

'Course it is,' he says indignantly. 'I've done the school run before.'

Well, if he has, I certainly don't remember.

And if Mrs Poulson didn't recognise him, why didn't she stop him yesterday? She had no qualms about delivering my daughter into the hands of the local paedophile then, did she? What gave her the right to be so bloody sancti-monious this morning? Let Richard be indignant. I quite fancy him going up there to have a row. Maybe I should wind him up. Get him really riled.

'Did anyone complain about their lunches, by any chance?' I ask, digging.

'I'd love to see them try. I made these really delicious chicken mayonnaise sandwiches.'

'Really?' My voice has shifted a couple of octaves beyond its normal range.

'I used that organic chicken in the fridge. Thomas loved them so much yesterday I made him an extra one today.'

'You made your own chicken mayonnaise first thing in the morning?'

'On granary. What's wrong with that?'

Where did this guy come from? This isn't the man I've been married to for the past twelve years. That man barely knew what a lunchbox was, never mind what to put in it. Come on, he just about knew where the *school* was.

'Nothing,' I say. 'I'm just impressed you managed to do all that first thing in the morning and get them to school on time.'

'Did I say anything about being on time? I think we got there just in time for them to eat lunch,' he says earnestly.

I laugh and he laughs too. But the moment we realise

we're both laughing, we stop. The awkwardness is broken by his mobile. He pulls a *sorry* face and walks into the hall to take the call.

Now, I'm trying really hard not to listen – *honestly*. It could be anyone. A colleague, a client, a friend. It doesn't have to be *her*. So I busy myself by banging pots, opening and closing cupboard doors. But of course, desperate curiosity overcomes me. I stop and listen . . . He's talking quietly. All I can make out are snatches.

'I'm so sorry . . . totally inexcusable, but . . . unexpectedly overran and . . . Is there anything I can . . . Please let me call you back . . .'

Well, that didn't tell me much. But so what if it was her? They get up to far worse than talking on the phone. But it is bothering me. *Ridiculous*. She's already split us up. What extra damage can one call to his mobile do? Because *Richard* and *his mobile* are in our house and that means if she's speaking to him, she's here too. And excuse me for not being very hospitable, but *here* is the last place I want her.

'Fran, do you think you'll be needing me any more today?' he asks, coming back into the kitchen.

It was her. I knew it. She wants him at her side immediately. He has that awkward, shifty look about him – the one I've come to know and hate.

I could drag it out, couldn't I? I could easily keep him here for longer, use his guilt to my advantage. Do an Angie Watts. I *love* that accent. '*I'm dying, Den! I've got six mumfs to live, gaw blimey.*' I could so easily . . .

'Don't worry. Michael's back now. I can manage from here,' I say instead. If he wants to be with her, I have no intention of standing in his way.

'If you want me to stay, I will. It's just that if I go now, I can try to sort this mess out.'

'What mess?'

He runs a hand through his hair. 'Nothing, nothing. Just, you know, work crap.'

He looks terrible. I was wrong. It *wasn't* her. It was work crap.

'What is it?' I say, taking an interest in his job that I haven't felt for, oh, years.

'I'm so *stupid*. That was Colin Harrison's PA on the phone.'

'Who's he?'

'Oh, only the chairman of Shell. I had an appointment – a sort of pre-pitch schmooze to get him on side. Do you know how hard he is to get to see? Took me weeks to swing it and now . . . I can't believe I missed it. What kind of idiot forgets an appointment with Sir Colin Harrison?'

Ha! Maybe the same kind that forgets an appointment with Sir Sony Pictures.

'What did you say to her?' I ask.

'That I'd been stuck in a meeting that overran – couldn't get out of it. *Shit.*'

'Maybe if you go now, you can still make it,' I suggest encouragingly.

He looks at me disconsolately. 'She said he's tied up for the rest of the day. Told me not to bother . . . But you're right. If I run . . . It's worth a shot. Reckon I can get to Waterloo in half an hour?'

'Go for it,' I say. 'But drive carefully.'

I feel terrible. This is all my fault because I needed him here.

He circles the island, gathering his things. 'Pompous arsehole. You can't afford to put a foot wrong with this guy,' he mutters. 'I reckon I've kissed goodbye to the biggest bit of business we'd have won for . . . *Jesus!* How could I have been so *stupid?*' He kicks at the wall and then yelps out loud in pain.

Now *that* was stupid.

'Richard, calm down. You'll kill yourself before you get to the first traffic light.'

'I know, you're right . . . But, shit, have I got some serious sucking up to do if I'm going to save this one.'

I can save this one, I think, my mind whirling. It's like improv at college all over again. 'Pompous, did you say he was?'

'Completely puffed up with his own importance . . . But he's chairman of a massive oil company; I suppose he has a right to be. Look, I'd better be off. I'll just go for a quick piss.'

As he walks from the kitchen, I pick up his mobile from the island. The last time I looked at it, GUCCI was on the display. And look at where that got me. I hold it now, aware of the trouble I could be getting myself into. Big trouble – for Richard too. But something's surging inside me and I just can't stop it.

I'm scrolling through the menu, looking for the call list. No, I'm not searching for Gucci. I'm looking for Sir Hotshot Bigcheese. There he is – though on the display he's simply called SHELL. I press the button to return the call and realise my hand is shaking. I'm excited, scared witless . . . buzzing with adrenaline.

In the booth, headphones on, script at the ready. 'From the top, Fran . . . '

'Good afternoon, Sir Colin Harrison's office,' an efficient voice announces after a single ring.

First, my all-purpose, busy-but-courteous PA's voice: 'This is Cherie Blair's office. I have a call from Mrs Blair. Is Sir Colin free to take it?'

'One moment, please.'

And it's the . . . longest . . . moment . . . of . . . my . . . life. As it drags, I seriously consider hanging up. Can I even do Cherie any more? It's been so long.

'Hello . . . Just putting you through now.'

Shit. Too late to bottle it.

I listen to the clicks on the line, as if I'm waiting terrified in the wings, awaiting my cue to stumble forward into the blinding spotlight. And briefly, I think how amazing it is that you can get anyone on the phone if you're someone important – though, of course, I'm nobody at all—

'Che*rie*, hello . . . !'

Shit, I am so not a *nobody* any more. Right now, I'm Cherie bloody Blair.

'. . . Lovely to speak to you again,' booms the supremely confident voice.

Did he say *again*? Oh, fuck and shit! He *knows* her! Well, of course he does. These people belong to the small and exclusive club whose members rule the world. Why the hell didn't the possibility cross my mind before I started this?

'Sir Colin . . .' I begin haltingly. But I *know* this voice. Used to be able to do it in my sleep – actually *did* once, according to Richard. 'How are you?' *Yes*, the tone and pitch sound pretty near perfect.

'Please, how many times have I told you? You must call me Colin,' he says, as oily as one of his company's slicks.

'Of course . . . *Colin*.'

'And what can I do for you, Che*rie*?'

'Oh, nothing, nothing at all. I'm simply calling to apologise.'

'What on earth do you have to apologise for?'

'Tony has been monopolising our favourite marketeer, hasn't he?' Cherie explains sweetly – and, yes, I *am* Che*rie*, I *so* am.

'Who's that?' Sir Colin asks, sounding clueless.

'Richard . . . Richard Clark. Tony's had him tied up all day. Poor Richard. He's been looking at his watch for the past hour. He really should have said something, but you know . . .'

I let it hang there because although I can do the voice, I'm not exactly sure what I should be saying. Well, there isn't a *script*, is there? And now I've got to wrap it up because – shit, shit, shit! – I can hear the toilet flushing upstairs.

'Ah, so Richard's been with the PM?' Sir Colin muses, obviously impressed, and so he should be.

'What an amazing mind that man has. Just incredible. His advice is highly prized,' I say, aware that I may be *slightly* overselling the man who has now finished his piss and is clumping down the stairs. *Got to wrap this up.*

'*Highly* prized,' Sir Colin agrees. 'Tell the dear man not to worry. In fact, I'll call him myself. Rearrange our meeting at a time to suit him. It really isn't a problem.'

'Thank you, I knew you'd understand,' Cherie says quickly. Richard is now in the hall, now in the kitchen, now right in front of me. 'I must go. Thank you again.'

Richard frowns, looking at *his* mobile pressed to *my* ear.

Must get off the phone. Must think of a way of explaining this. Must—

'One moment, Che*rie*,' Sir Colin says. 'I must thank you for your advice.'

Oh God. What bloody advice?

'It was nothing,' Che*rie* says.

'You're too modest. It helped Catherine enormously. In fact, she wanted to send you a copy of the draft report, just for your information. Which address is best?'

Aaagghh! Go away! I don't want to do this any more.

'Oh, why don't you just send it to . . . Number Ten?'

'Really?'

If Sir Colin is surprised, you should see Richard's face. *Oh God . . .*

'*Absolutely*,' Che*rie* says, maybe a bit too squeakily. 'Now I really must—'

'Tell me, will you and Tony be at the CBI lunch next month?'

This man does not want to get off the phone, does he? Hasn't he got anything else to do?

'Do you know, I'll have to look at the diary. Possibly . . . if Tony isn't in . . . *Washington*. With George. Now, I really *must* run because . . .' Because what? The milkman's knocking? The gasman's here? '. . . I really should get on. My apologies on Tony's behalf once again. And see you *very* soon.'

I press the red button to end the call . . . and feel the weirdest mix of elation and terror. The way Richard is *staring* at me . . .

'Who was that? Why were you talking in that . . . Hey, that was Cherie Blair.'

Ah-ha, I *have* still got it.

But how the hell am I going to explain this?

'You've just called Harrison pretending to be Cherie Blair, haven't you?'

No need for explanations, then.

'I'm sorry! But I couldn't resist it,' I gabble. 'You said you were stuck in a meeting and you said he's pompous and I knew it would work because—'

I'm cut off by the mobile. It's ringing again. Richard looks at the display and I crane my neck to see it too.

SHELL.

He snatches the phone away from my view and marches into the hall.

I cower in the kitchen, not trying to listen this time, just waiting for the inevitable explosion of anger . . .

Two minutes later, he's back. I can't read his face.

'I cannot believe you did that,' he says evenly. 'And I'd sooner not think about what's going to happen the next time he sees the prime minister and his wife.'

Ah, I hadn't thought that far ahead.

'No worries,' he says, breaking into a wide grin. 'I told him Tone would prefer that no one knows I'm helping him out. He said he wouldn't mention it. Not even to Tone and Mrs Tone. Strictly hush-hush sort of thing.'

'Glad to be of service,' I say. Relief washes over me, though it's quickly replaced by the urge to run around the island, whooping with joy.

I feel *great*.

Like I had no idea that I would. Or even *could* any more.

Richard kills the moment by picking his stuff up and switching slickly back to work mode. 'I'll call you later. To see how Sureya is,' he says awkwardly.

'You do that.'

And once again, he turns to leave.

But halfway to the front door, he stops and turns round. 'It's *incredible*,' he says.

'What is?'

'What you can do. Do you *know* what you can do?'

'I'm not thinking about that. I'm just going to focus on Sureya for now.'

He shakes his head. A look on his face that I've never seen before. 'Jesus, Fran, imagine if it had been us. Imagine if we'd lost Molly or Thomas.'

No. I've been there once today and I never, ever want to go there again.

6

The children are in bed and I'm having a sandwich. Forcing myself to do something I haven't been doing much lately: eat. It's essential, apparently. My goodness, is that a space between my stomach and my waistband?

Mind the gap? I *love* the gap.

After Richard left this afternoon, I made myself do stuff. I dusted and hoovered until it was time to pick the kids up. Better that than stop and reflect. Then the children took my mind off the horror. At least they did until I saw Thomas through the kitchen window, joyously kicking a ball, practising tricks for his trial, his future spread gloriously before him. *All that potential.* I took such pleasure from it, and then felt such guilt.

Poor Sureya.

Poor Rosa.

I forced myself to move on. I emptied some kitchen cupboards and cleaned the shelves. Displacement activity, avoidance, running away . . . It got me through to the evening. The exhaustion has hit me at last. What a day – two days, I suppose, though they seem to have merged into a single sprawling mass. But it's going to end soon because I won't be able to keep my eyes open for very much longer.

I haven't heard from Richard, but having been deprived of his office for a day and a half, I'm assuming he'll be lost to us for a while. I wonder how Sir Colin is? The thought makes me smile, but not for long. I'm reminded that as well as Richard, I haven't heard from Michael either. I want to know how Sureya is, but I don't want to intrude. Besides, I'm having the twins tomorrow, so I'll speak to him then.

I finish my sandwich and look at my watch. Not long past nine. I haven't gone to bed this early for years, but tonight I'm going to have to make an exception.

The phone rings and I answer it quickly, assuming it must be Michael.

'Darling, it's me,' says a breathy and extremely un-Michael voice.

'Who?'

'It's *me*! *Fiona!*'

I know only one Fiona. My sister-in-law-from-hell. What does she want? It can't be me. She only ever calls when she's at least half certain Richard will be here.

'Hi, Fiona. Richard's stuck at work,' I say reflexively, ready for her to dictate a message as if I'm his secretary.

'I know,' she says, which confuses me. 'I just spoke to him. I can't believe what's happened. I really am *devastated*.'

How bizarre. She doesn't even know Sureya.

'Really?' I ask.

'Fran, of *course* I am,' she says indignantly. 'It's terrible news.'

Perhaps they do know each other. Did I introduce them at the party?

'It is awful, isn't it?' I say. 'But these things happen and the important thing is to give her some space now. She needs to grieve in peace.'

'Fran, why are you talking about yourself in the third person?'

'I'm not.'

'*Who* are you talking about, then?'

'Sureya,' I say, though of course I know now that not

only am I barking up the wrong tree, I'm also in the wrong bloody forest completely.

'I'm talking about you and Richard,' she says. 'He *told* me, Fran. *Everything.*'

I'm surprised. No, scrub that, I'm totally stunned. What the hell did he tell her for? I can't speak, but Fiona – never one to hold back – fills the silence. 'I wanted to invite you both to drinks on Friday evening. I'm being made a partner. Honestly, I can't believe it.'

'Well, I can. You're brilliant at your job. I remember you telling me about that case you won when—'

'*Fran*, I'm not talking about work.'

She's getting pissed off because now I'm barking up a fresh tree, but it's still the wrong one and it's in a forest even further away from the one I should be in. This lack of comprehension between us isn't new. It's been a problem since the day we met. I must admit that maybe once or twice, I've been, you know, deliberately obtuse. But not tonight – I'm way too tired for games.

'I'm talking about your separation,' she explains. 'About him meeting someone else. I am so, so sorry.'

Now, I find that hard to believe. I shouldn't be surprised that Richard has told her, actually. His sister can be very insistent. I might be able to fool the entire population of North London that all is well in the Clark household, but not Richard. I can imagine him keeping up the pretence for only minutes before caving in and giving her every detail. Even down to what we were wearing and who was standing where at the moment we went our separate ways. What surprises me is that she's *so, so sorry*. She hates me. We're hardly what anybody would call close. I'm probably closer to Sir Colin and he thinks I'm someone else.

'Don't be sorry,' I say. 'You know how it is. These things happen.'

'Well, they bloody well shouldn't. How could he? All those years you've invested in him and his bloody career. It's terrible, Fran.'

And she does sound distraught. Much more of this and I might just have to start consoling *her*.

'It's all just so *obvious* as well,' she continues. 'She works for *Gucci*, for God's sake, she's ten years his junior . . .'

She's only twenty-nine? Jesus, the things I wish I still didn't know.

'. . . Honestly, I thought he was better than that. I never had him down as the type who'd go for the stupid, pathetic mid-life crisis thing. I'm ashamed of him.'

Bloody hell. Is she talking about the brother who turns water into wine and, on a good day, makes the dead walk? Is she *really* slagging him off?

'Well, it's not quite as simple as that,' I say.

And am I really defending him?

'Fran, you can't tell me about Richard. I *know* him. Better than anyone.'

That could be a sly dig at me, but I let it go.

'How are you coping?' she asks.

'Oh, you know, I'm just trying to keep things normal for the children.'

'Poor Molly,' she says. 'She's so young as well . . .'

No mention of Thomas?

'. . . What are you going to tell her?'

Obviously not.

'At the moment, nothing. Richard and I are going to talk and see if we can work things out, and, well, I guess we'll take it from there.'

'Why don't you talk to *me*?' she says gently. 'Maybe it'll help.'

Talk to her? I'd rather talk to my mother and that's saying something.

'Fiona, I'm so sorry, but I'm going to have to go. There's someone at the door.'

'You've got a cordless, haven't you?'

Damn.

'Yes, but it's the people campaigning against the, er . . . the new launderette.'

'At this time? What new launderette?'

Yes, what new launderette?

'Well . . . they're opening a launderette on the Broadway. The people around here think it'll lower the tone. Turn it into Albert Square or something. They look really angry. I'd better go and see what they want before they put a placard through the window.'

'Oh, shall I call you back?'

'Don't worry, I'll call you. Later. Or maybe tomorrow. Bye for now, *bye!*'

I hang up before she can say another word.

I can't believe I'm laughing. I can't believe Fiona either. When I was supposedly in the bosom of her family, she did her best to ignore me. Now that I've been cut adrift, she wants to be my friend? I'm too weary to try and make sense of it.

Go to bed, Fran.

I'm halfway up the stairs, halfway to sweet, hopefully dreamless oblivion, when the phone rings again.

Fiona? Ringing back to see if the Militant Anti-coin-op Tendency has left? I can't bear the prospect of talking to her again.

I know what to do.

Cherie Blair has inspired me.

I did the voiceover for a scary teen flick years back. That'll do nicely. I pick up the phone in the hall. 'Hello. You have reached the Potterton Asylum,' I intone with inhuman grimness. 'If you are calling about visiting times, please press one. If you are calling about job opportunities, please press two. And remember, you don't have to be mad to work here, but it hel—'

'Fran, stop it,' Mum says. 'What are you like? I thought you'd stopped that sort of nonsense when you were fifteen. Remember the trouble it used to get you into?'

She's right. The spoof calls didn't start with Cherie. I was nearly suspended after I'd phoned the headmaster as Cilla Black. I told him he'd been selected for a *Blind Date* teachers' special and it was going to be a *lorra, lorra laughs* . . . Oh, happy days.

'Sorry, Mum,' I say sheepishly. 'Just trying to relieve some tension.'

'What tension?' she asks, suddenly concerned.

'Oh, something's happened to one of our friends. No one you know,' I say breezily. I don't want to talk about anything horrible for the rest of the day. The rest of the year would be good, but I'll settle on just the one day.

As I listen to her tell me about her week – the local farmers' market, the bowls club social – something strikes me. I can kid the chairman of a multinational company that I'm the prime minister's wife, but I can't fool my own mother. Could I ever?

'So what do you think?' she asks.

Oh, dear. Missed that. 'Sorry, Mum, about what?'

'About the weekend,' she says. 'The children could sleep over on Saturday night, and you and Richard could go out. I'm sure he works too hard. I can't remember the last time we saw him . . .'

Should I tell her? And if I am going to tell her, wouldn't now be the perfect moment? Fiona knows. Why not Mum? And telling her won't exactly be like taking out a full-page ad in a national newspaper, as if I'm some celeb milking her personal tragedy for its PR value . . .

'*Hunk Hollywood and Starlet Sparkle regret to announce their immediate separation and would like to thank all their fans for their support during this difficult time. They also request that the media afford them some privacy, although Ms Sparkle can be seen doing damaged-yet-still-beautiful when entering the Ivy at seven thirty tonight.*'

She's my mum. I'm going to have to tell her sometime. Aren't I?

But if I tell her Richard has gone, it becomes definite. OFFICIAL. Would it be possible to suppress the news for ever? Not that she'd sob despairingly for her abandoned daughter. Mum isn't like that. But the stoic silence that she does so well would kill me. Do I really want to deal with that now?

'That's a great idea, Mum,' I say. 'I'll drop them off after football. Is that OK?'

'Lovely. Al wants to take Thomas to the kart track in Hadley Wood. It all sounds a bit dangerous to me, but you know, boys will be boys.' She laughs.

Al is a big fan of motor sports. A man at the wheel of something noisy and fast qualifies as an alpha of the species. No doubt he wants Thomas to begin his alpha-male apprenticeship behind the wheel of a dinky go-kart. Al's hero is Ayrton Senna. A guy who died as he'd lived – i.e. at two hundred miles per hour. Now that was a real man.

'Thomas would love that,' I say, deliberately *not* thinking about his tiny, mangled body being pulled from the twisted wreckage of a dinky go-kart. Oh God, why did I have to go and remember Ayrton Senna?

'I'll have them back in plenty of time on Sunday,' Mum says. 'You know, for the Autumn Fair.'

Shit!

After one recent visit from my kids, my mum knows their school events schedule better than I do. I'd completely forgotten about it. Never mind lethal go-kart pile-ups, now

I've got something *serious* to worry about. Sureya's tragedy has pulled me right out of the Arlington loop. Cassie, Annabel and the hateful Natasha have been out of sight and blissfully out of mind. But now they're right back in it. The Autumn bloody Fair. I wish it would just go away. But I've made a commitment. Hook a bloody Duck.

No particular expertise required.

Damn and shit. What do I do? Ring the head witch and tell her I can't make it? That will just get me slagged off all the way from here to the Broadway. Or do I turn up and ignore the nudges and sly looks? Which will also get me talked about all the way, etc. However I play it, I can't win. Damn and shit again.

Maybe I should do nothing. After all, I'm practised at bottling out of commitments. And if I can cope with Isabel and Harvey's wrath, I can withstand Cassie, can't I? The difference, of course, is that I never have to see Is and Harv again, but for the next six years at least, I'll have daily doses of Cass and co.

Mum eventually hangs up, unlike me, happy. I've hardly smoked today and the thought has me reaching for the packet. I light up, slump down on to a stair and take a long, despairing drag.

For God's sake, get a grip, Fran.

My best friend has just lost her baby and here I am losing the plot over stupid Hook a Duck.

Get yourself to bed immediately.

7

It's somewhere between Thursday and Friday. For argument's sake, let's call it very early Friday morning.

Yesterday was Rosa's funeral. Just Sureya, Michael and his parents, who had travelled up from Bath. And Rosa in a heartbreakingly tiny box. I sent flowers. Pink roses. Not terribly sombre, but somehow it felt right.

As I'd promised, I looked after the twins – one commitment I've come good on, then. My plan was tea at Pizza Express.

Let's just say it wasn't exactly a breeze.

Funny how you forget what it's like going out with toddlers once yours are no longer small, isn't it?

The waiters weren't exactly thrilled at the array of spilt drinks and smashed glasses and dropped salads, but I knew a bigger than usual tip would buy them off. Thomas was less easy to appease. If he has difficulty relating to kids his own age, his aversion to toddlers is total.

But all in all, it was good – relatively speaking. It wasn't until we got home that things went downhill.

I let Mina and Jasmin watch CBeebies until bedtime. Well, they watched some of it. In between, they explored. Or rather, they *wrecked*. I spent the evening following them, clearing up the trail of devastation and saving them from serious injury.

By ten o'clock, they were ready for bed. There were no cries of resistance as I took them upstairs. Mostly because they'd fallen asleep in front of the telly.

I think, somehow, they must be used to an earlier bedtime. Another thing I'd forgotten about small children.

I put them in blow-up beds in Molly's room. She was delighted. It gave her a chance to be mum – her favourite game. Good luck, sweetheart, I thought as I left the room.

Then I said goodnight to Thomas, who'd been holed up in his room all evening with his friend, the PlayStation. With his trial two days away, the excitement – and the nerves – were building. We talked strategy for a while.

'Do you think they'll let me play in my Arsenal kit?' he asked.

'Oh, I don't think they'll care what shirt you wear.'

'Yeah, but they're *Palace*. They hate Arsenal.'

'Just wear your blue tracksuit, then. You look great in that.'

'*Yeah*, but my Arsenal kit's *lucky*.'

He was growing exasperated. Mostly, it seemed, with me.

'I know! Wear your Arsenal shirt under your blue sweatshirt. Then they'll never know.'

'*Yeah*, but then I'll be too *hot*.'

I took a deep breath. 'Let's not worry about it now. We can decide on Saturday morning. Go to sleep now.'

He let me kiss him and I backed out of his room, pleased – this had been one of our better goodnight scenarios.

'Mum,' he said as I was pulling the door to, 'I can't wait, you know.'

'Neither can I.'

Downstairs, I managed two drags on my first cigarette since school pick-up before Armageddon kicked off. Mina and Jasmin were awake and were less than happy to find themselves in a strange room in a strange house. They were inconsolable.

'Why don't we read a story?' Molly suggested brightly.

Good idea, I thought. Well, it couldn't possibly make things any worse.

And it very nearly worked. Halfway through *The Three Little Pigs*, they were quiet and their eyelids were drooping. Then I blew it. I let Molly do the voice of the wolf. Her interpretation was brilliant – brilliantly terrifying, that is. As the twins' screams kicked off again, Molly joined in. Angry wails directed at the two hysterical baby-monsters who were not only ruining her night, but who also had no appreciation of the skill and effort required to do a really good, scary wolf voice.

'Will you tell them to SHUT UP!' Thomas yelled from across the landing.

Thanks, Thomas, I hadn't thought of that.

I don't wish to sound overly dramatic or anything, but an hour later, I thought I might kill myself.

Then I had a brainwave. Ice cream! The twins were practically junkies for the stuff. And you know what? *It worked.* They sat in their beds, eating chocolate ice cream at gone midnight – Molly too – and when they were done, they put their heads on their pillows and slept.

Just like that.

Parenting textbooks, eh? Maybe I should write one myself.

As I looked at their happy, slumbering faces, I felt overcome with sadness. For Jasmin and Mina, and for Molly and Thomas too. How little they knew of the shit that lies ahead and how little we can do to protect them from it. I swore to myself that whatever happens between Richard and me, my children will not suffer. I'll never forget how miserable my childhood home was. No dad, no money, a mum who was always at work. My kids have got every opportunity, and starting from now, I'm going to make sure they grab life and live it.

And real life can just fuck off.

★   ★   ★

But it won't, will it?

Real life has a habit of interrupting, even at the strangest times. Like now: 3.30 a.m.

The phone is ringing.

I'm in bed, but sleep has been fitful. I've got Sureya on my mind and she won't budge. And now – *oh God* – the phone is ringing. I'm not a lover of that sound at three thirty in the morning. I reach for the receiver, and of course, I'm not expecting good news.

'Fran, it's me,' says an echoey voice.

'Summer? Is that you?'

'That's what I just said,' Summer replies flatly. 'It's me all right.'

'It's gone three in the morning.'

'No it's not. It's seven thirty. A beautiful sunset.'

'*Summer*, it's the middle of the night—'

'Look, if I'd wanted a conversation about the time, I'd have called the speaking clock.' She sounds bleak.

'Well, what *do* you want to have a conversation about?' I ask, familiar panic rising. 'It's not the baby, is it?'

'No, why would it be?'

'Oh, it's just that . . .' What am I going to do? Tell her about Sureya now, on the phone, at this hour? I don't think so. As much as I'd been dying to give her the news about Sureya's pregnancy before, the news of her miscarriage will have to wait. 'No, nothing,' I say. 'Just wondering what's up.'

Silence. And is she crying? 'Summer? What is it?'

'God, it was fucking dreadful, Fran,' she says at last. 'They made me hang around for days and then they wouldn't even test me. Said there was no point.'

'What,' they gave it to Sharon Stone?'

'*That* I could have understood. No, they've got Angelina fucking Jolie. She'd signed before I got here.'

'Why the hell did they let you fly all the way out there, then?'

'Good question. The fuckers. Laurence pleaded ignorance, of course.'

'But isn't it his film? Doesn't he have some say?'

'Oh, yes, he has some say all right. And what he said was, "But, baby, it's Ange*leee*na!" Arsehole. Said the part had *grown* and they needed a *marquee name*, blah, blah, fucking blah. Said Sharon's pissed off too – like I care. Begged me to see the *difficult* position he's in.'

'And what did you say?'

'I told him the position he's in is on his knees with the studio's dick in his mouth. Oh, how he laughed.'

It's too late – or too early – to think straight. I'm stuck with an unwanted mental image of Laurence, on his knees, the studio's dick in his mouth, when Summer's voice cuts in.

'I hate the shallow, spineless bastard,' she spits. 'I hate his fucking guts.'

'So would anyone, Summer,' I tell her and mean it.

'Anyway, fuck him. I'm outta here. I'm coming home.'

'Right. God, so George Clooney. It's over, then . . .'

But hang on. When did Summer ever call me to cry over a rejection? She takes such things in her stride, part and parcel of being a working actress. Admittedly, this is a *big* rejection – a Hollywood-size rejection – but even so . . . Is there something else going on here?

'Have you told Laurence about the baby?' I ask.

A big, choking sob at the other end of the line.

I'll take that as a yes.

'What a *wanker*, Fran!' She's yelling now. 'What a total fucking *prick*.'

'What did he say?'

'He told me I'd done this *deliberately*. Can you believe it?

Like I'm part of some conspiracy to destroy his life . . . I told you, men are bad news. Should have listened to my own advice. How could I have been such an idiot?'

'You weren't an idiot, Summer,' I soothe. 'You went with your feelings, that's all. But you're right. *Fuck* him. You so do not need a man in your life, especially not *that* man. And it's not all bad. You're going to have a baby. Isn't that wonderful?'

Because *wasn't* it wonderful when we spoke about it last week?

Not any more it seems. 'What's so fucking wonderful? I can't have a baby. What was I thinking?'

'Listen, when are you coming home?'

'Plane leaves in a couple of hours.'

'OK, we'll talk about it then.'

Nothing.

'OK?'

I can actually hear her pulling herself together.

'Whatever,' she says. And then, 'You OK? How did it go with Big Dick on Sunday?'

'Fine. I'll tell you when you're home.'

'OK. I'll call you. Miss you.'

'I miss you too,' I tell her. 'I mean it, Summer. Everything's going to be fine. And don't worry about Angelina. She might have freak lips and snog her brother and wear vials of blood round her neck, but she's positively ordinary compared with you.'

I listen to the very ordinary sound of the dialling tone.

8

Friday. I mean *proper* Friday, with daylight and everything. It's eight o'clock now, but I've been up since just after six. That was when Mina and Jasmin woke, bright-eyed, bushy-tailed and apparently *thrilled* to find themselves in a strange room in a strange house. Three-year-old logic – I'll never get it.

We're all in the kitchen. It's breakfast time. I'm sticking close to the twins, who are on high stools at the island. I need to be close enough to catch anything that falls – cereal bowl, juice beaker, small child . . . Molly looks knackered. She's only had six of her mandatory twelve hours' princess-sleep. She's liable to slip into a coma at assembly. Thomas is half-heartedly chewing a slice of toast. They say a boy needs his father and I think this one definitely does. With two extra females in the house, the poor kid is drowning in a sea of oestrogen.

The phone rings, making me jump.

'It sounds noisy there,' Richard says.

'I've got Mina and Jasmin,' I explain.

'Oh, yeah, the funeral,' he says matter-of-factly. 'How did it go?'

How did it go? It's not a meeting, Richard. '*Oh, it went fine. Like clockwork apart from a slight overrun, but all targets were met by the time things wrapped up.*'

That's not fair. It's not his fault. How do we know what to say or how to be at a time like this? Unless you've lost a child, how could you know?

'I don't know how it went, to be honest,' I say. 'I haven't heard from Sureya or Michael. I expect it was grim.'

'Jesus, of course it was,' he mutters, his voice tinged with self-rebuke.

I wonder where he is. I listen for telltale sounds. Is she with him . . . ? *Stop it, Fran.* 'Anyway, what's up?' I ask.

'It's about Thomas's trial tomorrow. I was wondering if . . . well, I'd like to come with you . . . if that's OK with you.'

My heart leaps. Thomas will be thrilled. And, yes, I'm thrilled too. Mostly because . . . *Beckenham?* I have absolutely no idea how to get there.

'That'd be great,' I say, as coolly as I can manage. 'Be here at ten,' I say, watching Jasmin nudge her cereal bowl unnervingly close to the edge of the island. 'Look, I don't want to sound rude, but is that it? Only—'

'One other thing. I saw Sir Colin yesterday.'

'Oh, how did it go?' I ask matter-of-factly, which is OK because this time we *are* talking about a meeting.

'It went well. No, better than that. Fran, the guy *loves* me. Come the pitch, I reckon I could present Thomas's homework and he'll buy it.'

'Well done,' I say sincerely. 'I knew you'd be able to retrieve things.'

'Nothing to do with me. Thank Cherie. He didn't once mention Tone and me, but he was all nudges and knowing winks. Can you believe it? He's the chairman of bloody Shell and *I* make *him* feel— *Shit*, what was that?'

The smash of china on tiles was loud. The wail that follows is louder still.

'Gotta go, Richard. Bye.'

I hang up and run to Jasmin, who's on the floor, lying in a puddle of milk and Ricicles.

*   *   *

'Daddy's coming with us tomorrow,' I say to Thomas on the walk to school.

'Don't call him *Daddy*. God, Mum, I'm nearly eleven, not bloody two.'

'Hey, don't swear,' I say sternly, but then smile because *he* is (sort of) and I don't want to spoil the moment.

'After Palace, are we *all* going to Granny Ruth's? Daddy *never* goes there with us,' he says, tellingly reverting to Daddy.

I don't have the heart to say that no, Daddy won't be changing the habit of a lifetime. 'We'll see,' I say.

I watch him run on ahead, bouncing his football. I feel a glow because this is as close to *sorted* as I've ever seen him. See? Brushing things under the carpet does no harm whatsoever. Quite the opposite, it can actually be a good thing.

I push Jasmin and Mina along in their double buggy and we're only a hundred yards from the school gate. I almost jump when I hear the voice that calls out to me.

'Fran!' I can feel her Prozac-heated smile burning into my back.

Damn! I've managed to avoid her since Monday.

'Natasha,' I say, turning my head slowly.

'You didn't come to the ARPS meeting yesterday. Everything all right?'

'Not really,' I say, facing forward again and trying to pick up speed. But she keeps pace with me – no mean feat, considering the shoes she's wearing. I'm just thankful for the double buggy. It means there's no room on the pavement for her to pull up alongside me.

'Oh my God! What's wrong? It's not Richard, is it?' she cries, her voice saturated with concern.

I'm fucked if I'm telling you, bitch. 'No, not Richard.' I stop abruptly and stare her out. 'I didn't come to the meeting because nobody told me about it.'

'Count yourself lucky, my love,' she laughs. 'It was dull, dull, dull. Just Grupenführer Cassie giving us our final orders before Operation Autumn Fair.'

We're at the gate. I push my way through, but the path widens on the other side and now she draws alongside me. She looks down at the twins.

'They're Sureya's little girls, aren't they?' she says. 'Too busy for the school run, is she?'

'Something like that,' I say curtly. I'm damned if I'm giving her the truth. I know from bitter experience what she'd do with it . . . *'Well, it's terribly sad, but she only has herself to blame, the way she pushes herself with all those drama workshops. Some women need to be told they can't have it all.'* God, I can hear it now and the thought makes me sick.

As I peel away from her to go to the nursery, she has one last stab at meaningful conversation. 'Are you sure there's nothing you want to talk about? You know what they say: it's good to talk.' She throws her head back and laughs as if it's the funniest joke in the world.

She can keep her Prozac, I decide. I'd rather be fucked up *naturally* than fucked up on medication.

'No, really, everything's cool,' I say.

'Good, good. Here, take this.' She hands me a flyer. 'Cassie will never forgive me if I leave anyone out . . . And you know where I am if you want a chat,' she says to my back. I don't turn round.

Anyone still think Judas was the last word in betrayal? For what she's done, Natasha can go to hell. Judas is already there. At least she'll have a mate.

On the walk home, I unfold the sheet of paper she thrust at me. It bears instructions from ARPS; everything I ever wanted to know about the Autumn Fair but was afraid to ask. When and where to meet, what to bring, etiquette.

'Use of the word "autumn" is acceptable. However, please refrain from using such terms as "the gateway to winter" or "the harbinger of colder climes" as these belittle the September-to-November period, which under anti-discrimination legislation has the right to be judged on equal terms with the other three seasons.'

Well, not quite, but really, it wouldn't surprise me.

The leaflet and bumping into Natasha has made my mind up. I'm doing the fair. I'm not going to welsh on a commitment, even if it's only to run the Hook a stupid Duck stand. I'm not going to hide and I've got nothing to be ashamed of. I don't need a husband by my side. I can face those women alone, I know I can . . .

Besides, Mum rang again last night. She wants to bring the kids back early on Sunday so she can come with us, which is a good thing because it means I don't have to face those women on my own.

When I get home, I clear up the breakfast things, put a load in the washing machine and make myself a coffee, all the while aware that I am only putting it off. Now I've run out of excuses. I dial Sureya's number. Michael picks up.

'Thanks for having the girls,' he says with forced cheeriness.

'Oh, my pleasure. They were absolutely no trouble, honestly.'

'Did they sleep OK? They're not brilliant with change.'

'No problem. Slept like angels.'

'Good . . . Thanks . . .'

I listen to his breathing for a moment.

'Do you want me to pick them up from nursery?' I ask. 'I don't mind.'

'No, it's OK. I'll do that. I've got time off work and . . .' He trails off again.

'How is she, Michael?' The only question I've wanted to ask.

'I don't know . . . Terrible, really, if you want the truth.'

'Do you want me to come round today? Talk to her?'

A sigh that speaks volumes, yet barely begins to describe the sadness he must be feeling. 'God, Fran, not even I know what to say. What can I say . . . ? She was so tiny. That little box . . .'

I listen to his voice crack. Poor Michael. He of all people must know the appalling grief Sureya is going through, and yet even he finds it impossible to comfort her. And if he can't find the words, how the hell would I?

But this is Sureya, my *friend*. I won't, in my usual fashion, run away. For once in my life, I'm doing the right thing.

'I'll have the twins again tonight,' I say. 'Give you both a bit more space.'

'No. Thanks, but yesterday was more than enough. They need to come home. Besides, I think it'll do us both some good to spend time with them.'

'Yes, it will. They're beautiful, amazing girls, Michael.'

'They are, aren't they . . . ?'

I can hear him choking again.

'Look, I'll go,' I say. 'But if there's anything I can do, call. Promise me.'

'OK. Thanks, Fran . . . You've been great, you know . . .'

He puts the phone down and it's horrible to think there's nothing else I can do. Except be here if they need me, I suppose. And that's not really very much at all, is it?

After I'd put the phone down, I thought of Summer. She sounded more desperate than I'd ever heard her when she called last night. Now she was five miles high, flying home, agonising over what to do about her baby. I wondered if she

257

knew how lucky she was to have the choice. But I stopped myself going down that road. The comparison wasn't fair – Summer is not Sureya. Anyway, the last thing anyone in a pit of despair wants to hear is that there's someone worse off – even though there always is.

At that point in the morning, I needed to take my mind off the ghastliness of real life. I found escape in tackling the mess that is the study – the home office, as the estate agent described it. I didn't get very far. I opened a cupboard and out tumbled a stack of photo albums.

They surround me now. I'm sitting on the floor, smoking, revisiting happier times. Photos of Richard and me, a pair of twenty-somethings with our friends, making life resemble one long party. Most of the pictures, though, feature Thomas and Molly, and it's been good to look at those. They've reminded me that the good times didn't stop completely when children arrived. I *have* had some fun, post-kids.

Not on this holiday, however. An album of snaps taken at Disneyland Paris sits on my lap. We went when Molly wasn't quite two. She loved it, but she was a baby – she'd have been happy with five days in a plastic paddling pool. It was Thomas who hated it. Richard and I realised what a stupid mistake we'd made on our first morning. Every ride that Thomas wanted to go on came with a height restriction, and titch that he was (still is, bless him), he fell way short. But he was six going on seven going on seventeen and he was desperate to defy death. He wanted to be flung upside down, hurled sideways and twisted back to front, all at several hundred miles an hour, *pleeeease*. The baby rides that made Molly gurgle with delight made him sick. He did *not* want a cuddle from Mickey, thank you very much, and he spat on the ground Minnie walked on.

The holiday was so awful that I can't even look at the pictures without feeling tense. Turn the page quickly and . . . That's better. Portugal, two months later – an impulse purchase, made to compensate for the Disney disaster. This time, we played it safe and chose the most five-star, kid-friendly hotel we could find. With the children in the hotel's kids' club, Richard and I enjoyed our freedom like two drug-starved junkies given a free run of a crack house. That was the week we water-skied, windsurfed, paraglided and . . .

Jesus Christ, I cannot believe I did this. But I'm looking at the picture – irrefutable photographic evidence. Me in T-shirt and shorts, my arms outstretched before me, blue, blue sky behind me and below me – a hundred and twenty bloody feet below me – the Atlantic Ocean.

That was the week I bungee-jumped!

We were driving along the coast, looking for somewhere to have lunch, when we saw the platform at the top of a cliff. 'Let's stop for a quick look,' Richard said.

'Do we have to?' I asked. 'I'm starving.'

Why would I want to gaze at people *paying* to be pushed off a very high cliff with only a skinny bit of string tied to their ankles? Well, that's how it looked from afar. But I indulged him. We stopped. Just for a look.

'We have *got* to have a go,' he said as soon as we were out of the car.

'No *way* am I—'

'It's perfectly safe.'

'No, my love, safe is sitting at home and watching this sort of thing on the telly – preferably while strapped into the sofa.'

But he begged and cajoled, used every trick in the book. He is a very good salesman and I knew he wouldn't give up.

I think I did it out of guilt. He was so desperate for us both to do it, and I knew I'd been a pain to live with – did I mention the post-natal depression? Whatever. All I knew was that for the first time in ages – be it the sun, the sea, the sex (the *sex*!) or just the fact of having a break – I was having the time of my life and I didn't want it to stop there at the roadside just because I wimped out of one tiny-weeny bungee jump.

So we jumped.

Richard went first. I couldn't watch. I didn't open my eyes until he'd been winched back on to the platform, his head and shoulders wet from a brief dip in the ocean, his eyes wide with excitement. Then it was my turn. And it really was the most exhilarating thing I have ever done. OK, so Richard and the Grim Reaper (the guy who was running the show) spent half an hour talking me into it. And in the end, they virtually pushed me off the edge because the queue behind me was growing a tiny bit restless. ('Are you bloody well jumping, or what? Because if you're not, piss off and let someone else have a go.')

But I did it!

Afterwards, we had a long, sun-soaked lunch. Lobster, ice-cold beer and laughter as we relived the experience over and over. The thrill of *flying* and the better-than-sex rush that just wouldn't go away.

We both agreed we should live like that *all the time*. From now on, we were going to seize the moment, try new things just for the hell of it, see the entire world, be spontaneous, mad, wild, whatever.

Then, obviously, we had to go and pick the kids up and Molly was crying and Thomas was yelling at us for leaving him with a bunch of strangers and we kind of forgot about seizing the moment because real life had taken over. As it does.

But the memory is wonderful. More than that, the photograph of me *airborne* gives me strength. If I can jump off a bloody cliff, why should I be cowed by the ARPS witches? Even, for that matter, by Gucci Girl? OK, so just the thought of them makes my knees buckle, but that's all right. All I have to do is pretend they don't exist.

Pretending *works*. It's like a miracle cure.

And they thought Freud was clever.

I make a start on putting the albums away, but stop when the phone rings.

'Fran, hi. Chris at Saatchi here,' says Chris at Saatchi.

'*Chris!*' My beam must light the room. 'I thought you'd forgotten me.'

'I'm sorry. Been meaning to call you for a couple of days, but it's been mad here.'

Yes, I remember those days.

'Don't worry,' I reassure him. 'I understand.'

'No, honestly, I'm not bullshitting,' he says, reading me wrong. 'I really wanted to go for that drink. I wanted to thank you for a great party.'

'Was it? I think I was too . . . er . . . *merry* to notice,' I laugh.

'You were merry? I could barely get out of bed the next day.'

And suddenly it's just like old times. *Your hangover? What about mine?* That old routine. And it has to be said I'm thankful for it.

'Look, we have got some serious catching up to do,' he continues, 'but something's come up . . .'

Here we go. There's always a *but*.

'. . . You can really help me out with something. I think I told Richard when I rang, but I didn't give him the details. I wanted to speak to you first.'

Oh my God. There is no *but*. Where's he going with this?

'Are you still there?'

'Yes, sorry, just listening. Go on.'

'Right. We're doing something for the Commission for Racial Equality.'

'Yeah,' I say slowly.

'It's a huge international anti-racism thing. The Americans have made a two-minute film that's going to run on all the US networks and we've made a British version for the CRE. It's going to air on all five channels simultaneously – I can't believe we've got them to agree to it.'

'It sounds great,' I say, wondering where the hell I fit in.

'It is. It's fantastic. Basically, it's a two-minute tracking shot down a street lined with shops – corner shops, chippies, Chinese takeaways, sari shops, kebab houses, the lot. It's mobbed with people of every different colour and race. Anyway, as we pass all this different ethnic stuff, the VO changes seamlessly to represent each race. The line is "Sixty million people, one voice" . . . Sorry, it probably sounds shit the way I'm describing it, but it looks amazing . . . '

He's gushing. He sounds very excited.

'. . . You still there, Fran?'

'Yes, just trying to take it all in.' I don't add that I'm also feeling slightly nauseous – I can sense what's coming.

'We got a tape of the American version the other day. It's been voiced by Robin Williams and that's what makes it. He's done an amazing job. He goes from Alabama trailer park to Ivy League patrician in the space of a syllable. It's, like, *breathtaking*. We've got a hell of a lot to live up to with our version, I'm telling you.'

I have got to get a grip. I *know* what's coming now. My head is spinning. His energy and enthusiasm are making me dizzy.

'Anyway, Fran, that's our problem. The voice. We've tried

five or six people and we thought we had it cracked. John Sessions did a great read.'

'Oh, he's terrific,' I say. I've worked with him and he is.

'Yeah, we thought so too. But then the Robin Williams tape came in. He just isn't cutting it, I'm afraid.'

He's afraid? *I'm* afraid. Very afraid.

'We've tried 'em all. Rory Bremner, Roni Ancona, Catherine Tate, Jon Culshaw . . . None of them are quite right. Come on, you know what I'm getting at. This script has your name on it.'

'But I haven't worked for years, Chris.'

'Oh, don't give me that crap. Talent like yours does not fade away . . .'

Doesn't it?

'. . . You were the best and you still fucking well are.'

Am I?

'Look, it's yes or no time. We've got to record Thursday next week. I mean, feel free to say no . . . But when the blight of racism grows and society completely disintegrates, just because we couldn't get a VO as good as Robin Williams, well, I hope you can live with your conscience.'

He's joking, isn't he? Of course he is. But he's being serious too: it *is* yes or no time.

'Well . . . ?'

'Well what?' I ask stupidly. But I'm trying to buy myself time.

'You going to help us out, or not?'

Honestly, can I do it? I didn't show up for the last booking I had. Then I blew it with Isabel and Harvey. Do I seriously think I can go up against Robin A-list Williams . . . ?

I'm standing on a tiny platform, more than a hundred feet above the sea . . .

'I'm so honoured that you're asking me, Chris. Of course I'll do it.'

He whoops with delight and – just as I did when I plummeted towards the Atlantic – so do I.

9

Saturday. It's ten fifteen. We're running late – I think. We're supposed to be in Beckenham at twelve. Where the hell is Beckenham? I believe it may be in Kent. But . . . er . . . where's that? I have no idea how long it'll take to get there. Thank God Richard the navigator is coming. But why isn't he here yet? I'm beginning to panic.

'Molly, get your shoes on,' I yell.

'Aw, do I *have* to go?'

'Oh, would you like to stay here? Have the house to yourself?'

'Can I?' she asks excitedly.

'Absolutely not. Get your shoes on.'

Thomas – who normally has to be dragged forcibly from the house – has been ready since dawn. He's sitting in the garden, *focusing*. In the end, he went for the full Arsenal kit, right down to the Thierry Henry-endorsed shin pads. I wouldn't be surprised if he slept in it – I'll check the sheets later for stud marks.

I look at my watch. It's precisely one minute later than when I last looked. *Where the hell is Richard?* I hear the front door open and rock back, relieved, on to the kitchen counter.

'Sorry I'm late,' he says as he strides into the room. 'They're digging the road up just the other side of the Broadway.'

'Shouldn't we be making a move?' I ask – it's not so much a question, more a nudge back towards the front door. But instead he heads for the fridge.

'No hurry,' he says, pulling out a juice carton and a pork pie.

'But the traffic.'

'It's only bad on the Broadway. We're not even going that way.'

'Oh . . . OK.'

I watch him pour himself a glass of orange juice and unwrap the wax paper from the pie. He looks at me *looking*. 'You don't mind, do you?' he asks, his mouth full. 'Only I didn't get any breakfast.'

I shake my head.

But actually, I mind intensely. What does he think? That he *lives* here? Didn't he forfeit fridge rights when he walked out two weeks ago? Funny that, isn't it? I long for him to come back, but the moment he acts as if he has, I resent it. Sometimes the most unfathomable person around here is me.

'I needed to pick something up on the way here. Held me up longer than I'd bargained for,' he says casually, as if we've got all day. 'But what can you do, eh? When you've got stuff to do . . .' He leaves it hanging as he demolishes the pie. God, he's irritating. Like he's the most important man on the planet and God forbid anything should hold him up.

'Why? What *stuff* do you have to do?' I ask.

'Oh, you know, just stuff. What time do you think we'll be through today?'

'*Richard.*' I want to scream it, but suppress the urge so that I only sound the tiniest bit cross. 'If we're holding you back from doing anything *important* today, feel free to just bugger off and do it, won't you?'

'Oh, no, sorry, you've misunderstood,' he says, back-pedalling faster than an ant spotting the elephant stampede. 'It's just that I was going to go back to see Bel after. I've got some stuff for her, that's all.'

He sees my face go from cross to molten-red fury and back-peddles even faster. 'But you know it's really not important. At all. In fact, it can even wait until . . . until tomorrow. Or the day after. In fact, I don't even know why I mentioned it, it's so unimportant.'

I *hate* the sound of that woman's name. And with it, the reminder that she is now the love of his life. I'm not speaking. I'm – very noisily it has to be said – putting mugs back into cupboards and deliberately not looking at him. Stupid, stupid man with his stupid, stupid *things to do.*

'Er, where's Thomas?' he asks, sensing my annoyance – don't ask me how – and very sensibly looking for a way out.

'In the garden – doing some mental prepping.'

'I'll go and have a word.'

He heads outside and I watch them through the window. Father and son. What's he saying to him? 'Best not to get your hopes up too high' or 'Crystal Palace isn't the only football club in the world'? Like he'd know.

I feel resentment again. What makes him think he can just turn up and take over the parenting? He hasn't once shown an interest in Thomas's football dreams and now he's coming over all Kevin Keegan. Or whoever the latest football manager sensation is. OK, I don't claim to know anything about football either, but at least I've *been here.*

Molly comes into the kitchen, shoes on. As I kneel down to tie them, Richard returns from the garden and she runs to him, laces trailing. He bends down to hug her and a fresh wave of resentment replaces the last one. Richard has been here for ten minutes. In that time, he has acted as if he never left – as if he *owns* the place (which, of course, he does). I have positively *yearned* for this moment. What the hell is wrong with me?

'Shall we make a move, then?' he asks.

'I'm just going to get Myra,' Molly says. 'I'm taking her with us, OK, Mummy?'

Myra the disabled Cabbage Patch Kid. We finally had a talk about her this morning. I explained to Molly that Myra shouldn't be excluded because of her imperfections. No, I said, she must be embraced. Of course, Myra – one arm short of the full pair – will have problems embracing back, but Molly took my speech to heart. I hope she'll remember this important life lesson twenty years down the line when her mother is in a mental institution, her mind ravaged and her liver annihilated by years of alcohol abuse . . .

And *now* it strikes me.

When did I last have a drink?

It completely freaks me out. I haven't touched a drop since . . . When the hell was it? Monday lunchtime. I had half a glass of wine when I sat in Sureya's kitchen almost five full days ago. More amazing still, I haven't even *thought* about having a drink in that time.

Of course – just as the realisation at the hospital that I hadn't smoked had me reaching instinctively for my cigarettes – the thought has me immediately thinking about having a drink. Obviously, I'm not going to. For a start, it's way too early. And I'm about to accompany my son to the most important event of his life. Need to keep a very clear head. But I'm wondering how the hell I did it. How did I get through a week – a week like *this*! – without reaching for even a tiny glass of wine?

Maybe it's because for once in my life, I've been totally wrapped up in somebody else's problems instead of my own. Who knows? I'm no analyst . . .

But just thinking about the absence of alcohol in my life makes me smile inwardly. Outwardly too, apparently, Richard asks, 'What's tickling you?'

'Nothing much,' I reply. 'Ready, then?'

'Yeah, I'll just take a leak. Get the kids into the car. My keys are on the island.'

As he heads for the loo, I can't see his keys anywhere. I take his leather jacket off the back of the stool and fumble through the pockets. His keys are in there, but so is something else. Something hard to the touch. I lift it out.

A tiny black velvet jewellery box. Too small for anything other than a ring.

So here it is: the reason he needs to 'get on' today; the 'stuff' he needs to give Bel. Jesus, he's going to ask her to . . . *marry* him? My head is reeling, my stomach lurching. Because . . . *Shit* . . . The realisation rolls over me like a freight train. Our marriage. That's it. It's over. Official.

I hear the toilet flush, but for a moment I can't move. I'm frozen, the jewellery box stuck to my hand as if it's been glued to my palm. I give my head a brisk shake and I force myself to move. I slip the box back into his pocket and jangle the keys as noisily as I can. 'Come on, kids, we gotta go!' I yell.

That's right, fuck you, Richard, *fuck you*. Today is Thomas's day. I'm not going to let you blow it for him. As for me, well, I'll just have to fret over how *I* feel later.

Richard joins us in the hall. I throw him his jacket and we're out of the door. I'm about to slam it shut behind me when the phone rings.

'Let the machine get it,' Richard says, glancing at his watch agitatedly.

'It might be Sureya,' I say.

'OK, we'll wait in the car.'

I go back into the hall and pick up the phone.

'It's me,' Summer says.

'Hi, welcome back. When did you get in?'

'Yesterday afternoon. I was gonna call you last night, but, you know, jet lag.'

'Look, I'm just on my way out.'

'Oh . . . right . . . sorry. You go.'

And contained in those five words is something I can't quite put my finger on. It sounds like despair. It's confusing because I don't think I've ever heard Summer do despair.

'Summer, are you OK?'

'I can't do it, Fran. I can't have this baby.'

Outside, Richard has taken his seat at the wheel.

'Where are you?' I ask.

'The Portman Women's Clinic.'

'The *what*? What are you doing there?'

'Put it this way, I'm not getting my flu jabs.'

'God, *no*. Summer, are you sure you've thought it through properly?'

'What do you imagine I've been doing all week? What do you think I did on the entire flight home? I'm *sick* of thinking. I just want to get it over with.'

I hear the sound of Richard revving the engine impatiently. I look through the front door at Thomas, tiny and vulnerable in the back of the big car, looking as if he can't wait to get his ordeal over with either.

But Summer and I need to talk before she does something she'll regret for the rest of her life.

'Listen, where's this clinic?' I ask.

Silence. Like despair, not something that usually comes with a call from Summer.

'Summer, are you there?'

'I don't even know why I'm calling you, to be honest, Fran. Look, you go. We'll talk later.'

'No, we need to talk now.'

'I'm not going to change my mind. Listen, you go, I'll ring you when—'

'No, don't hang up,' I shout, looking at Richard looking at me, irritated. 'Tell me, where's this clinic?'

'Harley Street. Why?'

Slow down, Fran, be calm. I try to work out the logistics as Richard toots the horn.

'I'm coming, Summer. Just don't do anything until I get there. Do you hear me?'

'I told you, I've made my decision. You're not going to talk me out of it.'

'Whatever, you can't go through this alone. You need a friend there.'

'Someone to make me feel guilty, you mean? No thanks.'

'I'm not going to make you feel guilty. Please let me be there for you . . . *Please*, just do this for me.'

Silence . . . eternal bloody silence. Then, 'O . . . K.'

'Right, I'll get there as fast as I can.'

I run out to the car and fling open the passenger door. 'Richard, we've got to do a car swap. You guys take the Mini.'

'What, why, where are you going?'

'YouneedtogotoCrystalPalaceinmycarsoIcangotoSummer inyours,' I gabble, and it really does come out as one word, which Richard, to his credit, understands.

'Why? Where is she?'

I fill him in on Summer's phone call. Actually, what I say is, 'Hospitalnotimetoexplain.' The rest is just detail.

'Right,' he says, snapping to attention. 'OK, kids, out of the car.'

He doesn't need to ask why they have to cram themselves into the Mini while I get the palatial executive limo. He knows me. He knows that I'm unable to venture beyond our postcode without help. His Lexus possesses something miraculous called sat nav, which is my only hope of getting from A to B to C without ending up in the S, H, I and T.

As the children change cars he says, 'Right, where are you headed?'

271

'Harley Street, then Beckenham.'

'You're going to come to the trial afterwards?' he says, pressing buttons on the magical sat nav, feeding it a fresh set of destinations. 'Aren't you going to be too late?'

'I'll try my damnedest not to be. I'll just have a quick word with Thomas.'

I go the Mini and help him with his seat belt.

'Why aren't you coming?' he asks, his face dropping.

'It's an emergency, Thomas. Summer's in a bit of trouble. But I'll be there. I'm going to do everything I can to make it, I promise . . . You're going to be brilliant today, angel, I *know* it.'

Richard leaps into the driver's seat. 'Come on, let's go, go, go.'

I kiss Molly, then Thomas. 'I love you,' I say. 'Just remember that.'

It's barely audible, but I definitely hear it: 'Love you too, Mum.'

I don't have to search hard for her. I don't even have to go into the clinic. She's sitting on the wall outside, smoking. Judging by the pile of butts at her feet, she's either been chain-smoking or this is Last Fag Saloon. The place where women come for one final smoky ponder on what they are about to do.

She smiles. 'That was quick. What did you do? Fly?'

'Pah, flying's so last week. I power-walked. It's the new thing in North London. You should try it.'

She looks me up and down. 'Actually, if I didn't know you better, I'd believe you. You look positively thin.'

Do I? I've been described as a number of things lately. *Thin* has not been one of them. But she's right. My combats are clinging desperately to my hips. If I don't eat cream cakes soon, they'll be round my ankles.

I pull a cigarette from my own pack. 'Mind if I join you?'
She shrugs and I light up.

'You gonna give me the pro-life speech now?' she asks.

'You know I'm not like that. I've signed too many of
Sureya's pro-*choice* petitions. You know I'll support you whatever you decide . . . but . . . you can't do this.' I say it with
maximum conviction because it's what I feel. In my gut and
in my heart. I *am* pro-choice; I'm just convinced that the
one she's making is wrong. I feel it to the extent that I'm
prepared to risk missing the most important event in my
son's life. Not that she needs to know that.

She doesn't respond. I look at her properly. Red eyes
sitting on top of grey bags, ragged hair, bleached skin – she
clearly didn't spend her time in LA acquiring a California
tan. This isn't Summer. This is someone else, and by the
look of her, this someone else is going through hell.

I take her hand. 'It isn't right to do this,' I say. 'Not now.
Not when you're jet-lagged, knackered, emotional. You need
to let things settle a bit, get some of your equilibrium back.'

'Yeah, yeah, I knew you were going to say that. Look,
I'm going to finish this fag and go back in there. Get this
over with and get on with my life.'

I look at her cigarette. I reckon I have about three or four
drags to change her mind. Better get to work.

'Why did you call me this morning, Summer?'

'To let you know what I was doing,' she replies, looking
at me as if I'm stupid – which I may well be, but I have to
go with this.

'Rubbish,' I say. 'You called me because you weren't sure.'

'What are you talking about? I'm booked in. I've paid my
deposit. I've seen the doctor, the counsellor, and high-fived
the doorman. Of course I'm sure.'

'No, you're not. You knew I'd try to talk you out of it, or
at least tell you to slow down. I think that's why you rang

me. You needed to hear someone tell you that you're making a mistake.'

I look at her for confirmation, but she doesn't give me anything.

'Think back to that lunch we had the week before last,' I continue. 'Remember how wonderful it all felt? I know it's a complete bloody cliché, but you *glowed* that day. Having this baby felt right then. What's really changed?'

'*Everything!*' she cries out. 'Everything's changed. That lunch was a million years ago.'

'No, nothing's changed. Apart from Laurence.'

She winces at the mention of his name. 'God, I loathe that man. So much, you have no idea.'

'Fair enough, I hate him too. But so what? You never claimed to love him. You *awed* him. That was the best you could come up with. So who cares if he's done a runner?'

'I can't believe I've been such a prat. I fell for his whole *I love you* line. I've been all the things I love to mock. Weak, pathetic, fucking useless . . .'

'No, you haven't, Summer. You just went with your feelings,' I tell her.

'*Feelings*. Look where the hell they get you. Honestly, how am I going to take care of a baby? I can't even look after myself.'

'Listen to you. Who do you sound like?'

'I dunno. Who?'

'*Me!* You sound exactly like me,' I shout, feeling the frustration. 'And, God, let me tell you it's pathetic. I don't know how you've put up with me for all these years.'

She smiles at me weakly, then drops her cigarette on to the pavement . . . But she doesn't get up to go.

'What have you always told me, Summer? That I don't need Richard.'

'That's different,' she mumbles crossly.

'But it isn't! It's exactly the same. You've spent your entire adult life telling anyone who'll listen that men are dispensable. You can't go back on that now.'

She takes a moment before she answers. 'No, I guess not,' she says, grinding her cigarette out with her toe.

'So fuck Laurence,' I urge, and I think a bit of me is also talking about Richard. 'Let him go. You have to keep this baby because *you* want it. Simple as that.'

'What about work?' she says. 'It'll completely screw up my career.'

'Of course it won't. You think actresses don't have babies?'

'You haven't exactly been busy these last ten years.'

'Kids didn't kill my career, Summer. *I* did. I just used Thomas and Molly as an excuse. Don't you dare make my mistake. Don't you dare use your career as an excuse not to have this baby.'

She doesn't say anything, but I know I'm getting through to her. Mustn't blow it now. 'You're a brilliant, wonderful actress,' I tell her. 'Every casting director in town knows how good you are and now you'll be even more in demand because being a mum ups your range. Think of all that new experience you'll be able to draw on.'

She raises an eyebrow, smelling bullshit and I feel all my good work slipping away. 'Look, I've been able to play a perfectly convincing mum up to now, thank you,' she says.

'You're right. You have. But believe me, you'll be even more convincing in nine months . . . When you smell of Sudacream and baby sick and you haven't had a decent night's sleep for days.'

She laughs – thank God, because I could have so derailed this conversation with that comment. 'What are you talking about?' she says. 'I haven't slept for days as it is. I am shattered.'

'See, you're getting into character already. Look, I'm being serious. I know I haven't been the world's greatest advert for motherhood, but my kids are the most amazing, precious thing in my life. I regret a lot of things I've done – or haven't done – but I'll never regret having them. Life doesn't end with kids. It's just the beginning.'

She gives me the raised eyebrow again, but I'm not bull-shitting her now.

'Do you know what? I've just been offered the most fantastic job,' I tell her. 'Chris Sergeant called me. He's got a script that is so *me* it's not true. It's an anti-racism thing – I have to do, like, twenty accents in two minutes or some-thing. There's an American version. Robin Williams is doing it. Me and Robin Williams, eh?'

'I know I don't look it, Fran, but I'm so, so pleased for you.'

'I'm absolutely terrified if you must know, but this time I *will* at least turn up. If it kills me.' •

She gives me a faint smile. 'You're going to walk it. I know it.'

'But the point is, Summer, if the script of a lifetime can just fall into the lap of a waster like me, imagine the parts a trouper like you is going to land. Don't give this baby up, Summer, because you *can* have it all.'

'Jesus, what's happened to you, Fran? You sound like . . . *me.*'

'Well, you should pay attention, then. Your advice has always been excellent. Forget work, forget Laurence. Having this baby is the right thing to do because it's, well, it's the right thing to do. If you can't see it now, you'll see it in a few days. If you go ahead with this, you'll have nothing but regrets.'

My words hang in the air between us as Summer takes it all in.

I resist the urge to look at my watch. *Thomas.* Will they be there yet?

I also resist the urge to grab her by the shoulders and shake her violently. I am so right about this. Why can't she see that?

But she does and the fresh tears in her eyes tell me she saw it all along. She just needed the confirmation. She slides off the wall and hugs me desperately.

'I do want it . . . But it's scaring the shit out of me, Fran,' she whispers.

'Of course it is,' I soothe. 'It's all part of the programme.'

'I really don't think I can do it on my own,' she sobs, her tears making my face wet too.

'But you're not alone,' I tell her. 'And you never will be.'

And if you thought that was crying before, forget it. *This* is what you call crying. I let her get on with it. But I also gingerly raise my left arm and steal a glance at my watch. Eleven forty-five. Thomas's trial is fifteen minutes away. If I can pull myself away from this hug in the next five minutes, run back to the car and drive like a lunatic, I might just catch the end of it.

'I'd better go back in and get my stuff,' Summer says. 'Fancy going to lunch?'

'I'd love to, but I've got to get to Beckenham.'

'*Beckenham?* Why?'

'Thomas has got his football trial.'

'Jesus, Fran, why didn't you say something? What time?'

'Er, fifteen minutes.'

'*Fifteen* minutes? *Fuck.* What the hell are you doing here? Go! GO!'

'Are you sure you're OK?'

'Course I bloody am,' she snaps.

The old Summer is back. With a vengeance, it seems.

'Want me to come with you? You know, to navigate.'

Summer navigate? Summer is a diva. She doesn't *drive*. She tells the cabby where to go, closes her eyes and doesn't open them until she gets there. But of course I say, 'I'd love you to come.'

Bloody technology. Just what is the point of satellite navigation? Now, if it *talked* you through the streets of London, it might be some use. If it said, 'Next left . . . Not here. This is a petrol station . . . The *next* left . . . At the lights . . . Here . . . *Here!* TURN THE FUCKING WHEEL!' it might be worth having. And if it also dabbed at your fevered brow with a soft tissue, that would be a bonus.

But, no, it does none of that. It just sits there on the dashboard. Mute. I swear it's got the huff with me. It's silently muttering, 'It's hardly my fault if she can't follow some simple bloody instructions, is it?'

Where the hell are we? Didn't we drive past that pub five minutes ago?

Summer? *Useless.* She's just gripping the dashboard, her knuckles white as I ease the car towards the middle of the road, looking for a way past a huge delivery truck, which is pootling along at a completely inconsiderate forty. I glance at her. She's white as a sheet. And she hasn't said a word for twenty minutes. Maybe I'd better slow down because she looks as if she's about to have a coronary, which would make a complete nonsense of all my hard work earlier.

'That pub,' she says quietly. 'Didn't we just pass it five minutes ago?'

It's one twenty. I honestly don't know how we made it. After spending what felt like for ever driving around South-east London in increasingly small circles, suddenly we're here. The CRYSTAL PALACE FC sign by the gate is the most beautiful sight in the world. I drive through and pull into a parking space in front of a single-storey brick building. My red Mini is two spaces away. At least they're still here. I climb out of the car and rather than go to the reception, which is through the glass doors, I head straight for the training pitches I spotted on the other side of the building. I hurry, not waiting for Summer. I think she's still in shock. I took advantage of the drive here to fill her in on Sureya. She went from white-faced shock to red-faced anger at the injustice of the world as I told the story. I think the distraction of telling such a horrific story might have had something to do with us getting lost in the first place.

But we're here now. I see Richard and Molly first, standing beside a pitch, watching. I scan the players, then see Thomas. He's wearing an oversized yellow bib on top of his Arsenal shirt. He looks tiny. He always looks small, but next to the other players he seems pixie-like. How old are they? They can't be Thomas's age because they're bloody huge. Summer arrives at my side and we watch for a moment. Thomas scurries about the pitch purposefully, but no one gives him the ball – as if he's so small he's invisible.

We walk down the touchline and join Richard.

'Got here OK, then?' he says pointlessly.

I'm not completely useless, mate, I think, still angry and resentful that he's in perfect-parent mode even as proof of his love for his mistress sits in his jacket pocket.

'Got here fine,' I say sweetly.

'She all right?' He nods at Summer, who stands a discreet ten feet from us.

'She is now,' I say, feeling a surge of pride because she is, thanks to me. 'I'll tell you about it later.'

Twenty yards away from us, three men in tracksuits stand studying the action. Another older man in an overcoat is with them. It's FA Ron. I've only seen him once – the day he watched Thomas in a park match and afterwards suggested a trial – but you don't forget a shock of white hair like his in a hurry.

'How's Thomas doing?' I ask Richard.

He shrugs uncertainly. 'Hard to tell. They had him doing some skills stuff earlier. He was amazing. I can't believe what he did with that ball.'

'You have to look if you want to see, Richard,' I say and immediately regret it. It sounds like a line from the wise Kung Fu master in a cheap martial-arts movie. 'Or should that be *glasshopper*?' I add, just to keep my dignity.

He gives me a little laugh. 'Sorry, you're right. But really, he's incredible. God knows where he gets it from.'

I wonder.

My mind goes back to Saturday nights spent watching *Match of the Day*. Dad would roll home from the pub just in time for the start of the programme. Then he'd spend the next hour yelling at the screen, as if the players could hear him, as if the matches were live and hadn't finished several hours before and as if he knew a damn sight more about the game than England's best managers. Like Thomas, he was football crazy. Funny things, genes. You never know which ones you're going to get.

'Anyway, then they stuck him in this match,' Richard continues. 'He's hardly seen the ball, to be honest.'

'Why have they got him playing with teenagers?'

'They're not. They're all ten, eleven, twelve.'

'But they're massive. Do they feed them steroids?'

As the words are out of my mouth, Thomas finds himself at the end of a pass. My heart catches as he sets off with the ball, then leaps as he jinks past a player twice his size . . .

That's it, Thomas, go!

. . . and straight into another three times as big. *Foul*, surely! Thomas is on his backside, watching bewildered as the ball heads off in the other direction. I feel anger rising.

Why isn't anyone doing anything? Who's refereeing this match? I want to run to Thomas and hug him, but even more I want to grab the big bastard who knocked him over and give him a slap. Obviously, I don't. But only because Molly chooses the moment to take hold of my hand.

'Poor Thomas,' I say. 'This isn't fair.'

'This is what it's been like,' Richard says. 'Every time he gets the ball he's shoved off it. It's more like rugby than football.'

Well, he would know about that.

We watch for a few more painful minutes, during which I give thanks to Thierry Henry for his shin pads. Summer sidles up to me and says, 'He's a plucky little thing, isn't he? He doesn't want to give up.' She's right. I catch a rare glimpse of Thomas's teeth, but he's not smiling – they're gritted in determination.

A whistle blows. It's over. I'm relieved because that was agonising to watch. Thomas doubles over, his hands clutching his knees, his little face contorted with exhaustion. Again, I want to run to him, and instinctively, I make a move towards him, but this time I feel Richard's hand on my shoulder.

What's he playing at?

But he's right, because one of the tracksuited coaches is trotting up to Thomas. We watch them talk – or rather we watch the coach talk, Thomas nodding between panting. FA Ron walks along the touchline to us.

'Mrs Clark,' he says with a broad smile. 'Good to see you again.' He gives Richard a nod and turns to me. 'Terry'll be over for a chat in a moment.'

'What do you think, Ron?' I ask urgently. 'How was he?'

He grins at me. 'It's not for me to say, Mrs Clark. I just get 'em down here. It's up to the coaches to make the call.'

I give him a pleading look.

He laughs. 'I think he's got a bundle of talent,' he says. 'Guts too. That was a tough game he was playing in. These lads have all been with the academy for a while. He's a great kid.'

As he walks away, I cling to those words: '*bundle of talent*', '*guts*', '*a great kid*'. He so is a great kid.

On the pitch, Terry the coach leaves Thomas and rejoins his colleagues. Thomas, at last, ambles up to us and I kneel down to embrace his tired, sweat-drenched little body. 'You were *amazing*,' I say. 'I'm so proud of you.'

'Well done, Thomas,' Richard adds. 'That looked really tough out there.'

'*Tough?* They were a bunch of psychos,' Summer chips in. 'You were fantastic, Thomas.'

He gives us his you're-all-morons glare. 'I was *rubbish*,' he says, his head dropping.

'You were not. Ron said you've got loads of talent. *And* guts,' I tell him. 'What was that guy Terry saying to you?'

'Just well done and stuff.'

'*See?* Well done.'

He shrugs as if it all means nothing.

We watch in silence as the coaches talk. FA Ron is with them, but standing slightly apart, listening – it's not his call. I feel sick. This is worse than any casting verdict I ever had to wait on. I take Thomas's hand, but he pulls away – this is not the place to be seen holding Mummy's hand. I cling on to Molly's instead, more for my sake than for hers.

After an eternity, the man called Terry walks towards us. I try to read his face, but he's giving nothing away.

'You Thomas's dad?' he asks as he reaches us.

'Yes,' Richard says before turning to me. 'And this is—'

'Terry Kember,' Terry Kember says, thrusting out his hand and shaking Richard's. 'I run the academy.'

I feel my heart rate quicken. I just want to get to the end, the yes or no bit. I'm so scared I can hardly breathe.

'He's a great kid,' he says – to Richard. 'Good close control and quick feet. And he's got the beginnings of a good football brain, an eye for a pass.'

Richard nods, as if he knows what the man is talking about. I glance down at Thomas, who's threatening to burst, such is the praise from a football *professional*.

'I was well impressed with his skills, Mr Clark.'

That's great, but what's all this *Mr Clark*? What about *me*? The woman who has ferried Thomas to and from football practice every weekend. The woman who cheers his goals and washes his kit and nurses his injuries. In short, the woman who's taken an interest.

Choosing to ignore my mental rage, the coach crouches down to Thomas's level. 'How old are you?' he asks.

'Eleven,' Thomas lies. 'Well, I am in December.'

'Right. Like I was telling your dad, you're a terrific player. Where are you playing at the moment?'

'The North London Academy.'

'I know that one. Gary Holt runs it, doesn't he? He's a top coach. You keep up the hard work and he'll bring your game on.' He ruffles Thomas's hair, then stands up and turns to Richard – yes, *Richard*.

'Good. Right . . .' He shifts awkwardly from foot to foot. We've got to the yes or no bit and I've a horrible feeling it's not yes. 'He's got the skills, but . . .'

There it is, the *but*.

'. . . he's on the small side.'

'But he's got the skills,' I interrupt, not bothering to keep the desperation out of my voice.

Terry Kember looks at me for the first time. 'Football's a *physical* game. You saw the size of the lads out there. You've got to be able to handle yourself.'

'He's still growing,' I say, putting my arm out and pulling Thomas towards me. This time he doesn't resist.

'Yeah, of course, but I doubt he's gonna be a six-footer.' He looks at the despair on my face. 'A lot can change. He might shoot up. Some lads do. Why don't you bring him back in a year or two and we can take another look . . . ?'

No, why don't I place my hands round your stupid neck and squeeze really tightly until you change your mind?

He looks at his watch. 'I'm gonna have to shoot off now. Thanks for coming down. And well done today, Thomas. You keep up the practice, yeah?'

And with a brief shake of *Richard's* hand he's off, striding across the training pitch – a busy man with more young dreams to shatter. I *hate* him. Yes, for his casual sexism, but mostly for the fact that I can *feel* Thomas's heart breaking. I can't believe how upset I am. I've spent the last couple of days gently preparing him for the possibility of rejection, but it seems that I forgot to prepare myself.

'Arsehole,' I mutter.

'It wasn't all bad,' Richard says. 'He said a lot of positive stuff.'

'No, Richard, he's a complete arsehole.' I bend down to Thomas. He's chewing hard on his bottom lip, fighting back the tears. 'You are going to prove him so wrong, Thomas, just you watch. I'm going to feed you nothing but steak and you're going to grow like mad, and when you're playing for England, I'm going to write a letter to that man just to remind him how badly he screwed up today.'

I pull him into me and hug him tight, partly to wipe his tears away and partly to hide my own.

★　　★　　★

The kids are on their way to my mum's. Richard is taking them. I couldn't believe my ears when he offered. 'Well, you need to get Summer home,' he said. He was right, I did. I desperately wanted to be with Thomas, but the thought of putting Richard and Summer in the same car . . . Well, the interior would have frosted up without the help of flashy Lexus air conditioning.

I spent fifteen minutes with Thomas before we set off, trying to suck the anguish out of him.

'Crystal Palace are rubbish, anyway,' I said. 'I never wanted you to play for them. You're an *Arsenal* player.'

'But they only pick French kids.'

'So? You can learn French. And eat lots of steak.'

I decided then that I was going to get tickets to the next Arsenal home game if it killed me. Then I decided that Richard should buy Thomas and himself season tickets to make up for totally ruining our lives. I haven't made any demands yet – isn't that what bitter, deserted wives are supposed to do? Maybe now is the time.

The journey back into town is quiet – slow, too, compared with the outward one. Summer sits beside me, emotionally drained. She speaks for the first time in ages as we cross Waterloo Bridge, back to the relative familiarity that lies north of the river.

'What a bloody day,' she says. 'It's given me a fair old insight into the coming joys of motherhood. All that . . . *disappointment* to deal with.'

'Please don't let that put you off. You have to have those so you can enjoy the highs. There are highs, honest. I'll try to make sure you're around for one sometime.'

She laughs and says, 'You were brilliant back there, you know.'

'I was not. I let that man totally wind me up.'

'No, you were brilliant. You were really there for Thomas.

Just like you were for me this morning. And how you've been there for Sureya. You're a fantastic mum and a brilliant friend.'

'Stop it. Stop it right now,' I command. 'I've had enough of crying for one day.'

10

Home.

Alone.

I regret letting the kids go to my mum's now. Richard is on his way to his lover to give her the contents of that little black box. I can't believe the self-pity that engulfs me. She's about to put on her ring and I'm about to put on a Pot Noodle. How sad am I? And I'm talking teen-speak here – sad as in an unmitigated, waste-of-space loser. Although I suppose I mean it in the old-fashioned sense too. Sadness because I suppose, finally, I have to accept that my marriage is over. No more hiding from the truth. Single-motherhood beckons. Hey, Mum, we've finally come full circle.

And here I sit, a life alone ahead of me. And more immediately, a whole Saturday night on my own to endure. What shall I do? Hit the clubs? Pull a bloke? I don't think so.

It's nearly six o'clock – yes, I'm clock-watching already – when the phone rings. It's Richard, calling from his car.

'How's Thomas?' My first question.

'Quiet. But he'll be OK. He's tougher than he looks. I talked to him a bit. About rejection. How it's a good thing. He sort of understood, I think.'

Oh, yes, I can hear it now. *'Gosh, I hadn't thought of it like that. But you're so right, Dad. Having my only dream crushed has put me in a really positive place.'*

When I don't respond, Richard feels the need to defend himself. 'It's *true*. Rejection is good. If you get what you want too easily, it doesn't mean half as much as it does when you have to really work for it.'

There's an analogy about our marriage in there somewhere, I'm sure, if only I could be bothered to look for it.

'Was my mum shocked to see you?' I ask.

'Didn't seem to be. Al was the one who seemed surprised. Said, "Who are you? Oh, yeah, you're Fran's bloke." Sarky sod.'

'Oh, you know what he's like. Don't take it personally,' I say. Best not to mention that Al doesn't like him very much and *personal* is exactly what it was.

'Thomas will be fine, you know,' Richard says. The fact that he's returning to the subject unprompted suggests he's as worried about him as I am. 'I'm going to spend some time with him. Do some bonding.'

Ah, still in perfect-parent mode. Obviously, now is the moment to strike.

'You know what the perfect way to bond would be, don't you?' I say.

'What's that?'

'Arsenal season tickets.'

'Really? Well, OK, if you think that'll help.'

'No end,' I tell him and marvel at how easy it was.

Is that all you have to do to get what you want? Just be assertive? '*Richard, I want you to come home right now. I want you to tell me you love me and promise me you'll never, ever leave me again. And I want that new Kenwood blender Al bought my mum too.*'

'What are you doing now?' he asks.

'It's Saturday night. I'm hitting the clubs.'

'Really?'

'I was joking.'

'Right. It's just that I was wondering if I could stop by.'

'You want to stop by?' I repeat stupidly.

'Yes. If that's OK.'

I tell him it is, but my stomach surges slightly. It dawns on me that this is crunch time. He's going to do the decent thing. He's going to suggest I get myself a divorce lawyer *before* he gets down on one bended knee to Bel.

As we hang up, my head spins with panic. I told Summer that she was right. That any woman can function – and quite happily, thank you – without a man. But right now, I'm not sure I'd be able to back up that statement in a court of law.

We're sitting at the island in the kitchen, the place where most business seems to be conducted in this house. He pours himself a scotch. He offers me the bottle, but I don't drink spirits. I pour myself a glass of red instead. My first in a long time.

No divorce talk. *Yet.*

'It was good to spend time with the kids today,' he says. 'Even with Thomas being low . . . It was good.'

'You should do it more often.'

'I will. Look, I'm sorry, but I'm trying here.'

He looks hurt and so he should. Where was he when I was having my life ripped to shreds by a bunch of gossiping vultures? Where was he when his precious daughter was being branded a playground racist? Well, damn him. It's time I filled him in on the children he's suddenly taking an interest in.

'I know you're trying, Richard, and that's great,' I say, 'but it's not all fun-packed, happy parenting around here. There's *stuff* that has to be dealt with.'

'What stuff?'

'Molly has been accused of racism. The deputy head threatened me with Social Services the other day and—'

'Hold on, hold on, what the hell are you talking about?'

I tell him about my meeting with Gottfried. He looks

stunned when I've finished. *Ha, tell me how the hell you'd get out of that one, Perfect Parent.*

'Jesus, that is ridiculous,' he says. 'Utterly stupid. Molly isn't racist.'

'Of course she's not.'

'I hope you're going to do the right thing here, Fran.'

'Too right I am,' I tell him determinedly.

'Good. Because this is outrageous and you've really got to make it go away.'

'Well, of course,' I say, and I'm pleasantly surprised by the strength of his conviction. After all this time of feeling isolated and bewildered by Gottfried's accusation, it's good to finally have an ally.

Richard nods positively. 'Just make sure you tell them *exactly* what they want to hear.'

Immediately I hear the words, I explode. 'Are you mad? *Tell them what they want to hear?* That's the same as telling them they're right. Molly's done nothing wrong and I've got *nothing* to be ashamed of.'

'You're misunderstanding me. I'm not saying you have. All I'm saying is that you can't start a war with the school. They have procedures on this sort of thing. I mean, racism is *the* big deal these days.'

'They don't know what racism is. For God's sake, they'd have you up in court for calling a garden implement a spade around here.'

He laughs. 'That's funny.'

'I wasn't trying to be, Richard. These people are actively seeking out discrimination, which is all well and good. The trouble is, they're finding it where it doesn't exist.'

'Can't you see their point of view, though? They've got to jump on anything that anyone could misconstrue as prejudice or they'll end up in all sorts of trouble.'

'But there's nothing racist going on here!' I yell in frustration.

I can't believe what I'm hearing. I'm just as furious at Richard now as I was at Gottfried when she first raised the issue. 'You have no idea what it's like, do you? Everyone jumps on *everything*. It's so politically correct it's fundamentalist. I've had enough, Richard. I'm not giving in on this.'

'But it's a battle you can't win. It's not worth it.'

Is this really Richard speaking? It's more like listening to a lecture from Cassie. What the hell happened to the maverick I married?

'Clearly, I just don't know you any more. When did you become such a . . . such a . . . I don't know. You're pathetic. Miss Gucci's welcome to you.'

'Thanks for that,' he says, turning away from me.

I know, I know, that was nasty. But I can't believe he's on their side.

'Look, I'm sorry,' I say, backtracking. 'But it's been awful. And the fact that I haven't put an end to it is bothering me. I guess that's why I snapped. Sorry.'

He looks at me for a long moment, then says, 'Can we change the subject?'

'Probably a good idea.'

'Actually, you've already changed it . . . Miss Gucci.'

Here it comes. D.I.V.O.R.C.E.

He's going to tell me that he loves her and can't be without her. That they're getting engaged and moving in together. I brace myself on the edge of the island.

He does his thing: runs his hand nervously through his hair, prepares himself, mentally sorting out the right words – *it's not you, it's me, blah, blah*. Now that the moment has arrived . . . I just want to get it over with.

'Look, just get on with it, Richard,' I snap. 'Let's get this marriage over with so we can both get on with our lives.'

'What are you talking about?' He looks shocked. 'I just wanted to tell you that Bel and I . . . I've broken it off with her. You want a *divorce*?'

'No . . .' My turn for shocked. 'No, I don't. I just thought . . . Well, I thought that's what you wanted.'

'God, no . . . Not at all. Look, I don't know what's going to happen to us, but I wanted you to know that Bel won't have anything to do with it. It's over.'

Yeesss!

I'm past shock. I just want to punch the air in victory. I have no idea what's going to happen to us either, but at least I no longer have to endure a seizure every time I picture them together. I no longer have to imagine them holding hands across a candlelit table or sweaty and breathless from the sheer passion of it all. I no longer have to see them . . .

Hang on. He's lying. I don't believe a word he says any more. About anything, frankly. What about that little black box, eh? Even if it is just a parting gift, why couldn't he just have got her a token? Like a thank-you card, maybe? Look, whether they're still together or not, I hate the undeserving bitch. I'd like her arm to fall off *à la* Myra. And maybe a leg too. I want her to *suffer*. It sounds terrible, but what can I say? It's how I feel.

'So it's over, then, is it?' I ask sceptically.

'Yes. It was a mistake. Probably the most stupid, selfish thing I've ever done. I stopped trying . . . with you, I mean, and I shouldn't have. And I couldn't regret it more because . . . well, I feel like I've blown everything.'

Oh. He doesn't look as if he's making this up. Maybe they *have* finished and maybe that regretful look on his face really *is* what he says it is. I'm confused. About what this really means to him. To *us*.

'What's going to happen now?' I ask.

'I really don't know. She'll probably find a pretext to fire us. But if she doesn't, it might actually make the account easier to manage. The senior client being involved with the MD of her agency was a recipe for disaster, frankly, and— You weren't talking about the business, were you?'

'No.'

We sit in silence for a moment. I have a feeling I should speak, but I don't know what to say. I look at him. He seems to be grappling with something, as if he hasn't finished yet. I take a sip of wine. He can take all the time he wants – at least I know it has nothing to do with divorce.

'It's been a hell of a time, hasn't it?' he says at last. 'I've learnt a lot.'

'Like what?'

'I've missed the kids. I've missed you. I've missed home.'

I know he's missed the kids and the comforts of home, but was *I* sandwiched in the middle of that list?

'Look, I know things haven't been perfect,' he says, breaking the silence. 'That was more my fault than yours. I lost myself in work and took things at home for granted. And then there was Bel—' He stops and shakes his head. 'Weird . . . I know I haven't been here, but over the last couple of weeks, I feel as if I've got to know you again. I've seen a side of you tha—'

'You mean last Saturday?' I say, feeling my defences go back up. 'I told you, that was a one-off. I've hardly touched a drop since—'

'No, I'm talking about this last week. The way you were there for Sureya, for Thomas and Summer today, even for me with the Cherie Blair thing. You've been incredible, Fran.'

'Have I?'

'Absolutely. The thing is, you've always been this amazing woman. I've just forgotten about her.'

I forgot about her too, I think. I can't speak. Richard and

I haven't talked like this for years. And Richard hasn't said things like this to me for even more years. I feel so ... *special.* And I can't speak!

His hand slides across the island and moves on top of mine.

'I've really, really missed you, you know.'

There it is again. And not squashed between kids and home this time.

And the way he's looking at me, I want to hold him and kiss him and tell him I love him. But I don't. I don't move or say a word. Not because I've finally turned into my mother who never opens up to anyone, but because if I do, I'll cry. And as I told Summer, I've done enough of that today.

'I want this marriage to work. I'm going to change, Fran, I promise you that,' he tells me slightly gushingly. 'I'm going to work less hours, do more with the kids, show you how special you are.' He stops abruptly. 'If you'll let me . . . Do you think we can at least try?'

I don't know what to say. I want to scream YES! But I also want to punch him. *Hard.* What does he think? That I can just forget that he's been wining, dining and fucking another woman for the past few months?

He slides off his stool and takes a couple of steps towards me. Then he reaches into a pocket and puts down the velvet box in front of me.

'What's this?' I ask, surprised – I am *such* a good actress.

'It's for you. Go on, open it.'

I open the little box and gasp – and this time I'm not acting. It's *not* a ring. It's a tiny silver microphone. The type of charm you'd put on a bracelet. And it is beautiful. 'It's *gorgeous*, Richard. What's this for?'

'Well, it's a microphone. You know, with your talent, Cherie Blair and everything I thought it was really you.'

'Er, yes, I know *what* it is,' I say, just stopping short of adding *idiot*. 'But *why*?'

'Because I've fucked up and I owe you. I wanted to get you something to tell you how sorry I am. And how special you are. I went out shopping this morning. That's why I was late.' He takes the little trinket from the case and puts it in my hand. 'It's to go on that bracelet I bought you for your thirtieth,' he tells me.

'Richard, I lost my charm bracelet when we went skiing, remember?' How could he forget? 'You went down that black run four times looking for it. I wanted you to go back again, but you fell and dislocated your shoulder and we spent the whole day in hospital.'

'Yes, OK, I remember now,' he says, slightly embarrassed. At the reminder of the fall, or because he'd forgotten about the bracelet? I'm not sure. 'Jesus, what an idiot. Sorry. I can't even tell you how much I love you without screwing it up.'

I feel tears well up. At his obvious sincerity? Because he's finally telling me – *showing* me – how much he still loves me? I don't know.

'I'll wear it on a chain, Richard. And I *love* it, bracelet or no bracelet,' I tell him.

The moment is so electric I feel as if we're both wearing head-to-toe nylon. As he stoops, moving his face towards mine, I feel goosebumps rise. His arms go around me and I'm so ready for him to kiss me . . .

But I can't. I know he still loves me, but there are still too many unresolved feelings. Whatever he says, the fact remains he's been kissing someone else for the past few months. I move away from him.

'What's the matter?' he asks.

'Sorry, Richard. It's a beautiful gift. Thank you. But I can't do this now.'

'No, I'm sorry. I shouldn't have . . .' He trails off and looks down at his feet sheepishly. 'Look, it's Saturday night,' he mumbles. 'Shall we hit a club?'

He's smiling now and I smile back. 'I don't think so. But I couldn't half murder a Pot Noodle.'

11

The Sabbath. Day of rest? Rubbish. It's mayhem. The Arlington assembly hall has been taken over by a group of militant fund-raisers and turned into a war zone. So this is ARPS at work. The nation should be warned.

I stand in the middle of the hall and try to take it all in. Everyone appears to be rushing around purposefully. Stalls are being set up. Walls are being decorated with posters and signs. Bunting is being hung. But there's a distinct whiff of panic in the air. The tension is making my palms sweat. It's only the school fair, for God's sake. I really should get out more.

'*Francesca*,' a voice barks. I spin round to see Cassie. She's clutching an armful of fluffy toys. 'All volunteers were supposed to be here at *nine*,' she says, trying hard for a smile, like she isn't *really* furious with me, which just proves that she is. 'We really could have done with you sooner.'

'Oh, I'm sorry, I didn't know.' Are those my legs shaking? Forget getting out more. I knew I should have stayed at home.

'You didn't read my leaflet?' sing-songs a horrifyingly familiar voice. Natasha has appeared by my side. She's holding a big brown box that seems to be bursting at the seams. 'Fran, I've missed you!' she gushes. 'Haven't seen you for, ooh, days. Listen, I can't stop. I've got all the food I made to bring in *and* set up my other stall.'

'Your *other* stall?' I ask stupidly.

297

'Yes, designer gear! You should pop by and have a browse.' She beams, looking me up and down. 'Got everything from Gap to Gucci. All cut-price too. See you later.'

I suppose she deserves her look of triumph. Designer gear beats ducks, I suppose.

Cassie looks as shocked by her comment as I feel. I wouldn't have known what to say even if she'd given me a chance to respond. I'm still gasping when I hear a voice that shocks me more.

'Cup of tea, anyone?'

I spin round and see Richard, who's holding two steaming plastic cups.

'*Richard.* What are you doing here?'

'Just thought I'd come and lend my support,' he says, grinning winningly at Cassie.

'Cassie, I'm not sure you've met,' I say, trying to push Natasha from my mind. 'This is Richard. Can he do anything to help?'

'That would be *great*,' she says, sighing with relief, as if he's Moses and has come to part the waters so we can all cross to safety. 'There's a box of balloons over there. Would you mind blowing them up? Sorry, but the pump's broken.'

'Absolutely. No problem,' Richard says, turning up the smile a notch.

'Thank you. Thank you *so* much,' she simpers.

See? Waters parted, across we go.

'Where do you want me, Cassie?' I ask, breaking the spell.

'You'd better get to your stall. Doors open in ten— no, *five* minutes. You're over there. Far corner. I *must* get on. I've got a *ton* of carrot cake to slice.' And she's off, leaving a trail of fluffy rabbits in her wake.

Richard smiles at me. 'She seemed nice.'

'*Nice?* She's a witch – she's the worst of the lot.'

'I think you imagine half the stuff they're saying about

you.' He laughs, as if I'm Mia Farrow and I'm just fantasising that everyone wants my baby.

'Piss off, Richard. Anyway, what *are* you doing here?'

'Nice to see you too.'

'Sorry, but you're the last person I expected to see today.'

'Molly was going on at me to come yesterday. I thought I'd surprise her.' He smiles. 'I'd better get on with blowing up balloons for my new mate Cassie.'

I turn round and head for my date with the ducks.

In the remotest corner of the hall, I sit on a stool, clutching a stick with a small hook on the end. The stool is on a plastic sheet alongside a small, half-filled paddling pool containing six plastic ducks. Most of them have either heeled over on to their sides or lie at the bottom of the pool. In exchange for fifty pence, children get to hook one from the water and EVERY DUCK WINS A PRIZE. So far, only one child has had a go. And that was only because he was just three – too young to know a dud stall when he saw one. And also because I gave him a free go.

The hall is packed, but everyone seems to be keeping well clear of my corner. I think someone – let's call her Annabel – may be having a laugh at my expense.

I gaze out at the fun being had in the rest of the hall. Bells being rung with comically huge mallets, coconuts being shied, teachers being splattered with custard pies and Punch beating the living shit out of Judy . . . No, of course he's not. That would be spousal abuse. At Arlington, Punch has to sign a commitment to engage in non-violent entertainment. I think he's giving the kids his recipe for lentil soup.

Elsewhere, people throng the stalls, buying up handcrafted nick-nacks and homemade jams and cakes. And designer clobber, of course. On a stage at the far end of the hall stands a pretty woman with lovely clothes and one of those new handbags covered in buckles . . . Oh, yes, she's also black. She makes her announcements with the easy confidence of a trained TV presenter. She's a good MC, but I could so have done that job. But, no, I'm in charge of ducks that sink.

Sounds like I'm feeling desperately sorry for myself, doesn't it? That's because I am. I feel ridiculous.

I see a wart approaching me. It's attached to a nose. Annabel's nose. I fix my face with my best false smile.

'Is that your Richard over there?' she asks when she reaches me.

'That's him.'

Cassie has managed to talk Richard into taking charge of donkey rides. Not a real donkey of course – that would be animal abuse – but the headmaster and the PE teacher going head to arse in a panto costume. Richard is helping kids on to the beast's back, then leading it on a brief circuit round some stalls. He has at least a couple of dozen squealing children queued up for a fifty-pence ride.

'He's doing *brilliantly*.' Annabel beams.

Yes, thanks, I can see that.

'We don't normally see him at school. How's it all going, then?' she asks.

The shame of having your broken marriage become public knowledge is just too much to bear. I feel my face burn. 'Fine, thanks,' I say through clenched teeth. 'We're getting on just *fine*.'

'I meant with the stall,' she says snottily.

Oh God. Ground, please open up . . . At last I manage to say, 'Oh, *great*, thanks, no problem.'

'*Excellent*. See you later.'

Excellent. Marvellous. Wonderful.

I want to *die*.

Mum and Al arrived with the kids about half an hour ago. I hugged them all, but my focus was on Thomas.

'How's he been, Mum?' I asked.

'A bit quiet. But he had great fun karting with Al. He'll be all right.'

'Of course he will,' I said. 'Yesterday was just a minor setback. He's going to play for Arsenal, you know.'

'They only pick French kids,' Al said contemptuously.

So that's who Thomas got the notion from. I should have guessed.

They left me alone again after five minutes. Thomas went off with Al to search for stalls that involve throwing things. Mum took Molly in search of cakes from the café. But this is Arlington, remember. I warned them that if it was a sugar rush they were after, not to get their hopes up.

I now have fifty pence in my bucket. Put there by me. Molly wanted to hook a duck and I felt obliged to pay. I look at my watch. I don't think I can stand another minute of this. It isn't just the loneliness. I'm getting looks, I'm sure of it; I'm the subject of sly pointing and nudges; women telling their husbands not to bring their kids near me – '*Best keep away. She's a Neo-Nazi and she sells her body to feed her Pinot Grigio habit.*'

Or maybe I am going mad. Am I imagining it all . . . ?

But Mia Farrow was right! They *were* after her baby for their devil sect. All of them: the old sweetie Minnie, her husband Roman, their friends, even kindly Doctor Sapperstein. They *were* witches . . .

From nowhere John Cassavetes— I mean Richard appears at my side. 'All on your lonesome?' he says, still breathless from all that donkey fun.

'Yep.' I try to smile, but then drop it. What's the point? 'Actually, Richard, I've had enough. I can't stand here like this for another two hours.'

'But you can't give up. What do you want? For them to call you a quitter?'

'Oh, they've called me far worse lately. Honestly, Richard, I've had enough. I'll go home and make dinner. Come and join us if—'

'You are not going home,' he says firmly.

Thomas appears in front of us, glowering. 'Mum, I've only just started having fun. Don't tell me we're going home now?'

'Well, you stay with Daddy if you want. But I'm tired, and anyway, it'll be finished soon and—'

'Stop calling him *Daddy*!' he shouts. 'I'm not a baby. What's wrong with you? First, you're late for my trial, and now you want to leave. You're rubbish. This whole weekend is *crap*!'

His frustration is finally boiling over and it shocks me rigid. Richard bends down and puts an arm on his shoulder, but he angrily brushes it aside. He has tears in his eyes, but wipes them away frantically upon the arrival of a couple of his classmates – small boys drawn like moths to the sound of anger.

Mum appears too. 'Hello,' she coos, oblivious to the scene of imminent hysteria she's walked into. Molly is beside her, munching a carrot stick. So they found the café, then.

Mum rustles a paper bag. 'Anyone fancy a doughnut? Bit weird, if you ask me. They're low-fat and sugar-free. Doesn't make them very doughnut-y, does it?'

Thomas's body relaxes slightly. Sugar or not, he does like his doughnuts. As he takes a huge bite, I can't help myself and out slips my all-time favourite Homer-ism: '*Mmmm*, doughnuts . . . Is there *anything* they can't do?'

It works. Thomas smiles. OK, it's not a huge, ear-to-ear grin, but it's a start. And it broadens out when he looks at his classmates. They're gazing at me wide-eyed and slack-jawed. One of them recovers his power of speech and says to Thomas, 'Can she do that again?'

Well, she can, but right now she just wants to go home.

'Sure she can,' Thomas says nonchalantly, finishing off his doughnut and dipping into the bag for another. 'Go on, Mum.'

'I don't think so,' I say, feeling slightly foolish.

'Oh, go on,' pleads the classmate. 'Do Homer again.'

'Do *Bart*,' his friend says.

'Go on, Mum,' Thomas urges.

OK, one more time. Just for Thomas. I take a breath and come out with Bart's 'I am through with working. Working is for chumps' before switching to Homer's 'Son, I'm proud of you. I was twice your age before I figured that out.'

Thomas tries to contain his pride while his mates fall about, howling with laughter. Suddenly – if only for a fleeting moment – he has that rarest of things: a cool parent. I don't think I've ever been one of those before. 'She can do them all, you know,' he says as casually as he can manage.

'Yeah, Mummy, do Lisa,' Molly squeaks.

'OK, last ones,' I say. I quickly rattle off Lisa's 'Relax? I can't relax! Nor can I yield, relent or . . . Only *two* synonyms? Oh my God, I'm losing my perspicacity!' and Marge's 'You should listen to your heart, not the voices in your head' before finishing with a classic Bart: 'Aren't we forgetting the true meaning of Christmas? You know, the birth of Santa.'

And suddenly where there were two admiring classmates there are now half a dozen. 'Who else can you do?' one of them asks.

'She can do *any*one,' Thomas informs him.

'Anyone in the world?'

'The *universe*.'

'What? Even Mrs Gottfried?'

'*Mrs Gottfried?*' Thomas crows. '*Way* too easy. Hey, Mum, do that moron Mr Williams from IT.'

'Thomas, don't be so rude about your teachers,' Richard

says authoritatively. What is it with part-time parents? They think they can just step in and take control. It's good to see him have exactly the same effect as a full-time parent like me – i.e. none whatsoever. The boys carry on the teacher-bitch, tossing out names for me to take off.

I'm pulling my jacket on now, ready to quit while I'm ahead. It's rare that Thomas is the centre of attention – unless it's on a football pitch – and it seems like the perfect moment to exit.

'Fran, we watched that film the other day,' Mum says, seemingly out of nowhere. '*Whatever Happened to Baby Jane?* Horrible film. Do Bette Davies. Such an *evil* voice.'

Evil? Can I do evil? I can't resist the challenge. I fix her with a mad-eyed Baby Jane stare and drawl, 'Blanche, you know we have . . . *rats* in the cellar?'

Al, who's never heard me in action, hoots with laughter and Mum screws her face up so tight I can't tell if it's with delight or disgust.

'Hey, you ought to stick fifty pence in the bucket for that,' Richard says.

'That was brilliant,' Al whoops. 'I'll give her a bloody quid for it.'

But the children aren't interested in dead movie stars. They want teachers and they want them now.

'Please do Mr Williams.'

'No, Mrs Poulson.'

'*Gottfried!*'

My instincts tell me no. But their little faces – especially Thomas's. And even Richard is looking at me with what seems to be eager anticipation.

'Go on, Mummy,' Molly begs. '*Pleeease.*'

And suddenly it's just like being in the bungee-jump queue again. Everyone waiting impatiently while I froze, too scared to jump.

What am I talking about? It's nothing like that. There's no hundred-foot drop. Just a bunch of pumped-up kids with requests for a few comedy voices. A couple of teachers won't do any harm. Will it?

I take a deep breath and give them a burst of Mr Williams, who talks like a heavily sedated Billy Connolly, and segue smoothly into Mrs Gottfried. It's a subtle portrayal. Well, actually, I make her sound like Hitler's sister. You could say that my parody of the woman who accused me of racism is profoundly ironic. Or perhaps, insanely suicidal. Let the critics judge.

My audience loves it. The loudly shrieking children attract an even bigger crowd, as well as stares from parents, who want to know what the commotion is. I don't care, because Thomas is in heaven.

So of course, I give him more of what he wants. I rattle through all the teachers I know well enough to impersonate. And as I'm going, I notice Richard moving out with the bucket.

'Cough up, kids,' he says as he passes it around. Al chucks in a two-pound coin and it's followed by more jangling change as Thomas's friends follow suit.

'Richard,' I hiss. 'You can't take money off them.'

'Why the hell not? That's what they're here for. To part with their money. It's all for charity, you know . . . Right, anyone else want to hear an impersonation? Come on, roll up! Voices for a pound! Any voice you like!'

Listen to him. Who does he think he is? Del Trotter? Next he'll be telling me we'll be millionaires by the end of the day.

'Richard, stop it, please. You're embarrassing me.'

'No time to argue, Fran. Your public awaits.'

He's right. Where the hell did they all come from? My previously empty corner of the hall is suddenly packed fifteen deep. And the requests are flying in.

'Barbara Windsor!'

'Mariah Carey!'

'Sharon Osbourne!'

'No, Kelly!'

'Joan Bakewell!' (Which can only come from an Arlington mum.)

'I'll give you two quid for Jordan!' (Which can only come from Al.)

What else can I do but submit? Anyway, I couldn't escape if I tried. I'm cornered here, literally. I suppose I'd better just get on with it.

I'm exhausted. My throat is sore and dry, and my voice is husky. But the show's over. Fran Clark has left the building. Well, her voice has. Her body is still standing by the paddling pool, slightly dazed and only kept upright by surging adrenaline.

Richard stands beside me, gazing incredulously into the bucket. He reaches in and plucks out a tenner.

'*Wow.* Who put that in there?' I whisper.

'Some bloke. It was for your Hillary Clinton. Wonder what he'd have given you for your Cherie Blair?'

The hall is emptying, but the crowds around me were the last to go. No one, it seems, can resist an impersonation. And, it seems, I'm quite good at them. Most stayed to the bitter end – until they'd heard my fifth Victoria Beckham and I refused to do a sixth. Thomas and Molly – who, to be fair, had heard it all before – had had enough about half an hour ago. I gave Mum my keys and she took them home.

'You were fantastic, Fran,' Richard says.

I don't contradict him, and only partly because my voice is shot.

'You should hit the club circuit. You'd clean up with that act . . . Uh-oh, here comes the boss.'

I've already spotted Cassie marching towards us.

'Well, that was quite a performance,' she says when she reaches me.

'Thanks,' I say, though by the sound of her voice I'm not sure it's a compliment.

'I was watching you and it all looked like *terrific* fun . . . But you were supposed to be manning Hook a Duck,' she says, looking down at the paddling pool.

'I was,' I say feebly, 'but nobody seemed interested.'

She rolls her eyes. 'We've been run off our feet today, Francesca.' I notice she's not even trying for the mock smile any more. 'If you didn't feel up to running your allotted stall, well, I had plenty of people who'd have been happy to make a go of it. You know, we'll only reach our fund-raising targets if *everyone* puts in *maximum* effort. It's all about teamwork, pulling tog—'

She's cut off by the heavy clunk of coins – lots of coins. Richard has hefted the bucket on to the stool. Her eyes widen, as do mine. It's practically brim-full. I had no idea I was *that* good.

'Here you go, Cassie. Should go some way to meeting your targets,' Richard says. He gives her his finest mock smile, which, after nearly twenty years in marketing, is *very* good. 'We're off now. Have fun tidying up.'

He grabs my arm and out we go.

No, we don't *go*. We *swagger*.

Outside, I look round to check we're not being followed. 'Bloody hell,' I gasp. 'How much money do you think was in that bucket?'

'Oh, a lot,' he says casually. 'Three, four hundred maybe.'

'No way. People weren't throwing in that much, were they?'

'They *were*. It was an absolute frenzy . . . And I went to the bank earlier. Had a wad of twenties in my wallet – about two hundred. I slipped it in when she was having a go at you.'

'Are you nuts? What did you do that for?'

'Because you were right. She's a witch. I wasn't going to let her get away with talking to you like that. I was going to lay into her, but then I figured that money talks loudest with people like that . . . Anyway, fuck her. Fuck the lot of them. Stupid fucking fuckers.'

His foul-mouthed outburst shocks me, not because I disapprove, but because I thought *he* did. 'I thought swearing was for people who don't have the vocabulary to express themselves properly,' I say.

'Oh, I have the vocabulary all right, and *fuck her* is just about perfect.'

How did that happen? My Victorian kitchen actually *smells* like one. By the time we got home, Mum had a chicken and potatoes in the oven, and the table set for dinner. Thomas and Molly are playing in the morning room, Richard is at the Aga making gravy, and Al is outside sweeping up leaves on the patio. I have the sudden notion that we're on the set of a middle-class British remake of *The Waltons*.

'*Pass the balsamic vinegar, John Boy.*'

'*Sure thing, Jim-Bob. Pa, can I borrow the Lexus tonight?*'

It really does feel that idyllic. OK, I'm not an idiot. I know it isn't, not by any stretch of the imagination. Let's just say it's as idyllic as it could possibly be, given . . . Given everything, really.

I have a glass of wine in my hands and that's fine. I'm enjoying it, not a trace of guilt to be found. Bloody Natasha. I'm no sodding alcoholic. No more than she's a nice person, anyway.

'Do you know? That was a very good Bette Davies you

did back there, Fran,' Mum says, peeling a carrot. 'Have you thought about going back to work?'

I want to laugh. Have I ever thought of going back to work? I think I might have mentioned the post-natal depression. But suddenly it seems like a long time ago.

'Yeah, have you thought about going back to work?' Richard smiles.

'Maybe one day,' I say. I think about telling them both about Chris Sergeant's call, but the phone rings. I take it in the hall.

It's Summer. 'Thanks for yesterday,' she says. 'You didn't have to do that.'

'Oh yes I did.'

'No you didn't.'

'You don't understand,' I insist. 'I *did*. I had to try out the sat-nav thing.'

She laughs. 'I'm so glad you stopped me. I can't believe I was so close to . . . doing it. I do want this baby. How could I have not seen that? I'm so stupid sometimes.'

I'm about to reply with something Sureya-ish; how opening up helped her to clear away the clutter (I'm sure Sureya said something like that once, although I think she might have been talking about her new extension), but she's off again.

'What am I saying? I'm not the stupid one. He's the complete fucking moron. Do you know what he said to me?'

'I presume you're talking about Laurence?'

'Who else? He said, how could I be certain the baby was his.'

I laugh out loud and so does she. But she hasn't finished ripping Laurence to shreds. Not by a long shot. I let her get on with it, chipping in with the occasional 'God, what a prick' and even a slightly clichéd '*Men!*' It's obviously doing her good. She's cleansing herself internally, *getting all the crap out of her system.* And this one I know is *definitely* a Sureya-ism. It's what she told me when she gave me a 'miracle' herbal laxative that didn't actually work at all.

Summer has just about finished sounding off.

'That's it,' she announces. 'He's *history.* Mention the motherfucker's name again and I'll have to kill you, OK? Anyway, tell me, I want to know about Sureya.'

'I was just thinking about her, can't *stop* thinking about her. I'll go and see her tomorrow. Just to, you know, let her know I'm still here for her.'

'Tell her I'm thinking about her too. I haven't seen her for ages.'

We lapse into a slightly awkward silence. What is there to say?

I break the tension with, 'Listen, you and I should have a night out soon. Maybe Thursday. I'm in town anyway for that recording.'

'Definitely! Let's do it. But I won't be drinking. Oh, and I get pretty tired so can we make it earlier rather than later? And I don't fancy anywhere noisy. And nowhere smoky either.'

'The library, then.'

'The library it is. It'll be a riot.'

We hang up, each of us happy, I think.

I get up to return to the kitchen, but the phone immediately rings again.

'Mrs Clark? It's Ron. Ron Penfold.'

'*Ron.*' What does he want on a Sunday evening?

'Sorry to be calling you, but I wanted to say something about yesterday. I'm guessing Thomas was pretty gutted.'

'He was. But you know, these things happen. Look, I know the decision had nothing to do with you. It's really kind of you to call.'

'I'm telling you, Mrs Clark, if it had been down to me,

I'd have given him a chance. Thomas is on the small side, but he could easily shoot up. Even if he doesn't, talent like his can compensate for lack of inches. Terry's a good coach, but between you and me, I reckon he made the wrong call yesterday.'

'Thanks. I'll tell Thomas you said that. It'll do a lot for his confidence.'

'Would you mind if I told him myself? It'll be a great shame if he gives up now. Thought it might help if I had a word. If you don't mind, that is.'

'Of course I don't mind. And thank you.'

'No thanks needed. If Thomas ever makes it, I'll be known as the scout who first spotted him. That'll do for me.'

I call Thomas to the phone and leave him to it. Well, I leave him to it in as much as I walk away but stop to listen from the kitchen doorway. Thomas isn't saying much, but I can see the smile on his face and that'll do for me too.

12

My children skipped all the way to school this morning. Well, Thomas didn't quite skip, but the call from Ron definitely lifted him. Slightly. And today, there is another reason for his lack of a scowl; one for the record books, actually. For the first time ever, my children were being taken to school by *both* their parents.

Richard walked beside me and I almost wanted to skip as well. Honestly, not for any girlish ooh-everything's-fab-cos-I'm-in-love reasons. No, his presence made me feel considerably less nervous about what I'm about to do.

He got up ridiculously early this morning to make breakfast and the kids didn't realise he'd slept in the spare room. The smell of bacon woke them up.

Bacon on a *Monday*?

As we ate, we told them we had to go in for a chat with Mrs Gottfried. About fund-raising, extra finance for the school, that sort of thing, I explained. They tuned out at *fund* – I know how to get my kids uninterested.

We're sitting outside her office now.

'Ready for this?' Richard asks.

'As I'll ever be,' I reply.

Who am I trying to kid? I'm not ready. I *hate* confrontation. Why am I doing this? Why didn't I decide to take Richard's perfectly sensible advice – i.e. mumble, 'Sorry, Miss, won't happen again,' and just make it go away?

Because however fearful I am now, my original feelings

of outrage haven't gone away. I've got nothing to be *sorry* for. I AM NOT A RACIST, MY DAUGHTER IS NOT A RACIST, and I'll shout the fact from the rooftops.

The office door clicks open, making me jump. I look up at Gottfried. Almost imperceptibly, her nostrils flare when our eyes meet. Right, OK, I'm done shouting, thanks. Want to go home now.

Richard stands up and holds out his hand. 'Mrs Gottfried, I'm Richard Clark. We haven't met.' Then he fixes her with his hundred-watt smile.

And, my God, is she swooning? I remember looking at David Cassidy like that when I was about five. She takes his hand and looks as if she doesn't want to let go. 'You vish to talk about Molly?' she says at last. 'Please come in.'

As we follow her into her office and sit down, I'm wondering desperately how I'm going to play this. Why didn't Richard and I come up with a strategy? He's pitching to Shell this afternoon and you can bet he's rehearsed that one to death. OK, I know Gottfried doesn't control billions of pounds of oil money, but she's one of the most important figures in my world at the moment. We should have put some thought into this.

'I owe you an apology,' he said to me last night. 'You were right, this racism thing is ridiculous. You've got absolutely nothing to be sorry for. Let's go in tomorrow morning and sort out the old bat.'

And that was it! Our strategy: *sort out the old bat.* I wanted to talk about it, I really did, but the DVD was playing and there was no disturbing him. Sure, he's missed the kids and me these last two weeks, but Tony Soprano and Paulie were playing pool and there was only the black left on the table.

'I'm pleased you've come in,' she says. 'I am seeing the

head this afternoon and I know he vill be asking me for an update. As I explained to you, Mrs Clark, he is very concerned that this matter is resolved.'

'Mrs Gottfried, forgive me for jumping in,' Richard says, jumping in, 'but my wife and I have to leave promptly and I'm sure you're busy too. I'd like to get straight to the point if I may.'

Oh, so he's going to kick things off. Well, that's cool. As I mentioned, I hadn't quite worked out how I was going to start. I'll just let him get on with it and pick up the thread in a minute.

'I'd like to make our view perfectly clear,' he says. 'Racism is not an issue we take lightly. We won't tolerate it and we don't excuse it. In fact, we're actively involved in the fight against discrimination . . .'

Are we?

'. . . Fran is working with the Commission for Racial Equality . . .'

Oh, that's right, we are. So glad I mentioned that to him last night.

'. . . She's playing an integral role in a major international initiative that's going to get a lot of TV coverage over the coming weeks. In fact, Fran cares so passionately about the project that she's providing her services for free.'

Oh, I was just about to jump in with that bit, but he isn't giving me a chance. And actually, do you know what? That's fine by me. Looks as if it's fine by Gottfried as well. She is *enthralled.*

'And given our *proactive* stance on the issue, Mrs Gottfried,' he continues, 'we will not tolerate the accusations of racism that have been levelled against us. I must agree with my wife. Neither she nor my daughter has done anything wrong here.'

He sits back, pausing for a moment, crossing one long leg

elegantly over the other. Gottfried is transfixed – she's a *leg* woman! She manages to tear her eyes off his lower limbs and look him in the face. Then she clears her throat. 'Mr Clark, of course I *fully* understand your point of view, but this leaves me in a rather . . . awkward position,' she simpers.

Another one for the record books: Gottfried is *simpering*.

'Look, we're all reasonable people,' Richard says firmly but reasonably. Now he's Michael Corleone: vaguely menacing but ever open to reason. 'We're prepared to make a concession. We'll ask Molly to keep her very special talent to herself for now. She won't be running around making jokes in anything but her own voice. Fran and I give you our guarantee on that.' He pauses to dazzle her with a fresh smile, but he hasn't finished. 'And I'm sure that come the Christmas play, when a leading role requires a special acting skill – a gift for voices, say – you won't forget Molly. What do you think, Mrs Gottfried?'

What does she think? She *thinks* she wants to marry him and bear him several strapping sons – there really is no other explanation for that dreamy look in her eyes.

'Mr Clark, of course I accept your assurance,' she says slightly breathily. '*Thank* you, and I vill pass it to the head.'

'And the play?' Richard says, maintaining the smile at full power.

'It is rather unprecedented,' she says awkwardly. 'The leading roles are usually reserved for the older, more experienced children . . . But at Arlington, ve pride ourselves on fostering the children's gifts. Molly is clearly very talented and it vould be terrible if ve did not celebrate that. I vill talk to Miss Roberts about vich role might suit her. I vill call you *personally* ven it is arranged.'

Richard's smile turns into a humble little laugh. 'My children and their gifts, eh? It's just so great to know that the school feels this way about individual talent. I'm sure that in his final year here, Thomas's football skills are also going to thrive under Arlington's nurturing guidance.'

Gottfried chokes. 'Of course, Mr Clark,' she coughs. 'Of course.'

Richard's work here is done.

'*Excellent.* Please have this,' he says, sliding a business card across her desk. 'And please know that you can call me – on my mobile *or* my private line – any time. Any time at all.'

As we walk out of her office, I steal a backward glance and I see her clutching the little white card.

Jesus, is she *stroking* it?

'Sterling work, Richard, well done,' I say to him when we're outside. 'God, you're a smooth-talking bastard, aren't you?'

'You were right to stand up to her,' he says. 'I hope you didn't mind the concession.' He looks worried.

'That's what life's about, Richard – concessions.'

We're at the school gate. We have to part here – I'm going to Sureya's and he's catching the Tube to work. But as we're about to say goodbye, we hear the familiar click-click-clicking of heels. She's running towards us, double buggy in front, Quinn just behind. He's eating toast this morning.

'Morning! Sorry, can't stop,' she gushes as she runs past. 'Late again. We are going to be in so much trouble!'

'Who's that again?' Richard asks as she flies past us.

'Natasha. The one who started all the—'

'Yeah, yeah, I know who she is. I forgot to tell you, I heard an interesting story about her last week. From Adam, you know the designer whose girlfriend works with—'

'Yeah, yeah, I know who. Go on.' That's the trouble with men. Too much unnecessary detail.

'Well, a couple of years ago, Natasha got done for

shoplifting. Hard to believe a woman like that has got a criminal record, isn't it?'

Hard to believe? It's totally *un*believable. I'm too shocked to speak.

'Nice bit of information to have, isn't it? Do with it as you will, Mrs Clark.' He winks at me.

'I'd never stoop to her level. Never in a million years,' I tell him and I mean it. 'But my God, what was she stealing?' And I'm thinking it would be fitting if it were something Gucci. We all know how much Natasha likes her labels.

'A purse. From Accessorise. The one in Brent Cross.'

I laugh and Richard furrows his brow, confused. I could explain, tell him that everything she owns is attached to an expensive designer label. But I don't. I simply say, 'Unbelievable.' The rest is just detail.

'Good luck with Shell,' I say when I'm done laughing.

'Thanks. I don't want to tempt fate, but I reckon Cherie's already won us that one. Give Sureya my love, won't you?'

'I will.'

'And thanks for a great weekend.'

He takes my hand and leans forward, kissing me lightly on the cheek. This time I let him.

I stand for a moment, watching him walk away. He looks back at me and I call out, 'You were brilliant in there. Gottfried *loves* you.'

'*I jus' make 'er an offer she can't-a refuse-a,*' he shouts back. I really wish he'd leave the impressions to me.

Michael answers the door. He looks sad and tired, but not quite as haggard as he did five days ago. 'Hi, Fran, come in,' he says.

I step into the hall and say, 'So . . . how are you doing?'

'Oh, you know, not so bad I suppose,' he lies.

We stand in painful silence for a moment. Suddenly I feel I shouldn't have come. I should have left them in peace. Maybe I should go?

'Sureya's in there,' he says at last, pointing to the front room. 'Go through.'

I don't move.

'Go on,' he says. 'She's only had my mug to look at these past few days. It'll do her good to see you.'

Gingerly, I push the door open and stick my head round. She's on the sofa in her dressing gown, a cup of tea in her hand. The TV is on, the volume low. I go in and sit down next to her.

I take a little parcel from my bag and hand it to her. 'Here,' I say. 'I brought you this.' It's the little book of beautiful poetry that she gave me a couple of years ago. 'Read the inscription,' I tell her.

She opens it and looks at the handwritten note: 'Read this and weep. And then see how much better you feel. Your friend always, Sureya.'

I watch her face closely. She smiles slightly.

'And I want it back when you've finished with it, OK?' I say.

We sit in silence until Michael brings me a coffee. When he leaves us alone again, she looks at me.

'Poor man,' she says. 'He doesn't know what to say. And I've been dreadful to him. He doesn't deserve it. It's not as if he isn't going through his own hell.'

'Don't worry about him. He loves you. It's his job to take the shit,' I say.

She's quiet for a moment, then says, 'I can drink again now. What do you think about that?'

This gives me a brilliant idea. 'Hey, I'm going out with Summer on Thursday. Why don't you come too? Get you out for a bit. What do you say?'

'Sorry,' she says, looking away. 'I don't think I really want to see her for a while, if you don't mind.'

Well, I knew it was a long shot, but I didn't expect her to react quite so—

Then it hits me. How could I have been so stupid? So insensitive? Summer's still pregnant, isn't she?

'Oh God, I'm so sorry,' I say, shaking my head like the moron I am. 'I didn't think. I just, you know, thought that maybe you might . . .'

She gives me a forgiving look. 'Don't worry. It's no big deal. Just, you know, one step at a time.'

I take hold of her hands. 'Listen, Sureya, I'm not going to stay. I'm not going to offer you anything else either. To take you out, have the twins, bring you shopping, whatever. All that goes without saying. All I want to say is, well, you know where I am. OK?'

'That's all I need to know,' she says, squeezing my hands so hard it hurts.

I gulp down my coffee and stand up to go.

'By the way, Fran,' she says. 'Jasmin woke up at two this morning. Wouldn't go back to sleep. She wanted ice cream.'

I feel myself blush.

'I said, "Ice cream? In the middle of the night?" Then she hits me with, "Auntie Fran lets us have it."'

'I am really sorry,' I gush, suddenly feeling like the world's most inept mother. 'I had a few problems settling them when they stayed. Nothing major . . . just . . . you know . . . Sorry.'

'God, don't worry about it. I know how difficult they can be when they're out of their routine.'

'So, what did you do?'

'What do you think? I gave her some ice cream. It worked a treat. She went out like a light . . . You know, you should make the time to write one of those parenting manuals.'

13

(Unlucky for some, but only some)

I never really knew what it meant to walk with a spring in your step, but I do now. It's all bouncy and light and ever so slightly out of control.

Of course I'm nervous. Shitting bricks, I think we used to say when we were young. Obviously, not any more, though. I'm a respectable, pretty much middle-aged, North London housewife and we don't talk like that round our way.

I climb the steps and stand on the exact same spot where I stood . . . How long ago was it . . . ? Four and a half weeks. I'm at the door of Saunders & Gordon, a recording studio I've been to a hundred times before. But it feels like the first time. I'm nervous as hell . . . No, sod it. I'm shitting bricks.

My first proper job in, oh, for ever. So the nerves are forgivable, aren't they? Anyway, today it's different. Nervous energy is also *positive* energy. Note that a) I've remembered the appointment, and b) I've actually turned up for it.

Of course, I got this far four and a half weeks ago. I had my hand on this very door handle, before turning round and running away. And then I was only fleeing from a seven-word tag line. This is BIG. This is me versus Robin bloody Williams. I could so easily turn and run.

But this time it *is* different. Yes, I know you've heard it all before, but this really is the new me.

And it has nothing to do with the fact that last night I

had the most amazing sex with a man called Richard Clark.

It has everything to do with the fact that things have changed.

Everything has changed.

Thomas has suffered the first big rejection of his life.

Sureya has lost the baby she'd longed for.

Summer is keeping the one she never imagined she'd have.

And I have a husband who is sleeping in the spare room.

But the biggest change, of course, has been in me. I now know something I've never known before. I know that whatever happens, I can cope. Richard might end up moving back into the double bed. Or he might move out for good. I might hit the bottle and end up in rehab. Or I might go teetotal and quit with the smoking while I'm at it. Thomas might make the Arsenal squad. Or he might discover a new talent. Whatever happens, we'll handle it. No, *I'll* handle it.

And I might march into this studio and give the finest read of my entire life. Or it could be a complete dog's breakfast. If it is, I'll cope with that as well.

So I clasp the door handle and . . . *push.*

I walk in and head up the stairs for the first-floor reception. The girl behind the desk looks at me and smiles.

'Fran Clark,' I announce. 'I'm here to see Chris Sergeant.'

'Please take a seat,' she says.

Welsh. Caerphilly, if I'm not mistaken. I'm not usually wrong about these things.

Before she gets a chance to call him, a heavy sound-proofed door swings open and Chris emerges from a studio. He sees me and bounds towards me, his arms outstretched for a hug.

'Fran!' he calls out. 'You made it.'

Yes, it looks like I did.